THE IMMORTALS

THE IMMORTALS

A Story of Love and War

Karen Stokes

GREEN ALTAR BOOKS
SHOTWELL PUBLISHING

Published by GREEN ALTAR BOOKS, an imprint of
SHOTWELL PUBLISHING LLC
Post Office Box 2592
Columbia, So. Carolina 29202
www.ShotwellPublishing.com

Cover image courtesy of David J. Rutledge.

Cover design by Karen Stokes and Stephen Penner.

SECOND EDITION
ISBN-13: 978-1947660137
ISBN-10: 1947660136

10 9 8 7 6 5 4 3 2

Produced in the Republic of South Carolina

This book is dedicated to the memory of
William Porcher DuBose,
and to his causes, earthly and heavenly.

Contents

PROLOGUE

MAJOR TAYLOR LOOKED INTO THE MIRROR to observe what was left of him.

Pulling back his ragged shirt, he studied a thin neck rising above broad but emaciated shoulders, their large bones and joints clearly visible under the white flesh. He then lifted his gaze a little higher, to a face once youthful and supple, where the pale, pinched skin was drawn tautly over the contours and hollows of the skull. From prominent sockets, two somber eyes stared back at him, eyes once fine and clear—but now sunken, dull, vague, and marred by dark circles underneath.

Remembering Marguerite, the major wondered if he would ever see her again. But why wish for that, he asked himself–even if he did live to see her again, what would she want with this wasted scarecrow of a man?

A bony hand went to his mouth. His jaw had suddenly begun to ache and throb more painfully, and he realized that he was going to lose another tooth. Frowning at his reflection, he thought himself an altogether sorry sight, the worst among all the sorry specimens who occupied the bunks around his in the rough wooden barracks of Fort Delaware. Yet how different, how vital he had been when first brought to this place! Since boyhood, he had always enjoyed extraordinarily good health, yet even his strong constitution had not been able to outlast the rigors of more than a year's captivity in Yankee prisons.

Someone called his name.

"George!"

A moment later, one of his fellow prisoners of war, another scarecrow, appeared at his side looking concerned.

"What are you doing on your feet, George?" asked Captain Allen. "You ought to be in bed, sick as you are!"

The major tottered as he turned away from the looking-glass on the post, and would certainly have fallen if the captain had not caught his arm and helped him to his bunk. His friend covered him with a coarse blanket and felt his forehead, which was feverish. A little cool water was all the comfort he had to offer.

"You sleep now," he said.

Major Taylor closed his eyes. He was feeling so weak that drowsiness came to him quickly despite the aching tooth.

It had always been a habit of his to think of pleasant things before falling asleep, and even in the worst of circumstances, even in this place, he tried to keep to this practice. Hoping that sweet memories would usher in dreams as sweet, he let his thoughts drift back to a time some four and a half years in the past, to a day in 1860...a day that would change the course of his life forever, in his beautiful city by the sea.

CHAPTER ONE

IN CHARLESTON, SUCH DAYS IN DECEMBER were not uncommon. On that particular afternoon, the sea breezes were gentle, the sky was gloriously blue and clear, and the air mild now that the morning's chill had worn away. A handsome, well-dressed young couple was walking side by side on the Battery promenade enjoying the fine weather and each other's company, followed closely by another, slightly older pair acting as chaperones for the young lady.

As Marguerite Finley strolled along the elevated stone sea wall with her beau George Taylor, she reflected that it was a day so pleasant, so perfect, that it made one think of paradise. Though it was nearly winter, and there were no flowers in bloom except for a few camellias, the young live oak trees in the nearby park were as green and beautiful as ever, and the views of the shining harbor and the grand mansions facing it, bright and splendid. Everything appeared even more splendid than usual to Marguerite that day, always to be remembered as one of supreme importance in her life.

Looking seaward, the lovers gazed off toward the horizon, observing in the distance Fort Sumter, the stronghold in the middle of Charleston harbor rising up out of the waters like a geometrically perfect island mountain. A stray gust of air lifted the lilac-colored ribbons of Marguerite's hat and fluttered them against George's dark beard. He laughed a little (nervously, she thought) as he gently removed them.

Marguerite turned her head and glanced back at the couple following behind, and her brother and sister-in-law immediately nodded to her and smiled. She saw a whispered exchange between the two, after which she noticed that they slowed their pace considerably. George and Marguerite finally came to a stop to look out over the harbor, but after a few moments he led her a little farther off for a private conversation, then paused and faced her, squaring his shoulders.

"This is the spot where we first met," he said. "Do you remember?"

"I do remember, Mr. Taylor," she answered promptly. "I remember that day very well. It was really not so long ago, was it?"

He attempted a smile, but almost as soon as the semblance of one appeared, it faded, and he took a deep breath and spoke again.

"I have something to ask you, Miss Marguerite."

The petite young woman gazed up at her taller partner affectionately, and after enduring a prolonged pause, suppressed a smile at his nervousness.

"Will you marry me?" George finally asked, not in the suave, self-possessed way he had intended and practiced, but with a fixed, desperate stare, a slight involuntary twitch in the corners of his mouth, and a trace of perspiration on his brow–looking very much like a man on the verge of supreme joy or utter despair, which, in fact, he was. He had even forgotten to kneel in front of the young lady, something else he had intended and practiced.

Marguerite almost laughed aloud at his comically tortured expression. The poor fellow obviously did not know how much he was adored.

"George Washington Taylor!" she thought in amused exasperation. "How could you have any doubt as to my answer?"

Her answer was *yes*.

George smiled, laughed, and breathed an audible sigh of relief at the same time. His first impulse was to take Marguerite by the waist and swing her up and around in the air in jubilation, but he had to content himself with squeezing her gloved hands for a few moments. Very briefly, he held one of those hands against his broad chest so that she could feel his pounding heart. Then she received a whiskery kiss on the cheek that tickled and made her laugh.

The other couple was approaching now.

"Ah, ha!" cried Marguerite's brother, grinning broadly. "We know what has happened here, Rita! We can tell by looking at Mr. Taylor!"

"Well!" Marguerite protested with a smile. "Don't I look happy, too?"

"Yes, my dear," laughed her sister-in-law, "very happy, indeed!"

Five months before the day of their engagement, the two lovers had first set eyes on each other here at this same spot by the harbor, near a part of the Battery nearly opposite the Taylor residence, a large, beautiful house on East Battery Street where George lived with his father.

At the beginning and end of each day, George liked to take his exercise by walking on the sea wall promenade. Going out for his usual walk one breezy July evening at sunset, he was closing the gate behind him when he noticed a group of young ladies and a gentleman strolling along the Battery. He thought he recognized one of the young women as his cousin Bessie Lightwood, and followed after them to speak with her. Bessie, an attractive girl of twenty with bright red hair, happened to glance back in his direction, and smiled and called out to George when she saw him.

"Here is my cousin Mr. Taylor," she said to the others.

They all paused to meet him. Miss Lightwood introduced George to four of her friends, two of whom were sisters to the young man, and another young woman, a Miss Finley, who (he was informed) had recently returned to Charleston after several years of schooling in Philadelphia. Petite and slender, Miss Finley had lowered her head and was holding on to the wide brim of her hat as a sudden gust of wind threatened to dislodge it, so that at first George saw only a delicate chin and spiral curls of brunette hair dangling and brushing against it.

The sun was hidden behind a fiery cloud bank on the horizon, but at the exact moment Miss Finley looked up at George, its rays broke through and shone out in oblique shafts, creating a golden light that illuminated her strikingly pretty face—gilding her fair, perfect skin, and making her large brown eyes glow like jewels of amber. Those eyes flashed at him with a keen, candid look, and then narrowed in a smile as George realized that he had stared at the young woman a moment or two longer than politeness might allow. He tried to find his tongue, and something to say with it, but Miss Finley spoke first.

"You are the son of Senator Ephraim Taylor?" she asked him curiously.

"I am."

"Oh, my father admires him so. He says he is one of the state's greatest men."

"I happen to agree with your father," said George, "if it is not immodest of me to say so."

"Not at all," she replied.

When Miss Finley found out that George was following in his father's footsteps in the choice of the law as a profession, she nodded approvingly, and at the end of their brief conversation, their eyes remained locked on each other, until Miss Lightwood invited George to join them on their outing. He offered his right arm to Miss Lightwood, and they walked on, followed by the quiet young man and his talkative sisters. These two burst into a private conversation as soon as they were free to do so.

"Miss Finley has been our guest on Sullivan's Island for the past few days," George's cousin remarked. "I thought we might see you there, as Grandmamma is your neighbor in Moultrieville."

"I've been here in the city much of the week," he explained.

"Yes, I saw your father on the island, and he told me you were away in Charleston on business again."

"How long are you in the city?" he inquired.

"Just a day or two more," said Bessie. "We wished to stay for the fourth, to see the fireworks here at the Battery."

"Oh, yes, you must stay for that," said George, addressing the young lady walking to his left, of whose nearness he was acutely conscious.

Miss Lightwood told him that she and her party were going to a birthday celebration for a friend who lived a few blocks away. When they reached their friend's house, she insisted that George join them, but he politely declined, protesting that he was not expected.

"Perhaps I shall see you all at the fireworks," he said to them in parting.

"Yes, George," his cousin laughed. "I certainly expect to see you there. As you live on the Battery, you have only to step out your front door, after all!"

"True, it's a show I could hardly miss!" he replied merrily, not knowing why he suddenly felt so lighthearted and exhilarated, as he gave one final, lingering look to Miss Finley, who was smiling at him.

The next morning, George sat a desk in his room trying to read over an abstract of title for a piece of property his father was purchasing, but found that he was not able to concentrate very well on the document; he was feeling too abstracted himself. The image of the young woman he had met the day before–her face, her voice, her gestures–kept coming into his mind to entice him away from his work. He had thought about her several times the night before, and had even seen her again in his dreams. Savoring the music of her name–Marguerite–he remembered the jarring, keen sensation that he had experienced on first looking into her eyes, which were not only beautiful, but sparkling with intelligence and irrepressible energy. He certainly thought there was something very captivating about her.

George was still thinking of Miss Finley as he walked to his office on Broad Street. There was nothing pressing to attend to there, and he had been intending to return to the island that afternoon, but reflecting that the next day would be the Fourth of July, he had changed his mind and decided to do a little work. He sat down at his desk and, after reading some letters which had accumulated in his absence, began to write his replies.

His desk was a crowded but orderly arrangement of papers reflecting some recent case work, most of which he considered of no great significance or interest. The largest heap of documents concerned his most important work at present, the settlement of the estate of a wealthy planter. Another pile dealt with a contest over the guardianship of a minor child, and still another consisted of the records of a case in which a Charleston merchant claimed he had been inadequately compensated by his insurer for a fire-damaged wharf and buildings, and finally, on the outermost edges of the desk rested the forms, abstracts, and correspondence relating to several routine real estate transactions recently completed but not yet filed away. Everything pertaining to his work was neatly and meticulously arranged according to a system which George had tried to make as efficient as possible. This well-organized office was a tangible reflection of his logical and very orderly mind.

He was able to concentrate well enough to finish several letters, but as soon as he put down his pen his mind went back to the subject he had been thinking of earlier. His eyes were fixed on the bookcases of the opposite wall, and he seemed to studying a neatly arranged shelf of letterpress and account books, but he was in fact picturing the form of Miss Finley again and trying to remember every word she had spoken.

The rest of that day, and all the next, George suffered with an uncharacteristic restlessness of body and mind, and soon realized that these recurring thoughts of a certain young lady were the cause of it. That fourth of July evening, just before dark, after dressing himself with great care, he went downstairs, where he waited by a window until he saw people beginning to gather along the Battery. Soon he stepped out to the piazza and began to look around for his cousin and her friends.

The day had started out hot, but there had been a shower in the early afternoon, and though the rain had brought a premature end to the holiday parades and other festivities, it had also cooled the air considerably, so much so that the temperature was almost comfortable after sunset.

From his house George watched more and more people filling the promenade, mostly well-dressed ladies and gentlemen of the city's upper classes. They gathered on the raised walk of the High Battery and all along the Low Battery closer to the park called White Point Garden, where a brass band began to play patriotic tunes from a platform under the trees.

As it grew darker, George left the house and walked out among the growing crowds of spectators, where no less than a half-dozen friends and relatives detained him for conversations here and there, but as the fireworks began, shooting up into the air from a barge in the harbor, he moved in the direction of the park and finally caught a glimpse of his cousin Bessie Lightwood. She was standing arm in arm with the young lady he had been looking for, next to the young man and his two sisters who had been with her before. Like everyone else, they were gazing up at the first explosions of brilliant stars bursting overhead. George circled around behind them and made his way closer, until he was standing just a few yards away from Miss Finley. She was nodding in response to something Miss Lightwood was saying, and cooling her face with a small straw fan as she looked up, her mouth open in a smile of wonder and delight.

Bluish rockets went up, one after another, hissing and spiraling through the air before they burst into multicolored showers of light. A couple stepped up between George and Miss Finley, blocking his view of her, and he moved around them. He was preparing to make his presence known, and was looking at Miss Finley as he deliberated a casual greeting, when there was a lull in the pyrotechnical display for the preparation of a large stationary piece on the barge, and she happened to turn her head in his direction. As their eyes met, her fan came to an abrupt stop. He momentarily froze in embarrassment, long enough to leave no doubt that he had been staring at her, but quickly found the presence of mind to smile and bow his head in acknowledgment. She smiled back at him, and then he saw her speak to his cousin, who craned her head around, saw George, and waved at him. Seizing on the invitation, he approached.

"You remember Mr. Taylor, don't you?" Bessie said to Miss Finley.

"Very well," she replied, smiling more with her eyes than her mouth when she looked at George, who was relieved to see that she was amused rather than offended by his attentions.

He scarcely had time to greet his cousin's other friends before everyone's attention was drawn to a spectacle on the water. The large set piece on the ship had suddenly burst into dazzling light and movement, depicting a sea battle of an age past. Two fanciful men-of-war began exchanging volleys of cannon fire which exploded in stars of red sparks. After an exciting battle, one ship finally emerged victorious, as the other sank beneath billowing waves of light.

After this scene, more fireworks shot up into the night sky in larger and grander displays, then ceased, and all eyes were drawn again toward the harbor, where another large display was soon kindled into life on the barge. The shape of a huge temple lit up, its interior emblazoned with a soaring eagle flanked by two turning, screeching wheels of fire, and overarched by glittering sparklers arranged so that they formed letters spelling out the words *George Washington*. When that name appeared, hearty, prolonged applause went up from the spectators ranged along the Battery.

Once the fireworks show was over, the crowds dispersed rather quickly. George's cousin invited him to join her and her friends for ice cream. He walked with them to their carriage, and they drove to King Street. Some shops were still open, and a number of people were strolling along the sidewalks under the illumination of the gas lights.

They stopped at an ice cream shop and went inside its pavilion, but the tables were so small in the place that the party had to split into two groups. George was fortunate enough to have the company of Miss Finley and his cousin, while the other gentleman sat with his sisters, though he was obviously a little discontented with the arrangement. George had been so interested in Miss Finley he had hardly taken any notice of the young man, but now saw, by his looks cast in her direction, that he might have a rival for her affections. Up to then it had not occurred to George that the fellow was anything but an escort for the females. After briefly sizing up the callow youth, who was probably some three or four years younger than himself, George judged him unworthy, or at least unlikely, and, remembering Miss Finley's interactions with the young man, he decided that she had shown no interest in him other than that which politeness demanded, and so paid no further attention to him.

Miss Lightwood was a talkative young lady, and tended to monopolize the conversation, just as she had during their first walk along the Battery together, but since her subject tonight was Miss Finley, George listened to his cousin with patience and interest. Among other things, he learned that she and her family resided in a fine old house on Meeting Street, that her father was a well- known banker, and that she liked peaches in her ice cream.

When Miss Lightwood left their table for a few minutes to talk with an old friend she had spotted in the street, George had his first chance for a private conversation with Miss Finley. From the questions that she asked him, he discovered that she already knew much more about him than he did of her. She explained to George that his cousin had talked of him several times, and informed him that both she and Miss Lightwood thought it was quite extraordinary that at such a young age (twenty-five), George had compiled and published a digest of the rulings of the state court of appeals. The book had brought him much recognition in his profession, and

Miss Lightwood had also hinted to her friends that there was talk of "someone in the Taylor family" being considered for the Federal district attorneyship.

"Oh, she wasn't speaking of me," said George. He told Miss Finley that his cousin had been referring to his older brother, Mr. Albert Taylor, who was a serious candidate for that post.

"What a distinguished family you have, Mr. Taylor," Miss Finley said admiringly.

George could only smile and shrug, though he found all her compliments intensely pleasurable. Since the young lady seemed genuinely interested in his work, he told her about another book he was writing, tentatively titled, *The History of a Lawsuit,* tracing the development of a hypothetical legal case from beginning to end, and meant for the use of students of the law.

"That is very remarkable, Mr. Taylor," Miss Finley marveled. "Your cousin Bessie tells me that you are always so busy with your work, she can scarcely imagine where you find the time to write books."

"I'm afraid I have been accused of devoting myself too entirely to work," he admitted.

"And do you plead guilty to that charge, Mr. Taylor?" she asked, smiling softly. "Do you devote yourself too entirely to your work?"

"I begin to think I have, Miss Finley," he replied.

The wistful, rather helpless look George gave her when he made this answer, along with the matching tone of voice in which it was uttered, impressed Miss Finley very much, though she did not show it. She asked when he expected to finish his second book.

"I hope to complete it by the end of the summer."

"In Moultrieville?"

"Yes, I shall be going back there very soon," said George, adding, with an awkward clearing of the throat, "Perhaps I shall see you on the island."

His cousin Bessie had just returned to the table, and overheard their last exchange as she took her seat again.

"I'm afraid you will not see us on the island, George," she said. "We are going to Flat Rock. Miss Finley's family is there."

George's smile fell a little at this piece of news.

"We are taking the cars to Greenville tomorrow with my brother," Miss Lightwood informed him, "and from there we shall take the stage to North Carolina. It is a terrible time to travel, I know—so hot—but we were waiting for Mama to get better. Now that she has, the capricious thing has decided to remain on the island with Grandmamma. I much prefer the mountains in the summer, and so does Miss Finley, so we shall brave the cars and the stage to get there."

While Bessie was speaking, George's eyes were drawn to Miss Finley by a force stronger than his will. When he was able to look away, he was sure he had not successfully concealed the disappointment he felt.

"A long journey," was all he could think to say in response.

At the end of the evening, George declined a ride in the carriage and walked home instead, all the way reflecting on the sad reality that he would not be seeing Miss Finley again until September or October.

After Miss Lightwood had been away for about two weeks, George began to look for a letter from her, hoping that through one he might hear some news of Miss Finley. He lived so near his cousin in Charleston, and saw her so frequently, that they had never been regular correspondents, but she had sometimes written to him during her summer travels. After another week went by, he decided to take the initiative and write to Bessie. Sitting down at his desk one evening, he began a letter. He kept its tone light and cheerful, and tried to make it as interesting as possible. In the last paragraph, after describing some unusual objects he had found on the seashore after a storm, George wrote, "At dusk I always take a restful walk on the beach if the weather permits."

He stopped and thought, "No, that's not very interesting."

But he had already written it, and dared to add, "How are you and Miss Finley enjoying Flat Rock? It is so beautiful there, I imagine you are taking many walks together. I sometimes think of our last stroll on the Battery, and wish that I was in such pleasant company again."

George paused in uncertainty, thinking that he had perhaps been too bold, but then changed his mind. The next morning he sent off the letter to his cousin with the rest of the mail.

It was a lovely, sunny day, and Marguerite and Bessie decided to go out for an early walk and hike up the side of a nearby mountain, eager to take some exercise on the day after their long and tiresome journey to Flat Rock. By mid-morning, when they had been walking upward for a while on a trail through the woods, Miss Lightwood was winded, and requested that they sit down on an overturned tree trunk that formed a natural seat beside the path.

Marguerite sat down with her, but mumbled a protest, "Good heavens, Bessie, it isn't much farther to the top."

"Rita! If you will just allow me a few moments, I must catch my breath," Bessie responded, huffing and puffing a little as she tried to make herself comfortable on the trunk.

Her friend patted her hand and apologized.

"I haven't your energy, you know," said Miss Lightwood. "You are the most tireless creature I have ever seen! You quite exhaust me sometimes."

"Forgive me, Bessie. It's just that I find it so exhilarating to be here again. I do love this place! My family has come here every summer since I can remember. Father says that once a year, he simply must see something other than the flat lands of the low country, and I feel the same! He was raised in the upcountry, you know, in Greenville, and likes to be among the hills and mountains again."

After a rest, the two young women continued up the trail, soon reaching the summit of the mountain, where there was a massive, sloping expanse of granite. They sat down on a ledge of rock here and could see, over the tops of the trees rising from the base of the granite formation, a vista of forests and faraway mountains, bluish green in color in the morning mists. The two friends had talked constantly along the way, but Marguerite grew quiet now as she gazed off toward the surrounding countryside. After a long silence, her friend studied her curiously and asked her what she was thinking of.

"Oh...nothing in particular," she replied, though she was unmistakably preoccupied.

Bessie smiled.

"I think you are being evasive, Marguerite," she said. "I believe you are thinking of something very particular. I should say, *someone* in particular. I know you have been keeping something from me since we left Charleston. These spells of daydreaming have been quite frequent."

Marguerite reddened a little and laughed.

"I do like him," she admitted.

"Mr. Taylor liked you, too. I could tell."

"You really think so?"

"Of course! I must say, I was very struck by the way George looked at you. You are so beautiful, I suppose you are accustomed to such looks, but I know my cousin well, and I have never seen him look so–smitten, as they say–or anything close to such a state. I am quite certain that he is thinking of you, perhaps at this very moment."

"Oh, no," Marguerite demurred mildly, but her smile belied the protest. She tried to look less pleased, but was not very successful as she went on, "I am sure Mr. Taylor has quite forgotten me by now. He is, no doubt, at this very moment, busily engaged in some important legal matter, or working on his book."

"Well, perhaps," Bessie responded skeptically, "but I should wager that when he is at leisure, his thoughts turn to you."

Marguerite smiled again, but this time offered no contradiction. She had been harboring a strong suspicion that Mr. George W. Taylor, Esquire, was interested in her, and now that Bessie had confirmed it for her, she was certain, and felt very happy about it. She even felt confident enough to remark how handsome she thought his eyes were, and that they "had such an intensity about them."

"That's his feverish mind showing through," Bessie replied. "George works much too hard and much too long, and never seems to rest."

"Why is that?" Marguerite wondered. "Is he ambitious?"

"I suppose. He loves to work. He is very capable, and so he works to the utmost of his capabilities. Perhaps he wishes to see just how much he can accomplish."

"I'm sure he is capable of accomplishing a great deal."

"I shouldn't be surprised," Bessie agreed.

"Do you think Mr. Taylor suspects that I am younger than you?" asked Marguerite, her brow contracting with some concern.

"I don't know," answered Bessie. "He probably thinks you are at least my age, or close to it. You certainly look and act older than your seventeen and a half years."

"Then you needn't mention it to him," Marguerite suggested.

"Oh, I shan't, dear. Besides, by the time we return to Charleston, you shall be on the very threshold of your eighteenth birthday–a most unobjectionable age!"

Less than a month later, when a letter from Charleston arrived for Miss Lightwood, she had the proof in hand to win her wager about George, which had not been forgotten.

"Why, George never writes to me!" she marveled, as a servant held out the envelope to her one afternoon.

"Perhaps there is some important family news," Marguerite speculated.

"I think not," said Bessie, opening the letter.

She read the first few lines and looked up at Marguerite.

"Nothing important," she said, suppressing a smile. "Why don't we read it together?"

The two young women left the company of Marguerite's dozing grandmother and went upstairs to their room, where they sat down on the bed. Miss Lightwood read aloud, rattling off George's casual observations about the health and activities of various family members and mutual friends, tidbits of goings-on in Charleston, and a few remarks on a summer storm that had caused some damage on Sullivan's Island. Her eyes widened as she came to the part of the letter in which he asked about Miss Finley and mentioned "such pleasant company."

"Oh, Marguerite," she sighed, "I told you he was thinking of you."

"It does seem so..."

"Seem so! Why, my cousin hardly ever writes to me, and never without some good reason. The only reason for this chatty little epistle is you, my dear. Why, for my cousin George to say such a thing–*such pleasant company*–is practically a profession of love!"

Marguerite's face broke into a wide smile of delight.

"Let me read that part for myself again," she requested, taking the letter.

Her eyes pored over the letter until she found the reference to herself, and she read it several times.

"I do like Mr. Taylor's handwriting," she finally remarked. "It is very strong and clear."

"So is his meaning, my dear!" laughed Bessie. "Shall I pen a reply?"

The following week, George received the anxiously awaited letter from his cousin. Its arrival was a great event. She reported on the delightful time she was having with the Finleys in Flat Rock, and how beautiful the weather had been lately. In her closing lines she wrote, "Miss Finley sends her regards, and wonders how you are progressing with your book."

George immediately started a reply. He kept it somewhat short, but again tried to make it interesting and entertaining, and carefully added as a postscript, "Tell Miss Finley that I spend my days hard at work on my book, and have completed more than three quarters of it. As she has been kind enough to express an interest, I hope to have the honor of presenting her with a copy of the finished product by the end of this year, or at the least early next year."

About a week later, another letter from his cousin Bessie arrived. In this way, George kept up an indirect correspondence with the beautiful Miss Finley for the rest of the summer.

On their first meeting, Marguerite had been very favorably impressed with Mr. Taylor's outward qualities. George's looks were just the sort she liked. He had dark, glossy brown hair, and clear hazel eyes which she found beautiful and stirring. He was somewhat tall, but not absurdly tall for her, strongly-built, and handsome of face–at least what she could see of it beneath a heavy, well-groomed beard and mustache. She preferred clean shaven men, but overlooked this slight defect in him as one that could be easily corrected.

When it became clear that Mr. Taylor was beginning to court her through his correspondence with Miss Lightwood, she became more curious and inquisitive about his unseen qualities. One afternoon, the two young women took another hike on the mountain near the Finley house, and when they sat down to rest, at nearly the same spot they had stopped before, Marguerite asked her friend what she thought of her cousin George. Bessie told her that it was well known in the Lightwood family that George revered his father and aspired to be like him in every way, and also said that she would not be surprised to see him have as distinguished a career in the law and perhaps even politics.

"But I am partial, you know," she added. "I love George as a brother–his brother Albert, too. Albert has often remarked to me how much George is like his father. He has the same honest face, which inspires such confidence in his clients."

Marguerite was looking down at the ground and digging up clods of dirt with a walking stick she held in one hand, tapping them into smaller clumps until they were reduced to dust again. Her attention seemed to be focused on this useless occupation, but her friend could tell she was still dwelling on other things. Finally, Marguerite looked up and said, "So many young men are disappointing in one way or another. Don't you find it so?"

After some consideration, Bessie answered, "I think they might say the same thing of young ladies."

"Yes, that is true."

"We perhaps live too much in the ideal, and expect too much of each other. Really, we are all poor creatures."

Marguerite turned an amused smile on her friend.

"Dear me, Bessie, you are too much the philosopher! I was merely trying to find out if you would mention anything disappointing about Mr. Taylor."

Bessie laughed and said, "Oh, I see."

After another thoughtful pause, the worst she think of to offer about her cousin was that he could be testy and temperamental, that his sense of humor tended toward the sarcastic, and that people sometimes found his conversation too blunt and his manner a little brusque.

"George can be blunt to rudeness at times, but only with his equals, and never to ladies. He claims it is not rudeness, but forthrightness. But really," she explained, "I think he hides a soft heart beneath that manner."

"Yes," Marguerite agreed. "I can see that in his face. It is a kind face. I did not find him brusque at all."

"Oh, Rita!" Miss Lightwood laughed. "You must know that George was on his very best behavior in your company!"

"Oh, that may be, but–"

Marguerite hesitated, and her expression grew very serious.

"That may be," she repeated, "but if–now I tell you, in strictest confidence, you understand, Bessie–if Mr. Taylor is what he seems to be, I think he is someone whom I could wholeheartedly love and admire."

While she was away, especially after the first letter from Flat Rock, George was frequently thinking of Miss Finley. Because of her interest in it, he was more determined than ever to complete his book by the end of the summer, and despite the distraction she presented to his mind, he managed to finish a first draft of the manuscript in the latter part of September.

On the last day of that month, another letter from his cousin Bessie arrived. In it she mentioned that she had painted a little watercolor picture of the Finley house and was going to have it framed for Miss Finley.

"Please say nothing of it, George," she wrote. "It is a surprise for her upcoming birthday–a remembrance of what will likely be our last summer together as unattached and free young ladies. Miss Finley turns eighteen in November, and once she goes out into society this season, she will no doubt be engaged to be married by the spring, if not sooner."

"Eighteen! She is not yet eighteen," George thought, surprised.

The idea caused him some concern, but only briefly. He had never pictured himself courting a girl so young, but then reminded himself that there was really nothing very unusual about it–many young women were engaged or married at that age. Besides, he was already in love with Miss Finley, or as he had recently expressed it to his father, "greatly possessed in every manner with the young lady."

One cool evening George's elderly great aunt from next door paid a call to the Taylor's summer cottage on Sullivan's Island. She hobbled in on the arm of a servant woman, also elderly, but not so ancient as Mrs. Lightwood, who had been born a British subject in Charleston.

George was alone at home that night, and entertained his aunt by a small fire in the parlor. Though she was frail and feeble, her mind was still very clear, and she kept herself well informed about a great many of her relations and descendants. George was a favorite of the old lady, who was beginning to grow concerned that her nephew, now closer to thirty than twenty, was still a bachelor. They had not been talking long during her visit when she asked him if he had found a suitable young woman to marry yet. She was expecting to hear the same reply as usual, but this time his answer surprised her.

"You never know," he said, with a certain sparkle in his eyes, "I may find one soon!"

"Hmm," Mrs. Lightwood responded, lifting her pale, withered, aristocratic face in great interest. "And what do you mean by that, George?"

"Perhaps I shall tell you soon," he said.

"So there is hope after all!" his great aunt cried in her weak, warbling voice.

"There is certainly hope."

"Do I know this young lady?" she inquired.

"I believe you do."

"Hmm...and why do you not tell me her name?"

"Once the matter has progressed a little further, perhaps I shall."

A final "hmm" seemingly brought this part of the conversation to a close. Then Mrs. Lightwood began to talk about her grand-daughter Bessie. For years she had secretly hoped that George would choose Miss Lightwood for a wife, but could soon tell by his reactions to the subject that his cousin was not the young lady in question.

When George mentioned that he had received letters from Bessie in North Carolina, this brought up the subject of her friend Miss Finley. Mrs. Lightwood shook her head at the name. An opinionated person, she expressed some disapproval of the young woman, whom she characterized as "headstrong" and "too highly pleased with herself."

His aunt's criticism of Miss Finley was unpleasant to George's ears, but otherwise had no effect on him, and did nothing to diminish his growing interest in her. Knowing that the stern, humorless old lady always disapproved of most everyone in some way, he easily brushed off her remarks. On the other hand, he was very gratified to hear what his aunt had to say when she began praising Miss Finley's mother, who was well known and highly respected for her devotion to her church and a ladies' charitable organization in the city. He was very willing to believe that Mrs. Finley must be every bit as fine a creature as her daughter.

The look of displeasure that momentarily crossed George's face when his aunt expressed her opinion of Miss Finley had not been lost on the old lady. Mrs. Lightwood paused and studied her nephew shrewdly from under her lashless eyelids, and, remembering how beautiful the young woman was, began to harbor her suspicions.

In a letter received by George in early October, Bessie wrote how happy Miss Finley was to be returning to Charleston soon, and that she looked forward to seeing him again. With such encouragement, he did not hesitate to call on the young lady when he learned that she was back in town. Two months later, they were engaged to be married.

CHAPTER TWO

EXCEPT FOR MARGUERITE'S BROTHER and his wife, who were average in height, the Finley family tended toward diminutiveness. Her father was a short bald man of fifty-nine, her mother a petite matron still beautiful in her early fifties. Marguerite's little sister, an eight year-old, was a tiny pixie who seemed incapable of being still or quiet.

Their three-story house, which had been in Mrs. Finley's family since the turn of the century, had been enlarged once or twice over the decades, and was elegantly, but not ostentatiously furnished. The floors and stairs of the older part of the house creaked and groaned more emphatically under George's heavier tread, and that of Mr. Finley's butler Titus, a stocky, irascible old black man who, for some reason, took an instant dislike to George and always greeted him coldly.

As George's affection for Marguerite grew, so did his liking for her family, especially her brother Frederick, who tended toward his father's plainness rather than his mother's beauty. Frederick worked in Mr. Finley's bank, and was still considered a newlywed, having been married less than a year. Marguerite's father was a devout, quiet, courteous man, usually mild-mannered, but sometimes given to harmless outbursts of temper. He worshiped his little wife, a person constantly in motion, perpetually occupied in the management of the household and servants, and in receiving and entertaining guests, whether business associates of her husband or visiting friends and relations. Outside the home, Mrs. Finley kept as busy in the administration and worthy projects of her church and the Ladies' Benevolent Society. The better George knew Marguerite, the more he saw how much she admired and revered her mother, and sought to please her by sharing her interests and working by her side in her charitable pursuits, realizing that Mrs. Finley was not only her daughter's model, but also her closest friend and confidante.

Most of the second floor of the Finley house was taken up by two drawing rooms which mirrored each other across a hallway off the stairs. One afternoon, during one of George's earliest visits as a suitor, one of the drawing rooms was occupied by Mrs. Finley, who was seated at a desk, engrossed in correspondence and household accounts. Her youngest daughter Charlotte, always called Chassie, was nearby in a corner full of her toys, playing with dolls. She had a half dozen or so of various sizes propped up in a line before her, and was making miniature school books for each. When she was finished with the books, and had distributed them to each doll, she could be heard lecturing her pupils on the subject of spelling.

From the far end of the opposite room, Marguerite happened to notice her little sister, and smiled. George, seated in a chair next to hers, followed her eyes and also saw the tiny books and the doll school in progress.

"Educating her toys?" he asked with a soft chuckle.

"Yes, but I'm afraid, very poorly. Chassie's spelling is quite awful. She usually prefers to sing to her dolls. I suppose in her imagination they are singing with her."

A few moments later, after resuming their conversation, they heard the little girl's voice breaking into song, and watched her pick up a doll to serenade.

Marguerite glanced over at a table nearby where she had left a small album covered in dark green silk. She asked George if he would like to see her keepsake of her summer in Flat Rock, and brought it to a sofa, where they sat together.

"Bessie and I began collecting things for our books from the first day we arrived in the mountains," Marguerite began, turning to the first page, which was inscribed, "Flat Rock, July through October, 1860, Marguerite Peronneau Finley."

Seeing her middle name, George asked, "Are you related to Mr. Frederick Peronneau, the attorney?"

"He is my mother's brother," she replied. "My brother Frederick is named for him."

"Your uncle is a fine lawyer," George remarked. "I lost one of my first cases to him, but I learned so much from the experience, I didn't begrudge it."

Marguerite turned a page in the album to reveal a watercolor painting of a lake surrounded by forests and mountains. George was very impressed with the beauty and skillfulness of the work.

"Are you the artist?" he asked.

She nodded. "Do you like it?"

"It's very beautiful," he complimented her, and after admiring it and commenting on various points of the work, he lifted his eyes to her face to admire another kind of beauty.

"Do you know Flat Rock at all?" she inquired.

"I have been there a few times. An uncle of mine has a summer house there."

Marguerite asked his name, and discovered that the gentleman was one of her father's friends.

"We have all sorts of connections, don't we, Mr. Taylor?"

As George recovered from the powerful effect of the smile accompanying her observation, he was surprised to see, on the next page, one of his letters to his cousin Miss Lightwood.

"That was your first letter," said Marguerite. "I hope you don't mind that Bessie gave it to me."

"Not at all."

"She was quite surprised to receive it, you know."

"Was she?"

"She said that you never wrote to her without some good reason."

"I had good reason," he admitted with an awkward smile, going a little red in the face, which was turned down to the letter.

"Not knowing you very well then, I had to rely on Bessie's interpretations. She said that I was the reason for the letter."

"Well, of course," George murmured, still keeping his eyes on the album.

They both smiled and laughed, and she went on to another section of the book to show him a little mountain landscape Bessie had painted. George did not think it was as well done as Marguerite's painting, and said so, but then, fancying that his frank remark had struck her as rude, he quickly turned his attention to a poem written below Bessie's watercolor and asked who the author was. Marguerite looked a little embarrassed as she spoke about it.

"Bessie and I collaborated on this poem all summer. It was the last thing I wrote into my book, but I don't think it is very good. We could never rhyme the word 'chinquapin,' no matter how hard we tried, and I forget now why we thought it was so important. Isn't that silly?"

"Won't you read your poem to me?" he urged her.

"Oh, no! It's too poor. I ought not to have put it in my book."

"You needn't be afraid to read it to me," George assured her. "I am no judge of such things. There is no poetry in me."

"None at all?" she asked, looking a little surprised.

"Not very much at all."

"Oh," she said, with a shade of disappointment in her voice. "I adore poetry. I have a whole library of it. Have you heard of the new book of poems by Mr. Timrod? They say he is a true poetical genius."

"I am not familiar with that gentleman, no."

"Perhaps we might read it together sometime. I have ordered a copy."

"I should like that."

"Even though you don't care for poetry, Mr. Taylor?"

"It's not that I don't like poetry, it's just that...well, I'm afraid it is lost on me sometimes."

Marguerite looked back to her album and fingered another page. Pulling back a piece of tissue paper, she revealed an array of pressed flowers from the mountains, then another sheet of leaves and fir needles pressed flat and labeled and dated in her neat, delicate handwriting. There were two more of her paintings further on, both of which George admired, more pages of pressed flowers and leaves, passages of copied poetry and prose, and inscriptions by friends and relations. George noticed one written in a decidedly masculine hand which included a poetic meditation on the beauty of Marguerite's eyes. It was signed "Leonard Haywood."

"Who is this Mr. Haywood?" George asked a little sourly, his smile disappearing.

"Oh, a neighbor in Flat Rock. An old friend of the family."

"How old? I mean, how old is he?"

"He is a little older than me, and a little younger than you."

"I see."

Marguerite suppressed a smile at George's evident jealousy, which she found very pleasant, but she quickly put his mind at rest about the young man.

"I have known Leo all my life, and unfortunately, I cannot say he has turned out very well. He is a rather conceited, haughty young man, and much too fond of his own pleasures. He spends all his time in the mountains shooting."

The next page she turned to, one full of shiny, colorful feathers, offered proof of what she said.

"Leo brought us these from one of his shooting excursions on Baring's Pond. Heaven knows how many poor waterfowl he sent to their reward that day! The feathers are very beautiful, though, aren't they?"

"Very," George agreed, feeling more charitable toward Mr. Haywood now that he knew Marguerite had no liking for him. "He must be a very good shot."

She skipped a few more pages of inscriptions and found the last painting in the album, a miniature portrait of Bessie. They were both so absorbed in their observations about the likeness that they did not notice Mrs. Finley enter the room. George's face was very close to Marguerite's as they studied the portrait, and when her mother spoke he moved away from the young lady instantly, feeling like a culprit for some reason, and rose to his feet. Mrs. Finley invited him to stay for dinner.

That afternoon, only the adults sat at the long, mostly empty dinner table. Chassie had already eaten and gone out to play with friends. Mr. Finley was seated at the head of the table, his wife to his right, and Marguerite and George to his left.

"How is your honored father, Mr. Taylor?" he asked as their plates were being served by two handsomely dressed servants.

"I regret to say that his health is not very good," said George, "although he has improved since last month."

"I was very sorry to hear that Senator Taylor was suffering from heart troubles. I hope he may make a full recovery."

"That is my hope, sir."

"We need such men in these times. I have followed your father's brilliant career in the law, in our senate, and the senate in Washington. I believe there is no man who holds the welfare of our state and union higher in his heart. He is a good and wise man. We need more such men, especially in Washington! What has been going on there–"

As his voice began to rise to an excited pitch, his wife interrupted in a gentle but firm tone, "Oh, Charles, please don't begin one of your tirades against the Yankees."

"As you wish, my dear," said Mr. Finley, calming. "But I should like to know, Mr. Taylor, what your father thinks of the upcoming presidential election."

"I'm afraid he is not very optimistic about it," George answered.

"Ah, I feared as much. I am of the same opinion. The Republicans will have it. The party of the North will triumph! Then we will have no choice but to secede. It seems there is no reasoning with them! President Buchanan, well, he is a reasonable man, and an honorable one, I think, but this man Lincoln, is not to be trusted."

"My father is of a divided mind on secession, sir," said George, with a fleeting smile to acknowledge his unintended pun. "He certainly thinks we have the right, as all reasonable men do, but wonders about the wisdom of it. He fears a war, as the North will not wish to let the most valuable section of the country go."

"War!" Mr. Finley exclaimed vehemently. "Well, yes, I know there have been such rumblings, but such a course on their part would be a monstrous injustice–a crime!"

Suddenly, he was almost trembling with anger.

"The worst sort of despotism," he sputtered, "to threaten us with the sword!"

His wife placed her hand on his.

"Charles," she said, stroking his fingers. "Calm yourself. Please don't lose your temper in front of our guest."

Mr. Finley took in a quick breath, huffed it out, and shrank down in his chair as he glumly turned his attention to the food on his plate.

"War," he mumbled to himself again after a few moments, chewing on a mouthful of rice. "Our sons must go to war!"

After this remark, which everyone heard, Mrs. Finley noticed Marguerite looking at George with a momentary expression of concern, and then, thinking of her son Frederick, she burst out irritably, "There will be no war! And there will be no more talk of one in this house!"

Mr. Finley, as always, deferred to his wife, and there was no further conversation about politics at the table that afternoon.

One morning shortly after the announcement of the engagement, while George was talking with Marguerite during one of his visits to the Finley household, her little sister ambled into the drawing room and announced that their mother wished to speak with

Marguerite for a moment. Mr. Finley, seated far across the room next to a window, was so absorbed in a newspaper that he did not even look up at the sound of his other daughter's voice.

"Excuse me, dear," said Marguerite, rising from her place beside George on the sofa and leaving him in Chassie's company.

Marguerite's sister was a pretty little girl with soft brown hair and eyes much like her sister's. In fact she resembled Marguerite so much that George imagined that when he looked at her, he was seeing his fiancée as she must have looked at that age.

The child plopped herself down in a chair opposite his and looked at George with a puckered, impish smile.

"Do you absolutely adore my sister Marguerite?" she suddenly asked in a gushing tone, making dramatic, languishing gestures with her thin little arms.

"I do," he laughed softly. "Are you trying to embarrass me?"

"Yes!" she giggled, covering her face momentarily and squirming with satisfaction.

"Well, you have not succeeded, young lady."

Chassie opened her mouth and then snapped it shut, and made a great effort to change her expression to one of sincerity and innocence.

"Are you going to be my brother?" she asked him sweetly.

"I am," George replied.

"Oh, good. I am glad."

"Thank you."

She leaned forward in her chair and beckoned George closer with a movement of her fingers. He inclined his head toward her a little.

"Shall I tell you a secret about my sister?" she asked in a confidential tone.

"Well, I don't know," George replied warily. "Perhaps you ought not to."

Ignoring his reservations, the little girl revealed the secret, declaring, "Marguerite does not care for whiskers and beards."

"Is that so?" he responded after a pause, unsure whether to believe Chassie or not.

"It is. I know it for a fact. I have heard her tell her friends so."

"Hm-m," George mused, eyeing the child dubiously, although he was now inclined to believe her.

She assured him again that she was telling him the truth.

"And do you like whiskers and beards?" he asked Chassie.

"I like your beard," she replied. "It's a very handsome one."

"Perhaps I ought to marry you, then," he suggested in mock seriousness.

The little girl rocked back and forth in her chair emitting peals of laughter.

"I can't marry you!" she cried. "You're going to be my brother!"

"Well, I certainly can't argue with that logic," he answered, amused, "but I shall very proud to have such a charming little sister."

Chassie simpered at the compliment.

"Do you have any sisters?" she asked.

George's expression sobered a little.

"I had one," he said quietly, "but she went to heaven a long time ago."

"Oh!" Chassie sighed, producing a sad face of commiseration.

Marguerite came back into the room at that moment, and her sister instantly brightened and jumped up from her chair.

"Mr. Taylor says that I am charming!" she told Marguerite, smiling triumphantly.

"He may change his mind once he gets to know you better, my little pest," she replied.

Chassie put out her tongue at her sister and then skipped off, humming loudly.

"Miss Marguerite," George said reprovingly, "your little sister is very charming."

"That may be, but you mustn't tell her so," she replied, taking her place beside him again. "It may make her vain. The little creature is already too well satisfied with herself."

"Like another little creature I know?" he wondered privately.

George studied Marguerite for a few moments with a cryptic smile, and then remarked, "Chassie told me something interesting."

"And what was that?" she asked.

"She thinks my beard is very handsome," he said.

"Does she? Well, it is, Mr. Taylor," Marguerite replied–rather archly, he thought.

Chassie soon reappeared in the doorway and offered to sing a new song she had learned from a friend.

"We do not wish to hear you sing right now, Chassie," her sister promptly responded.

The little girl raised her arms and warbled out her favorite lyrics anyway, "*She's a young thing, and cannot leave her mother!*"

A look of disapproval and irritation from Marguerite only sent her laughing and running over to their father. She climbed into Mr. Finley's lap, and though he seemed very interested in something he was reading, she made him put down his paper and then insisted on singing the whole song for him, while he listened with a complacent smile.

George had observed that Marguerite possessed the same ability to charm and manipulate her doting father, and suspected she had exercised it over him throughout her life. It seemed to him that Mrs. Finley was the stronger disciplinarian in the family, at least where her daughters were concerned, and that it was her firmness and force of moral authority which had kept them from being completely spoiled by such indulgence.

At times, especially in the first few weeks of their courtship, George had been so infatuated with Marguerite that he found it difficult to see any characteristic of hers as a fault, actual or potential. Sometimes, in his fascination, he could only see this little brunette goddess, with her chiseled, upturned nose, curving coral lips, and the most beautiful brown eyes in the world. But in more lucid moments, as he became better acquainted with Miss Finley, he discovered that, at least to some degree, his stern old aunt had been right in her assessment of the young lady.

In November, Marguerite had celebrated her eighteenth birthday, and at a party given in her honor by a cousin, George noticed how naturally and easily she took to being the center of attention, and how she reveled in it. Among her female friends, and even many of her younger male relations, Marguerite was unquestionably the queen bee, her judgments and opinions usually being considered the best on most every matter. With her confident, energetic personality, she seemed to take this order of things for granted as natural and fitting, and she could in fact be somewhat domineering, though with such humor and charm that none of her young friends seemed to take any offense. George was already so hopelessly in love, it seemed useless to worry about such things, but he wondered sometimes if Marguerite might someday try to hold sway over him the way she did with her father.

After the birthday celebration, as George was escorting her back to her house, Marguerite asked him if he had enjoyed himself. He answered yes, but with some qualification in his own mind. He had taken more pleasure in seeing Marguerite's enjoyment than in the party itself.

"Nearly everyone there was my age or younger," she remarked. "Did you feel out of place, Mr. Taylor?"

"Perhaps a little."

"It is not as though you are so much older, still..."

"What?"

"You must have thought we were rather childish, the way we carried on and reminisced, and became a little foolish sometimes."

"You are young–why shouldn't you enjoy your friends?"

"I saw that you were watching me. Once or twice, I fancied that you were looking at me disapprovingly."

"No! No, Miss Marguerite," he assured her.

"But you were observing me–studying me. What were you thinking? Now be honest, Mr. Taylor. Consider yourself under oath."

He hesitated to answer, but went ahead with it, carefully.

"I was thinking...how admired you are among your friends."

"And?" she prodded, after waiting for more.

"And...and that you are quite the queen of your set."

"Oh."

After a long pause, Marguerite asked George if he had been surprised to be invited to a celebration of her eighteenth birthday.

"Surprised by the invitation, or by your age?" he asked.

"The latter."

"Well, no. My cousin Bessie told me about that before you returned from Flat Rock."

"And were you surprised then?"

"A little," he admitted.

Looking serious and thoughtful, Marguerite was quiet again for a while, then asked about a conversation he had with one of her male cousins at the party, knowing by their looks that she had been the subject of it.

"Your cousin Harry, the cadet?" said George, smiling. "He was telling me how you used to give him thrashings for his misdeeds."

Marguerite colored in embarrassment.

"When we were very young, you understand," she explained. "I was a little older than Harry, and often had to look after him. He was always misbehaving in some way."

"He also told me that you were a bit of a tomboy," George added, still smiling.

"Well, I suppose I must admit to that," Marguerite responded irritably, a little provoked as she recalled her cousin's teasing glances from across the room–but after a pause, when she spoke again more calmly and seriously, there was note of entreaty in her voice.

"That was a long while ago," she said. "But we are no longer children...and we must all put away childish things eventually, mustn't we?"

From her tone, and the way she looked at him, George had the idea that she was speaking of something more than old tomboy ways. He wondered–but did not ask–did she imagine that he thought her too young to marry, too immature or childish?

Marguerite could not explain to him why she had indulged herself so much that afternoon, why she had let herself have free rein at her party that day. She kept it to herself, that her party had not only been a celebration of her birthday, but also a kind of farewell to the past. A farewell, because she was closing the door on one part of her life–girlhood and youth–and preparing to open another. The door that was opening was the rest of her life, which was to be centered on George, because she loved him. But Marguerite could not say any of these things to him that day, because he had not yet asked her to be his wife.

"Don't put all childish things away just yet, Miss Marguerite," he said, gazing at her tenderly. "I like to see you so lighthearted and careless with your friends, as though there were no troubles in the world."

He added in his thoughts, "The troubles of this world may be upon us soon enough."

Marguerite seemed to hear the words he did not speak–to read his mind–and, thinking of the possibility of war, which had grown more likely after the recent election, she felt a greater rush of love for him than ever before.

After her birthday, Marguerite expected Mr. Taylor to propose to her. When he was not prompt enough in doing so, she began to give subtle indications of disappointment which he misinterpreted as coolness. For many days George was tortured by suspicions that Marguerite did not love him as much as he loved her, or that she had decided he was unsuitable for her, or had found some other gentleman more preferable. On the afternoon he asked her to marry him, his usual self-confidence crumbled, and up to that time, he had never experienced more anxiety in his life than he did during those few moments of suspense as he tried to produce the all-important question.

Earlier that same day, when George had asked Marguerite's father for his permission to propose marriage to her, Mr. Finley had expressed a reservation about the matter. Only a month before, his darling daughter had been seventeen ("Seventeen!" he had cried out incredulously), and he found himself reluctant to part with her at such a young age. After giving the matter some consideration, he thought it best that they wait a year before they married. George had hoped for a somewhat shorter engagement, but he readily agreed to Mr. Finley's terms, realizing that such a delay was for the best, after all. He was in the middle of several important cases which promised to be very lucrative, and which might, by the end of a year's time, make him a small fortune, or at least enough to set up his own household and support a wife and family.

Marguerite and her mother were great lovers of music. Mr. Finley did not share their enthusiasm, so when they expressed a desire to attend the upcoming performance of a famous Norwegian virtuoso violinist, he saw an opportunity to avoid it by suggesting that George accompany the ladies. After an acclaimed public performance, this musician had agreed to give a private one at a neighbor's house. George did not really care for classical airs (he preferred a more folksy type of music), but to please Marguerite and her parents, he dutifully escorted her and Mrs. Finley to a house down the street one evening and pretended to enjoy himself. A precedent having been set, Marguerite seemed to expect him to accompany her to all similar engagements in the future. At the third such musical soiree in so many weeks, just a few days after they were engaged to be married, George finally began to express some dissatisfaction. Just before the performance began, he admitted to Marguerite that he did not care for these entertainments. Surprised, she told him she was simply unable to understand how anyone could not love such beautiful music, but before she could say more, the concert began.

After about an hour, George began to grow extremely restless, having only so much tolerance for cultural refinement at one time. Besides, he did not like to sit still for long periods. He shifted his legs, inspected his fingernails, preened his mustache, scratched at his neck around a collar which was a little too tight, and let his shoulders rise and fall with exhalations of ennui. This fidgeting annoyed Marguerite, but at the same time, because it was George's fidgeting, she could not help but find it charming. It went on so long, however, that she felt she had to put an end to it, and did so by tapping his arm with her folded fan and tilting amused but scolding eyes at him. He responded by making an insincerely contrite face. This made her laugh, but only a little, and she immediately regained her composure and resumed a serene, appreciative expression as she continued to listen to the music.

After a piano concerto, a plump lady seated in the front rose to sing a canzonet called "The Little Golden Ring." A lady seated next to Marguerite's mother proudly whispered to Mrs. Finley that she had once heard the famous Jenny Lind sing this song.

"It is Schumann, is it not?" Mrs. Finley inquired, also in a whisper. "Oh, to have heard the Swedish nightingale sing it! How unfortunate that we missed her when she came to Charleston."

An air from "Lucia di Lammermoor" followed this performance, and then a gentleman took his place beside the plump songstress to join her in a duet she called "Moonlight, Music, Love and Flowers," accompanied by the pianist. George visibly cringed at the title, and while they sang, diverted himself by watching the slow, fitful descent of the bald head of a sleepy old man sitting in front of him.

"*Oh,*" they sang, "*this is one of life's fairy hours, of moonlight, music, love, and flowers...*"

At its conclusion, during the applause, Marguerite leaned over to George and asked what he thought of the song.

"Terribly sentimental," he replied, suppressing a yawn.

"Mr. Taylor!" she said, drawing out his name in a reproving, disappointed tone. "Have you no sentiment? I am very sentimental concerning you."

"Well, *that* is all right!" he beamed at her, then, looking toward the bowing performers, he applauded more heartily as he realized that the soiree was finally over and added, "About me, you may be as sentimental as you like, Miss Marguerite."

"I see!" she drawled waggishly, narrowing her eyes. "Extravagant sentiment is acceptable as long as it concerns you."

"Yes, that's correct," said George, and for this answer, and the smug smile that accompanied it, he received another corrective tap of her fan to his arm.

In the latter part of December, the entire city was in a state of breathless excitement over the arrival of the Secession Convention delegates, the men elected from every part of the state to cast their votes for or against this momentous decision. The convention had begun in the capital city of Columbia, but a reported outbreak of smallpox there caused the assembly to move to Charleston, where they gathered at St. Andrew's Hall on Broad Street. This building was not far from George's office, and each day on his way to or from work he paused to chat with some of the gentlemen who were following the proceedings closely. Whatever news he heard was promptly reported to his father.

Although Mr. Taylor was still recovering from recent heart troubles, and mostly confined to home, he was very eager to hear anything about the Secession Convention. The old gentleman was reasonably certain what the outcome of the vote would be, but he was still anxious to know that this great step had in fact been taken–that his state had declared her independence.

On the afternoon of December 20th, Mr. Taylor received word that the vote had been taken (a unanimous one in favor of secession), and that the hour of the ratification of the Ordinance of Secession was drawing near. The Convention had moved into the larger venue of the South Carolina Institute Hall on Meeting Street for the signing of the Ordinance, and the final announcement, he was told, was imminent. As the afternoon wore on into evening, he grew tired of waiting, and after an early supper, sat down in a comfortable chair, and while attempting to read a newspaper by lamplight, nodded off.

Well after dark, George came home and found his father asleep in the library, and hesitated a moment before waking him. As he faced Mr. Taylor, he raised his eyes to a portrait of the senator which hung on the wall and was struck again, as he had been many times lately, by the sad contrast that existed between the image and the actual man. The painting depicted a vigorous, stout, bearded gentleman of middle age; the shrunken figure in the library chair was only a shadow of him.

Orphaned at an early age, Ephraim Taylor had inherited no wealth, but, blessed with friends and patrons who saw his potential and guided him into the right profession, he had become a successful attorney and built up a considerable fortune through his law practice. Through marriage, he had acquired a large amount of land, and for a number of years added planting to his interests, until he found it too burdensome, and sold the property to a relative. He loved the fine home he had built on the Battery for his late wife, and enjoyed his cottage on Sullivan's Island, a place he regarded as a resort necessary to good health during the hot summers. Beyond these things, he allowed himself few luxuries, and never abandoned his habits of thrift and moderation even when they were no longer necessary. During his prolonged illness, Mr. Taylor had clung to his old wardrobe, stubbornly refusing to buy new clothes, though they were at least two sizes too big for him now. It pained George to see how his father's slender, withered neck no longer filled his collar, and how his cuffs gaped around bony wrists. It also worried him that he slept so much during the day, but George was consoled by the fact that Mr. Taylor had been improving lately, getting stronger, and showing more of an appetite, so much so that their physician now held out hope of at least a few more years of tolerable health.

Still staring at the portrait, George heard a sigh, then his father's voice.

"What's the news?" the old gentleman asked, drawing himself up in the chair.

"Any moment now, I'm told."

"Good heavens, how late is it?"

"Not even nine o'clock, Father. Would you like to go down to Institute Hall? It's not very cold tonight."

"I don't know that I am up to such a walk," Mr. Taylor said doubtfully.

"We could take a carriage most of the way. I've asked Albert to bring his around for you."

"That's good of your brother."

"We knew you'd wish to go, Father. After all, how often is such history made before our eyes?"

"True! And I do wish to go. I feel quite rested, and can certainly tolerate a little walking and standing."

As Mr. Taylor stood and straightened his clothes, George went to a front window and looked out to the street.

"Albert's here," he said.

In the moonlight he could see a tall, well-dressed man approaching the house, walking with the help of a cane, and with a peculiar, hobbling gait. George's older brother Albert had been lame for many years from a boyhood riding accident that had left one foot crushed and mostly useless. Having married young, he was already the father of four children. Like George, he was an attorney, and the senior partner in the firm of Taylor & Taylor since their father's retirement. He had served as the United States district attorney for several months, but recently resigned the position in view of his state's intention to leave the union.

The carriage took the Taylors as far down Meeting Street as the congestion of other carriages and people would allow. George helped his father out, and the three men approached a large crowd, mostly composed of gentlemen, gathered outside Institute Hall, waiting for the formal announcement of the outcome of the convention's deliberations. Mr. Taylor's suspense did not last much longer; a few minutes after he and his sons arrived, the president of the convention stepped out of the front entrance of the building to address the people. The gentleman declared in a solemn, sonorous voice, that the Ordinance of Secession had been signed by all the delegates, and that the state of South Carolina was now "an independent commonwealth."

Wild, deafening yells, whoops, and cheers, and thunderous applause rose up from the crowd. George put his arm around his father, who was trembling with excitement, his face alternately joyful and sad.

"So it has come to this," Mr. Taylor said in a whisper. "So it has finally come to this!"

George could not hear his father for all the clamor, and applauded with the rest of the crowd. Although not usually given to outbursts of emotion in public, he felt a sense of relief and happiness so soaring that he joined in the hurrahs and threw his hat up into the air with scores of others that were sent flying in every direction. Church bells were ringing all over town, and overhead, fireworks rocketed up into the sky.

Judge Yeadon, an old friend of the Taylors, seized George's hand and pumped it forcefully.

"Well, George, do you feel giddy?" he asked, grinning broadly. "We are afloat!"

The elderly judge did not wait for an answer, but quickly went on to the next acquaintance he saw to share his exultation. After a few minutes George saw Marguerite and her brother and parents a few yards away. She and her mother were fluttering their handkerchiefs high in the air in celebration. He elbowed his way through the crowd, on the way receiving slaps on the back, handshakes, and smiles and cries of congratulation from friends and strangers alike. Marguerite rushed up to her fiancé when she caught sight of him.

"Mr. Taylor!" she cried. "Isn't it wonderful?"
George was so transported that he forgot himself and embraced Marguerite in sight of her parents, but Mr. and Mrs. Finley were equally caught up in the excitement and commotion, and only laughed, and after George released their daughter, they embraced him themselves.

"What a day this is!" Mr. Finley exclaimed in his ear, to be heard over the noise of the crowds. "Never to be forgotten! The day of our independence!"

Like many others in the crowd, George was wearing a secession cockade, a blue and white rosette which had in its center a little straw ornament fashioned in the shape of a palmetto tree, the symbol of the state. When Marguerite admired the emblem he took it off his lapel and pinned it to her hat.

"A remembrance of the day," he said, leaning down to her.

After the Secession Convention had adjourned, the street remained crowded for a while with people still celebrating and eagerly conversing over the announcement of secession. Mr. Finley saw some of the delegates walking toward the Mills House Hotel, just a short distance down Meeting Street, and at his urging, his family, along with George, Albert and Mr. Taylor, moved in that direction, too. Outside the hotel an audience had gathered, and began to cheer loudly as one of the convention delegates stepped out on the second floor balcony to address them. The gentleman, a dignified, middle-aged man, was from an upcountry district, but as a former senator, he was well-known to the citizens of Charleston. He held a sheet of paper in one hand, and raised the other to quiet the audience below him on the street.

"People of South Carolina!" he began. The noise of the crowd diminished, and he waited until they were silent before he spoke again.

"You all know me–I am for the Constitution!"

Prolonged cheers went up with this statement, and when they finally died away, the speaker went on, "All of the proceedings of our convention will be published in due time, but for now, I believe it fitting to recount some of the reasoning which has led to the bold step taken today. Just as our forefathers held grievances against the Crown of England in the century past, we have our own against our former government. And I tell you that the one great evil of which we complain, and from which all other evils have flowed, is the overthrow of the constitution of the United States! This is why we have dissolved our connection with them! Friends, let us state it plainly–the government of this country is no longer a government of sovereign states, but a despotism!"

More cheers broke out from the hearers at this, and they were quieted again by the speaker's upraised hand.

"The Revolution of 1776 turned upon one great principle, that of self-government. Today, the Southern states stand exactly in the same position towards the Northern states that the colonists did toward Great Britain. The Northern states, being the majority in Congress, claim the same power of omnipotence in legislation. The Southern states are a minority in Congress, and their representation there is useless to protect them from unjust taxation. The tariff and freights imposed by legislation raise the prices of both our foreign and domestic goods, and thus we as consumers are heavily taxed — not for revenue, no, but to promote, by prohibitions, Northern interests in their mines and manufactures!"

Here the crowd produced some boos, and an excited young man shouted out, "And now Congress will raise the tariff even higher!"

"Intolerably high, sir!" the speaker agreed indignantly. "Abominably high!"

"We will be cheated no more!" another gentleman cried out.

"Can any man," asked the senator, nodding in acknowledgment of this outburst, and extending his hands dramatically, "can any man believe that our ancestors intended to establish over their posterity, exactly the same sort of government they had overthrown? When the union was first established, there was then no tariff, and African slavery existed in all the states but one. The idea that the Southern states would be made to pay that tribute to the North which they had refused to pay to Great Britain, or that the institution of slavery would be made the grand basis of a sectional organization of the North to rule the South, was never imagined by our ancestors! The object of the Constitution was to secure a limited free government, yet over the years, by gradual encroachments upon the reserved rights of the states, the government has become consolidated, centralized, with a claim of limitless powers in its operations!"

The speaker left off as the audience once more expressed its disapproval. George had heard many speeches like this one lately, and though thrilled by the events of the day, he was too distracted by the proximity of Marguerite to listen very attentively. They were standing next to each other, and he moved even closer to her, so that when he took her left hand in his right, this was mostly concealed by the folds of her skirt. Everyone in the crowd was smiling and ecstatic, but George and Marguerite shared smiles of a private happiness as he intertwined his fingers with hers.

After the audience quieted again, the senator resumed, "The Northern states have for decades violated the compact among the states. To ensure their dominance, they have announced that the South shall be excluded from the common territories. They have nullified all laws made for the recovery of fugitive slaves. Moreover, they have allowed individuals and societies to agitate against our institutions—even to the point of sending books and pictures into our midst to incite the horrors of a slave insurrection in our land! Once this sectional party takes possession of the government on the fourth of March next, constitutional guarantees will no longer exist, and the equal rights of the states will be lost! The Republican Party is manifestly in league with the tariff, with internal improvements, and with three Pacific Railroads! My friends, you cannot overthrow such a party as that."

The senator stopped, reverently raised his hands and eyes upward momentarily, and then continued solemnly, "The Constitution of the United States was a grand experiment, but the experiment has failed. The South is not and cannot be safe under a common government with the Northern states. Numbers, with them, is the great element of free government, yet the very object of all constitutions is to restrain the majority. This rule of numbers may be harmless in a small community of identical interests and pursuits, but in a vast and various union of states, it is a despotism!"

The speaker paused to clear his throat while the audience vociferously expressed its agreement, and then concluded, "In separating ourselves from them, we invade no rights, no interests of theirs. As an independent state in the days of our fathers, this state made the constitution with the other sovereign states, and now, again acting in her sovereign capacity, South Carolina has deemed it proper to secede from that union. Our right to do so is denied by the Northern states. They desire to establish a sectional despotism omnipotent over all the states, and their Wide Awakes march in their city streets to threaten with the sword, to coerce submission to their rule! But we will not submit! We have severed our ties, and all we ask is to be left alone to work out our own destiny!"

While the crowd was busy cheering, waving, and applauding, George satisfied himself that no one was looking his way, and quickly leaned down and pressed a kiss to Marguerite's cheek, and as his lips brushed past her ear, whispered in exhilaration, "I love you!"

Later that evening, George sat with his brother and father for a while in the library of the Taylor house, and they talked of the day's great event, and what might happen next. Mr. Taylor speculated about the reaction of the outgoing president, Mr. James Buchanan.

"The difficulties of his position are very great," he mused. "If he allows the revenue collections of this port to cease, he virtually annuls the tariff laws of the country, and cuts off the only certain source of income to the government in Washington."

"Do you think he would employ the federal army and navy to support the revenue department?" asked George.

"I don't know," his father replied, "but upon your question, George, rests the probability of a collision between South Carolina and the United States."

Albert brought up the subject of the Federal soldiers who garrisoned Fort Moultrie on Sullivan's Island. Now that they were on foreign soil, he wondered if they would leave South Carolina peacefully.

"Their commander Major Anderson is a Southern man," said Mr. Taylor. "I am told that his sympathies are with us, and since all our South Carolina congressmen met with President Buchanan last week, and received his pledge that the federal forts here would not be reinforced, I don't see how Anderson can do much of anything."

"Surely President Buchanan will evacuate his troops from Charleston now," George remarked.

"That is my hope," his father responded. "And the sooner, the better."

"What if they should be gone by next week?" Albert speculated happily. "What a Christmas gift that would be for us all!"

Although she seldom entertained so lavishly, on the day before Christmas Eve, Marguerite's mother had overseen the preparation of a magnificent meal for nearly fifty guests, and arranged an evening of music and amusements for afterwards. As her guests entered the house, they saw on a rosewood table in the entrance hall a small Christmas tree made of goose feathers dyed green, and festoons and garlands of greenery hung over every doorway and window. In the dining room, an array of delicious dishes were brought to the table, including wild turkey, ham, oyster pate, partridges, pheasants, duck, bread and butter, rice and vegetables, and finally, desserts of rum cake, cherry pie, coconut cake, and confections called sugar plums.

George was annoyed when Marguerite had to leave his side to participate in some of her mother's entertainments. He was already upset that evening, having learned that his fiancée was leaving Charleston the next day with her family to visit relations in Savannah–for two entire weeks!

After everyone had finished dining, an audience gathered in the parlor opposite the dining room to watch the *'tableaux vivantes,'* or living pictures. The participants arranged their scenery and took their positions on a low wooden stage behind curtains set up on a frame, and when the curtains opened, a motionless, picturesque arrangement of people and props drew applause and appreciative murmurs from the onlookers. Most of the tableaux depicted a Christmas theme, beginning with a nativity scene with three gorgeously clad wise men, one of whom was Titus the butler.

This part of the evening's entertainment ended on a musical note, again with a theme in keeping with the season. A choir of twelve children, all boys, walked up to the platform. They were dressed in tunics, sashes, and floppy feathered hats reminiscent of medieval dress. As soon as they were in their places, a tall, portly man wearing kingly purple robes strode forth, followed by another "boy" (played by Marguerite) dressed as a page, but modestly robed to the ankles, her hair gathered up into a green velvet cap. The musicians behind the stage began a familiar tune, and the sweet, clear voices of the choir began the carol of "Good King Wenceslas," describing that monarch's good deed on the night of the Feast of Stephen. As they sang, another character appeared—a thin, hooded, ragged creature who walked with difficulty in the artificial snow and shivered in the imaginary cold.

The rich, deep, booming voice of the king sang out to inquire of this poor peasant in the snow, whom he indicated with broad, dramatic gestures. The high-pitched, bell-like voice of the page answered him in song. With graceful and appropriate movements and expressions, the king and his page sang and acted out the moving story of the carol, to the delight of everyone in the audience.

The whole scene was so touching and so beautifully sung, that George forgot his annoyance and watched in pure enjoyment. When they were finished, everyone applauded vigorously. Comments of "Charming!" and "Enchanting!" and so on, filled his ears, and he felt very proud and happy, until he remembered that Marguerite would be leaving for Savannah the next morning.

Away for a half a month! George hardly knew what he would do with himself in Marguerite's absence, although in the holiday season there was no lack of diversion. The day she left he went to a party given by his uncle John Hutchinson. The next day, Christmas, he went to church with his father, and they spent the rest of the afternoon at Albert's house with his family, where he enjoyed watching the children open their gifts. The following evening, after bringing his father home from another family gathering, George went next door to visit with David Macbeth, one of his oldest friends.

David lived on a plantation in a nearby district, but had come to Charleston to spend Christmas with his parents. The Macbeth family congratulated George on his engagement and wanted to know all about Marguerite. After Mr. and Mrs. Macbeth went to bed, George passed several hours talking with his friend, who had also recently become engaged. The time slipped by so pleasantly that George did not realize how late he had stayed until he began to yawn and grow profoundly sleepy. In the darkness and cold, everything around him was very silent and still as he walked the short distance back to his own house.

Early the next morning, the peace and quiet of the Macbeth household was suddenly disrupted by a group of alarmed citizens who burst through the gate and rushed up to the house. Their voices, and the hammering of their fists on the front door, were loud enough to wake up George in his bed. He went to the window and opened it to hear and see what was going on below. Mr. Macbeth, who was the mayor of Charleston, was being informed by these men that Fort Moultrie was on fire. Hearing this, George quickly dressed himself and hurried downstairs.

The mayor made the decision to dispatch two city fire companies to render assistance to Major Anderson, the commander of the fort. His son David offered to alert the firemen and go with them. Out of curiosity as well as a desire to help, George also offered his services and accompanied his friend. Within a quarter of an hour they were boarding a steamer for Sullivan's Island with the firemen.

As the last volunteer fireman was scurrying up the gangplank, a rowboat was seen approaching the steamer. The lone young man in it had just come from the island, bringing electrifying news. During the night, he said, Major Anderson and his garrison had secretly departed from Fort Moultrie by sea and removed to Fort Sumter. The cannons at Fort Moultrie had been spiked, and some men Anderson had temporarily left behind or sent back had set the gun carriages on fire and destroyed ammunition and other military materiel at the fort on Sullivan's Island.

Hearing all this, but hardly comprehending it at first, the firefighters looked to one another in speechless astonishment.

The steamer left the wharf, and in a little while, a large column of smoke rising from the direction of the fort was visible to the men on board. As they disembarked at the island, an acrid burning smell was very strong in the air, and soon made their eyes begin to water. When the fire companies reached Fort Moultrie, they could see dark clouds of smoke soaring up from behind the massive brick walls. David Macbeth immediately went to work with the firemen, but George stopped briefly to talk with an acquaintance, an elderly gentleman who lived year-round in Moultrieville. He had been watching the fires since dawn, and had taken a peek inside the fort, and noted that the flagstaff had been broken.

George fully intended to lend a hand in the firefighting, but first he wanted to take in the whole scene for himself. He went inside the walls of the fort and walked past the empty barracks as the firemen rushed to the gun carriages to extinguish the flames.

Even with the shouting and bustle going on around him, George was impressed with an eeriness about the place–so strangely and suddenly deserted in the secrecy of night–and its guns, deliberately disabled! Though the flames were in his eyes, and the smoke in his nostrils, it took him a few moments to overcome his lingering disbelief.

George climbed up to one of the parapets that faced seaward and standing there, he first looked up at the billowing, ominous smoke rising up into the cloudy sky and then turned and gazed off toward Fort Sumter. It was only about a mile across the water from one fort to the other, and the formidable structure in the harbor loomed much larger at this place of observation than it did when viewed from the sea walls of Charleston.

As if paralyzed, George stood transfixed in astonishment and bewilderment, staring at Fort Sumter—and soon he felt his heart chilled by something other than the cold morning winds blowing in off the ocean.

CHAPTER THREE

WHEN GEORGE GOT BACK to Charleston his first thought was to see his father, and he found him in his library. The old gentleman knew of Major Anderson's removal from Sullivan's Island to the new harbor fort, as did the whole city by now. A Charleston guard boat had brought the news that morning.

Mr. Taylor was angry and exasperated.

"It is a breach of faith!" he exclaimed to his son. "Our congressional delegation understood from President Buchanan that there was to be no change in the status of the forts, but now Anderson has crippled Fort Moultrie and is likely strengthening Fort Sumter!"

"But surely the president will evacuate the garrison now," said George.

"If that is his government's intention, then why did Major Anderson take this warlike action? Clearly, they are preparing for hostilities!"

Mr. Taylor threw up his hands in frustration and abruptly seated himself at his desk to write some letters of inquiry.

From his years in the state legislature and in Washington, the senator had developed a multiplicity of connections with important men, and still communicated with them often. Now that a terrible crisis was in the making, he wanted to know all he could, and began sending more telegrams and letters to old friends and colleagues in New York and Washington, including one of the three commissioners sent by the South Carolina governor to negotiate with President Buchanan. He also took measures to keep in constant communication with close friends and relatives in the South Carolina government, and made sure that he knew of the governor's decisions and actions as soon as possible. Though he was retired from the law and politics, and no longer in a position of authority, quite a few officials of his state, and others, had continued to consult him for his thoughts and advice, especially during the past few months.

The day after Fort Sumter was occupied, Mr. Taylor heard that the three South Carolinians who had been sent to Washington to discuss the removal of the Federal troops at Fort Moultrie, and to offer a peaceful settlement concerning Federal property in the state, had been forced to terminate their negotiations because of Major Anderson's unexpected, startling, and apparently unauthorized action. It was later learned Anderson had feared that the steamboat patrolling the harbor would land men on Sullivan's Island to attack Fort Moultrie, the more vulnerable of the two forts, though there had been no such intention on the part of the South Carolinians.

"We should have taken possession of Fort Sumter long ago," Mr. Taylor fumed, hearing this report. "There were no troops in it until Anderson moved there, and there was nothing to prevent us, except that we were foolish enough to trust in the honor of the government in Washington!"

Soon the new year of 1861 began, and Mr. Taylor continued to follow all news and events very closely. In February, after the formation of the Confederate States of America in Montgomery, Alabama, President Jefferson Davis sent three peace commissioners to Washington to seek the removal of the U.S. garrison from Fort Sumter, to offer an equitable payment for the seceded states' share of the public debt, and to establish friendly relations between the two countries. Mr. Taylor anxiously waited to see if these men would be able to effect a peaceful separation, but he was soon disappointed. Though they communicated through a go-between with Mr. Seward, the Secretary of State, Mr. Lincoln, the new president of the United States, did not meet with the Confederate commissioners, nor would he recognize the legitimacy of their government.

One evening in March, the Finleys hosted a special supper in honor of the publication of George's new book, *The History of a Lawsuit*. It was already being sold in the bookstores, and was receiving favorable reviews. After a long, enjoyable meal, and much conversation at the dinner table, Marguerite claimed George for herself for a while and took him into the parlor opposite the dining room.

"I have begun a scrapbook for you," she said, picking up a handsome leather album embossed with Greek key borders.

She sat down beside George on the sofa and opened the album in her lap. Several newspaper clippings were pasted on the first page.

"Those are mainly about your first book. I found them in some of Papa's old newspapers. All are very complimentary. Shall I read one to you?"

"Yes, I should prefer to hear my praises sung in your voice," he replied, with mingled embarrassment and pleasure.

She began, "The lawyers who have occasion to consult the decisions of the law court of this State, will doubtless be gratified to hear that George W. Taylor, Esquire, a highly talented and diligent young member of the Charleston Bar, has prepared and published a Digest of the cases decided by the Court of Appeals during the last twenty years. To prepare a suitable Digest requires unusual qualities of mind, and analytical powers of no common order. Mr. Taylor has brought to bear upon his task, an extensive and thorough acquaintance with our cases, great discrimination, excellent judgment, a well-balanced mind, and inexhaustible industry. He has produced a work philosophical in its arrangement, complete in all its parts, and invaluable as a work of reference. We predict for him an established reputation, and for his Digest, a very high rank as a legal authority."

"I remember that review," said George. "It was one of the first."

"It must have been gratifying to receive such recognition of your hard work and abilities."

"The book sold pretty well. It didn't make me much money, but I didn't write it for that reason. I only wanted to create something useful."

"And so you did!" said Marguerite, smiling and turning to the next page, where there were clippings about his newest book. She read part of another notice aloud.

"Mr. George W. Taylor, Esquire, of this city, well known to our citizens as one of the most talented and promising of the younger lawyers at our Bar, has published another valuable legal work. *The History of a Lawsuit* has recently appeared, and is doing more than claimed for it, in affording 'aid and comfort' to those entering upon the study of the law. His first publication, a Digest of our law reports, and this book, have been regarded with great favor by the profession. Mr. Taylor graduated at South Carolina College, in the class of '54, studied law at the office of the Honorable Joseph J. Pettigrew, and was admitted to the practice of his profession in 1856. From his first appearance at the bar, he has been distinguished by energy, persevering industry and legal capacity, that have secured for him a high position among his professional brethren..."

Marguerite paused, beaming with pride.

"Shall I go on?" she asked.

"I don't think I can bear anymore tonight," he said, laughing awkwardly. "You and your family have been far too kind and complimentary to me this evening, far more than I deserve."

Marguerite's brother walked into the room as George was answering and heard much of what he said.

"Ah, Rita is making you read the scrapbook, too," he observed facetiously. "My dear sister, what are you thinking? You will make Mr. Taylor vain and conceited, and then we'll not like him anymore. Now, let's break up this mutual admiration society and take a boat out into the harbor."

"Tonight?" his sister responded, surprised.

"Why not? It isn't even nine o'clock yet. The weather's fine and the moon is full. Come, get your coats and let's go rowing."

"Shall we, Mr. Taylor?" Marguerite asked George.

Though it was early March, the evening air was somewhat cool but not chilly, and the sea breezes were mild and only intermittent. Everyone seemed pleased with Frederick's idea of a rowing party in the harbor, and they stopped by Bessie Lightwood's house to pick her up. One of her female friends accompanied them, and when George and Marguerite took their seats, and Frederick helped his wife Elizabeth into hers, the small boat was nearly full. George and Frederick each took an oar, and two of the ladies also rowed. Marguerite traded places with Miss Lightwood when she grew tired, happy for the exercise.

Once they rounded the tip of the peninsula, the lights of the city at their backs, the dark outline of Fort Sumter could be seen on the horizon. A full moon was rising in a sky dotted here and there with fleecy fragments of clouds. It smoldered with a ruddy hue as it first appeared, but this reddish coloring gradually faded as the moon climbed higher, until it was a luminous ivory ball, its brightness reflected on every surface.

They rowed farther out into the harbor. Eventually the rowers ceased, and while everyone enjoyed a lazy repose as the boat drifted along with the tide, they admired the beauty, quiet, and serenity of the scenes around them. Lights could be seen from the Battery, Chisholm's Mill, and various houses and streets in the city. In the opposite direction, some lights were visible at Fort Sumter now, reminding them of an ominous presence in that place, but that night, everything looked so peaceful and magical that the menace of war seemed more dreamlike than reality.

Seated facing Marguerite, George put down his oar and leaned closer to her. In the moonlight, her fine features looked even more chiseled against her pale skin, and her dark eyes, even more captivating than usual, even mysterious.

"What are you thinking of?" he asked her quietly, as the others talked among themselves in lowered voices.

"I am not thinking at all, really," she replied, "only taking in all this romance."

"So am I," said George, adding in a whisper, "especially the one I see before me."

Marguerite laughed a little in embarrassment when Miss Lightwood leaned over and said roguishly, "We heard that, George."

"Shame on you for eavesdropping," he chided her.

"Good heavens! We are all at such close quarters in this boat, I don't see how you could think you would not be overheard."

The two cousins traded some banter, but as the exchange ended with affectionate smiles, George said, "Bessie, I can never be vexed with you for anything, ever again."

"Ah, and I know why," she laughed, glancing at Marguerite.

Some unthinking impulse of happiness made Marguerite laugh, too, and she made a movement which rocked the boat slightly, flinging out her arms as if she meant to jump into the harbor waters.

"I feel so grand," she declared, "I think I shall swim back home!"

"You will not!" her brother promptly objected, though he knew she must be joking.

"You know, I was thinking of doing the same thing myself," George joined in, making the same movement with his arms.

"You will not!" cried Marguerite, catching one of his hands, then she and everyone else laughed at their nonsense.

Marguerite let go of George's hand and put an arm over the side of the boat to dip her fingertips into the water.

"Oh, it's very cold," she remarked. "Too cold for swimming tonight, but it is refreshing to the touch."

She pushed up one of her sleeves to the elbow, revealing enough of a slim, shapely bare arm to make George dream of the continuation of those curves. When he saw that she was about to put her hand down into the water again, he begged her not to do that.

"Why not?" she asked.

"You might catch a chill, if the water is so cold," he said.

"Well, if you wish it," Marguerite relented, pulling down her sleeve.

"George is so protective," Miss Lightwood observed approvingly. "He will make a very good husband, I think. And he is so attentive! How he has hovered about you–"

"Bessie," George interrupted in a cautionary tone, catching the teasing note that had come into her voice, and feeling that she was about to say something that would irritate or embarrass him. His cousin laughed at his touchiness and turned away to talk with her friend.

It was true that since their engagement, Miss Finley had become the center of George's life, but he did not like to think that this made him an amusing spectacle for his friends and relations. For the past few weeks, the social season in Charleston had been in full swing, and he had been going out more often in public with Marguerite. On one of their first outings together, Bessie had teased him a little about the way he looked at his fiancée, and after that, reluctant to put his feelings on display for others, he affected more reserve with Marguerite whenever they were in company—and yet there were times when he could not help but show them. At the Saint Cecilia Society ball, where Marguerite wore a lovely, delicate dress of sea green tarleton, her hair adorned with white japonica flowers, she looked so fresh and verdant that George could not help but say to her, within the hearing of all those around them, that she looked like spring itself.

The month of March went out like the proverbial lion rather than a lamb, leaving in its wake storms and a few last days of cold weather, but after the first week of April passed, a beautiful spring began unfolding. The first flowers of the season were in bloom, and George breathed in their perfume with a swelling chest. Though deeply troubled by the profound political tensions in the air, he was too much in love to be depressed.

One afternoon, as he was eating dinner with his father at home, their meal was interrupted when a servant delivered a note to Mr. Taylor. The senator read it with a grim expression.

"Important news?" asked George.

His father nodded silently as he reread the brief message. He looked up at George with tears in his eyes.

"I am informed by the Governor that the government in Washington means to bring supplies to Fort Sumter, by force if necessary. An armed squadron of ships is on its way to Charleston."

Mr. Taylor wiped his eyes with a handkerchief, and his face grew red as sorrow gave place to anger.

"All the while, their Secretary of State has been assuring our commissioners in Washington that the garrison would be withdrawn from the fort. Now we see what a piece of deception that was. This is nothing but treachery! They have been using the time to prepare their warships!"

George hung his head speechlessly. His heart had suddenly become as heavy as a stone. Mr. Taylor rose from his chair and nervously paced back and forth on the carpet.

"Some of the Northern papers put it out as a relief expedition, bringing food to starving men. Of course we know this is nonsense, as the garrison has regularly received food from the city markets. Major Anderson has the same grocer we do! These ships are not coming to bring provisions—they are coming to provoke a war!"

"What do you think will happen, Father?" George asked.

"I do not think our government can allow Fort Sumter to be strengthened. It will have to be rendered powerless. Otherwise, the garrison there could join forces with the fleet when it arrives, and I do not see how we could successfully oppose such a powerful combination should they try to attack Charleston. They say their only intent is to provision the fort, but how can we take their word on that, when they have lied to us before–promising us that the fort would be evacuated? For months, we have waited, preparing to defend ourselves if necessary, tolerating the intolerable, in the hope that Anderson and his men would be removed, so that bloodshed could be avoided–but now that no longer seems possible."

Later, Mr. Taylor received news that there was some fierce opposition in President Davis's cabinet to firing on Fort Sumter, and that his own secretary of state was desperately advising against it. As several tense days dragged on, the senator kept in constant communication with old colleagues and government officials, but there was no change in the situation in Charleston harbor. Major Anderson repeatedly refused to leave the fort, and General Beauregard, the commander of the Confederate forces defending the city, awaited orders from his government in Montgomery.

In the early morning hours of the twelfth of April, George was suddenly roused from his slumbers before dawn by the noise of cannon fire. He lit a lamp beside his bed and looked at the clock. It was about four thirty a.m. Making his way to the window of his bedroom, he looked out to see the shadowy figures of people gathering along the Battery. Major Anderson, the commander of the garrison at Fort Sumter, had made a final refusal to evacuate the place a few hours earlier, and the bombardment of the fort had begun. Shot and shell were being thrown into Sumter from Fort Moultrie and the encircling harbor batteries.

George quickly dressed himself and went downstairs, knowing that Marguerite and her family would probably wish to watch the spectacle from the upper piazza of his house. Mr. Taylor was already there, watching the bombardment. As soon as George reached the foot of the stairs, his brother and sister-in-law came rushing in through the front door in a state of great excitement, and about fifteen minutes later, the Finleys arrived.

Mr. Finley had a spy glass with him, and Marguerite and her mother had brought their opera glasses to get a better view of the proceedings, though it was difficult to see anything except the distant flashes of artillery fire until the dawn began to lighten the cloudy skies. It was a windy morning, and the northeast gusts carried the booming sounds of the guns clearly into the ears of all those watching from the city. The crowd along the Battery became immense, and every upper window, piazza and rooftop which afforded a view of the harbor was peopled with spectators. Mr. Taylor's house was almost directly in front of Fort Sumter in the distance, so that he and his family and guests had, from the third floor piazza, one of the best viewing places in the city.

Within a few hours, Anderson's men began to return fire, and as the morning wore on, a spectacular duel of artillery continued.

As soon as daylight appeared, several ships could be seen off to the right of Fort Sumter, out of the range of the guns. These vessels were the transports and warships sent down from the North to bring supplies to Major Anderson's garrison. They were full of provisions, ammunition, and troops, but they kept their position and made no move to intervene. Hour after hour, the combatants and non-combatants alike watched and waited for them to take some action.

"Why don't the ships come to the aid of Fort Sumter?" Mrs. Finley asked her husband. "Did they not come here to help Major Anderson?"

"I do not know, my dear," he said. "Perhaps they deem it too dangerous, or are waiting for more ships to arrive. Then again, perhaps the winds are against them. What do you think, Mr. Taylor?"

"It hardly matters now," George's father remarked gravely. "At any rate, they have no need to render any assistance to Major Anderson. They have already fulfilled their mission."

Marguerite looked at the senator intently.

"I believe I know what you mean, Mr. Taylor," she said, "but will you state it plainly?"

"They have commenced a war, Miss Finley," he replied.

As the day wore on, and the thunder and smoke of the bombardment continued, many in the watching crowds began to wonder, like Mrs. Finley, why the armed vessels off the bar did nothing. Her husband, gazing through his spy-glass, pointed out that the besieged garrison had lowered the flag of the fort to half mast as a signal of distress, but to no avail.

A crowd of non-combatants who had gathered on the beach of Sullivan's Island to watch the bombardment had a much closer view of Fort Sumter. They were standing in an area well away from Fort Moultrie, and far removed from the line of fire being sent there from Fort Sumter. About four hours into the bombardment, one of Major Anderson's gun crews decided it would be fitting to send something in the direction of these spectators, and so—perhaps offering a taste of things to come—they aimed their fire at the observers on the beach and sent off two rounds from their 42-pounder. The first shot landed in front of the crowd on the beach, missing them by only about 150 feet, and then vaulted over their heads and crashed into a hotel building behind them. The second ball did much the same, as the people frantically scattered in all directions except seaward to escape.

The bombardment went on throughout the rest of the day, to a lesser extent that night, and continued the following morning. Finally, when no further resistance could be offered, a white flag of truce was raised at Fort Sumter, and the firing came to an end. In the entire action, no deaths had been inflicted on either side.

Not long after the surrender of the fort, George and his brother Albert stood on the High Battery with spyglasses to watch Major Anderson and his men board the steamship which would take them home. On that same day, April 15, they learned that the president of the United States had called for the state militias to supply seventy-five thousand men to suppress the "insurrection."

In the latter part of May, George came home from his office one afternoon to ask his father's advice about a particularly complex estate settlement he was handling. He found Mr. Taylor in his library, engaged in an occupation which had become something of an obsession with him over the past few months. He was sitting at a desk, surrounded by letters, newspapers, pamphlets, and periodicals, mostly of Northern origin, but a few of them European, and was holding a pair of scissors, cutting out a column from a Northern journal he had just received. It would be pasted into a scrapbook of clippings he had been collecting, as he followed opinion and events in the North. George was about to ask his father a question about the estate case, but hesitated when he saw him put down the clipping and lower his head in meditation, sitting quiet and still as a statue. Mr. Taylor was obviously preoccupied with much weightier matters than those on George's mind. When he looked up from his work, his eyes were heavy and bloodshot.

"You have been reading too much, Father," George gently reproved him. "You will strain your sight."

"You are right," Mr. Taylor answered wearily. "I have seen too much–already, much too much."

The old gentleman slowly rubbed his eyes and sighed, then took up the clipping he had just cut out.

"The Northern radicals have become even more bloodthirsty than before! They hate us more than ever!" he said wonderingly. "Have you read these papers?"

"Some of them, yes."

Mr. Taylor sighed.

"It was my hope that the North and South could separate peacefully, but that will not happen. The union will be preserved, but by force of arms now. They will not let us go."

The old gentleman tossed aside the scrap and leaned over the desk with his head in his hands.

"I see no hope for us," he muttered, almost inaudibly.

"You don't mean that, Father," George replied. "You have spent too much time poring over the ravings of the radicals, and have made yourself depressed."

Mr. Taylor lifted his head and studied his son's face with a serious, deliberative expression, as if trying to make up his mind about something concerning him. Looking more and more troubled, he rose from his seat, walked over to a window, and stood there looking out, his hands clasped behind his back. George waited for his father to speak, and was shocked when Mr. Taylor suddenly swayed as if about to fall, and put out his hands to take hold of the window sill and steady himself.

"What is wrong? Are you ill?" George asked anxiously. He took his father's arm and helped him into a chair.

Mr. Taylor brought his hands to his chin, laced his fingers together tightly, and tapped them against a frowning mouth.

"I am not ill, George," he said, with a slight waver in his voice his son had never heard before. "No more than usual, at least."

"Then what has disturbed you so?"

As he looked at his son to answer him, his eyes welled and glittered with a strange intensity, but no tears fell.

"What else? War!"

Mr. Taylor's look of horror momentarily infected George, and he remembered his own feeling of dread that fateful day at Fort Moultrie, as he contemplated the other harbor fortress–but he quickly recoiled against these feelings, and tried to reason with his father to reassure him.

"Some of my friends have predicted a very bloody conflict," said George, "but surely it cannot last long."

"As to its duration, that I do not know, but as to its extent...," Mr. Taylor paused, then, gesturing toward his scrapbooks, went on, "as to its extent, I fear it will be more bloody than we can even imagine. There are many people in the North who wish to let us go in peace, and even some abolitionists who would say good riddance to us, but all these have no real power. Those who are in power know they can and must defeat us. If they fail, great financial loss stares them in the face–hence their madness! They must also show that the union cannot be dissolved, to save them from future secessions. Now that they have declared war on us–though they will not call it that–the South will have to fight, and knowing our people as I do, I know that they will not submit, nor admit defeat unless and until utterly crushed. So you see, our enemies will not only defeat us in this war–they will invade and destroy us."

George wondered for a moment if his father's mind had been affected by his illness, yet Mr. Taylor was not raving or even irrational; if anything, his manner was more subdued than normal, though from dread and despair.

"Surely not," George protested. "You always said that we had the best fighting men in the world, Father. You really see no hope of our winning this war if the North persists in it?"

"No, George. They are more numerous. They have manufactures, a navy...They will be able to draw on the resources of the world, while our ports will be blocked, and we–"

Mr. Taylor stopped. George was shaking his head in contradiction.

"Father, when they come up against our armies, get a taste of real fighting, and see their comrades and sons die in battle, they will make peace with us."

Mr. Taylor rose to his feet and walked over to his desk, where he picked up a handful of newspaper scraps and held them up.

"They will not make peace with us until they prevail, I am convinced!" he exclaimed. "There will be no peace–until we are utterly ruined!"

George was momentarily taken aback by his father's passion and conviction, but he was soon shaking his head again in disbelief. The old gentleman went back to his chair and limply collapsed there, as though all his bones had gone soft and no longer supported him, his face a picture of hopelessness. George had only seen his father like this once before–when his wife died.

George could see that recent events had taken a heavy toll on his father. Mr. Taylor had lost more weight in the past few weeks, and looked even frailer now. His son kneeled beside the chair and tried to comfort him with some good news.

"Albert may be vexed with me for telling you first, but I am going to tell you anyway. President Davis has appointed him as the Confederate States District Attorney for South Carolina. I saw the letter this morning."

Mr. Taylor brightened a little, and a smile slowly lifted his lips.

"Ah, that is good news," he said quietly. "Tell Albert I am very proud of him."

"You may tell him yourself. I'm sure he will come by to pay you a visit today."

"This is a position of great responsibility," Mr. Taylor mused. "You must do all you can to assist your brother, George. I am sure he will be depending on you to do that."

"I shall be proud to offer any service I can."

They talked about Albert for a while. Then George remembered the reason why he had stopped by and sought his advice about the complicated estate settlement. They conversed about several difficult aspects of the matter for a full hour, until the old gentleman began to grow drowsy, and George left him to nap in his chair.

Since the beginning of the year, nearly every able-bodied man in Charleston had been enlisting to swell the ranks of militia companies newly formed for the defense of the state. They were busy repairing the forts and building up the other harbor defenses, drilling and training, and manning outposts on the sea islands along the coast. Almost all of George's friends and contemporaries were now in uniform, and he had been seriously considering his own obligations of this kind for a long while. In March he had talked about it with his brother, but Albert asked him to wait. Because of his new responsibilities, he had turned over the firm's ongoing cases to George, and hoped to see most of them resolved before the end of the year. He also told George that he needed his help in taking on the district attorneyship.

"You will be serving your country in that capacity, just as soldiers serve in another," Albert argued.

"I suppose...," George said hesitantly.

"I know how you feel," his brother assured him. "If my lameness did not prevent me, I should wish to go into the army, too. I am only asking you to postpone your decision a little while."

Albert was persuasive enough to convince his brother that his help was essential, so he agreed to put off enlistment for a time. George was so busy in the spring and first part of the summer that he gave the matter little further thought; in late July, however, when the casualties of the first major battle in Virginia were brought home to Charleston for burial with solemn, grand public ceremonies, he made up his mind that he must enter military service, and began to look for a suitable place.

One afternoon the following month, as he was walking home from his office, he saw a young man who looked familiar. He hesitated to speak to him until he came closer and recognized his cousin, Franklin Stephens. He had been abroad several years studying medicine, and looked very different from the slim, beardless youth George remembered. Frank wore a thin mustache and a short goatee now, and was no longer so slim, but his dimpled smile and light blue eyes were unmistakable. They greeted each other with an embrace and walked together arm in arm talking of their lives for the past few years.

"When did you return to South Carolina?" George asked his cousin.

"Well, I wanted to come home last December, when my brother Philip went into state service, but Father insisted that I finish my studies, so I did not get back until last month."

The young man informed him that he would be serving in his brother's new regiment.

"Not a regiment, though, really," he explained. "The governor has given Philip permission to form something of a small army. It's to be called the Holton Legion, in honor of Mr. Richard Holton, the

Charleston gentleman who is equipping us. We are to serve in the state defenses for now, near the coast I should think. We shall begin recruiting next month, to be in place by the middle of October."

George was very interested in the Legion; the timing worked out well, as he was sure he could finish up most of the work he had promised to do for Albert by October. Frank Stephens was a physician, and would serve as the Legion's surgeon. His older brother Philip, who had extensive military experience, would be in command with the rank of colonel. George hinted that he had been looking for a place to serve.

"You ought to join us, then," his cousin encouraged him. "I'm sure my brother would be happy to have you as one of his officers. The three of us have always gotten along famously, haven't we?"

"That's true," said George. "But give me a little time to think it over."

"Nonsense!" Frank protested, slapping George's back. "It's all settled–you're in, my man! I'm going to tell Philip that he has one of his lieutenants."

When he was alone that evening, George thought about Holton Legion and came to the same decision his cousin had already made for him. It had first occurred to him to enlist as a private. Like almost all the young men of his state, he had experienced some military training in the militia, but he wondered whether such training was adequate preparation for service as an officer in wartime. The thought of entering the army as an officer made George feel a little uneasy, and he wondered if it was wise, but after consulting with his father, he decided to leave the call to Colonel Stephens. Philip was not the sort of man to show favoritism to relatives, and would not make George an officer if he thought him unfit for the rank.

A week later, after several conversations with the colonel, George was commissioned as a second lieutenant.

With the same thoroughness and diligence that he applied to his profession, George threw himself into the study of every book on military tactics and practices he could lay his hands on, preparing himself for his duties. In late September, he put on his gray uniform and wore it in public for the first time as he walked to the Finley house, smiles and stares of respect meeting him all along the way. He had been so busy finishing up work on several cases which had just concluded, or were about to, that he had not seen Marguerite in several days.

As he walked down the street, his mind was still full of the legal work he had been unusually busy with for weeks, especially a lawsuit he had been forced to hand over to another attorney—a complicated affair that had gone on for years and unfortunately promised to go on for at least several more—but George was very glad that, the day before, he had been able to finish with one particularly distasteful case so that he would not have anything more to do with it. One of the defendants in this affair was a man who, though nominally a gentleman, was of a very low character and a violent temper. A bankrupt, he had squandered his own fortune and put his wife's in jeopardy when creditors came after him. The couple were estranged because of the man's profligacy and other vices, but George had been engaged to protect the wife's property, and it was necessary for him to correspond with the husband, who lived in a district over a hundred miles from Charleston. In his letters, the man repeatedly claimed that he loved his wife and wished to reconcile with her, but his attorney suspected that the man's principal motive was only mercenary. When the court of equity rendered a decree in the matter, George was relieved to be rid of such a sordid business.

The case also had one other unpleasant aspect: it had not turned out as well as he had hoped. The court's decree had not been entirely unfavorable to his clients, but he regarded the outcome as something of a failure. When the chancellor handed down his decision, George looked over the arguments he had presented and came to the conclusion that they could and should have been made more cogently and clearly–that it was a case he could and should have won. He drew up an appeal, but had to turn that over to a friend to handle in his absence. He was disappointed in himself, and it occurred to him that he might have been too distracted during the proceedings. Besides thoughts of Marguerite, news of the wounding and deaths of friends and relations in the army had preoccupied him and caused him to grow more anxious about his own military obligations, so much so that he could hardly pass an hour without dwelling on the matter.

He had always done very well professionally, and though in the past he had, like any other attorney, suffered setbacks and failures, this little blow to his confidence came at a particularly bad time. He was wearing a uniform now, about to enter into very grave matters of life and death, and, going into the great unknown of war, he felt somewhat unsure of himself. He did not know how he would measure up as a soldier or a leader of men, and his misgivings about this, together with his drive to excel in whatever he did, had led to a decision concerning Marguerite. It was a decision he knew she would not like, and so as he approached the gate of her family's house that morning, his happiness to be with her again was mixed with some dread.

On seeing George in uniform for the first time, Marguerite reacted with such admiration and pride that he had to laugh out loud for nervous relief.

"You look so handsome and dashing, Mr. Taylor!" she cried.

She took his hand and led him over to a sofa, where they sat down to talk. Marguerite asked him about the Legion, and as he answered her questions, she slowly ran her fingers over the gold braid of his lower sleeves. During a pause, she could tell that there was something serious on his mind other than the war. She asked George what he was thinking of. He hesitated, frowning, but forced himself to say what he had to.

"Miss Marguerite," he began, lowering his eyes.

A thought came into her head, and she spoke out impulsively, interrupting him.

"I wish you to wear your uniform for the wedding," she said. "I can think of no finer thing for you to wear."

George looked at her strangely.

"About the wedding–," he said tensely, catching his breath.

"What about the wedding?" she asked, her tone falling with her smile as she observed his uneasiness.

His expression grew solemn, even grave, but Marguerite suddenly remembered something else important she wished to tell him and spoke again before he could answer.

"Oh, I meant to tell you, Papa wishes to make us a wedding present of a house! He is looking into purchasing the Logan mansion for us. It is a beautiful home, and not very old. If this house is not acceptable, he says he will build us a new one, though that may be difficult just now. Papa said that he knows of a lot on a very pleasant street, and will purchase it for us, though we may have to wait until the war is over to build on it. Perhaps we might live in a rented house until then."

"I...I don't think it is a wise thing to do," said George.

"Which? To buy, or to build?"

"Neither, I mean–"

He hesitated again

"Please tell me," Marguerite urged. "Is something wrong?"

"No, but there is something unpleasant I must ask of you."

"What is it?"

"I know that everything is set for December, but I must ask you–will you consider postponing our plans to marry? Would you wait for me?"

Marguerite's mouth opened in astonishment.

"But why?" she asked anxiously.

"I think I shall do better if I can devote myself entirely to my duties," he explained reluctantly.

"You have a duty to me," she reminded George after an awkward pause.

"We are engaged, yes. But the marriage can be put off. The war–over the war I have no control–it is upon us. But I don't think it will last long much longer. I don't see how it can. It will be decided one way or another very soon, in a matter of months, certainly less than a year."

"You really think so?"

"I do."

After ruminating over his reasons in silence for a few moments, Marguerite said, "I don't see why we ought not to marry. We are already bound to each other. What difference will it make?"

George expelled a sigh of frustration.

"Miss Marguerite," he said, "my nature is such that I must be single-minded in this thing. Can't you understand? We are at war, for our very existence. Is there anything more important than that?"

"No," she admitted, looking away.

"Then I ask you to allow me this bit of obstinacy, whether you understand or not."

"I see I must," she replied, meeting his eyes with a gloomy look of disappointment. "Because you ask it, I must. If I insisted otherwise, you would be resentful."

"I could never resent you."

"Oh, but you would. You have a fixed idea in your stubborn mind, which, to my misfortune, has to do with me."

"Miss Marguerite," he said in a pleading, persuasive tone, taking her hand as he tried to explain himself. "You know how much I love you. You must know that you are on my mind a great deal. If we were married, I think it would only be worse torture for me to be separated from you. And then, if we did marry...and were...blessed with the expectation of a child, I should be able to do nothing but worry about your health and safety. While I am in the army, let things remain as they are. Your father and your family will be able to protect you and provide for you while I am away, relieving me of that worry. You should stay with them, under their protection, not in some house your father has promised us."

Marguerite suddenly held his hand in a tighter grasp, brought it to her lips, and kissed it repeatedly. Her eyes were closed, and he could feel the wetness of her tears on his skin.

"I think you are wrong, but I will give in to you on this," she said, hanging her head, "because I must. But I will not cease to hope that you will change your mind. After we are separated for a while, I think you will."

"You are making this more difficult for me," George protested. "You mustn't do that."

"Forgive me!" she begged him. "I know you are doing what you think is best. I think you are wrong, but I shall wait for you. What else can I do?"

"I don't wish to see any more tears," said George, assuming a sternness he did not really feel. "I can't bear it."

He had never seen Marguerite weep before, and never had she looked so girlish and immature as she did at that moment, but she soon raised her chin and faced him with composure.

"I promise," she said, "there will be no more tears."

"That's better. Now, I shall want a likeness of you to take with me, something small I can keep in my pocket."

"I shall have one made for you. If it is not ready by the time you leave, I shall send it to you. But I shall want one of you, too, not just your face, but all of you, in your uniform. Will you do that for me?"

"Of course. Shall I speak with your father or–"

"I shall tell him."

"You must stress that it is only a postponement, because of the war, nothing more, and that you are in agreement with me. I don't wish him to think that I have any doubts where you and I are concerned."

"He knows you don't, dear."

George hesitated, looking troubled again.

"No, I ought to speak with him myself," he decided aloud. "Is he here?"

He went to look for Mr. Finley. When George returned to his fiancée after about a quarter of an hour, he appeared relieved and calm.

"Your father agrees with me. He says that it is best we wait."

"Then we wait," she replied, trying not to frown.

CHAPTER FOUR

MARGUERITE KNEW QUITE A FEW engaged couples, and some merely contemplating engagement, who had rushed to the altar before the men had to go off to assume their military duties. Some other courting couples of her acquaintance had married on the man's first furlough, after a separation which, as might be expected, had made hearts grow fonder. Marguerite believed that the same thing would happen to George–that he would change his mind after spending some time apart from her and hasten home to marry her.

In October, all the officers and soldiers of Holton Legion assembled in Charleston and then departed from the city to begin their service over sixty miles south in Beaufort District, where they were to defend the railroad connecting Charleston and Savannah. The weather at that time of year was beautiful and cool, and George's first taste of camp life was not unpleasant. It was a sort of adventure, after all, and though he began to experience a nervous anticipation about what may come, he felt no fear as yet. The only thing that made him uneasy was his inexperience.

George found most of his fellow officers congenial, and some of them, it seemed, were exceptionally fine men. In his first letter to Marguerite, he joked that the Legion was "swarming with clergymen." A number of the officers and soldiers were students from seminaries, or ordained men who had temporarily left the ministry for military service, or earnest laymen of various denominations who were intending to enter the ministry after the war. The commander, Colonel Stephens, was a strikingly handsome man of thirty with dark hair, blue eyes, and a strong, straight frame. In face and physique he resembled a young Robert E. Lee, and looked so much the soldier every inch that few would have guessed that he had recently been ordained as an Episcopal priest.

After much soul-searching, a young friend and distant relation of the colonel, Alexander Dwight, had given up his studies at an Episcopal seminary to serve as Stephens' adjutant in the Legion. In his second letter to Marguerite, George told her about young Adjutant Dwight.

Holton Legion

20th October 1861

Dearest Miss Marguerite,

You asked a great many questions in your letter, the first of many I hope to receive from you.

My first letter to you I fear was not very informative or interesting. I also received a letter from my cousin Miss Alicia Porter of Beaufort, who particularly wished me to promptly seek out and meet her fiancé, Alexander Dwight, which of course I have done. Aleck (as we call him) is Adjutant to Colonel Stephens, and upon learning that we are to be related by marriage, he immediately took a great liking to me. I find him an extraordinary young man—really the most amiable fellow in the world. His family is from St. John's Parish. He is two years younger than I, very devout, and quite the scholar. He took a degree at the University of Virginia, and was lately studying for holy orders at the seminary in Camden. Before all that, he graduated the Citadel with first honors, and seems to be a very good officer, though I think he would make a better chaplain. We have been thrown together quite a bit already, as he shares the same mess as Frank Stephens, whom I see often. We are becoming very good friends.

Aleck is utterly in love and wishes to marry soon, but Alicia's father, my uncle, the Rev. Dr. Paul Porter, says they must wait until he is ordained <u>and</u> the war is over. Aleck has already written to Alicia several times, with feverish devotion (like mine). He is a more cheerful lovesick soul than I am, and tries to make the best of circumstances, though he is separated from the object of his affection (like me). Being a minister's daughter, and very like Aleck in mind and temperament, I think Alice is admirably suited for him. Rev. Porter disapproves of clergymen entering the military service except as chaplains, so I suppose this is the root of his objection. And yet his own son, my cousin Robert, who was a fellow student with Aleck at the seminary, has, against his father's wishes, joined the army, and is already in Virginia. He is engaged, too, so there will be no marrying for him either, I imagine, for a good long while.

We are far from any village, in something of a wilderness near the Coosawhatchie River. Our camp is fully set up and organized, and our pickets are well situated, but for now this place is much like a camp of instruction. Adjutant Dwight spends most of his time as the drill master, bringing our awkward, untrained troops into fit shape. It has been amusing to watch the soldiers drill and see how independent they are of each other.

Whenever one is out of step, he blames it on the fellow next to him.

Yesterday I received the likeness you had made for me, Miss Marguerite, and jealously keep it for my eyes alone. You are not quite smiling, but you look as if you are about to. I have shown it only to Aleck, who pronounces you "exquisite." And of course, having seen the "real thing," I know you are, in every way. I like the handsome little case that encloses it, and keep it near me as much as possible as my most treasured possession. I am sorry I did not have time to have my likeness taken again before I left Charleston, but I promise that on my first furlough I shall allow you and your mother to march me down to Mr. Cook's and let him have at me. I shall try to look more natural this time, and dispense with what you call the "hypnotic stare" of my last attempt. I don't know why you should think that I would wish to use powers of mesmerism on you. As I already have your heart, and your promise to marry me, what more could I want? When I look at your likeness, it is your charming gaze that mesmerizes me.

Colonel Stephens has just sent for me, so I close now. Write to me soon! I must have at least the conversation of your letters. You know that I miss you very much, my dearest.

Yours very affectionately,

George W. Taylor

As the month of November began, the weather continued mild and fair; the evenings were cool, but not unpleasantly so. One night, George was sitting by a campfire with Aleck Dwight, who was asking him questions about the man who was going to be his father-in-law. The young adjutant had been composing a letter to Reverend Porter, but had changed his mind about it, and was holding the crumpled piece of paper in one of his hands, crushing it smaller and smaller so that it disappeared in his fist.

"I'm afraid I cannot offer you much hope, Aleck," said George. "My uncle Porter is quite inflexible on matters of principle. As much as he dotes on Alicia, I don't think he will give in and let her marry while you are in the army."

"Yes, I think you're right," Aleck answered glumly, staring into the fire. "Miss Alicia told me much the same thing. It is all very unfortunate, but I am resigned. Perhaps it is for the best."

After tossing the wadded letter into the flames, he turned to George with a faint smile and a rueful look in his piercing gray eyes. Aleck's face and nose were somewhat long and of a delicate mold, and his high forehead was smooth and clear of any lines. His hair was dark, his complexion pale, and he was slight and shorter than average. He had suffered a long spell of ill health the year before, and did not look strong, but had been able to convince his friend Colonel Stephens that he was fully recovered and much stronger than he looked. When the adjutant was among the troops especially, perhaps to compensate for his small stature, he carried himself with a rigid military posture, but now, in the company of his friend and future relation, he was quite relaxed, and sat slumping with his elbows on his knees and his collar and coat unbuttoned.

George had been wondering how Aleck had met his cousin Miss Porter, and asked him about it. A broad smile broke out on the young man's face at the memory.

"You know that Robert and I were fellow students in Camden, and we became great friends there. Miss Alicia wrote to him regularly, every week, and he used to read me some of her letters– with her permission, of course. He always asked her to critique his sermons and papers, and from hearing the opinions and thoughts she expressed in her letters, I began to appreciate what an extraordinary young lady she was. You mustn't tell Robert, but I think she has a finer mind than his, and I must say I have great respect for his abilities. Well, I think I was already a little in love with her before we met, and when I went home with Robert on holiday, and saw her, you might say that my fate was sealed."

"Did my cousin feel the same way so quickly?" George asked.

"She did. Later on, after we became engaged, she told me so."

"Were you engaged before you decided to enter into military service?"

"Yes, long before. We were only waiting for me to finish my studies at the seminary. It was after I joined the Legion that Mr. Porter demanded the postponement. I tried to reason with him, but he would not be persuaded. I don't think I angered him, but he was not pleased with my objections, and I'm afraid I was not very eloquent or persuasive. What could I do? He has such an imposing presence, and I–I do not."

Aleck looked up at the black, clouded night sky overhead and sighed, "Ah, if not for this war, I should have my wife, my ordination, and my parish by now."

"If not for this war, I should have been married myself soon," said George.

Aleck looked surprised.

"You mean you've put it off? Why did you do that?"

"I thought it best to wait."

"*That* I do not understand," the adjutant reacted wonderingly. "I should marry Miss Alicia immediately if her father allowed it."

"I wish you could, Aleck."

"Ah, George, if only I were in your position, and could simply change my mind, and make it so, like that!" he laughed, snapping his fingers, and adding wonderingly, "You must have a will of iron."

George smiled.

"I'm afraid I do," he said, "rather like my uncle Porter."

A few days later, after hearing some good news, George wrote a letter to Marguerite to tell her about it.

Coosawhatchie

4th November 1861

> *I am very happy to inform you, my dear Miss Marguerite, that we shall soon leave this area, as there are orders for us to remove to Adam's Run. This puts me much closer to Charleston (less than thirty miles away!) and to a better probability of seeing you soon. Do you think it would be possible for us to meet at your uncle's plantation? I believe you told me it was in St. Andrew's Parish. Perhaps you could arrange to visit him in the next few weeks. It would not be such a long journey for me to ride there, and I think I stand a better chance of obtaining permission for that, rather than going to Charleston.*

> *The news of our imminent removal did not sit well with Adjutant Dwight, as it takes him much farther away from Beaufort, and Miss Alicia–but, resilient fellow that he is, he only moped a little while, and has since dutifully resigned himself to his fate. He is seated near me just now writing a letter to her.*

> *Other than the happy development I have just shared, there isn't much of anything new to report since my last letter, except for a little incident which might amuse you.*

A few days ago some officers of the Charleston Light Dragoons paid our camp a visit. One of them, my cousin John Hutchinson, challenged our best horseman to a race at their encampment (near the railroad, not too far from here). It so happened that Captain Peyre, the cavalry officer with the fastest horse, had just returned from a long reconnoitre, some of it through swampy lands, and both rider and animal looked so spiritless, bedraggled and muddy that the Dragoons laughed at them when they were presented as our finest contenders for the race. "This is your best horse?" they jeered. Captain Peyre's mount, a somewhat thickset mare, looked all the worse for the fact that she was just getting her coarse winter coat. "She is faster than she looks," Peyre assured them, pretending to be affronted. "We shall see about that on Thursday," they said very confidently, though some of the Dragoons, including my cousin John, looked a bit conscience-stricken about the challenge. The horse they usually race is a thoroughbred champion, but they were not aware that Peyre's mare is a famed quarter horse.

On Thursday, the Captain showed up with his mare in much the same state of poor grooming, and was once again an object of some derision and hauteur. However once the race began (a quarter mile dash), the Dragoons were amazed to see our mare flying far ahead of their champion. She won by at least two lengths. They soon found out about our little subterfuge, but took it in a good-humored, sporting manner. Even John laughed heartily at the trick, though I suspect he lost some money on the betting. When we told Colonel Stephens about the incident, he was very amused, and also pleased to learn that so few of his officers had placed any wagers. The

Dragoons' expressions of dismay and astonishment were our best reward. I must say it gave me some satisfaction to see the look on the face of my cavalier cousin, when our horse triumphed so handily.

Please write to me very soon and let me know if our rendezvous is possible at your uncle's plantation. You described the place to me once, and I have heard from other sources that it is one of the most beautiful estates on the Ashley River. I should like to see it, but of course I am much more anxious to see you. Tell Chassie that I received her sweet little note. I shall enclose a reply with this letter.

Yours most devotedly,

George W. Taylor

The following week, when Holton Legion was just about to leave for Adam's Run, word came that the enemy was fighting for a foothold on the South Carolina coast at Port Royal Sound. A few days later, in early December, reports were confirmed that the area was under enemy control. George and Aleck were concerned about Alicia and her family, who lived in nearby Beaufort. They soon learned that all the inhabitants of the town had been forced to evacuate upon hearing that enemy ships were on the way up the river.

George wrote to Marguerite, "We have not heard from the Porters as yet, but I suspect they have taken refuge with Rev. Porter's brother, a planter in Prince William Parish. We know at least that everyone was safely away before the Yankees entered Beaufort."

In the church, a young soldier from Connecticut was probing piles of rubble and the scattered, useless leavings of the pillagers who had long since departed. Private Griswolt grumbled, cursing his luck, having arrived too late to be among those who had found and carried off the best stuff first.

The church building was to be used as a hospital, and the dismantling of the interior had already begun. Most of the pews and chancel furniture had been thrown out or destroyed, and the gallery rails cut away. A fine old organ of English make had been disemboweled, smashed, and stripped of its ivory keys, and any other portable objects of obvious value had also been stolen. Outside, the high wall which enclosed the church and its grounds and cemetery was being torn down in several sections, its bricks to be used in the construction of a large baking oven for the needs of the occupying army.

Private Griswolt had been ordered to remove the trash from the floors, but, seeing no great need for any hurry, he began to entertain himself by looking through the scatterings of books, papers, and other odds and ends left behind after the gutting of the larger furnishings. His new uniform–a blue-black coat and trousers of a lighter shade of blue–was wrinkled and a little soiled, but as yet unscathed by any hardship or contact with the enemy, the army and navy of his country having won a fairly easy victory that week. From aboard one of the ships of a massive Federal fleet, the private had witnessed the U.S. forces overpower the much weaker Confederate defenses at Port Royal Sound. Afterward, some ships had proceeded on to Beaufort, a town on the Beaufort River less than twenty miles away.

As soon as this part of coastal South Carolina, which included the islands of Port Royal and Hilton Head, was in Union possession, news of the outcome of the battle had traveled quickly to Beaufort, and its people had abruptly evacuated.

When Private Griswolt came ashore and walked into the town, he and his companions were surprised to find it devoid of almost every white inhabitant. It was very strange, he thought, to walk into a place where there were no families in the houses, no owners or workers in the stores and businesses. Only some slaves had remained behind, many of them wearing fine clothes they had taken from the empty residences.

The soldiers and officers were impressed with the beauty and elegance of the town, admiring the handsome live oak trees shading streets paved with shells, the lush semi-tropical gardens and ornamental trees, and lovely houses and mansions with broad piazzas facing south. It was plain to see that a wealthy and cultured people had lived here. The parish church, the one Private Griswolt had been assigned to clean up inside, was beautiful and stately, and a public library, the pride of the town, was housed in another elegant building. Just that morning, he had been told that its collection of over three thousand volumes was being crated and shipped to New York.

Tired and bored, he sat down on the floor in a spot which had once been the juncture of a pew and an aisle, and soon noticed, within arm's length, a small leather-bound book which looked very old. His curiosity aroused, he picked it up and saw inside its front cover some lines handwritten in an old English script. They read: "Parish Prayer Book, Beaufort, St. Helena, Port Royal Island, South Carolina." Below this, in the same hand, were written the names of some vestrymen of the church, and the date "1773."

He turned to the title page and read, *The Book of Common Prayer and Administration of the Sacraments, and other Rites and Ceremonies of the Church, According to the Use of the Church of England...* The title went on, but he stopped here and looked down to the bottom of the page, noting that the book had been printed in London in the year "MDCCXXIX," which he correctly rendered as 1729. He thumbed through the pages and saw that some of the words and phrases had been crossed out here and there, and other words and phrases written in above them. It interested him to see in the prayers for those in authority, that the name of King George had been inked out and replaced with "the delegates of our American States."

After a little more perusal, Private Griswolt slipped the book into one of his pockets and decided to hunt for more such interesting finds. He got to his feet again and walked around slowly, making a more careful survey of the church floor. After a few minutes he came across a small heap of hymn and prayer books and kneeled down to take a closer look. One volume among them of a different color and size had caught his eye. The corner of this large book bound in fawn-colored leather protruded beneath the jumble of black devotionals. He grasped it and pulled it out, and was surprised by its size and weight. It reminded him of the massive account books that sat on a shelf in the store where he had clerked before the war. It was a handsome volume, and like the other book he had found, looked very old.

He opened it on the floor. Antique handwriting of the previous century met his eyes. The name of the parish, "Saint Helena," was inscribed in large letters on the first page. On the following pages were lists of names and dates under the headings of "Births," "Baptisms," "Marriages," and "Burials," as well as the names of officiating ministers. The earliest date he saw was 1724.

For some reason the names of these hundreds, perhaps thousands, of strangers recorded in the book fascinated the young man, as did the beautiful script in which they were written. He turned the well-preserved pages with intense interest.

Another, older soldier from his regiment entered the church and was curious to see his young friend seated on the floor poring over a book. The older man sullenly gazed around the ruined interior as he approached the private.

"Nothing worthwhile left, I see," he complained. "What's that you have there, Griswolt?"

"It's a register, I suppose," said the soldier, not looking up.

"Griswolt, you're a fool. Why do you waste your time on such a thing?"

"I like to read it. I don't know why, but I do."

"Well, I suppose you might as well. Those who came here first got the best things, and no doubt the officers took the finest of all for themselves! All they leave us are these worthless books."

After a pause, he emphasized his resentment by giving the pile of prayer books and hymnals a lively kick.

"This is a very fine book," said the young Connecticut man quietly. "I shall keep it, and after the war, perhaps the people of this parish, if any of them are left, will buy it back from me."

The older man made a thoughtful grimace.

"Well, that is a notion!" he said. "Griswolt, perhaps you are not such a fool after all! Where did you find it?"

"Among those books you just scattered."

"I'll look elsewhere," he muttered, and he set off on a quest for more valuable church records which had possibly been overlooked in previous lootings.

The young soldier turned to the latter pages of the register where, in a smaller, more contemporary handwriting, the entries ended in November of 1861. The rector's name on these final inscriptions was that of the Revd. Dr. Paul Trapier Porter.

It was twilight, and the evening shadows were coalescing into a general gloom. Having been deprived of any opportunity for solitude and reflection over the past few days, Reverend Porter had left his brother's plantation house and walked out into the gardens just before sunset. Finding a wooden bench in a far corner, below which lay a cushion of moss for his knees, he had knelt in prayer beside it, and prayed so long and with such concentration that he did not notice the transition from day into night. He was surprised to open his eyes in near darkness.

Candles and lamps had long since been lit inside the house, and he could see their reassuring glow in all the windows. A door opened, through which more yellowish light flooded out, and he recognized the figure of his plump little wife at the threshold. She called his name, and he answered her as he rose to his feet slowly and with evident difficulty. The air was damp and cool, and his knees, along with most every other joint in his body, gave him some pain in movement.

Mrs. Porter stepped to the edge of the piazza and peered out in the direction of his voice.

"Here I am, dear," said her husband, approaching the house.

Though she could not see him at first in the darkness, she soon discerned his tall, spare frame emerging from a path bordered by towering hedges.

"This night air will not do your rheumatism any good, Paul," she said.

"I was just coming inside," he answered, moving into the illumination from the open doorway behind her.

Now clearly visible was a wiry man with a long face. His thick hair was a mixture of copper and brown colors that made an abrupt transition to silvery gray at his temples, where a pair of bristling mutton chop whiskers began, nearly meeting at the point of his prominent chin, and growing whiter the closer they came to it.

He stopped at the foot of the low steps to the piazza, climbed the first two, and stopped, standing at a height which put him nearly eye-level with his petite wife. She reached out to him, and he took both her hands and cradled his face in them.

"You have been praying?" she asked gently.

He nodded.

"And now I seek my only other comfort," he said, almost in a whisper. "May we sit on the piazza for a little while? We'll keep each other warm."

They found a comfortable place on a wicker settee and sat down, her shoulders and an elbow enveloped by his long arm, which was holding her close.

"I think you have been a little sad these past few days, Sarah," he remarked softly. "Are you feeling better now?"

"Yes," she replied, but in a sigh that contradicted her answer.

"Already homesick, my dear?" he asked.

"I've been pining for home since we left it," she admitted. "How can I help it?"

"We shall have to be strong," said Rev. Porter. "We are not so far from home here in this parish, but it may be a very long while before we can return to Beaufort."

"You think so?"

"There is no way of knowing for sure, dear, not yet."

The clergyman suspected that there would be nothing much left of a home to which they could return, but kept these thoughts to himself.

"It's very good of your brother to offer us refuge here," said Mrs. Porter, "but I fear we are an imposition. It was not expected that his daughter and her children would also be here, and now it is quite a full house."

"It is a little crowded, isn't it? I shall write to the bishop tomorrow, and a few of my brethren, to see if there is some church, some place of temporary service for me...until we can go back home."

The clergyman felt his wife's little round shoulders rise and fall in another long sigh.

"It is hard to believe that our home is in the hands of the enemy! Oh, how could that be!" she said wonderingly, shaking her head.

"But it is a fact," he replied, "and we must make the best of it. Evil has come upon us, yes, but surely some good will come out of it."

"Alicia is so distressed now," Mrs. Porter fretted, "wondering if Mr. Dwight and his regiment may be sent against the Yankees at Port Royal."

Her husband's face took on the solemn look of the pulpit she knew so well.

"Mr. Dwight has chosen to be a soldier," he said, "and if he is sent against them, he must go. If God sees fit to spare him, his life will be preserved."

Though Rev. Porter liked the young man and approved of him as a husband for his daughter, he felt it was very unfortunate that their romance had budded just at the start of the war, knowing there was a great probability of heartache in store for a girl in love with a soldier.

Thinking of the two young lovers, Mrs. Porter suppressed a smile and said quietly, "Our daughter has tried again to persuade me to speak to you on their behalf."

"And what did you say to her?"

"I refused."

"Good!" said Rev. Porter, a little sharply, but he quickly added in an affectionate tone, "Alice knows what person has the most influence with me. If you two were to join forces–well, I might begin to waver."

"That is your daughter's hope, I am sure," said his wife.

"Then I hope you remain on my side, dear, for I believe I am right in this thing."

"I am always on your side, Paul," she assured him.

For a long while they sat together without talking, and while they listened to voices from inside the house, and the sounds of insects in the surrounding gardens, woods and fields, Mrs. Porter pondered the immediate future of her family, wishing that it could include a visit to Charleston. She had many friends and relations there, and she was particularly anxious to see her brother, Mr. Ephraim Taylor, whose bad health worried her, but after giving the matter some thought, she decided not to bring it up just yet, knowing that the city where she had been born and raised held some painful memories for her husband. He had pain enough as it was now, as he lamented the church he had been forced to abandon and grieved for his scattered flock.

Charleston was the city in which Rev. Porter had been given charge of his first church. Though young and inexperienced in those days, he thought he had made a good beginning as the rector of an old, established, wealthy congregation–but troubles soon began for him, and only grew worse. He worked tirelessly in conducting services, in visiting the sick, and in every other ministerial duty, and when he perceived a spiritual lifelessness in many of his parishioners, he tried, with evangelical fervor, by preaching, exhortation, and example, to awaken those souls who held to religious observances and doctrines merely as a matter of good form and tradition. It concerned him that so few of the men were communicants of the church, and it grieved him to hear that some of his parishioners, especially the young people, frequented the theater and the race course, as well as fancy balls and operas, and to see how coldly they received his sermons on the impropriety of indulgence in such worldly amusements.

While antagonizing part of the congregation with these views, the young clergyman also began to clash with the vestrymen on a number of matters both practical and doctrinal. His first year in the church was full of conflict, and nearly four more years of the same followed. Eventually, towards the end of his fifth year as rector, the strain of all this strife, as well as that of his duties, began to take their toll on his somewhat delicate constitution and highly-strung temperament. His health failed, and he resigned.

Having some personal wealth, Rev. Porter took his family abroad for a year, to places considered to have a healthful climate. He knew that his leaving had not been unwelcome to those in the congregation who had come to regard him as strait-laced and stern, and for this reason, and others, he later looked back on those years with self-reproach and regret. He did not regret holding fast to his convictions, but felt that he should have tied to bring about changes in a more restrained and prudent way.

When Rev. Porter returned to South Carolina, he was elected rector to the Beaufort parish, where he ministered more happily and fruitfully for the next twenty-four years. He was nearly sixty now, and had not expected at this late time in life, to be seeking another place of ministry, just as he had never expected to find himself a refugee of war.

Admiring the autumn hues of the leaves, Alicia had gathered several and arranged them on a wooden bench opposite her own. They were to be the subjects of her next watercolor sketch. She had just dipped her brush into the water and was about to touch it to a little square of sepia, when she heard footsteps approaching the garden house, followed by a male voice calling her name. She recognized the voice as that of her first cousin Julian Porter, whom she had not seen in more than a year. He had been abroad all that time studying medicine.

Alicia put down her brush, turned to the open doorway, and the next moment, saw a familiar face looking in on her. A young man with curly auburn hair and a boyish face dominated by a toothy smile, was putting his lowered, tilted head around the door frame, so that it was all she saw at first.

"Ah, here you are," he said. "I was told I might find you in this place, cousin."

"Julian!" she exclaimed happily. "I didn't expect to see you so soon. Why do you hide yourself? Come and kiss me."

"You will be surprised when I show myself," he cautioned her, just before standing up straight and letting his body follow his head over the threshold.

"I am surprised!" said Alicia, as she took in a lanky frame over six feet tall. "You must be a full head taller than when I saw you last! Why is it that the men in our family tend so large, and all the ladies so little?"

"What, has the young parson suddenly grown taller?"

Julian was referring to her brother Robert, a short young man who, like Alicia, strongly resembled their mother. Her two oldest brothers, the first and second born of the Porter children, were tall, and favored their father.

Julian leaned down and kissed the face of a small, graceful girl with light brown hair and olive green eyes. Her figure was so slight and girlish that, though she was twenty years old, she hardly looked seventeen.

"It's very good to see you, Alice," he greeted her. "May I sit with you?"

"Please do, but not on those leaves," she requested, nodding toward the bench.

"I'll sit beside them, but perhaps you will prefer me as more inspiring subject," he joked, carefully placing himself at the far end of the seat.

"I think not."

"What! You do not find me resplendent? I'll have you know these clothes are the very latest in European fashion," said Julian, smoothing the fine material of his coat complacently.

"Your attire is very handsome, and you are impressively tall, and even a little better looking these days, but I am not skilled in depicting the human figure."

"So, you say I am even better looking than before!" he responded, grinning and nodding with comical self-satisfaction.

"That is not exactly what I said," she corrected him.

"Oh, how she puts me in my place!" he groaned, making a *moue* of disappointment. "The young lady will not allow me my little illusions."

"It is best not to have any illusions."

"Now I hear your father speaking in you," he laughed, "who, by the way, is occupying my old room. I surprised him at his letter writing when I walked in unannounced. It was very rude of me, but I didn't expect to find him there. I only wanted to get some of my things."

Alicia looked apologetic.

"You must forgive us for making your house so crowded," she said. "I'm sure it is a great inconvenience for you and your family."

"Nonsense! Mother likes nothing better than a houseful of guests, especially our favorite relations. I shall share a room with your little brother William and my brothers. I think I shall have some fun with them, and terrify them at night with stories of medical horrors."

"Willie does not frighten easily. He will only laugh at you."

"That's true, he's a feisty little fellow. Perhaps I shall take them all out shooting one morning. We'll have a grand time while I'm here."

"How long have you been back from Europe?" she asked.

"Not long really. I've been in Charleston taking care of some business for my father, but now that's finished, I intend to exchange this elegant attire here for a uniform."

"You will offer yourself as a surgeon?" Alicia wondered.

"I hardly think one year of medical studies qualifies me for that position. I have made application to a Charleston regiment of regulars, and well, there are other possibilities. I think whoever is willing to take me first as an officer shall have me. I don't care how low my rank may begin, but I do wish to be an officer. A few of my friends who enlisted as privates have complained too much of their lot to me. All your brothers in service are officers, aren't they?"

"Paul is a captain, yes. Richard is on General Beauregard's staff, and Robert is a second lieutenant."

"Well then," said Julian, languidly crossing his long legs and arms, "I shall be an officer, too."

He noticed a large portfolio next to her on her bench and asked if he could look at it. Alicia handed it to him a little reluctantly.

"I remember how you used to make fun of my early attempts at artistry," she said, "my crude little drawings of flowers and trees, and how you used to tease me about them, and call me a bookworm."

"Did I? If I did, I am very sorry for such meanness. You were something of a bookworm, though, you must admit, and I hear that you still are."

He opened the cover of the portfolio, and was impressed to see a beautiful watercolor painting depicting water birds wading in a marshland.

"Well! You have certainly become an accomplished painter. This is very fine work, Alice. I pronounce you a great artist."

"I am only an amateur," she demurred laughingly, "but painting does give me great pleasure and satisfaction."

"I see you are still quite the lover of nature," he observed, turning another page to reveal a painting of a handsome palmetto tree.

"I am that," she said.

"Yes, a great admirer of nature–I remember that you once said you wanted something to that effect written on your gravestone."

"I did, and you teased me for that, too," she reminded him in a slightly scolding tone.

"How beastly I was! What was that epitaph, now? I can't quite recall."

"Are you making fun of me again?" she asked, studying him a little suspiciously.

"No, no!" Julian assured her. "I was just trying to recollect it. It was a poem, wasn't it?"

"Yes, some verses of Mr. Vaughn, which I altered slightly."

"Why ever were you even thinking of such a morbid thing as an epitaph, Alice?" he wondered.

"Don't you remember? I was very ill about eight years ago. For a short while, though the doctors assured me otherwise, I feared that I might be dying, and that is when I thought about it," she explained.

"Let me see if I can recall part of it," Julian mused, his eyes turned upward. "It was religious, of course, something like...oh Lord, give one among thy works a place, who in them loved and saw thy face."

"Yes, something very like that," Alicia laughed. "You have a remarkable memory, Julian. You always did."

"Anyway, I thought it was a lovely epitaph," said her cousin. His expression grew a little more serious, and stayed that way when he remarked, "I know something else that will be on your gravestone."

"What is that?"

"Beloved wife."

"There are few better epitaphs," she responded quietly.

Julian smiled, but his eyes were sad.

"I think Mr. Dwight is a very fortunate man, and selfish fellow that I am, my first impulse upon hearing of your betrothal was envy."

"But you told me that your first impulse was suspicion. Remember what you wrote in your letter, asking me so indignantly, how do I know this fellow is worthy of you?"

"I am informed Mr. Dwight is very worthy," he said. "Robbie wrote to me and told me all about him—so many outstanding qualities! And now that the glory of a uniform has been added to these other attributes, I suppose I cannot object to him. I do envy you both your happiness, though. It is what I have wanted for myself."

"Your sister thought you might fall in love with some European lady and bring her home to us," Alicia suggested humorously.

"The idea!" he cried indignantly. "There were certainly no temptations of that sort while I was abroad. I should never think of marrying any lady but one of home."

Alicia remembered a young lady of home who had interested Julian not so long ago.

"I thought you might propose to Miss Barnwell before you left for Europe," she said. "You seemed so taken with her last year."

Julian closed his eyes with a heavy exhalation.

"Ah, Miss Barnwell! I ought not to tell you, I did think of proposing to her–but at that time, my course was set, so to speak. Even so, I thought we had an understanding–I thought she would wait for me. But I was so taken up with preparing for a profession, so eager to please father, that I put off any thought of marriage, as he asked me to do–until I was established. I told myself I had to be practical, just as father advised. But it seems I have been too practical for my own good. You know, I like things to follow a certain course, and I expect them to, except that I have learned that life is not really like that, is it?"

"No, sometimes–no, frequently, it is not."

"Nothing is going along the course I had planned and hoped for," he complained. "Miss Barnwell is now Mrs. Cuthbert, and any other plans I had are to be swallowed up by this war. I shall go and join the army now...or perhaps the navy. I'm quite a good sailor, you know."

Julian suddenly thought of something, and his eyes widened eagerly.

"Your brother-in-law, Peter Johnstone, is the captain of a blockade runner. He is working for Mr. Trenholm's company. I think I shall see if he can use me. Yes, I shall certainly do that. After all, they also serve who–run the blockade!"

He laughed at his own poetic twist. The vague prospect of adventure, excitement, and escape had consoled him, and his mood instantly brightened.

"If Philip will take me on as an officer, I shall try to send you and your family some little luxuries which are becoming scarce. You like Dickens, don't you? I'll see if he has something new and send it to you," and he went on, describing other things he could possibly obtain for her family, and talking as if his future as a blockade runner was a settled thing already.

Alicia moderated a smile at her cousin's mercurial temperament. Though Julian was a steady and reliable young man in many ways, she knew he could be fickle in his affections and enthusiasms, remembering how often he had changed his mind concerning a profession, and how many times in the past he had been infatuated with one girl and another.

"I think you are very brave and daring," she said admiringly, showing no surprise that he seemed to have gotten over his disappointment about Miss Barnwell so quickly.

"I still have your likeness, Alice. May I keep it with me?" he asked.

"Of course, Julian."

"It will help me to look on it sometimes, and think of your friendship and love. You do love me, don't you?"

"You know that I do, Julian," she answered. "You are my dearest friend."

"Except for Mr. Dwight, of course," he laughed.

"Of course."

"I hear that our Robbie is also engaged to be married, and has gone against his father's wishes and joined the army."

"Both are true, but I fear neither of us shall marry soon."

The young man's expression turned serious again.

"I think that's hard of your father," he said, with a disapproving, sympathetic look.

In her heart, Alicia agreed with her cousin, but she loved and respected her father too much to say anything against him, and so said nothing.

Later, when Julian left her alone again, she sat still for a long time only thinking. She was no longer in the mood to paint; she and her cousin had been talking about her home, and she was homesick and sad now. For some reason, perhaps because of their talk of epitaphs, she was thinking of the churchyard at Beaufort, picturing the diminutive headstone of a little brother who was buried there, and remembering his short life, and death.

After a while she heard the voices and laughter of children, and soon, a little girl of eleven, one of her cousins, popped into the doorway of the garden house and stood there with her hands behind her back.

"Cousin Alice," she said, "we saw you through the windows. Are you sad?"

Alicia smiled affectionately.

"I'm fine," she replied.

The little girl slowly moved her right hand from behind her and held out a letter. Alicia could see Aleck Dwight's handwriting on it.

"Your mama asked me to give this to you. She said it would make you happy."

CHAPTER FIVE

ON THE 19TH OF NOVEMBER, George composed a letter to Marguerite for her 19th birthday: "I could not let this day pass without some remembrance of you, dear Miss Marguerite. Though we are apart, it is a day I celebrate with gratitude and joy, because it brought you into the world. I only wish I could see you today, to make my happiness complete. Our move has been put off for a week or two, perhaps longer, so I cannot give you a definite time for our hoped-for meeting at your uncle's place, but if things remain so uneventful, I think I shall be fortunate enough to spend a few days at home at Christmas, which is not so far away. You must promise to devote as much of your time to me as possible while I am in Charleston. I intend to be very greedy and selfish with your company, so let others be forewarned."

About a week later, Holton Legion traveled by train to the Adam's Run depot, and immediately after their arrival, began to clear an area in some nearby woods for a camp. A courier from the military headquarters soon brought orders for them to march in support of another command. They were told to expect a fight, but after they had marched less than a mile, another courier arrived and conveyed instructions for them to return to camp and wait.

That evening, in Colonel Stephens' tent, George watched him poring over maps and discussing the immediate possibilities of their movements with his officers and staff. Not having received any explanation from the commanding general in the area yet, the colonel could only wait and be ready to respond to further orders when they came. The Legion, he declared, had to be prepared for anything, and ready to move fast. In the meantime, while they waited, Colonel Stephens told his officers that he would not abide any "useless idleness" among the soldiers, and ordered the continuation of the rigorous drilling and training they had endured since the beginning of their service.

One morning in the second week of December 1861, news came that a terrible fire had ravaged Charleston. Additional reports trickled in that day, each more dire than the last, until George was very worried about Marguerite, his family, and hers. The next day, Frederick Finley, who was serving in another company in an area closer to Charleston, rode into the Holton Legion camp and brought George the news that both families were safe, and their homes unharmed. The fire, however, he said, had been disastrous, destroying a large swath through the central part of the city from Market to Broad Street.

Frederick also brought a letter from Marguerite. It was opened and read immediately, and after dark, as soon as George was finished with his duties for the day, he sat down in his tent, read it once more, and penned a reply.

Holton Legion

13th Dec. 1861

The letter you sent by your brother, my dearest Miss Marguerite, I have just read again, and I am very much relieved to hear that you and your family are well and safe. I hardly slept last night for worrying about all of you.

Knowing you are all right, I shall be better now, though I am much distressed to learn of the devastation. Frederick tells me that you and your mother, with all the other ladies of the Benevolent Society, are already busy helping those who suffered from the fire, making clothes and providing food at a soup house. I am keeping somewhat busy, too, but by comparison, things are rather quiet and dull here.

Your brother said that there was no damage in our neighborhood, and that the fire stopped just a few doors down from my Uncle John Hutchinson's house on Tradd Street. Ah, but to think of the devastation he described elsewhere, makes me very sad. Do you not think we have the most beautiful city in the world? Even though I have not seen all the great cities of Europe, I shall hold to that opinion. Whatever harms Charleston, seems to put a little dagger through my heart. Perhaps I am too attached to her.

It is very cold tonight, and my fingers are so numb that I can hardly write. This weather quite numbs the mind also to some degree. How I should love to be in a warm, cozy house in your company! The thought of it warms my heart, at least. In your last letter you expressed some concern about the roughness of camp life, but you needn't worry. Since childhood, I have never been sick a day in my life, and so far have not suffered as much as a sniffle. I cannot say the same for my servant Toby, who has been ill to some degree or another since the weather turned so cold. I was a little concerned at first about Aleck Dwight, too, as he had suffered some poor health last summer, but it appears that the exertions and exposure of camp life have physically toughened, rather than weakened him. And the more he is given to do, the more energetic he seems. His color has grown rosy and darkened with a tan, and he is now looking as hale and hearty as any of his comrades in arms. I told Aleck he had finally been cured of his recent illness, but he insisted on giving all the credit to my cousin Alicia. In his case, apparently, falling in love brought about a sudden and complete restoration of health.

Despite the cold, on a few clear nights Aleck and I have walked out beyond the camp to see the sky. In this wilderness, it seems that every star is visible, even stars beyond stars, and we contemplate the whole as an unsurpassed work of art. Are you surprised to hear that of your unimaginative fiancé? In my younger days I recall that I had some susceptibility to the beauties of nature–not that of a poet by any means, but at least a due appreciation, some of which I trust is still with me. Aleck has much more of the poetic faculty, which I suppose is closely related to the religious. It is in his case, anyway. He also has a surprising knowledge of astronomy. I wish you could hear him speak, as he often does when we are in admiration of such things, of God and creation, etc.–you would perceive what a rare intellect he has. I do not wish to attribute my present susceptibilities to his eloquence and influence, however. I think it is more to do with you, my love, for all beautiful things remind me of you, and that is a very pleasant association, indeed.

Colonel Stephens has just asked us to prayers in his tent, so I shall bring this letter to an end. I will understand if your letters become less frequent for a while, as you are very much occupied in your work for those burnt out by the fire. They are much more in need of your time and *efforts, but do think of me when your fingers are busy at sewing, knitting, etc., and know that I am certainly thinking of you.*

Yours affectionately,

George W. Taylor

When George received permission for a brief visit home for Christmas, he jotted a quick note to Marguerite to tell her the good news. "Expect me in a few days, on Monday most likely if all goes as planned. Aleck is going to Mr. Richard Porter's plantation in Prince William Parish for the holiday–no great surprise, as Alicia is there."

The Christmas holiday was over, and the miserably cold, rainy weather that prevailed on the morning Aleck departed made Alicia feel even sadder as she watched him riding away. He had been able to spend only two days with her and her family, and beautiful days they had been for her, but they were over now, and he was now on his way back to the Holton Legion camp at Adam's Run.

Everyone else was inside the warm house. Wishing to be alone in her melancholy mood, Alicia stayed on the piazza for a while, wrapped in a shawl. There was one last glimpse of Aleck as he turned his horse on to the road, one final wave of the hands, and finally, a hurried blowing of kisses as he disappeared behind a line of trees. Feeling drained after the emotion of their parting, she dropped into a chair and drew the shawl up around her chin with a sigh.

Her thoughts continued to center on Aleck, and she remembered the first time they had met. At her home in Beaufort, she had looked out a window one morning to see Robert and another young man walking toward the house arm in arm, talking and laughing. Her brother's description of Mr. Dwight had been accurate, she thought, seeing him for the first time. Like Robert, he was in his early twenties, but his stature was more suggestive of a teen. From a distance, she saw that long strands of dark, almost black hair had fallen across his brow as he shook his head in response to something Robert was saying, and that he raised his hand to brush them back into place with an air of self-consciousness.

As the two young men came closer, Alicia had a better view of Mr. Dwight's face. Not handsome, but pleasant-looking, her brother had described him, but this was not so accurate, it seemed to her. He had an engaging smile, and she thought he was at least a little handsome. She was already attracted to her brother's friend, but could not tell if this feeling came from what Robert had told her of him, or merely the sight of him.

When she came face to face with Mr. Dwight, there was an immediate attraction between the two, especially evident to Robert, who found it funny and had to turn away to hide his amusement.

Pulling the shawl more tightly around her, Alicia smiled as she remembered Aleck's nervousness when he proposed marriage two months later. Her father had given his permission for the engagement while Mr. Dwight was still a student at the seminary, and the couple made plans to marry within a year, but when the young man decided to join the army, Rev. Porter, disapproving, insisted that the wedding must be put off indefinitely.

Everything in life seemed indefinite to Alicia now. Uprooted from her home, a refugee of war, she had no idea how long the war would keep her from that home and her wedding, or where her family's wanderings might take her. But more frustrating and troubling than these uncertainties, was the anxiety for three brothers and a fiancé whose lives were in danger at every moment. Every letter or telegram from one of them was received by the family with a mixture of relief and dread–relief that the writer was still alive, dread that the letter might report a wound or illness, or that the next letter, in some other handwriting, might bring news of something even worse.

As the cold, dreary rain slackened a little, the front door opened, and Mrs. Porter put her head out.

"Alice!" she scolded. "You will catch a cold out here in this damp and frigid weather! Come inside, dear."

Alicia reluctantly obeyed and went into the house, noisy with the voices of children and the conversation of adults. She went to the fireplace to warm herself and looked down at her brother William, a gangling boy of thirteen who was playing with toy soldiers on the hearth, along with two of his young cousins. Then a hand encircled her shoulder, and a female face surrounded by masses of auburn ringlets appeared close to hers, as Lydia, a cousin her age, drew her away to a sofa for a conversation. As they sat down, she studied Alicia with a sympathetic smile.

"You are sad for Mr. Dwight's leaving?" she asked, patting Alicia's hands, but went on, without waiting for an answer, "He is such an intelligent, agreeable young man. I think you are very fortunate, cousin."

Alicia gave a slight smile of concurrence.

"I am so disappointed that your father will not allow you to marry Mr. Dwight until the war is over. Good heavens, it could last for years!"

"Are you trying to cheer me up, Lydia?" Alicia asked ironically.

The young woman apologized.

"Oh dear, I am such a goose. It's just that I should so love to be one of your bridesmaids! And to help with all the preparations for a wedding, and have something fun to do and something so happy and exciting to look forward to. Everyone would wish to come here for your wedding. The garden is perfectly beautiful in the spring. Can't you picture a wedding in mother's garden?"

"Yes," Alicia murmured, allowing herself to daydream for a moment.

"Do you remember your sister Caroline's wedding in Beaufort? That was the last time I saw all our family together, all the cousins and aunts and uncles and grands. How I should love for us all to be together again for such a happy occasion," Lydia sighed. "Almost everyone was present, except for Uncle John Hutchinson, who was out of the county at the time, I believe. Uncle Abel Hutchinson was there, though, and his good-looking sons!"

Here she rolled her eyes blissfully and sighed again.

"Though Uncle John was away, I remember that he sent Caroline and Peter the most exquisite wedding gift."

"An Italian painting, wasn't it?" Alicia recalled.

"Yes, by a very celebrated artist. Everyone was so happy that day, it quite breaks my heart to think of it now."

Lydia's happy expression had turned a little glum, but then, suddenly remembering something, she brightened and said, "Speaking of paintings, have you seen Papa's miniature of our great-grandfather?"

"I believe I saw it many years ago," Alicia replied.

"Papa has had it put into a new frame and case. Let me show it to you."

Lydia went to a little table, opened a drawer, and returned to the sofa with the family portrait. She sat down next to Alicia again and opened a small leather case which held a miniature painting on ivory.

"Our great-grandfather Mr. Trapier," Lydia murmured, and they peered down at a diminutive, masterfully painted image of a gentleman wearing a white wig. "It has always grieved Papa so, that Mr. Trapier became so ill in Philadelphia in 1776 that he had to return home to South Carolina."

"Ah, yes," said Alicia. "Papa laments it, too. If not for that, his grandfather would have been one of the signers of the Declaration of Independence."

"But didn't one of Mr. Trapier's great nephews sign our Ordinance of Secession?" Lydia asked.

Before Alicia could answer, Lydia's older sister called her name from the next room, and the young woman excused herself. Alicia's thoughts wandered back to a garden wedding, but a few moments later, she was brought back to reality when she noticed a servant approach Rev. Porter with a letter. Showing great interest, he opened it immediately. As soon as he had read it, an animated conversation followed between him and his wife, and the subject quickly spread to others seated nearest. His brother and sister-in-law seemed to be offering congratulatory sentiments. Alicia quickly crossed the room to find out the nature of this good news. She first overheard her father speaking of "leaving next month" and then learned that at least one uncertainty in her life had been resolved. He had been appointed as the assistant rector to a church in Columbia and would soon be moving his family there. Rev. Porter's older sister, Mrs. Crawford, had already written to him several times inviting him and his family to come and live with her and her husband. There was plenty of room in her spacious house, sparing the Porters the expense of renting one of their own.

"So, that's settled," thought Alicia. "We're going to Columbia."

She had never been to that city, but liked the idea of it. She was getting tired of living in an overcrowded house on a somewhat remote plantation, and besides, Columbia was connected to the rest of the state and country by railroads–railroads which made it easier and faster for soldiers on furlough to get there.

Mrs. Porter seemed a little disconcerted at the thought of moving to a district in the center of the state, since it put her an even greater distance from home. Somehow, it seemed to her that the farther they moved from Beaufort, the less likely it was that they would ever return. To cheer her up that evening, Alicia looked through her old letters from Mrs. Crawford, found a clipping about Columbia which had been sent with one of them, and asked her mother to read it and tell her if it was true. The article, clipped from a horticultural journal of 1860, was a letter from a Northern gentleman who had visited the capital city in the spring of that year.

"Oh, I don't wish to read," Mrs. Porter sighed. "You read it to me, Alice."

After scanning the first few lines, her daughter smiled and cleared her throat.

"Mr. Editor," she began, "I like this place surpassingly well. There is about it an air of neatness and elegance. The seat of government in South Carolina, Columbia is situated on the banks of a river called the Congaree, and is certainly one of the most beautiful rural towns in the United States–a true garden spot of the South. At this season, the handsome evergreens, which adorn and shade almost every street, have put on the new and bright livery of spring, and the air is rich with the perfume of a thousand flowers. A dwelling without a garden, in this place, is hardly to be met with, and this passion for the beauties of nature must certainly be viewed as an evidence of the cultivated and refined taste of its inhabitants."

The article continued, "The seat of Colonel Preston is one of the most interesting in this neighborhood. His house is a large and respectable mansion of stone, surrounded by pleasure grounds of fine evergreen and deciduous trees. Among the latter, our attention was arrested by a fine specimen of that curious tree, the Japanese Gingko, twenty feet high. Many of the large old trees are now venerable specimens, over eighty feet high, whose huge trunks and wide spreading branches are, in many cases, densely wreathed and draped with masses of English ivy, forming the most picturesque sylvan objects so rarely met with. The grounds—a type of the ancient school—are laid out strictly in the geometrical style. All the symmetry, uniformity of the old school, introduced in Europe several centuries ago, are displayed here, in formal walks and small figures, trellises, grottoes, artificial water, etc. The effect of this garden is striking, and its liberal proprietor, Col. Preston, by opening it freely to the public, has no doubt increased the popular taste of the city.

"In Columbia the *Camellia, Pittosporum, Gardenias, Magnolias,* all the new *Pines, Spruces, Thuyas,* &c., are perfectly hardy, and very common in nearly every garden, under the protectorate of accomplished gardeners. There is a *Magnolia grandiflora* here sixty feet high, with a top whose diameter exceeds seventy feet—a perfect colossus of arboricultural grandeur and beauty. Roses are in great profusion, flouting their beautiful heads from miles of hedge, exulting in balconies and parapets, enshrining cottages, and making nature generally exceedingly gorgeous; in fact, it is just the place to locate a paradisiacal garden. As soon as I can steal a little time from my present labors, I will send you a further description of some of the charms which make me love this place."

"Very pretty," Mrs. Porter remarked, brightening a little and looking reminiscent. "It makes me look forward to seeing the city again. I have been to Columbia several times, though my last visit was many years ago, and I do remember it as a very beautiful, elegant town. I am sure you will like it there, Alice."

Alicia also reminded her mother that many of their old parishioners from Beaufort were in Columbia now, and would no doubt attend her father's new church when they heard of his being there.

"True!" said Mrs. Porter, smiling broadly now. "It will be just like a homecoming!"

After reading the article again, Alicia remembered how impressed she had been with the writer's descriptions of Columbia, and how it had made her wish to go there and see all these things for herself. Mrs. Crawford had sent her the clipping to lure her for a visit, and at the time, just before the war, she had asked for and received her father's permission to go and spend a few days with her aunt, but, for various reasons, the trip never materialized. Now she would have her wish.

The Porters arrived in Columbia on a bitterly cold, gloomy afternoon in early January. The skies were so dark that Rev. Porter speculated that snow might be on the way. Alicia experienced a strange sense of foreboding on entering the city, but ascribed this feeling to the depressing weather.

The family had traveled most of the way by railroad, and as the train cleared the top of a low hill and brought the city into view, despite the gloomy skies, Alicia looked out on the scene with pleasure. The inland city of Columbia was very different from Beaufort, and, having been established for only about three quarters of a century, was not so old, but it was beautiful in its own right, she thought. The capital of South Carolina was a larger city with stately churches and public buildings, neatly laid-out streets lit by gaslight, a fine college, three railroad depots, and a magnificent new state house under construction. And yet, in Alicia's eyes, the city still retained an aura of bucolic beauty, nestled as it was among the rolling green hills of the midlands, and filled with beautiful trees, parks, and gardens, just as the article she had read to her mother described it.

Unlike Beaufort, Columbia had so far remained untouched by the uglier aspects of the war. No enemy army had occupied or assailed it, and the place hummed with undiminished social life, commerce, and numberless activities and industries geared toward the support of the cause. It had boasted a population of 8,000 just before the war, but that number had doubled with refugees and soldiers.

In the spring of 1862, Holton Legion was still stationed near Adam's Run. In late April and early May, elections for officers were held during a reorganization of the unit, and George received a promotion. He wrote a letter to his father about it first, then one to Marguerite.

> *Holton Legion*
>
> *Near Adam's Run*
>
> *2nd May 1862*

Dearest Miss Marguerite,

The election for company officers has just concluded, and I am happy to report to you that I have been elected Captain of Company A. Though I think a few others did so on my behalf, I did not engage in any electioneering. It is gratifying to know, however, that the men have such confidence in me. I have endeavored to do my best as an officer, and believe that I give general satisfaction.

The Legion has been assigned to General Evans' brigade. We are in for the war.

Other than this news, I have little else of interest to tell you. We have been called out on a number of false alarms, when we were supposed to see some fighting, but we have yet to encounter the enemy. Just yesterday, Col. Stephens sent Adjutant Dwight over to General Evans' headquarters, and Aleck was told the moment he showed up, to convey an order to the colonel to form his Legion and march towards White Point. Enemy gunboats were steaming up the river, shelling thickets and probing for our batteries. We marched as ordered, heard that the enemy had retired, then encamped in the woods, and never saw a fight. Few of us really expected the Yankees to land here, but we are all still so green that we half-believed we were on the eve of a skirmish, and so as we marched, there were many serious, thoughtful countenances to be seen, mine among them.

I have been sleeping on a bed of pine straw lately. That is not so bad, but we are beginning to suffer a little from the sand flies, fleas and other pests. I have made use of the mosquito net you sent to me, and at night I sleep in glorious freedom from the miserable little wretches. A few of our men have fallen ill lately. My man Toby has been very sick for over a week with something I fear may turn more serious, so I shall send him home. Camp life does not agree with him. I have decided to do without a body servant of my own for now, and have struck a bargain with Zachary, Aleck's boy, to work for me. His hire is reasonable, and the arrangement works out quite conveniently for all concerned.

Aleck, Frank and I rode into Wiltown with some others last week. It is a beautiful place, and there is something of a beach along the river there. The weather is already growing warm, and if we are still here in the summer I imagine we shall go bathing in those cool waters.

I must have told you what a comical fellow my cousin Frank is. Like his father, he is very skilled in the telling of tall stories, and often competes with our other raconteurs in attaining the highest realms of absurdity. Among other devices, he has a funny trick which never fails. Sometimes, at the end of one of his stories, as he is finishing on a happy, humorous note, he raises his hand above his face, and as it quickly passes down, his face instantly changes to the most grave, stern and rigid expression, like that of a solemn judge about to pass a death sentence. This comically instantaneous change elicits much laughter on the part of his companions, but none of that affects him, which only makes us laugh the more. Then he will suddenly pass the same hand upwards over his face again, and reveal a merry, smiling countenance, which, of course, only leads to more laughter. I don't think I describe it well enough to amuse you–it is something which must be seen to be fully appreciated. It certainly amuses us.

There are rumors that Evans' Brigade will be sent to Virginia in the summer. If this talk proves to be true I shall certainly ask for at least a week's furlough in Charleston before we depart, and you know that I shall contrive to spend as much time with you as possible. Give my love to your family. Believe me, Miss Marguerite, to be

Yours affectionately,

George W. Taylor

Letters of reply and congratulations arrived promptly for the new captain. George read the one from Marguerite first.

Charleston 4th May 1862

Dearest <u>Captain</u> Taylor,

We were all delighted and proud to hear of your promotion, but not surprised in the least, especially Papa. It would make you blush to hear all the grand predictions he makes for your future! Do let me know immediately if a furlough is likely in the next two months or so–Papa wishes to send us to Flat Rock for the summer, but I will beg him to let us put off our departure if you are coming to Charleston. Bank business, and his new responsibilities in the Soldiers' Bible Society, will keep him here in the city longer than usual. I shall send you and Mr. Dwight some of the little devotional books the Society is printing for the soldiers.

Mr. Taylor, I too have something to report, for which I hope you will be proud of me. Mama and I are among the ladies who have resolved to raise funds for a gunboat. Having read of the ladies in Mobile who have done the same so successfully, we decided that the ladies of Charleston could do no less. Already we are busy planning fairs and bazaars and raffles. We have solicited the help of the newspapers, printers, etc., and have met with the greatest enthusiasm and interest. I send you a handbill advertising our first concert at Hibernian Hall. How do you like it? It is a handsome little notice, I think. The tickets were all sold in no time. We have been soliciting donations of money and valuables, and besides some money, your brother has contributed a beautiful silver cigar case for a future raffle. He told me to tell you that it was given in your honor. Papa made a generous contribution to the fund, and some of his rich friends have promised to match it. Isn't it grand? I have sometimes wished that I were a man, so that I might do my part for our cause, but I think I am doing something now.

My dear Mr. Taylor, is it possible I shall see you again very soon? I wish your colonel would send you on some official business to Charleston, that I might spend but an hour or two with you. You see? I do not ask for much, but the occasional sight of you has become a necessary food for my soul, and it begins to waste away when I am so long parted from you. Oh, I know I am being foolish. I give in to these heartaches occasionally, and write very foolish things. Mama says I ought not to say how much I miss you; she fears I shall discourage you. Do I? Let me tell you instead, how much I love and admire you. I am tempted to tear up this letter and begin another, and not make mention of my sorrows, but I shall not do so, but leave it as it stands, and resolve to do better in the future. I shall look forward very much to your visit here, though it pains me to think of your going so far away afterwards.

Yours very affectionately,

Marguerite Finley

In June, Evans' Brigade had not yet received orders to go to Virginia, but the prospect was looking more and more likely, so George asked for, and received, a week's leave of absence in the latter part of the month. July finally brought the expected orders, and George managed one final, brief visit to his father and brother in Charleston, but did not see Marguerite again before he left; she and her family were already in Flat Rock. George's father was feeling very weak that day, and was not well enough to accompany him to the depot. Albert drove him there, and was introduced to Adjutant Dwight, and stayed and talked with him and George until there were signs that the train was about to depart. After Albert was gone, George and Aleck continued to linger on the platform for a while, looking for someone or anyone they knew other than their fellow travelers, hoping to catch a glimpse of some acquaintance, friend or relation, and wistfully observing numerous ladies who were seeing off beaux and husbands.

They had already put their gear on board the train and claimed their seats, and paced up and down restlessly, thinking of the long journey that lay ahead of them. They walked up to the engine and watched the men who were fiddling with machinery and controls, apparently dealing with some minor problem which had caused a delay. A brawny fireman on the tender car, grimed with soot from head to toe, showed his big white teeth in a smile and saluted the two young officers as the steam engine hissed more loudly. George looked up at the smokestack, from which a swirling cloud rushed up into the air then diminished and slowed to a steadier stream of whitish smoke punctuated by puffs.

The hisses of the engine seemed to grow more emphatic. Someone shouted, "All aboard!" and George and Aleck obeyed. They took their seats, and the train made its screeching, lurching start. Within a few minutes, they were moving along at a good speed, the wheels clacking at a regular rate as they rolled over the joints in the rails. Aleck took up a book to read, and George, who was seated by a window, looked out aimlessly on the passing countryside. They were in one of the first passenger cars, and he could see the clouds of smoke billowing from the engine ahead. The shadows that they cast on the ground below rushing past began to hypnotize him. His eyes grew heavy, and before long, he was sound asleep.

They arrived in Richmond on a Saturday. Early Monday morning, George sat down to write a hasty letter to his fiancée before his duties for the day began.

Richmond, Va.

30th July 1862

Dearest Miss Marguerite,

I promised you a letter as soon as we reached Richmond, but could not write until today. Richmond is a fine city, situated on the banks of the James River, and the surrounding countryside is very handsome. This is a busy, bustling place, and the streets are full of Confederate uniforms. Aleck and I went to church at St. Paul's yesterday. Mr. Minnigerode preached a fine sermon, and we saw President Davis there. Afterwards some of Aleck's old friends from the University of Virginia pounced on him and took him captive for the rest of the day, insisting on bringing me along, too. We dined together, and I enjoyed their company very much. A more brilliant set of young men I have seldom seen, mostly well-to-do fellows bound for the law or medicine or the ministry—and every one a private! They all reminisced a great deal about their college days together, but did not leave me out of the general conversation. They wanted to know how Alexander was comporting himself as an adjutant. I praised him highly, of course (and you can be sure he will remind me of what I said the next time I am displeased with him for some reason).

Towards the end of our time together Aleck got himself into an intense discussion with another seminarian. It turned into something of an argument, though a friendly one, over some theological or scriptural point which I'm afraid I did not quite follow. "I'll bet you five dollars you're wrong about that!" Aleck cried, to end the thing, which I found very amusing and a bit incongruous of our young clergyman. But he is rather excitable in this way on occasion.

I wonder how you are faring in Charleston. I do think it grand that the ladies (especially mine) continue to exert themselves so magnificently for the gunboat. What did my brother's cigar case bring at auction? No, you said it was a raffle. In any case, I hope it brought a princely sum. It will no doubt take many thousands of dollars to pay the cost of an armored vessel, but I have no doubt that the ladies of Charleston are up to the task.

We are expecting orders to move out very soon, and I am confident we shall see some fighting then. Another battle is expected at Malvern Hill. You will probably read of it in the papers before you hear any news from me, unless I can send you a telegram.

As usual, I have your likeness before me as I write so that I can gaze upon your lovely face. I always keep this most treasured possession next to my heart, along with some of your letters, but I shall not take them into battle with me. I shall leave them behind with my other things for safe-keeping, and God willing, return to claim them again.

I was very tired Sunday night, and do not have much time to write this morning, so you must forgive my brevity. Give my love to all the household, and a kiss to Chassie from me.

Yours with much love,

George W. Taylor

The following week, the men of Holton Legion briefly experienced their first taste of warfare in Virginia at Malvern Hill. Later in the month of August, General Longstreet's Corps, which included Evans' Brigade, was ordered to the vicinity of a railroad bridge across the Rapphannock River. George was certain now that Holton Legion would finally engage the enemy in earnest, and the sense of nervous anticipation and exhilaration he had experienced during his first days as an officer came back to him, multiplied many times over.

By the end of the month, the Legion had participated in two significant and costly battles. George wrote to his brother about them.

5th September 1862

My Dear Albert,

Since I wrote to you last we have seen two very bloody fights, and have suffered heavy losses in the Legion and the brigade. Doubtless you have already seen some account of them in the papers. Our first real fight was at Rappahannock Station, where we arrived on August 22nd. The enemy artillery were firing on us from a hill, and we were ordered to attack them. After crossing a stream with great difficulty, we charged the hill, but found no enemy! They had crossed the river, and from the other side opened fire on us again with artillery. Some skirmishing followed, and we finally drove them off in retreat, but not without considerable casualties in our ranks.

Towards the end of the month, we won a great victory at Manassas, but so much blood was spilled there that we are practically decimated as a regiment. Only about a hundred of us are left in Holton Legion now. There are orders for us to recruit, but that will take some time. We pursued the enemy as far as Leesburg, and the next day, crossed the Potomac into Maryland. This march is proving a hard and trying one, and I expect we shall soon see another major engagement, our destination being a mountain pass near Sharpsburg.

You have probably had word by now that Colonel Gadberry was killed at Manassas. Strange to say, he expected to die. Another officer told me that the colonel had had a presentiment that he would be killed in battle very soon. He died in a courageous attack on one of the strongest points of the Federal lines. Colonel Means was mortally wounded in the same action, while leading a charge. Both of them are deeply grieved in the brigade. I could not begin to enumerate how many South Carolinians perished in these battles.

This letter may see some delays before you receive it. I was fortunate in getting it off to you at all. Please reply soon—I was distressed to hear from you that Father was so ill again, and I am anxious to know if he is better now. I hope the news of Lee's great victory at Manassas will cheer him. Only tell him good news. Tell him I am well, and give my love to all at home.

Your loving brother,

George W. Taylor

CHAPTER SIX

IN THE SECOND WEEK of September, what was left of Holton Legion took part in another battle at South Mountain in Maryland. After a difficult, exhausting march, Evans' Brigade, temporarily under the command of Colonel Stephens, arrived on a Sunday afternoon and began their ascent of the mountain under furious enemy cannon fire, the Legion leading the way as skirmishers. They fought until after dark, and when it was apparent that the enemy could make no further advance that night, the colonel ordered his men to retire. On their way back down to their encampment in the pass, many of the soldiers were so overcome with fatigue that they dropped by the roadside to sleep.

George and Aleck returned to camp ravenously hungry, and sat down by a fire to eat a meal Zachary had prepared for them. Many of the men around them were already asleep, their beds the ground, with a blanket if they had one. The two young officers soon joined them in their slumbers.

A few days later, Evans' Brigade was once again in the midst of a fierce battle, this time at Sharpsburg. Soon after the fight, Lee's army was once again on the move, and George only had time to compose a brief note to Marguerite.

Holton Legion

18th Sept. 1862

Dearest Miss Marguerite,

Finding an unexpected, immediate opportunity of sending you a note, I write hastily to inform you that I am well. I know you will hear of a large number of casualties in our brigade, but thank God, I am not among them. Aleck Dwight is also well. Our corps (Longstreet's, you recall) fought bravely at Sharpsburg. General Jackson's corps joined us from Harper's Ferry. I caught a glimpse of him with General Lee on the same day (yesterday). Some say we prevailed in the battle, but the enemy was at least pressed back, so it could not be said that we lost. My heart is full of many things I wish to tell you, my darling, but I must close.

In haste, ever your affectionate,

George W. Taylor

The following month, George wrote to his brother from a camp near Winchester, Virginia.

Holton Legion

11th October 1862

Dear Albert,

I was very glad to receive your letter of the 2nd. You inquired about our losses, and we have recently heard some of the details of General Evans' report. Since the end of July, we have lost nearly half our brigade—over a thousand men.

A few days ago, Colonel Stephens submitted his resignation and will return to his parish at home at Black Oak. His ability and courage are unquestioned;

I have no doubt he is acting according to the dictates of his conscience. We shall all be sorry to lose him, but I for one am glad that such a man is removing himself from this terrible war. I wish his adjutant would do the same. I have never known two finer men, and would wish to see them both preserved for better things. They have a higher calling and purpose than most of us.

I did not tell Marguerite, and hesitated to tell you, that I had a narrow escape at Sharpsburg. A ball flew past my head and came so close that it scratched my ear. My hand went to the wound immediately, and when I saw the blood my heart beat fearfully fast, as it took me a moment to realize that I had not been shot in the head. I thought I would have a notch in my ear, but fortunately the flesh has healed nicely, with little disfigurement. Do not mention this to Marguerite, or anyone else.

I have not quite reconciled myself to the fact that I may die any day now. It is hard to be willing to die when one has so much to live for, but for so sacred a cause as ours, I must be willing. Do you remember our visits to Father's good friend Mr. Rivers, and how we used to admire his medals and sword from his time in the Palmetto Regiment? We made semblances of them and played at soldier when we were boys, but he would never tell us stories of those days no matter how we begged him. Now, having seen the unspeakable, I know why he never wished to talk of war. The evil of it is indescribable, and what is left after a battle is more horrible than the battle itself.

May victory and peace come to us speedily!

Your affectionate brother,

George W. Taylor

In early November, Evans' Brigade boarded trains in Richmond bound for North Carolina. Within the week, after some intermediate stops, they continued on to their final destination, a town called Kinston. George, like every other man in the brigade, was glad to be so much closer to home, and near a railroad at that. He wanted very much to visit his father, whose health was still precarious, and of course to see Marguerite. He wrote to her soon after they set up their new camp.

Camp Evans' Brigade

Near Kinston, N.C.

16th November 1862

We arrived here, Dearest, two days ago via the Newbern railroad, and I think we will surely remain in the area a number of weeks. Our stop before this place was Goldsboro, about twenty-five miles away. Kinston is on the Neuse River, in low marshy country, but we are encamped north of the town, in a beautiful grove on more elevated lands.

General Foster's forces are at Newbern, and it is expected that he will attempt to advance on Goldsboro to attack the railroad there. The Legion has increased in numbers, and some North Carolina troops are joining us, but even so, I do not see how we will be enough to match Foster's army of twelve thousand (so I hear). We shall certainly need reinforcements.

I am sharing a tent these days with Aleck, Frank Stephens, and Mr. Vardell, our quartermaster. It is late afternoon, and has been a sunny, brisk day which promises to turn off right cold after dark. I am ensconced in the tent as I write, and Aleck is at his desk just outside, also penning a letter. A golden setting sun is gilding the trees *on a hilltop not far from us–glorifying them, as Aleck put it, when he drew my attention away just now to admire them. He must be writing to someone in his family, for nothing ever distracts him from a letter to Alicia. I told him I was writing to you, and he begged my pardon, and made a little joke. "No wonder you are so <u>intent</u>," he said.*

I have been appointed Judge Advocate in a court martial to begin this week, and shall be glad for the distraction. It is only another kind of tedium, but one more suited to my predilections and temperament, and I much prefer some such activity and occupation to the more irksome tedium of camp life. The quartermaster tells us we shall fare very nicely in the way of rations in this place, and promises us plenty of vegetables, sweet potatoes, and fowl. We have been without vegetables so long that some of the men are suffering from a touch of scurvy. We shall fatten ourselves up while we are here, in anticipation of leaner times which may lie ahead.

Albert tells me that Father is no better, but thankfully, no worse of late. How I wish to see him! I hope to obtain a leave of absence for Christmas, but cannot say yet if that is likely. It fills me with longing to remember last Christmas in Charleston at your house–the lovely tableaux, and your singing. I hope you will sing the same carol again, just as you did that evening. But I must put away those memories for now and reserve them for later. I try to think of only pleasant things at night when I have gone to bed. It helps me to sleep, to conjure images of past and future happiness, of which you are, of course, the chief ingredient.

This letter should reach you in time for your birthday, Miss Marguerite, so let me convey my heartiest wishes to you for that best of anniversaries.

Yours with much love,

George W. Taylor

Marguerite received his letter on her birthday, in the late afternoon. After a supper party at the Finley house attended mostly by family members, she went up to her room to read it in private. As she wrote her reply, George's photograph was propped up on the desk before her eyes.

Charleston 19th Nov 1862

I was very glad to hear of your safe arrival in North Carolina, my dear Mr. Taylor. I thought of you a great deal today, and thank you for your good wishes. It is good to know that you are so much closer to home, but still, I miss you terribly. The whole household misses you. Mama says I ought not to write such things to you—that it might be "demoralizing," but I should think it would give you some pleasure to think that others long for you when you are absent, most of all, me.

I have your likeness before me always when I write to you, and when I am especially lonely for you, I sit and talk with your portrait. You say delightful things to me—always what I wish to hear. Your photograph is very compliant! The real George Taylor is not so; he scolds me sometimes, and would never be so yielding, or indulge me so, but I like him better nevertheless. He is flesh and blood, not a mere image. How I wish you were here! I could enjoy a real conversation with you, and bask in the light of your eyes and your smile, and feel the warmth of your hand in mine. Perhaps Mama is right about not putting such sentiments in letters–I find I am making myself quite heartsick for you.

Let me find some other subject, before tears begin to mar my letter. This morning, one of my cousins, Miss Smith, called to wish me a happy birthday, with several of her friends in tow. We have not seen her in a long time, and she began her visit by saying that she wished to know all about you, the latest family news, etc., and yet for the most part talked of nothing but parties and dinners she has attended and plans to attend, and all the preparations for her wedding. After she was gone Mama remarked that she used to be a level-headed girl but is now grown quite giddy. She is engaged to another cousin of ours, a young man you might know, Mr. Percival Creighton, at whose name my mother always used to roll her eyes. Mama has more respect for him these days, however. Many of the young gentlemen of Charleston who were such do-nothing dandies before the war are now, in her opinion, behaving themselves quite admirably in their enthusiastic dedication to the defense of state and country, but she still believes there is a little too much frivolity among some of our young people which she regards unseemly in such a time of crisis.

Let me tell you something more pleasant. I saw Judge Yeadon on the street yesterday, and he asked after you with great interest and solicitude. I told him how they had put you on several courts martial and that you found them very tedious work, indeed. The army is lucky to have such a man, he replied. He also made great predictions for your future. "No doubt George will follow in his father's footsteps. I shouldn't be surprised to see him as a judge or senator not too many years from now." I assured him that I had the very same confidence in you and your abilities.

I neglected to send you the newspaper article concerning the baptism of the gunboat Palmetto State in my last letter, and enclose it now, as it contains Mr. Holton's speech, which seemed to interest you. It was a delightful ceremony, and the collation afterwards, very enjoyable. To show their appreciation and gratitude, the gentlemen managers of the Ladies' Gunboat Fair served the ladies in attendance. Mama and I were introduced to General Beauregard, Captain Wemyss, and Captain Ingraham, a naval officer. Captain Wemyss, of Beauregard's staff, is an Englishman, formerly of the British Army, who ran the blockade to enlist in our army. We spoke with each of them only briefly, as they made their rounds to meet all the many ladies and gentlemen managers. The Palmetto State is an impressive ironclad vessel, and we were all very proud to have had a part in it. I wish you could have seen it.

In December, I look forward to seeing you. Your presence is what I wish for my Christmas gift.

Very affectionately,

Marguerite Finley

In the middle of December, early on a cold, bright Sunday morning, a long-anticipated encounter with the enemy finally took place at Kinston. Across the river from the town, part of the brigade formed a line of battle at the edge of a large field, behind a rail fence. Holton Legion was on their right, about a half mile from the bridge over the Neuse River, across the road leading to it, and an artillery battery was nearby at another position on the public road.

Adjutant Dwight had again been put in temporary command of the Legion, and after many long, watchful hours of waiting for the enemy's approach, he found his men somewhat unnerved and demoralized. All of them were aware that they would be badly outnumbered by the Federals. When they were all suddenly roused by the fire of musketry close by, an order came for them to fall back and take up a better position on some higher ground. It was all Adjutant Dwight could do to quell a momentary panic among the men and get them into the new position about fifty yards away. As they took their places there, he calmly walked up and down the lines giving orders and offering encouragement.

Seeing Adjutant Dwight so cool and self-possessed, the men shook off the panic and readied themselves for battle, but just a few minutes after it began, they saw their commanding officer shot down. A minie ball had entered Aleck's body near his hip. Stretcher bearers soon came for him, and he was carried across the bridge to the rear.

George and his company had been sent out as skirmishers at the main road to the bridge. In the middle of the morning, after enduring heavy fire from the approaching enemy, they were driven back into their own line at the edge of some woods, where several regiments were positioned in concealment. George was almost to the cover of the trees when he felt an impact and an excruciating pain in his leg. Despite the pain, he was able to go on, and managed to continue on towards the rear.

On his way he saw a group of men kneeling around the prostrate body of an officer and approached them, seized with a sudden fear that it might be Aleck. To his relief, he saw that it was not Aleck, but another officer he did not recognize. Severely injured, the young man was lying on a stretcher soaked with his own blood, his brains oozing out of a shattered forehead, while one of his friends, or possibly a relative, was weeping over him and bathing his face and lips with brandy to ease his passing. He had not been killed instantly, but was still dying, apparently in great agony.

"God take him quickly!" George gasped in pity, turning away, although he had by now become more accustomed to such horrific sights.

Almost ready to collapse with exhaustion more nervous than physical, he began to stagger as he walked. Others saw his bleeding leg and helped him get to a hospital tent, where a surgeon immediately examined him.

"You're fortunate, Captain," said the doctor. "It's not very serious, just a flesh wound. The ball tore off a bit of your leg, but did not make a direct hit. You'll be all right."

After his wound was cleaned and bandaged, George said he felt well enough to return to the fight, but the surgeon forbade it. He waited in the field hospital, and did not hear that Aleck had been wounded until after the battle, which had not gone well for the Confederates due to some blunders and miscommunications. In the early afternoon the brigade had been forced to retreat across the bridge, which had been set on fire before all the men could cross it, and a number of them trapped on the other side of the river were captured by the Federal troops.

Late in the afternoon, when George heard that Aleck had been shot while leading the Legion, he borrowed a pair of crutches and went looking for him. Those who were badly wounded were being transferred to ambulances which would take them toward Goldsboro, but another officer told him that Adjutant Dwight was still in a hospital tent. There, George found Aleck in the care of General Evans' chief surgeon and his assistant. They had just finished binding up the wound in his hip with fresh bandages. A basin held the bloodied ones they had just removed. Aleck looked pale and limp, but he was conscious. He saw George and beckoned him with a feeble movement of his fingers. As soon as the surgeon and his assistant went on to other patients, his friend was by his side.

"I've been looking for you," said George, peering deeply into Aleck's eyes, hoping not to see a dying light there.

"I thought the wound was mortal. I was preparing to die. But the doctor says it is not mortal, and that I should recover."

"Thank God!"

"I have," said Aleck. He tried to smile, but the attempt only produced a grimace of pain. He asked George about the crutches.

"It's nothing," he said. "I have these just to spare myself some pain. I'll be fine in a few days."

George stayed with Aleck until it was time for the ambulances to leave. While he waited with him, a letter came for the adjutant, and when Aleck saw that it was from Alicia, he asked George to open it for him. In his weakened condition, he found it difficult to read. After making it through the first few lines with great effort, he asked for another favor, and had George read the rest to him. Her letter continued:

"I have not approached my father again about our getting married. He has been grieving over two of our cousins from Abbeville who were killed in battle. Though it has not been seemly for me to do so lately, others have been speaking up on your behalf since I last wrote. Even the Bishop has put in a good word for you with my father, but I am afraid that so far, it is to no avail. Papa remains resolute. I hope you do not mind, but I asked him to read the sermon that you wrote and sent to me a while back. He did read it, and praised it grudgingly. But I know my father well, and could tell that he was quite impressed with it. He is really very pleased with you, except for the fact of your wearing a uniform. I persist in my hope that he will relent and let us marry when you become a chaplain, instead of insisting that we wait until the war is over.

"My cousin Julian has run the blockade again and is sending us some necessities and a few luxuries. I shall soon be sending you some quinine powders you may need sooner or later, and two pairs of socks which I made for you myself..."

Aleck began to laugh quietly, and George paused and looked at him.

"More socks!" he chuckled. "They never fit, but I wear them anyway. They are always too large! I'm afraid she ascribes me more heroic proportions than I can fulfill."

The battle at Kinston had ended in something of a draw. Afterward, Evans' Brigade and the North Carolina troops with them retreated towards Goldsboro. Near this town, just a few days later, there was another engagement with the army of General Foster, who, unfortunately for the Confederates, soon succeeded in carrying out his intention of disabling the railroad line there. His army then fell back in the direction of Newbern without being pursued.

George was deeply disappointed by the brigade's failure at Goldsboro, and at the first opportunity, he poured out his frustration in a letter to his brother, complaining, "The whole affair was badly handled, and there is a good deal of dissatisfaction among the officers concerning our leadership. Despite the reinforcements, our numbers were inadequate. Still, had our troops been more skillfully handled, I think we could have prevailed."

Aleck's wound got him a long furlough home for convalescence. When he returned to the Legion about two months later, he seemed to be fully recovered, though a little weakened from so much bed rest. During his time at home in St. John's Parish he had enjoyed two visits from Alicia, and claimed that her presence there accounted for his remarkably speedy recovery. After Aleck's close brush with death at Kinston, some influential friends of his, including a cousin who was a general, and the bishop of South Carolina, began working on his behalf to have him taken off the front lines and appointed to the chaplaincy.

A new year was well under way when the adjutant rejoined Holton Legion, now stationed near Wilmington, North Carolina, where George was busy with several courts martial arising out of the Goldsboro fiasco and some earlier incidents which had been the cause of tension and resentment in the brigade. Charges and counter charges had flown among certain officers, and now they, along with the commanding general, were to be put on trial.

The first court martial took place in early February and lasted about two weeks. During this time George stayed at a hotel in Wilmington, but came back to the brigade camp for a few days to prepare for the next trial scheduled for the following month. He found Aleck looking and feeling healthy and strong again, but more restless than usual. There were few active military operations going on, and in their winter quarters, the men of the brigade had little more than camp and picket duties to occupy them. Some companies, including George's, were on provost duty in the port of Wilmington, and others were guarding nearby salt works, as well as an area on the coast where an enemy landing was expected sooner or later.

In March, George returned to Wilmington for another court martial proceeding which lasted about three weeks. One Sunday, the day after the trial ended, Aleck met him at his hotel, and they attended church together. After the service, Aleck happened to see one of his old friends from the University of Virginia, and the young man took possession of him and George for the afternoon, insisting that they come to his house for dinner. There was other company there, too—a number of ladies, the young man's numerous sisters and cousins. They all seemed very pleased to entertain the two officers from South Carolina with conversation and music until nightfall, and invited them back for supper the following evening.

Early on Monday morning, George received orders to return to the camp with his company. His men began the march there as soon as possible, but their captain remained in Wilmington with Adjutant Dwight, and the officers enjoyed another evening in the company of Aleck's friend and his female relations, though they kept George and Aleck in town much longer than they had intended. The two rode back to camp after dark, with only a sliver of moon to light their way.

When they were close to the end of their ride, Aleck gazed up at the stars dreamily and let out a sigh of satisfaction. They had been talking of their pleasurable evening in Wilmington.

"I do love the company of ladies, don't you, George?" he said wistfully.

"They were very pleasant," George agreed, and, clearing his throat, added, "One of them was very pretty, too."

"It makes one feel so civilized and peaceful again to be in their presence. Much preferable to being in war."

"Almost anything is preferable to being in war!" George responded, wide-eyed.

When they returned to their quarters for the night, they found both of the other occupants of the tent already asleep, one of them quietly snoring on his back. George and Aleck crawled under their blankets and continued to discuss the evening they had spent with the ladies.

"The little one, Miss Jamison, had such a lovely singing voice," Aleck went on, in the same wistful tone as before.

George looked over at his friend with an expression of surprise and amusement.

"Are you going to tell Miss Alicia about your new acquaintances?" he asked.

"George!" Aleck responded reprovingly, turning a look of mock sternness on him. "Of course I shall. I tell her about everyone I meet."

"And she doesn't mind your spending time with charming young ladies?"

"Certainly not. Are you going to write to Miss Marguerite about your new friends? You were awfully attentive to one of them."

"Yes, I shall write to her about the ladies, but I don't plan to mention how pretty they were."

Aleck laughed.

"Perhaps I ought to write to her then. Will you enclose a note from me in your next letter?"

"Yes, do write to Miss Marguerite, Mr. Dwight," George answered dryly. "Give me your note, and I shall see that it meets with the fate it deserves."

As they both laughed again, and Dr. Stephens abruptly rolled over to face them with an irritated, groggy expression.

"Though I have been so very charmed with your conversation, gentlemen," he said wearily, "I hope it is at an end."

"It is," said George. "Sorry that we woke you, Frank."

Not looking very soothed by the apology, the doctor turned his back to them again, mumbling, "I think certain persons around here have a touch of spring fever. Well, sweet dreams to you."

Smiling, George and Aleck blew out the candles by their beds, ready for sleep, and dreams.

One sunny, cool afternoon, as George was returning to his tent, he saw Aleck sitting under a tree at a camp desk reading a letter with an open-mouthed expression of astonishment. George immediately approached and asked what the news was. The adjutant was ecstatic over this communication he had just received from Alicia. Her father had told her that she and Mr. Dwight had his permission to marry whenever they wished.

Aleck's hands were trembling as he read that part of the letter a second and third time to make sure he had not misunderstood her words.

"Am I dreaming?" he asked in a shaky voice. "It's almost too good to be true!"

"Read it to me," said George. "This is no dream."

"Papa," he read aloud, "has given us his blessing to marry as soon as we wish."

"Then you may marry as soon as you wish!" laughed George.

He congratulated his friend, but wondered why Rev. Porter had suddenly relented in his opposition.

"I don't know," said Aleck. "I was so stunned by what I read to you, I haven't been able to read past it."

"Read on!" George urged.

Aleck read silently for a few moments, and then explained that Rev. Porter had apparently undergone a change of heart concerning clergy in the military. He read aloud a little more of Alicia's letter.

"Papa has been simmering with indignation since June, when the Yankee General Butler so grossly insulted the ladies of New Orleans, and executed a civilian gentleman there for no good reason–and now, some other outrage he read of in the papers has finally tipped the scales in our favor. I was so happy when he informed me that we may marry that I did not even inquire what it was! Papa is so provoked that he says he is now willing to take up arms himself if need be, though he is over sixty years of age, and not in the best of health."

"That is very like my uncle," George chuckled. "He tries to be patient and longsuffering, but if he simmers long enough, he will boil over."

"So much the better for me!" Aleck exulted.

Smiling, George shook his head, remembering an incident from his childhood involving Rev. Porter.

"When Albert and I were boys," he recalled, "we were left to stay with the Porters when my parents went away one summer. Mother was ill, and Father was taking her to a health resort to consult with a celebrated physician. Rev. Porter felt sorry for us, and for our mother's sake, he tried to be patient with us, though I'm afraid we behaved ourselves very badly. He bore with us for a long while, until one day, seemingly out of the blue, he gave us both a thrashing I shall never forget. I don't recall exactly what we did to bring it on, but it must have been the last straw. I do remember what he said to us, though–he said, 'the rod of correction will benefit you boys immensely.'"

"And did it?" Aleck asked laughingly.

"I believe it did. I don't think we stopped our mischief altogether, but we were much more discreet about it."

Aleck looked down at Alicia's letter again.

"I shall ask for a leave of absence," he said. "I think one should be possible before long, don't you?"

"I don't see why not. You should put in for one immediately. There's no telling how long we shall have to be stuck at Wilmington, and there's certainly not much doing here."

A few days later, during the last week of March, Aleck left on a twenty-one day furlough. The same afternoon of his departure, George received a letter from Albert containing distressing news about their father. He immediately requested a leave of absence for himself, and the next day, he was on a train bound for South Carolina.

A family servant was waiting for him at the Charleston depot with a carriage, and from his expression, George could tell he had arrived too late. Mr. Taylor, he was told, had passed away on the previous morning.

CHAPTER SEVEN

THE LATE SPRING OF 1863 found Holton Legion on its way to Mississippi, where General Grant was laying siege to the city of Vicksburg in an attempt to gain final control of the Mississippi River. At the end of May, after a long, arduous journey by steamboat and railway from the Carolinas, the Legion arrived at their destination at night and set up camp a few miles away from the town of Jackson.

George wrote to Marguerite on his first day in Mississippi, in response to a letter he received from her from Charleston, and wrote again the following week.

Near Jackson

10th June 1863

We have been in this place about a week, Dearest, at the beginning of which I received your last letter, and now I anxiously look for another to arrive today or very soon. I was a little surprised to see that it came from Charleston, thinking that you must have already departed for Flat Rock, but rather glad to learn that your mother has refused to leave Mr. Finley alone in Charleston. I was sorry to hear that he had been somewhat ill lately, but thankfully, your letter indicates he is beginning to make a recovery.

We are all beginning to suffer a good deal with the heat, dust, and drought, though nightfall usually brings some relief, and last night was a mercifully mild, almost cool one. That evening we were treated to the music of an excellent regimental band. When they began "The Bonnie Blue Flag," cheers and singing broke out among the men, but the singing tapered off, as the band was playing it at a quickened tempo, a little too fast for singing the words properly. You have no idea how much good it does the men to experience these pleasant diversions. If not for such entertainments, and a regular supply of letters from home, with a furlough thrown in now and then, service in this war would be nearly intolerable, especially for the private soldiers.

There are some very good musicians in the brigade, and they often entertain us in the evenings. I should say, they entertain themselves, but everyone else gets the enjoyment of their talents, too. One Private Mann, a banjo player, is particularly admired, along with his brother, a fiddler. When they are joined by other fellows with guitars and more fiddles, etc., it is quite a rousing sound they produce. "Soldier's Joy" is my particular favorite. The lively music inspires many feet to tapping, and before long, a dozen or more men are dancing jigs and cutting such capers that they draw a crowd of spectators, and then some of the onlookers join in.

One fellow, an Irishman, is strictly a solo performer, and draws his own crowd when he dances a hornpipe. He does so with such skill and grace, I am sure people would pay to watch him. Aleck's boy Zach has learned the hornpipe by observing him, and is now greatly admired in his own right. He has added his own variations to the *dance, some of which are so eccentric and acrobatic, I think he is as impressive as the Irishman.*

In the temporary absence of our chaplain, Aleck holds a prayer meeting each night which has been very well attended. Last Sunday he preached for the first time, in an informal service, and his congregation, though not large, was very attentive. Because he is an officer, and has been through the same marches and fights as our soldiers, it is evident that the men respect him much more than an ordinary parson, and give greater weight to what he says. He preaches in a simple but profound style which all can understand, knowing that our men are from many different denominations, and of varying degrees of education.

The redbugs in these woods are becoming quite an annoyance. Aleck seems to find them particularly distressing. He loathes insects of any sort, especially those which like to make meals of us. When we were at Adams Run, he used to spend an inordinate amount of time trying to rid his blankets of fleas, especially after he had a mortifying dream one night, in which he was sitting beside his beloved Alicia and saw a flea jump from his clothes to hers.

You asked how the "married man" is doing. He is well, and receives more letters than ever from Alicia (from whom we learn that the Porters are also well, and will probably spend the duration of the war in Columbia). There is a question commonly asked by the soldiers of new acquaintances, which Aleck says he may now answer proudly, if anyone dares to ask, "Are you a married man, or a dog?" The married men, of course, are not insulted by the inquiry, but the dogs are abashed or take offense.

One young private, hoping to be held in higher status, protested that he was engaged to be married, but was told that "this don't signify." Fortunately officers are generally exempt from such abuse.

Thank you for the writing papers you sent. Stationery can sometimes be scarce, so I shall use them sparingly until I can avail myself of a good supply. Miss Marguerite, I send you and yours my love and remain

Your devoted dog,

George W. Taylor

In Mississippi, George had been without reasonably current newspapers for weeks, and was longing for news from the east, some word on Lee's army, and the latest from Charleston. The mail had become irregular, and letters from Marguerite were less frequent now. He had read, and read again, or loaned out all his books, and was reduced to raiding the libraries of his friends. Only Aleck had a significant number of books with him, but they were generally not to his taste. George was not much interested in the thoughts of Blaise Pascal, the writings of Aristotle, or the sermons of English divines, but he did borrow a book of ancient history by Xenophon, and was able to find some distraction in it. Other wars, he discovered, especially those of long ago, were not so depressing as the actual one going on around him.

One day he received several letters at once, along with a little parcel which contained a pocket edition of the poems of Tennyson, a gift from Chassie Finley. Not a great reader of poetry, George tossed it aside on his cot as he thumbed through several letters from home, pulling out Marguerite's first. Aleck came into the tent, and when he saw the book on the bed, picked it up with interest.

"Ah, Tennyson!" he said enthusiastically. "Something good to read! May I borrow it?"

"Certainly," George replied carelessly, quickly absorbed in his fiancée's letter.

As Aleck began to peruse the little book, he noticed an inscription inside. George had not even opened the book to see it.

"From your little sister to be?" he inquired.

"Hm?" George responded to his question, not looking up.

"Oh, nothing. I shall look forward to reading this," Aleck mused, admiring the little volume of Tennyson.

"Yes, certainly," George repeated absently, envisioning Marguerite's face as he read her words.

"Tell me what you think of this, George," said the adjutant. He had just had his hair shorn to less than an inch in length all over his head, and was grinning and exhibiting the new haircut.

When George did not respond he repeated more emphatically, "Well, what do you think?"

George looked up from Marguerite's letter, surveyed his friend, and rendered a verdict.

"You look like a convict," he said.

"You're so droll!" the adjutant laughed. "But I do look a bit like one, don't I? Well, thanks, but it's certainly much cooler in this heat! I can wash my hair just as I wash my face. You ought to try it, my friend."

"No, thank you."

The new style really was not so bad on Aleck, who was still somewhat boyish-looking, but George was certain he would look quite ridiculous with such short hair. Besides, he was too proud of his thick, lustrous locks to part with them, even for comfort's sake—or so he thought at that moment. The next day, however, his thinking on the subject began to change. By noon, the heat had grown so intense that George was beginning to have serious second thoughts about Aleck's suggestion. They had been marching since dawn in the direction of the Big Black River, on dusty lanes through farming country in which there were few woods to give shade, and the continued dry weather had made water even scarcer than before. If they had not soon reached a place called Livingston, where there were shade trees and springs, George might have sought out the adjutant's barber.

Here the brigade made camp for about a week, short of food and awaiting supplies.

At the Holton Legion camp, reports came in one day that the besieged town of Vicksburg had surrendered to General Grant. Aleck observed George's devastated expression when he heard the bad news and tried to cheer him.

"Only believe good news," the adjutant advised him.

"But we've lost Vicksburg," George protested.

"Yes, I know, but you must look at it this way, that some good may come of that. Rejoice in the good news, and tell yourself that even the bad may turn out to be to our advantage."

"I'm not that sanguine," sighed George.

"Neither am I! But this is my system against hopelessness, at least where the war is concerned. I haven't used it long, but it's been working very nicely for me lately."

"Well, I'm glad the system works for you, at least. Heard any good news lately?"

"There's a rather wild rumor going around that we're to be sent to Charleston soon."

"Oh, I don't believe that!"

"Wouldn't it be nice, though? Miss Finley is still there, isn't she? And perhaps my Alice could come and see me."

"Ah, Aleck, if only!"

That evening George sadly and hurriedly jotted another letter to Marguerite by candlelight, reporting that Vicksburg had fallen. He also related the same news to his brother, including some details he had left out of his letter to his fiancée, writing to Albert: "We heard that civilians had been killed in Vicksburg by Grant's relentless shelling day after day. Some died from the effects of the prolonged siege, others by the shells thrown in. The people of the town were driven to take refuge in underground shelters they had dug for themselves. They were all very hungry, close to starvation, and were reduced to eating the meat of rats and mules, when that could be found. Our soldiers defending the town were also starving, and greatly weakened by disease, we were told. One of our reports said that the Yankee ships in the river were directing much of their fire not at the town's defenses, but into Vicksburg itself, which was full of women and children! God preserve us from such a people.

"Before General Pemberton's surrender, General Johnston was moving us toward Vicksburg, but today we have been retreating on a forced march, having learned that a large enemy force was moving in our direction. We are heading back to Jackson, and will probably see some fighting there. Between the two armies, I think we are outnumbered about three to one, and our men are very low on rations. Some of them could not finish the march in the heat of the day today, staggered off to the side, and crumbled to the ground at various points along our route. After dusk the stragglers could be seen dragging into camp one by one, a few having crawled part of the way..."

He ended the letter in the same disheartened mode he had begun it, describing the loss of Vicksburg as a catastrophe. The next day, Evans' Brigade was on the march again with the rest of General Johnston's army.

Not long after George sent off these letters, the brigade was occupying trenches at Jackson again, awaiting the approach of the enemy at an open, grassy area bordered by a forest. Holton Legion was positioned to support a battery commanding the public road, and when the enemy finally appeared, it was not long before a prolonged fight began. Beginning in the early morning, and continuing all day except for a brief lull just before noon, bullets, balls, and shells flew over their heads from sharpshooters, skirmishers, and opposing batteries.

In the afternoon, nearly exhausted, Aleck was lying on the ground in a trench when a minie ball flew in, struck the dirt between his legs, ricocheted in an explosion of dust, and narrowly missed George, who was next to him. Both men sprang up to a sitting position in shock.

Wide-eyed, Aleck pursed his lips together and blew out a "Whew!"

"That was close," George panted, grimacing.

A shell suddenly whistled overhead, and they went back to their stomachs on the ground, re-energized with a rush of adrenaline.

About an hour later, when the battle seemed to be at its highest pitch so far during the day, they heard another man in their trench gasp loudly. They turned to see Lieutenant Jennings, who was standing up, clutching at his side.

"Great gods, I am shot!" he exclaimed, thinking himself a dead man.

The next moment, however, he probed the spot with his fingers, discovered that he was only scratched, and immediately cried out, "No, I am not shot!"

As his mask of extreme tragedy changed into one of astonished relief, the sudden transition and its accompanying narration proved too much for George and Aleck. They burst into helpless, almost hysterical laughter.

The lieutenant's face underwent another transition, this time to wrath.

"You find that amusing?" he demanded, trembling with nervous excitement, and blushing a fiery red.

"I'm sorry," laughed Aleck, "but it was, rather."

"Damn you both!" he hissed through clenched teeth.

All three men survived the battle that day, and afterwards, in the calm of the evening, George and Aleck went to Lieutenant Jennings' tent and apologized to him with sincere regret. By this time the lieutenant had fully recovered from the shock of his experience and was willing to forgive them and laugh about it himself.

The fighting went on for another week. Some of the Confederate and Federal lines were so close to each other that the men on both sides could yell out and converse with each other, usually to exchange more or less facetious insults. At times, truces were called, and some of the soldiers would go out to meet the enemy to fraternize and barter, quite willing to be civil, sometimes even friendly, to men who were there to kill them–for at least a little while.

The officers took no part in these often unauthorized, informal parleys, and George never ceased to wonder at them. One day he overheard an exchange so amusing that he wrote to Marguerite about it. While things were relatively quiet, one of his men called out to the enemy picket, saying, "Hullo, Yanks! Why don't you shoot?" The reply came back, "This shooting of prisoners is all up! We are just here to guard you!" And laughter erupted on both sides of the lines.

General Johnston continued to hold off the Federals, but his men were in no condition to withstand a siege, and were not strong enough in numbers to mount an attack, so one night in the middle of July, his entire army quietly and secretly evacuated the lines and marched off to Brandon, some twelve miles from Jackson. From there, for the next few days, they kept moving until they reached Forest Station, where they would board a train bound for Meridian.

The loss of Vicksburg had been bad enough, but George was almost as shaken when news came of General Lee's forces at Gettysburg. He had hoped for much better from the great commander, but his failure to gain a victory in Pennsylvania made George heartsick. For a while, the strain and concerns of command during the fight at Jackson and during the retreat afterwards, along with sheer physical exhaustion, had kept George from dwelling on these dispiriting subjects, but as he sat beside Aleck in the train car and watched the passing countryside, he found he could think of little else. For the first time since the start of the war, he was beginning to fear that it would all end in defeat for his country.

Still grieving for his father, George thought of him more often now, and remembered the appalling predictions he had made even before the first drop of blood had been spilt. For nearly two and a half years he had not given Mr. Taylor's dire prophecies much thought, but since early July, after the fall of Vicksburg, they began to come into his mind regularly to haunt and oppress him, even more so when he heard that General William Tecumseh Sherman's army had sacked and destroyed the city of Jackson, a place left defenseless after the Confederate forces removed from the area.

In his letters to Marguerite, George did his best to conceal his discouragement. He minimized setbacks and defeats, magnified any encouraging news, and tried to divert her with the narration of anecdotes and amusing incidents. He was disciplined enough not to show any of his apprehensions or emotions to the men who were under his command, and never allowed them to affect his judgment or actions, but in his private dealings with those closest to him, especially Aleck, it was becoming evident that something was troubling him deeply.

Though George struggled against his growing pessimism and dejection, it sometimes happened that when he was most successful at keeping these feelings at bay during the day, they would manifest in his dreams, in strange, inexplicable scenarios of disaster. One night he dreamed that Marguerite had written a letter to him breaking off their engagement, and after this, he began to be harassed by unfounded fears and suspicions about her. He scanned her letters, old and new, to detect any signs of cooling affections, or any indications that she might have feelings for another man, picturing some eligible officer on duty or on furlough in Charleston, young and dashing, and as handsome as she was beautiful, and imagining that this new suitor might turn her head and steal her heart.

Because George was in this particular morose frame of mind when he heard from her again, something that usually cheered him up, a letter from Marguerite, only served to irritate him and make him feel even gloomier. He was very displeased to see the subject matter, which was a new acquaintance of hers, a gentleman she had mentioned in an earlier letter, and he experienced a senseless surge of jealousy as he read her words: "I think I have told you that my dear friend Miss Julia Cordray is engaged to an Englishman, Captain Wemyss. He resigned his commission in the British army and ran the blockade into Charleston about a year ago, and is now Captain Wemyss of the Confederate Army. He is serving here in Charleston on the staff of General Beauregard."

"Yes, yes, the Englishman," George muttered. "You told me about him before."

Marguerite went on:

"Except for a few brief visits to her in Savannah, the captain has been separated from Julia for many months. She is now in Greenville with her family, and writes to me that she misses him terribly. Julia does go on about her English gentleman! I met the captain again yesterday. He is very handsome. He had some business with my father and was asked to stay to dinner. Captain Wemyss is a little bashful at first, but once he has sized up his company as congenial, he is talkative and very entertaining. He says he has been a soldier all his life (first in the British army and now in ours) and told us many interesting tales of service. Lately he had to go down to Florida on a rather mysterious mission for the Department and amused us very much with his descriptions of some of the characters he met with there.

"Julia tells me that he calls her his 'pet' and she seems to adore all the more him for that. While they are separated they have apparently settled on a 'non-flirting policy' to which, I assure you, Captain Wemyss strictly adheres. Isn't it strange that I haven't the slightest anxiety about you on that account? I am sure you have followed this policy as a matter of course without having been asked to do so."

As he put away her letter, for the first time since he had known Marguerite, George felt angry and cold toward her.

"She's a selfish little thing," he thought. "Selfish and spoiled! This is the second time she has written of this captain, and she is trying to make me jealous and miserable. Yes, she resents the postponement of our marriage and is trying to punish me."

He pulled out paper and pen and began a reply. After composing a few conventional phrases, he launched into a petulant, disconnected tirade: "You seem so very delighted with this Captain

Wemyss and his ways. Am I to begin calling you my little pet? I don't like all this talk of flirting..."

For the moment he forgot how Marguerite had, many times, denied harboring any resentment toward him, and how often she had fervently reassured him of her devotion and love. He forgot all this, but then he remembered, and felt ashamed of himself. He stopped writing, tore up his letter, and began another, this one more civil and rational.

George was interrupted in his letter writing that afternoon when his superior officer asked to see him about some reports, and when he returned to his tent, it was dark. Aleck was so absorbed in writing something that he hardly acknowledged George, who quickly resumed his letter to Marguerite. As soon as he finished it, he went to bed. He was very tired, but could tell the moment he closed his eyes that sleep would not come easily that night.

Aleck kept writing. Nearly an hour later, he was still writing, and George was still awake.

"That's a long letter," George remarked in a sigh.

"It's not a letter. It's a sermon," said Aleck. "Am I keeping you awake?"

"Certainly not. I enjoy the blazing light of your candle in my eyes."

Aleck laughed at his response.

"It really isn't so late, you know, George."

"It's almost ten o'clock," he said. "But do go on. It's all right. I don't think I shall get to sleep any faster if you stop."

"Why not?"

But he received no answer to his question. Instead, George asked him what his sermon was about.

"Oh, he wants to talk," thought Aleck, who replied, "It's about the City of God."

"Saint Augustine's City of God?" George queried, surprised. "Surely you're not going to preach about that to the men."

"Oh, no. I'm writing this for one of my old professors from the seminary. I'd like to have his opinion on it, and someday I might preach it to a congregation."

"Read it to me," George urged him. "I'll give you my opinion."

"No," Aleck chuckled, shaking his head.

"Well then, what's the gist of it? What's your text?"

"It is based on scriptures from the book of Hebrews," said Aleck. "Here we have no continuing city, but seek one to come, a better, even an heavenly one–one that is to come someday on this very earth."

"Let's see," George mused, "Augustine was writing his book at the time that Rome was being overrun by the barbarians."

"Yes, in the 5th century–the Visigoths."

George propped himself up on one elbow and looked at Aleck with sudden seriousness.

"Think our city is going to fall?" he asked.

For the first time, George saw a look of discouragement, even something close to despair, cross the young man's face. Apparently the adjutant's program of believing only good news, his "system against hopelessness," was not always entirely successful.

"I don't know," he answered quietly.

George studied him and asked, "Are you writing that to comfort yourself, Aleck?"

"I am writing it to remind myself of a great truth," he answered earnestly, "that the eternal is more important than what is temporary."

"I should hardly think that you needed to be reminded of that."

"In the temporal mess we are in, I need to be reminded of it very much."

"And what if our city should fall?" George wondered somberly.

"Then perhaps it shall be for the purpose of reminding us of this truth," Aleck replied.

Towards the end of July the men of Evans' Brigade received orders which would put them in the vicinity of Savannah, Georgia. Wild exclamations of excitement and joy went up all over the camp. Even if that city was not home, it was very much closer to home. In early August, after a short march, they boarded a train bound for Mobile, eventually reached the Montgomery depot, and continued to travel across Alabama and then to Georgia. When they reached the coast, however, instead of going into Savannah as they had hoped, they were directed to make an encampment on an island about ten miles from the city.

Adjutant Dwight passed on the orders to the other officers.

"What's the place called?" asked George.

"Isle of Hope," Aleck informed him.

"If only it were," he grumbled.

"What's that, George?"

"Nothing."

"We are to be held in reserve here for a while," said the adjutant, "but I shouldn't be surprised if we were sent on to Charleston soon."

"Do you know something we don't know?" George asked somewhat anxiously.

Aleck only smiled knowingly.

Contemplating the happy prospect of Charleston, George brightened, and he was able to shake off the gloomy mood which had begun plaguing him again during their journey east, despite the fact that it had been bringing him closer than ever to home, and to Marguerite.

Two days after their arrival at the island, George put in a request for a furlough to visit either Charleston or Savannah, depending on whether Marguerite could make a trip to the latter, where she had relatives with whom she could stay.

Other things lifted his spirits at this time, too. The Isle of Hope was a pretty, pleasant place, in fact a summer resort, with bathing houses on the beach, and several families occupying attractive cottages near the water. Food and water were plentiful here, and the Legion had a comfortable camp by the side of a creek, in the cool, deep shade of beautiful live oaks. George was also gratified by being informed that he was to be promoted to the rank of major within the month.

In reply to his first letter from Georgia, Marguerite promptly wrote to George and informed him that her father was not willing to let her travel to Savannah, so he made plans to spend a week in Charleston. A few days before his furlough was approved, news came that the enemy had begun shelling the city of Charleston from a nearby island. George soon learned details of the bombardment in another letter from his fiancée.

Charleston, 23rd Aug. 1863

Dearest Mr. Taylor,

No doubt you have already received some word of the events which have taken place here. I know that you will be interested in the particulars, so I shall tell you what I have learned. The Yankee General Gillmore, thwarted in all his attempts to take Battery Wagner, demanded its surrender, and indeed the surrender of Fort Sumter and all the harbor defenses! No surrender being given, he turned his guns on unoffending women and children in the city in the very early morning hours of August 22nd.

General Gillmore claims to have given fair warning of his intention to shell Charleston from the swamps at Morris Island, but Papa said this was not so. Apparently at nine o'clock on the evening of the 21ˢᵗ, a note was sent to the commander at Battery Wagner to be forwarded to General Beauregard. The note demanded that the harbor defenses should be immediately given up to the Yankees, and if not, the city would be shelled. General Beauregard was given four hours to reply, and to remove the women and children to safety, but the note he received was not signed. It did not reach him until midnight, and he naturally returned the anonymous communication for signature and verification, and with no answer. About an hour and half later, the shelling began in the middle of the night.

After daylight Papa spoke with our friend Captain Wemyss. It is the captain's opinion that it was a rather extraordinary proceeding, to say the least, that Gillmore should bombard the city because he cannot take the harbor defenses three and four miles away from it, and that the Yankees' attempt to destroy it with Greek fire is very abominable. But their hatred for Charleston, he says, "the hotbed of the rebellion" as they call it, is so intense that they would do anything to gratify it.

Now, despite Mama's objections, Papa is adamant that we must leave the city. A cousin in Greenville has offered us a house to rent, and we must, says Papa,

leave Charleston and go there immediately. He thinks
Greenville a safer place than Flat Rock, and though it is
really no closer to Charleston, it is accessible by railroad.
Do you know Greenville? It is a pretty town, and before
the war, contained some two thousand persons, though I
should think that refugees are swelling its numbers now.

It makes me very anxious to think I must leave my
dear city, which I fear may be taken by our enemies. May
God save the Confederacy! Independently of my love for
my country, the fate of all I love better than life, is bound
up with it.

How I long to see you! I am hoping and praying that
you will be able to come to Charleston within the week, so
that I may see you before we leave for Greenville. Please let
me know very soon if your furlough has come through—as
soon as possible.

I hope the weather is pleasant for you on your island.
It must be nice for you to be at the coast again and bathe
in the sea whenever you like. I am glad to hear that you
and your men have better food now after the hardships
and deprivations of your Mississippi campaign.

We received word from your brother that your house
on East Battery was not harmed by the shelling. I am
sure he will write to you with more details. All here send
their love to you, and Papa begged me to send you his
best regards. He is very pleased and proud to hear of your
promotion, as indeed we all are. We look forward to seeing
you very soon.

Yours most affectionately,

Marguerite Finley

Five days of George's leave of absence in Charleston was spent mostly in Marguerite's company. Throughout his visit, the weather was hot and sultry, and there were numerous thunder storms in the evenings. On the sixth day, in the early morning, George accompanied his fiancée and her family to the railroad depot and saw them off. Mr. Finley was traveling with them as far as Columbia, where he had some business to take care of for the bank. Two days after their departure, George was on his way back to the Isle of Hope.

It had been wrenching for him to part with Marguerite again, and he was close to tears as he watched the train slowly pulling out of the station, carrying her away from him. The next morning, on his last full last day in Charleston, George visited his father's grave at Magnolia Cemetery, and afterwards, he began to suffer again with his former depression, which had only temporarily abated during his time with Marguerite.

Not long after his return, the brigade was ordered to Charleston. Some regiments were posted to James Island, and a few companies were assigned to garrison duty in the city and at Fort Sumter, while other units, including Holton Legion, were encamped east of the Cooper River at Mount Pleasant and Sullivan's Island.

September and October passed somewhat uneventfully for the Legion. Their main duties were to guard the bridge from Mount Pleasant to Sullivan's Island and to build up fortifications in the area. For some reason, George's promotion was delayed. It finally came through at the beginning of November, and he was given new quarters–in a house–but his new, higher rank and its attendant privileges did little to cheer him. He felt himself sinking lower and lower, and though he eagerly seized on any bit of good news that came along to buoy himself up, his discouragement always returned, and sometimes grew deeper.

In the middle of November, the bombardment of Charleston was resumed with a vengeance. From the shores of Mount Pleasant and Sullivan's Island, George could only watch helplessly as the enemy relentlessly threw in hundreds of shells from their guns on Morris Island. After obtaining permission to visit the city, he went to the house on East Battery (which was now his) and removed many of his belongings, all his father's papers, and some family heirlooms, taking them to his brother's house. Albert lived on Elizabeth Street, in an area which had so far proved to be just out of range of the shelling.

On his way in and out of the lower part of the peninsula, George was shocked by what he saw there, particularly in the business district. Several stores with brick, stone, and iron fronts had gaping holes in their facades, and one was a shattered wreck; nearly every windowpane was shivered to countless pieces; and bricks and fragments of plaster and glass were scattered everywhere. He passed by many fine residences which had been hit by the shells, and he feared for his house, but there was nothing he could do to protect it.

One cold, overcast evening Aleck called on George at his house to discuss some reports. They talked for a while, and just as Aleck was about to leave, a heavy rain began.

"Why don't you stay the night here?" George suggested. "There are two beds in my room. You are welcome to one of them."

Aleck hesitated, considering that George was not the best of companions lately, but the allure of a dry, warm house and a comfortable bed was too much to refuse, and much preferable to the leaky tent he had been sharing with two other officers. When they retired, Aleck lit the lamp beside his bed and pulled out a little book from one of his coat pockets. He covered himself, propped his head on the pillows, and soon looked deeply absorbed in his reading. Sometimes he paused and jotted notations in the book with the stub of a pencil. George had put out his lamp, but was restless as usual, and watched his friend from the other bed.

After a while he asked, "What's that you're reading?"

"Aristotle," answered Aleck, not looking up. "To brush up on my Greek."

"And other things, I suppose."

"And other things, yes."

Aleck glanced at him quizzically, wondering why his tone sounded so sour.

"I've forgotten most of my Greek, but I suspect you actually understand all you're reading there," George remarked.

"I try," said Aleck, making a face of exaggerated nonchalance.

George stared at the adjutant, looking displeased.

"Look here," he said, "why haven't you pressed harder for the chaplaincy? When's that transfer coming through for you? "

"I have certainly not pressed for it, and would not even if I could. You know there isn't much I can do personally. I imagine it will come through for me soon, if it is God's will."

"You are a good officer, Aleck, but I should think that God could make better use of you as a chaplain."

"Perhaps," he mused, putting the book down and looking thoughtful. "It is a great responsibility, though. Sometimes I shrink from it, and wonder if I am fit for it."

Impulsively, he had confided something that had concerned him deeply for a long time, and immediately regretted having done so, seeing that George was in such a foul, irritable frame of mind.

"I don't know who could be more fit than you," George grumbled. "If you're not, then no one is."

"Look here, George," said the adjutant, mimicking his irascible air. "Why don't you go to sleep, or write to Miss Marguerite or someone? I ought to write to her myself and tell her what a grumpish old bear you've become."

George gave an angry huff and turned his back to Aleck, who went back to his reading with a satisfied smirk.

The next morning, George noticed that Aleck drug himself out of bed with some effort and seemed less energetic than usual.

"You don't look rested, Aleck," he remarked as they dressed and prepared for the day.

"Well...you woke me a few times last night," he said hesitantly.

"I thought you said I didn't snore very loudly."

"You don't. You were talking in your sleep, though–to, or about, Miss Marguerite."

George's face flushed red.

"What did I say?" he asked uneasily.

"I only heard her name clearly. The rest was rather garbled."

"Oh."

"Do you dream of her often?"

"Quite often."

"I dream of Alicia, although not as often as I would wish," Aleck confessed, a smile raising one corner of his lips. "And very sweet dreams they are, too."

"I suppose a dream now and then is better than nothing," George sighed.

"Always the optimist," his friend laughed, patting him on the back.

Although George had done his best to conceal his low spirits from Marguerite as much as possible, he realized that she had somehow become aware of them anyway–so much so that she seemed to be affected by them, and sometimes revealed a similar gloominess in her recent correspondence. Her latest was full of news about her activities in a sewing circle in Greenville, and her work assisting her mother at a military hospital which had been set up in a school there. The letter was reasonably cheerful at first, but towards the end she began to complain of the town having no telegraph or daily newspaper, then described how crowds gathered at the railroad depot to await newspapers from Columbia for the latest reports, and how a minister would stand on the platform to read off the names on the casualty lists–the same platform where the coffins of dead soldiers were brought off the train to be claimed by their families.

She also remarked, "How I dread the reading of those names."

In her next letter to George she wrote, "Chassie instructs me to scold you for taking so long to answer her last communication. There, you are scolded! I think it is generous of you to answer any of her little scrawls. She begins a letter, labors over it for a while, goes back to it, and in the end produces less than a page of large, awkward handwriting, full of ink blots, misspellings, and corrections. Her last one, I believe, was all about her pigeons, one of whom nearly met a tragic fate when a hawk attempted to carry it off for dinner. She is composing a letter to you now about her goat cart. These are subjects I am sure you find fascinating. I am quite put out with my little sister today! I was to tutor her as usual this morning, but after breakfast she ran off to play at a neighbor's farm, and did not come home until the afternoon. The little thing has gone rather wild here in the country. Mama begins to despair of her education..."

The letter went on to say how much she missed him and longed to see him again. "Shall we see you at Christmas, or before?" she asked, adding plaintively, "How long must we endure this painful separation?"

Aleck had brought George his mail, and lingered at his house while they both read letters from home. He noticed George wincing as he finished reading Marguerite's letter, and asked if something was wrong.

"No, nothing's wrong," he murmured, and sensing that he was being watched, George folded up the letter and put it away. He saw that Aleck had a new letter from Alicia and asked about it.

"How are the Porters?"

"They seem to be doing well. There really wasn't much family news in this letter. Alice was telling me about her latest reading"

"She writes more frequently since you were married," George observed.

"Yes. I find myself writing to her more often, too. I am always thinking of her, even when I am not thinking of her–somehow."

Aleck drew his wife's letter a little closer to his face and studied her graceful handwriting.

"She and I are so alike," he went on meditatively. "In our thinking and inclinations, our tastes–nearly everything. In our letters, it is as though we anticipate each other's thoughts and needs. A while back, I lost a favorite book which I had never mentioned to her, and not long afterwards, she sent me another copy. Alice said that it was something she was reading, and thought that I would like it–the very book!"

"That is a remarkable coincidence."

"I think so. She...she is like a second self. I don't think Alice would mind my confiding that to you."

"Is it–" George hesitated, not finishing the question.

"What?" Aleck urged him.

"Is it more difficult for you to be apart from her now that you are married?"

"I must admit, it is. It was very difficult to part with my wife. I felt as though I were being torn apart, pulled in two, and I don't feel complete without her anymore, but as long as I know she is safe and well, I am content. I must confess–I am more than content! I am not ashamed of being so happy in these evil times. Even if I were to be struck down tomorrow, in my dying moments, I would thank God for the happiness He has already allowed me in this life. But I think you live too much in the future, George. You are anxious for all this terrible disruption to be done with, so that you can enjoy peace and happiness and love, but you might enjoy some of those now, at least in some measure, if you did not insist on perfection. You expect that of yourself, I know, but you can't expect it of circumstances over which you have no control."

George looked thoughtful, and turned away from Aleck as he considered what he said.

"Why don't you marry, George?" Aleck asked in a delicate, quiet tone.

During the long silence that followed, George asked himself the same question.

"I didn't think this war would last so long," he said. "I thought it would be over long before now."

"So did I, at first," said Aleck. "Now...now I think it may go on for years more. You ought to marry, my friend."

George turned back to the adjutant with the beginnings of a smile on his face.

"Since we are confiding in each other," he said, "I shall tell you, I think you are right, and what you have said to me just now, makes me begin to think I will."

"Good!"

The next morning, as George opened his eyes in a comfortable bed in his sunny, pleasant bedroom, it occurred to him as his very first thought that if he were married, Marguerite would be here waking up beside him. He was sharing this house with another officer, but it also occurred to him that he might be able to rent a private house in the village. Though the enemy's bombardment of Charleston had been renewed in November, there was little danger at present in the immediate area. For all he knew he could be stationed here for several more months, and it seemed unlikely that the brigade would be sent anywhere else with winter approaching. Thinking of Marguerite's recent letters, he asked himself why he continued to make her and himself so miserable. Where else could any happiness be found except with her? While George rose and dressed himself, he was already so possessed by the idea of getting married that he found it difficult to decide if such a scheme for a honeymoon in this place was actually practicable, or even possible— but marry he would, whether she could live with him here or not.

Once he had determined to marry Marguerite, he could think of little else. A feverish anticipation took hold of him, and deep in his heart, he nurtured a hope that the comfort of her companionship would break the spell of melancholy in him, and strengthen him in his struggle against it.

Before breakfast George sat down at a desk and wrote a letter to her.

Mount Pleasant

5th November 1863

Dearest Miss Marguerite,

You will be surprised, but not displeased I think, by a decision I have made of late. If it is agreeable to you, I should like for us to marry at the earliest opportunity. I believe a furlough can be had, and for so laudable a purpose as matrimony, I am sure I can obtain one of at least three weeks or more.

When this war began, I firmly believed it would not be of long duration, but I see now it will last another year or two, if not longer. Although I entered the army with some trepidation as to my abilities as an officer, I am long since accustomed to my duties and comfortable in them, and I think my becoming a husband will in no way impair me as a soldier. This change of heart and mind must seem sudden and astonishing to you, I know, but what does that matter? I have lately realized that the only remaining obstacle to our being married was my own obstinacy, and perhaps even a little pride. When we first parted you said to me, as I recall, 'I think you are wrong,' and 'you will change your mind.' Well, I humble myself and admit it. You were right. Thus far your family has kept you safe, and I know that they will continue to do so whether we are married or not. Now that you are all in Greenville, I feel much easier about your safety and well-being, for it seems an unlikely place for the enemy to bother with. He does seem intent on taking Charleston, however unlikely that may be.

Write to me immediately, and tell me when we may fix the day. Next month may be the best chance for a furlough; I don't see why I could not be spared for a while. I think a private wedding would be best, but I shall leave all that to your preferences, since you must make all the arrangements. There is not much time to obtain a ring for you, but if you will measure the size you need for me I shall make every effort to obtain one in Charleston before the wedding.

The idea of seeing you again, and the thought that I may soon be your husband, is almost more happiness that I can bear. Now that the idea is settled in my mind, you must marry me, or I shall become a useless wreck. You see, I leave you no choice.

Yours with great love,

George W. Taylor

After reading George's letter, Marguerite sent off an immediate reply.

Greenville 9th Nov. 1863

My Dearest,

Your last letter was so much like a dream, I scarcely know how to begin a reply. 'If it is agreeable,' you wrote. How could you think there is any doubt? You know I would have married you long ago, but for your own obstinacy. Oh, forgive me—I ought not to call it that (though you did) – it was no such thing, and I am truly not resentful. I know you did what you thought best for both of us, but I am so glad you have come to a different view now.

A quiet and private wedding is fine with me. Mama has said before that we ought to take a wedding trip somewhere, but I really do not think such an idea advisable in such times. In any case, I should prefer to remain here in Greenville. There is a pretty little house on the property we rent, an old hunting lodge, I think, but I prefer to call it a cottage. What would you think of us setting up housekeeping there? I shall ride out to the place tomorrow to see if it is satisfactory. By all outward appearances, it seems a pleasant little dwelling, and is surrounded by many ancient, beautiful trees. If it needs some interior improvements, there would be time to for that to be done before you arrive. It will give me such delight to prepare a comfortable home for you!

As for a ring, you need not trouble yourself about that. If it is agreeable to you, my mother wishes to make us a gift of her mother's ring, which is very lovely, and very acceptable to me.

The day that seems best is December 2, but if that is not convenient for you, a date of the 5th would be the next best choice for the day of our wedding. Wedding—the happiest of words to end on!

> *Yours ever affectionately,*
>
> *Marguerite Finley*

P.S.

My heart is so overflowing, I must add another line or two. No need to tell you how much happiness your letter gave me. I am pretty certain you know how much I love you, my dear Mr. Taylor. I sometimes think I ought to

*conceal it more, show more reserve, but truly that is not
my nature, and I would not play at that as a stratagem,
even if I thought it might make you love me more. I know
you value honesty and candor, and so I tell you honestly,
I think I love you too much.*

"Don't say that," George murmured as he finished reading her letter.

CHAPTER EIGHT

THE CLOSER THE TRAIN BROUGHT him to Greenville, the more ecstatic George felt. Yet, for some reason, he found it hard to believe that the happiness he expected was really awaiting him. It all seemed too good to be true–a furlough of more than three weeks, a wedding, and a honeymoon with his beautiful Marguerite–it was like being transported from a kind of hell to a kind of heaven, and he had not yet absorbed the shock of it. The pessimistic voice that frequently managed to spoil even his happiest moments, kept whispering to him in his mind that something bad was bound to happen. It had whispered that thought most emphatically to him the day before when his train had been delayed along the route, making him a day late, but now that he was nearing his destination, he felt hopeful again, though somewhat nervous.

He was seated by the window, and as the train pulled into the depot, he pressed his face against the glass, peering toward the platform, where a number of gentleman and ladies were standing. Marguerite had told him so many times in her letters how anxious she was to see him again, that he was sure her face would be one of the first he spied, yet he saw no one like her in the small crowd.

When George got off the train, he was surprised to find Marguerite's brother waiting for him there, but then realized that

Frederick must have arranged for a furlough to attend his sister's wedding. George shook his hand heartily, and had to restrain himself from embracing the young man in a great outburst of affection. In the euphoria that filled him on his arrival, he found himself feeling affectionate toward everyone and everything he saw, especially anyone connected with Marguerite. He gazed at her brother with moist eyes, thinking what an amiable, fine young man he was, and that he was fortunate indeed to have such an excellent fellow as a brother-in-law. It took him a moment to perceive that Frederick's smile was a forced one.

"We expected you yesterday," he said.

"There was a problem just outside Branchville," George explained. "My train was delayed overnight there."

"I don't suppose you received my telegram," said Frederick, as his smile gave way to bitten, trembling lips.

"What telegram?" George asked, his spirits suddenly sinking as if weighted with lead.

"I sent it from Columbia. You must have just missed it. It was about Chassie. She's been ill. We didn't think it serious at first–only a mild fever– but then, just a day or two ago, very quickly, things began to turn very serious, and now–"

"She's dead?" gasped George.

"She may be dying. It is diphtheria, and the doctor does not hold out much hope for her."

"Frederick!" George said feelingly, grasping his hand.

The young man sniffed back tears and looked away.

"I have a carriage. I'll take you to our house."

On the drive, both men were very quiet, but George asked Frederick how his parents and Marguerite were holding up.

"Not very well," he answered.

The house Mr. Finley had rented sat at the very outskirts of the town, on the top of a broad hill surrounded by a small farmyard and woods. It looked to be a comfortable place, but impressed George as rather quaint and humble quarters for such a refined family. Frederick's wife Lizzie met them at the door. She was expecting, her baby due any day now, and she looked pale and weak.

"Any change?" Frederick asked her anxiously.

"Not much since you left, dear. The doctor came by again, but said she is no better. He says it is only a matter of time."

Choking back tears, Frederick kissed his wife and immediately went upstairs to Chassie's room.

Lizzie went into the parlor adjoining the hall and collapsed exhausted into a chair. George followed her a few steps, stopping in the doorway.

"Mr. Taylor," she murmured sadly. "I hardly know what to say to you. I'm sure Marguerite will be down directly."

In a few moments George heard light footsteps on the stairs and turned to see Marguerite walking down quickly. He rushed to the foot of the steps, and she fell into his arms.

"My darling," he whispered. "I am so sorry, so sorry..."

"She is dying," Marguerite sobbed. "We shall lose her!"

Towards dusk Marguerite's brother drove George back into Greenville, and he took a hotel room there for the night. He was so tired from his long train journey, and so emotionally drained, that he slept a full, sound night's sleep, though bad dreams troubled him towards morning. When he woke, he was bewildered at first to find himself in a strange room, until he remembered the events of the day before. He returned to the Finley house early, and that day, and the day afterwards, tried to comfort Marguerite as she and her family sorrowfully watched and waited, hoping against hope. He visited Chassie's room several times, but the little girl was so ill that she did not seem to know him.

On the third morning, George hired a man with a mule and a wagon to take him to the Finley house, and when he arrived, he found Frederick's wife waiting for him at the door. She was wiping her eyes with a handkerchief.

"She passed away a little while ago, Mr. Taylor."

He walked inside and looked toward the stairs.

"Should I go up?" he asked.

"Yes, perhaps you should," Lizzie answered after a pause.

George felt twice his weight as he slowly put one foot in front of the other ascending the steps, and gravity seemed to drag on his soul as well as his body. At the top of the stairs he saw Marguerite and her parents huddled outside the open door of Chassie's bedroom.

Marguerite had been weeping. Her beautiful eyes were bloodshot, their lids and delicate surrounding skin reddened. When George silently enfolded her in his arms, she began to cry again. This brought on more tears from her mother, and Mrs. Finley had to leave the hall and go into another room, supported by her husband.

George glanced into the bedroom, where Frederick was kneeling against the bed, holding the motionless little hand of his sister. Her nurse was quietly moaning and weeping in a corner chair, hiding her face in an apron. Chassie's face was hidden from view by a curtain of the canopy drawn back and tied to the headboard, and George was glad of it.

How could it be, he wondered, that this lovely little girl, so full of life, was no more? It was hard for him to believe it.

The next morning, when George returned to the Finley house again, he found Marguerite alone in the yard, seated on a bench in a little rose garden, and sat down beside her.

She was subdued, quiet, and melancholy. George had repeatedly offered his condolences to her and the whole family, and did not know what else to say to comfort her. He asked her a few questions about her little sister, but her answers were laconic, and she did not seem to want to talk about Chassie. She told him that she did not wish to talk at all.

"Put your arm around me, dear," she requested in a faint voice. "That's all I want."

He did as she asked, and they sat together in silence for a long while, until Mrs. Finley called to Marguerite from the house, seeking her counsel on some of the arrangements for the burial.

That afternoon, there was a service at the church. Afterwards, the pall bearers carried her casket out to the grave which had been prepared for her in the adjoining churchyard, where the priest uttered the final words and prayers.

The arms of Mr. and Mrs. Finley were tightly interlocked as they stood by their daughter's grave side, their eyes fixed mournfully on the little casket as it was lowered into the earth. George was holding Marguerite's arm, and felt her go limp for a moment. He slipped his arm around her waist and supported her as the priest began the final prayers.

"O merciful Father," he solemnly intoned, "whose face the angels of thy little ones do always behold in heaven, grant us steadfastly to believe that this thy child hath been taken into the safekeeping of thine eternal love..."

When the service was finished, George accompanied the Finleys back to their home. It had been a cold, overcast day, and the house was chilly. Frederick lit the wood in the fireplace, and everyone sat together in the parlor and watched the spreading, rising flames in silence for a while. Though they had just seen Chassie buried, and keenly sensed her absence, everyone seemed to experience the same stunned disbelief, and with it, a numbness of feeling after all the agonies of the preceding days. Is it possible, their eyes asked as they looked to each other, that she is really gone?

Slowly, and with difficulty, conversation began, in trickles at first, with observations about the beauty of the burial service. Soon they heard the patter of a light rain outside, and Mr. Finley expressed his gratitude that the showers had held off until now. His wife and the others quietly voiced their agreement. After this, the conversation gradually turned from matters of death to matters of life. They spoke of the child who was expected soon, as Frederick's wife took up her knitting needles to continue work on a tiny white blanket.

One morning, about a week after the funeral, Marguerite had two horses saddled and asked George to go riding with her.

"The exercise will do me good," she said.

They rode out from the house, toward a path which led into the woods. Marguerite was an expert horsewoman, and George admired her as she sat gracefully in the side saddle and confidently handled the reins and a crop. He imagined how handsome she would look in a new riding habit of velvet, instead of the plain, homespun dress and old jacket she was wearing today.

Although Marguerite's horse was elderly, he was still strong, and she had pronounced him a good old fellow. George's mare was a younger, but not particularly admirable animal, being somewhat broken-kneed and swayback. So many horses had been taken for the use of the army, these two were among the best specimens left in the area.

After a ride of about a quarter of an hour through the forest, they came to a meadow which stretched over several acres. On the other side of it, George could see a cabin nestled among some towering trees.

"Our cottage," said Marguerite, with a faint, mournful smile. "Shall we go and see it?"

George gave a nod, and she prodded her horse into a canter across the open field. He followed at a slower gait, and when he reached her side, they sat still for a long while without speaking, looking at the little house. George imagined that it had indeed once been a gentleman's hunting lodge, and Marguerite explained that it had once belonged to the largest planter in the area, who had sold a wooded portion of his plantation to a cousin of the Finleys many years before. Though the house was not really a log cabin, it had been quaintly finished to look like one, and was altogether a charming little residence, embowered in the shade of beautiful oak trees.

"I had a very cozy home prepared for us," she remarked, after a long silence. "Chassie helped me. It delighted her to do things for us."

"I can see that," said George. "I can see, it is a very lovely place."

"Shall we ride on?" asked Marguerite, abruptly turning her horse.

They set off at a trot, rode back across the meadow, then slowed to a walk on the trail which continued through the woods. Moving at this leisurely pace, they talked for an hour before turning back toward home, then resumed their conversation for as long on the way back. As they were nearing the edge of the woods, riding side by side, George attempted to get close enough to Marguerite to kiss her. She leaned forward to meet him, but before their lips touched, the horses decided they were too close together, and shied away from each other.

"Ah," he sighed, "I have missed my chance."

Marguerite smiled, and even laughed a little, replying, "A kiss is not so easy to maneuver on horseback."

He returned her smile.

"Still, I am content," he said, his eyes traveling over the lines of her beautiful face. "I have had you to myself for a while today. As things are now, I could not ask for any greater happiness than that."

She lowered her eyes, her smile fading.

"Forgive me," he said. "I ought not to speak of happiness at such a time."

"It's all right," she murmured. "I know what you meant."

George had not spoken of their disappointed hopes before, but now expressed regrets that they had not married at the time they had originally planned. Looking troubled, he wondered aloud if she had perhaps become resentful, or regretted her promise to him.

Marguerite interrupted him to deny both speculations.

"I do not think that I have given you any idea of such feelings," she protested.

"No, you have not," he admitted. "But sometimes, I am fearful of losing you."

"Oh, how can you fear that? Don't you believe that I love you?"

"Yes..."

"How could I be resentful when I have what I most desire? When I read the lists of the dead and wounded, and do not see your name? If you are spared to me, that is the most I dare to ask for. As long as that is granted to me, I ask for nothing else."

He reached over to her, took her hand, and kissed it in gratitude.

That evening, the house was quiet. Marguerite had been sitting with her mother, who was suffering with a severe headache. When Mrs. Finley fell asleep, she went downstairs to look for George, but found the first floor apparently deserted. Marguerite looked in several rooms, but saw no one until she noticed a movement outside the front parlor window, where a curling wisp of whitish smoke was rising up. Then she caught the sweet aroma of a cigar.

"Ah, they are on the piazza," she thought.

She walked to the window and looked out, seeing first the shoulder, and then the sleeve of a dark coat as George raised the cigar to his lips again.

"Mr. Taylor," she said.

He turned in the chair and faced her, folding his arm on the window sill.

"Is Papa with you?" she asked.

"No, I am alone out here. I believe he went for a walk with Frederick."

"When did you begin to smoke cigars?" she inquired curiously, pulling a chair up to the window.

"Oh, I haven't, really. Occasionally I indulge, especially when I am made a gift of so fine a cigar as this one. Your father gave it to me. Do you mind the smell?"

Marguerite wrinkled her nose a little in mild distaste.

"The smell of it is pleasant, but I can't imagine that the taste of it is."

"I'll get rid of it," George offered, but she reached out the window and put her hand on his arm to stop him.

"No, please don't. Please continue if you enjoy it. I don't mind. But aren't you cold out there?"

"I'm all right. I didn't wish to smoke indoors."

George shifted himself a little more in her direction and admired her with smiling eyes. They looked at each other without speaking for a while, the glow from a parlor lamp illuminating George's face, and Marguerite's in part, making it an interesting study in light and dark, lines and shadows.

"You look very pretty in the window, Miss Rita," he said. "It frames you like a picture."

Her hand traveled from his shoulder to his head, and her fingers caressed his hair, until he spoke again.

"How is your mother?" he asked.

"Finally asleep," she said, letting her hand fall against George's shoulder and rest there. "She has been weeping today, thinking of Chassie, and it gave her a headache, but I think the rest will help her. Mama misses her so. She woke up this morning, thinking that her darling's illness and death had only been a terrible nightmare, and was about to go to her room, when she realized it was not so. She tried to keep herself busy throughout the day, so as not to dwell on the pain too much, but when she lay down for a nap this afternoon, the tears began to flow. She could not help it."

"Ah," sighed George, feeling, he imagined, at least some of Mrs. Finley's sorrow, but not really knowing what to say. "All of you must miss Chassie a great deal. I do. It is sad to think that I shall never receive another letter from her."

"I do miss her, terribly."

Marguerite was quiet for a few moments, but then said to George, "I missed you terribly. I don't think you realize how much."

"I think I have some idea. I'm sure I feel the same."

"But it isn't the same for you. You are very busy and preoccupied with important matters all the time–"

"Not all the time."

"Most of the time, then. While I–I have nothing more important to do than knitting stockings and sewing–"

"But those are important things," he interrupted, "especially your work at the hospital."

"Yes, they are. Still, they do not occupy the mind, not enough. I am not a nurse, you know–they won't allow it, as I am not married, so they put me to work rolling bandages and washing and–yes, these things are important, but while my hands are busy, my thoughts are constantly turning to you. I wonder where you are... how you are, knowing that every day, nearly every hour, you are exposed to great danger."

"I see, dear. I see what you mean. It must be very difficult for you."

"It is."

George put his head down to one side, drew up his shoulder closer, and pressed his lips against her hand.

"Miss Rita," he said gently, after another kiss, "it wouldn't be any different if we were married, now would it?"

"No," she answered, "I don't suppose it would."

They both fell silent as George drew in the smoke of the cigar twice and twice slowly released it. Marguerite watched him with an uncharacteristically heavy expression, and then spoke to him in a low, confidential, almost plaintive voice.

"I think you are hiding something from me," she said. "I sense something unspoken in your letters. I think you have some sorrow you will not share with me."

George turned his face away, denying this.

"How is it she knows that?" he wondered. "How is it women divine such things?"

"I do not think you would lie to me," she pressed.

He heaved a long breath and tossed away the cigar in a gesture of frustration.

"If I do have some...sorrow, as you call it, there is no need for you to be burdened by it. I have my fears, like any man, but no one can know the future. You needn't concern yourself with the unknown, Miss Marguerite," he said. His tone was testy, but he spoke her name more tenderly, to soften his sharp answer.

He felt her fingers tighten their hold on his shoulder.

"Whenever a letter comes from where you are," she said, "my heart beats fast until I see your handwriting. I dread to see the handwriting of your colonel, or some other officer, bringing me some terrible news about you. I have tried to yield you to God's will, but it is very hard. You see, I have my fears, too. My greatest one is losing you."

George turned and studied her somber face.

"We know that is a possibility," he said. "We have always known that. But if something happened to me, I think you would be able to bear it. You are young, and strong, and others who love you would need you, and you would not fail them, I know."

She hung her head, but then quickly raised her face with a different expression, attempting a smile.

"You must forgive me," she said. "I am much too gloomy. You mustn't worry about me. You have enough worries without that. I ought not to be so ungrateful and selfish."

"You are not selfish, and it is no surprise that you are gloomy. You have suffered a great loss."

Marguerite looked off into the darkness thoughtfully.

"I think I shall begin to do more reading. Perhaps books will better distract my mind. I used to read a great deal."

"That's a good idea," he encouraged her.

Marguerite's sister-in-law came into the parlor and was a little perplexed to see her sitting at the window at night.

"I am talking with Mr. Taylor," she explained.

"Oh," said Lizzie, grimacing as she leaned on the arm of a chair to seat herself.

Marguerite thought she looked very pale.

"Are you unwell?" she asked.

"I was having pains again."

"Oh, dear!"

"Just another false alarm, I think. I am better now."

Mr. Finley and his son were just returning to the house from their walk, and George came inside with them. The five sat and talked together in the parlor until Mrs. Finley came down. Her headache had eased, and she was hungry. Marguerite brought out some little cakes and light foods that kind neighbors had prepared for the family, and they continued their conversation in the dining room, lingering over the crumbs and teacups until it was time for bed. Then, once again, George returned to his hotel for the night.

One morning the following week, Marguerite's brother had to return to his regiment in Virginia, and her father left on the same train to go to Columbia, where some bank business would keep him for a few days. After seeing them off at the depot, George accompanied Marguerite and her mother to do a little shopping in town. Inside a shop he left their company briefly, purchased several books for his fiancée and had them wrapped as a Christmas present, and while Marguerite and Mrs. Finley looked over some goods in another store, he left them again for a few minutes to go off on a more mysterious errand.

Mr. Finley returned to Greenville the day before Christmas. The family's celebration of that holiday was not a happy one as usual, and Chassie was missed most painfully of all on Christmas morning. Just before dusk that evening, Mr. Finley went out for a walk, and his wife lit the lamps in the parlor and went upstairs to find a sewing basket she had left there, and to check on her daughter-in-law, who was resting in her room. During the few moments they were alone together, George seated himself beside Marguerite on a sofa and took her hand.

"I must leave tomorrow," he said quietly.

"But surely you have another day here," she protested.

"No, I must leave tomorrow morning. It will take the rest of my furlough to get back to Charleston."

She expelled a breath of frustration and slouched in discouragement.

"Your mother will scold you for such posture," said George, smiling a little. Marguerite straightened her back and leaned closer to him.

"My mother isn't here," she said, with a meaning look.

Understanding that look, George immediately put his arms around Marguerite and kissed her passionately.

"I shall remember this," he whispered in her ear. "I shall live on it until I see you again. When I do see you again, Miss Rita, I intend to marry you."

"I should like nothing better," she answered.

When they heard Mrs. Finley's footsteps on the stairs, George resumed his chair by the fireplace. As the lady took her seat again,

Marguerite informed her that Mr. Taylor would be leaving on the morning train.

"Oh, no," she lamented. "I am so sorry to hear it. You have been a great comfort to Marguerite, and to all of us, Mr. Taylor."

"I am very sorry to go," George replied. "I certainly wish I could stay another week, believe me."

"So do I," she sighed. "Marguerite and I shall be so lonely for–"

Mrs. Finley suddenly choked with tears and covered her eyes. Seeing her mother's sorrow, and thinking of Chassie again, Marguerite also began to cry, and threw herself at her mother's knees, putting up her arms to her to enfold her in an embrace.

It made George's heart ache to see their grieving, but he knew there was little he could do or say to console them. He kept his place, remaining quiet until they had done with their weeping and regained some composure. While he was waiting, he remembered the gifts he had for them.

As Marguerite made her way back to the sofa, George pulled out a little leather case from a pocket and handed it to Mrs. Finley.

"What is this?" she asked tremulously.

"A keepsake for you," George explained. "I asked for a lock of Chassie's hair, and had two of these made. I was told there was a very skilled hair worker in town, and she finished them today."

He reached in his pocket and pulled out an identical case, which he gave to Marguerite. The two women opened them, and each found a tiny ring, intricately and exquisitely braided and shaped, of the little girl's fine brown hair enclosed in glass and rimmed with gold.

"The lady said it can be worn as a locket if you wish," he added.

Marguerite and her mother gazed silently at the little memento of their loved one in private memories and meditation for a long while, then placed the cases on the table next to Mrs. Finley, opened like pictures.

The next morning they accompanied George to the depot. Marguerite had resolved not to cry, and did not, though her mother could not help dabbing away a few tears with her handkerchief as they said their goodbyes.

"When you return to us, Mr. Taylor," said Mrs. Finley, "it will be for a happy occasion, I trust."

George smiled and kissed her cheek. The conductor made a final, insistent call for boarding, and Marguerite was forced to let go of George's hand.

"God bless you and keep you safe," she whispered, pressing a kiss to his face.

A few moments later, she and her mother were watching the train pulling away from the station, carrying him back to the coast.

When George got back to his house in Mount Pleasant, outside Charleston, Aleck was waiting for him there, having just returned from a furlough in Columbia.

"Here's the married man!" he exclaimed jubilantly, slapping George on the back.

"I'm not married," he said.

"What!" Aleck was about to laugh at him about this, but something in his friend's expression stopped him.

"What's happened, George?"

"Marguerite's little sister died a few days after I arrived."

"Ah! George! I am very sorry to hear it. How sad for Miss Marguerite and her parents. Your presence must have been a comfort to them, though."

"I think it was. They are all devastated. It was very sad. That child was the darling of the family."

"You were very fond of the little girl, weren't you?"

"I was. She sent me that book of Tennyson. Do you still have it?"

"Yes, of course. I'll return it to you directly."

"Thank you," said George. "I'd like to keep it."

The day after his return, George received a letter from Marguerite announcing the birth of a niece.

"Lizzie has a little daughter," she wrote. "She was born the evening of the day you left. For a girl, she is a fat, strapping little thing, and of course we all think her the very perfection of infant loveliness, a real cherub. She proves to be a great consolation to Mama, who has lost her heart entirely to the child."

Reading over some reports that had collected in his absence, George learned that on Christmas day itself, the enemy had shelled the city of Charleston more furiously than ever before, causing a major fire and more injuries and deaths among the inhabitants. One of those killed was an elderly gentleman who had been seated at his fireside when a shell ripped through a wall of the house and took off one of his legs. The cemetery of St. Michael's Church had been ploughed by shells and the chancel struck.

Over the winter, Holton Legion remained in the Charleston area, occupied with much the same duties as before. As spring approached, George and Marguerite began to make plans to marry in the summer, but at the end of March, the brigade received orders to move north again, under the command of a new general. The Legion also had a new commander, Colonel Elliott, who told his officers to expect to find themselves in the thick of major engagements in Virginia before long. Hearing this, George realized that the prospect of a June wedding now looked very dim indeed, but, telling himself that some great, decisive victory for the Confederates was possible, he held on to this hope of happiness, and let Marguerite do the same.

The day before the brigade boarded a train bound for the north, George wrote to her, "I dreamt of you last night. It was one of those dreams in which one has some purpose which is continually thwarted. Do you have such dreams? We were to go somewhere together, but were constantly being interrupted and foiled by a series of absurd contingencies which arose. These made sense in the dream, but made none at all as I reflected on them in my first waking thoughts. Frustrating as it was though, I was <u>with you</u>, and felt your arm around mine, and looked into your eyes. I will take even nonsensical dreams if you are in them. When this war is over I shall take you away on a wedding trip and never let you out of my sight."

CHAPTER NINE

THE BRIGADE ARRIVED IN VIRGINIA in the latter part of April 1864. In the first week of May, under the command of Major George W. Taylor, a detachment of about fifty men from Holton Legion was sent to a place called Stony Creek, to guard an important railroad station on the Petersburg and Weldon railroad, and a bridge over the Nottoway River in that area. Aleck was among the officers in this detachment, and was as concerned as his commander that such a small force of men could adequately defend the position. As soon as they arrived, they learned that the enemy was already threatening, and the major immediately sent off a request for reinforcements.

That night around the campfires, the men were unusually quiet. If any of them felt fear it was not shown, yet there was an unspoken but palpable sense of foreboding shared by most.

Late the next afternoon, enemy cavalry were sighted by the Confederate pickets near Stony Creek, and soon afterwards, a fight began which lasted for a few hours. After a number of his men were killed and wounded, Major Taylor was forced to surrender. Just before the surrender, while the bullets were still flying, George heard Aleck cry out and turned to see him falling to the ground. He went to his knees and scrambled over to his injured friend. There was blood on one side of his face, which he was covering with one hand.

"Let me see," said George, pulling away Aleck's fingers to inspect the wound.

He moved aside some hair matted with blood and sighed in relief.

"You're only grazed, Aleck," he said, panting hard. "It's just a scratch."

He pulled out a clean handkerchief and pressed it against the wound, then let Aleck hold it himself, though he could press only lightly, feeling weak and close to fainting. George saw another man down a few yards away and went to offer him some help, but found that he was already gone, having bled to death from a gunshot wound in the artery of his neck.

When George got to his feet the victorious Yankee soldiers were already within their lines, and he surrendered his arms. A moment later he saw an enemy soldier kneeling beside Aleck and going through his pockets. The sight aroused such ire and indignation in him that without thinking he walked away from his captor and approached the man, who immediately turned a pistol on him.

"Is this how you treat the wounded?" George roared hoarsely, half-choking from some dust he had inhaled.

"He's not hurt so badly," answered the soldier, slowly rising.

"Don't touch him again! This man is an officer, as you can plainly see."

"He's just a damned rebel to me, and so are you."

A young Yankee captain who had overheard the conversation walked over and reprimanded the soldier. The officer signaled for litter bearers, but by the time they arrived Aleck had come to his senses again and was sitting up. He tied the handkerchief around his head as a bandage.

"I am able to walk," he said, as George helped him to his feet.

George kept supporting Aleck with one arm as they were rounded up with the rest of their company and marched off a short distance to a wooded area where some supply wagons were pulled off to the side of a road, and here they were ordered to sit down on the ground and wait. Aleck patted his coat, sensing the absence of something, and put his fingers into an empty pocket.

"That soldier took my pocket testament!" he said, amazed, adding a little peevishly, "Well, I hope it does him some good!"

Aleck also discovered that his silver pocket watch was missing, and bemoaned its loss to George as they sat together.

"My father gave me that watch," he said, looking somewhat dejected. "I had hoped to keep it for the rest of my life. Now I suppose I shall never see it again, or my pocket testament."

But the adjutant was proved wrong about this when these items were returned to him a little while later by the officer who had intervened on his behalf. After the Yankees finished destroying the railroad station and bridge, the young captain walked over to Aleck and handed him his watch and Bible.

"I believe these are yours, sir," he said.

"They are! Thank you, sir," Aleck answered with a catch in his voice. "The watch was my father's."

The officer acknowledged him with a smart snap approximating a bow, and turned and left without another word. A few moments later, George saw Aleck closing his eyes and grimacing.

"Are you in pain?" he asked him.

"Oh, it's not bad," said Aleck. "It just stings a little, that's all."

When the surgeons were finished taking care of the immediate needs of the more severely wounded, one of them cleaned Aleck's head wound and put a proper bandage around his head. As they left the area, the adjutant was allowed to ride in a wagon with other injured prisoners, but George had to walk alongside with the rest of the captured men. They marched until dark, and then made camp, passing their first night as prisoners of war in fitful, uneasy slumbers.

They were first taken to Fort McHenry in Maryland. It was a miserable, overcrowded prison, but when the men of Holton Legion learned that they were soon to be sent on to the prison at Fort Delaware, most of them wished that they could stay where they were. As bad as Fort McHenry was, Fort Delaware was reputed to be far worse. It was in fact a dreaded place; some had heard it called "the death pen." Within the past year, two of the Holton Legion privates had lost several relatives there to smallpox.

Early on a rainy Monday morning the prisoners were ordered to form a line of march and led to a small steamer waiting at a wharf in Baltimore Harbor. The ship was not too crowded, and the voyage was smooth, almost pleasant, except for the gloomy weather.

As the steamer emerged from a dense bank of fog, George caught his first glimpse of their destination, a fortification in the middle of the Delaware River. Fort Delaware was a massive stone edifice, and it reminded him of Fort Sumter, but unlike Sumter, which seemed to rise up out of the waters of Charleston harbor, Fort Delaware was situated on a sizeable marshy island, or rather a mud shoal, and surrounded by a moat. This pentagon of granite and brick enclosed a large parade ground, and a hundred and fifty-six guns were mounted in its casements, guarding both sides of the Delaware River.

As a defense, the fort may have been well designed and well placed. As a prison camp for thousands of men, it was a breeding ground for misery and disease.

Aleck looked out on the low island with some concern.

"I hope it is high tide now," he remarked. "If the waters rose much further, well–it looks as if a strong storm could swamp this place."

George was also a little alarmed to see how flat and low the land of the island lay. He later learned that its acreage had been reclaimed from swamp lands by the building of levees, and soon discovered that the spongy soil became a quagmire of mud, sewage and filth after any amount of rain.

Only Confederate prisoners of the highest ranks, along with some political prisoners, were kept inside the walls of the fort. The others resided in drafty wooden barracks outside its walls. The enclosed yard, or pen, for the imprisoned Confederate officers was an area of about two acres containing the barracks and a mess hall. It was surrounded by a high wooden fence and was directly under the guns of the fort. The officers' area was separated from that of the private soldiers by a wide alley and two plank fences topped with catwalks, where sentries walked and kept watch night and day. A number of ditches ran in all directions across the prison yards. Their brownish green, nearly stagnant waters, controlled by flood gates, served to float off the waste and offal of thousands of prisoners, sometimes barely adequately.

After taking away most of their possessions, the guards gave George and Aleck one blanket each, led them though the prison yard through a light rain, and directed them to a room inside the barracks designated as "Division 22."

"Find yourselves a hole to sleep in," said the guard.

Like all new prisoners, on their arrival in the barracks, they were met with cries of "Fresh fish! Fresh fish!" and immediately surrounded and besieged with questions about news of the world outside. The old prisoners were particularly eager to hear of Confederate victories, or any possible prisoner of war exchanges in the works.

"What of Lee?" they asked eagerly. "What of Johnston's army?"

George was nearly penned to the wall by several curious prisoners, and after answering some of their questions, reciprocated with one of his own.

"How is it here?" he asked warily.

"Oh, not bad," answered Captain Allen, a thin man with a short blonde beard, who then added waggishly, "that is, if you like vermin, brutish guards, and bad food–the last in small quantities, of course."

"Sounds just fine," George remarked drily after a pause, eliciting hearty laughter from his new companions.

When they finally left him alone he took a look around the dreary barracks room in dismay. It was reasonably large, but housed so many men (close to a hundred, he guessed) that it was very cramped and crowded. In its center was an aisle about five feet wide with a table and a large cast iron stove, and nothing else except the rows of wooden shelves against the walls which served as beds. George and Aleck found two empty spots on the lowest level in a tier of three shelves and put down their blankets there.

Within each division, the prisoners were divided into groups of eight to ten men called messes. George and Aleck became part of a group which consisted of South Carolinians, including Captain Allen, and two gentlemen from Charleston, one of whom George recognized as an old acquaintance. This was Captain Joseph Levy, a Jewish officer, and the son of a wealthy Charleston merchant. George had met him before the war, and had gotten to know him better during his early service in Virginia, in Evans' Brigade. He recalled Levy as a serious, dignified young man of thirty with jet black hair and a sharply-defined, pointed mustache and chin beard. A prisoner of several months, his appearance had become rather shabby, of course, but he retained his former air of dignity and reserve. He recognized George immediately, and greeted him with a firm handshake and a polite bow, but no smile. Though Levy seldom smiled or exhibited any merriment, and was somewhat aloof except with one or two close friends, he was nevertheless well-liked and respected among the other officers.

"I am told that the food here is excellent," George remarked to the captain, as he spread out his blanket on the rough piece of wood which was to be his bed.

"Then you have been misinformed," Levy replied, languidly lifting his dark brows. "It is superb."

"That bad?"

Captain Levy slowly nodded and shrugged.

The other officer in their mess from Charleston was Captain Thomas E. Wells, known as "Ned" to his friends and family. He was a member of a prominent family of New York City, but had moved to Charleston at the age of twenty, married there, and joined the Confederate Army soon after the war began. Having arrived at Fort Delaware only a few days before, Wells looked healthy and cheerful. The handsome young officer was clean-shaven except for a little tuft of hair below the center of his lower lip, and below that, a short, neat chin beard as black as the thick, wavy hair on his head. Already restless and bored with prison life, he was trying to organize a theatrical club, and was working on a script for a play. He tried to interest George and Aleck in participating in his dramatic venture, but they laughingly declined.

"What sort of play are you writing?" Aleck asked him curiously.

"I am adapting one of Mr. Dickens' works for the stage," he replied, smiling proudly, and affecting a histrionic tone.

"Which one?"

"Nicholas Nickleby. Do you know it?"

"Oh, that's a very amusing book," said Aleck. "We shall look forward to your play."

"I'm having trouble finding men who can imitate an English accent," Wells complained. "Your confounded Southern drawl is too strong."

"Perhaps you might change the setting of the story," George suggested, at that moment highly conscious of his Charleston brogue.

"Take Dickens out of England?" Wells protested, mock indignation emphatically displayed on his mobile, expressive face. "Never!"

George and Aleck had arrived too late for the morning meal, but were in time to partake of the only other offering of the day, a "dinner" served at three p.m. They left the barracks and followed a long line of other prisoners across a walkway made of wooden planks leading to the mess hall. Breakfast for the prisoners normally consisted of a small slice of bread and one smaller piece of boiled bacon or beef about two inches long and a half inch thick. The afternoon meal was much the same, with the addition of a tin cup half full of a watery soup.

There were no chairs in the mess hall. The prisoners stood at the tables to dine. Many took their food back to the barracks with them to eat it there, and, seeing some other men in their mess do this, George and Aleck followed their example. When they got back to Division 22, Captain Levy was sitting in front of the coal stove heating some potatoes. He had cooked them earlier on a little kerosene stove he had, and shared them with George and Aleck, along with the luxuries of butter and salt for seasoning. The captain told them he had purchased the items from the prison sutler. Having friends and family in the North, he was among the more fortunate prisoners who regularly received money from persons on the outside.

As they ate, Aleck looked down at the tin cup he was holding with an expression of repulsion.

"What kind of soup is this?" he asked Captain Levy.

"That, sir, is known as rice soup," he replied. "I must admit, I have occasionally found a grain of rice in it. It more often contains rice worms and pea bugs. These are always dead, and the joke here is that as the soup is too weak to have drowned the little fellows, they must have died of starvation."

Unamused, Aleck took a sip of the stuff with obvious distaste, and then forced himself to quickly drink down the rest.

"Did you have any money with you when you arrived here?" Levy asked them.

"Both of us had a little gold money," said George. "We were given sutler's checks in exchange for it."

"You'll want to write home for more money as soon as possible," Levy advised the two new prisoners. "If you don't receive food from outside, or buy it from the sutler, you will probably not have enough to eat. The commander here, General Schoepf, has already cut our rations more than once. He is a Hungarian, or German, I think, and enforces rather strict discipline, but of course all prisons are like that, I imagine. In my opinion, this place is probably the best of the Yankee prisons."

George wondered about the private soldiers held prisoner at Fort Delaware.

"Well, we hear the privates have it worse," sighed Levy, shaking his head. "And we hear it quite often. They often manage to send messages into the officers' pen by tying notes to pebbles and throwing them over the fence to us. A few days ago, one of the privates addressed a note to our highest ranking officer. The poor fellow complained that the soldiers are continually robbed, and are very hungry and sick, and he asked if the officer could intervene on their behalf with the commandant. That was tried, but I understand nothing came of it."

Hearing all this, George winced. It pained him deeply to think of his own men in such circumstances.

"Can't anything be done for them?" he asked.

"Sometimes things are smuggled in to them," said the captain, "and if they come into our area on work details, we try to give them what we can spare, but I'm afraid there is little else to be done. Those of us who have money are at least fortunate to be able to make purchases from the sutler. The one here is a greedy, cheating wretch who charges exorbitant prices, but it's better to pay his prices than starve."

Levy explained how many officers who were desperate to supplement their meager diet and provide themselves little comforts, found ways of making money. Some took to barbering, cobbling and tailoring; others carved pieces of jewelry and other trinkets from bone and other materials which they peddled to the Yankee guards, and a few prisoners made and sold beer, or caught rats to produce a stew. The most menial form of paid labor was practiced by the "wash women," officers who washed and ironed clothes for fellow prisoners. The water they had to use was so dirty that the clothes never really looked clean, but the pressing at least imparted some neatness to their appearance.

"How bad is the water here?" asked Aleck.

"The water from the tanks of rain and creek water could be called tolerable, I suppose," said Captain Levy. "Though it is often not sanitary, it is far superior to the ditch waters. Unfortunately, in dry times, the ditches must be resorted to for drinking water, and also very unfortunately, the ditches are the only place to wash one's body and clothes. I always go out early each morning to wash, before the waters are made even worse by so many others who are using them. I would advise you gentlemen to do the same."

George was curious to know if there had been any successful escapes from Fort Delaware.

"Quite a few have tried, but few that I know of have succeeded," Levy informed him. "Since we are on an island, one of the few ways to get off is of course by swimming. We are a mile and a half from the nearest land, however. A few have made life preservers for themselves out of empty canteens tied to their bodies, and have floated off after dark at high tide. The body of one poor fellow who tried this was found just yesterday. They fished his corpse out of the water, his eyes and lips eaten out. Since I have been here, the only prisoner I know of who made a successful escape somehow procured an enemy uniform and marched out with a regiment who had finished their service here. He saw his opportunity and seized it. I wish I had thought of that!"

The delicious aroma of the buttered, baked potatoes the three men were finishing up did not go unnoticed by others in the room. Those who had nothing but the prison rations to eat that afternoon sent hungry glances in their direction, and George and Aleck, seeing these, exchanged an uneasy look, both feeling a pang of guilt at the same time. Captain Levy noticed, and, leaning forward, said in a low, confidential tone, "It is difficult, I know. I share with others as much as I can, though I can tell you there are some who are too proud to accept such charity. I often purchase more than I need from the sutler, so that I can give some to my friends. Doing this eases my conscience."

George asked what this prison vendor sold besides potatoes and butter, and Levy rattled off a list: coffee, tea, sugar, eggs, molasses, rice, sardines, cheese, ham, Scotch herring, canned fruit, tobacco, wood for cooking fuel, and pots and pans.

"And," he added, "up until very recently, if you were desperate enough to pay the sutler's price, even liquor. Sometimes, one can also purchase ice cream."

"What about vegetables?" asked Aleck.

"No such thing is served here," answered Levy, shaking his head. "They must be bought from the sutler. Just last week, some kind Delawareans, hearing that there was scurvy among the prisoners, tried to raise some money for the purpose of buying vegetables and medicines for us, but their gathering was broken up by soldiers, and a number of them were arrested and sent to prison for their efforts! I wasn't aware that charity had become a crime now."

On their first night at Fort Delaware, after the lights were put out at the appointed time of curfew, eight o'clock, George and Aleck lay side by side in their wooden bed, both very wakeful. Absorbed in their own private ruminations, they did not speak for a while, but the rest of the place was far from quiet. Some prisoners were conversing, more or less loudly, while those blessed with the ability to fall asleep quickly despite noise and discomforts, had already set up a chorus of snoring. The sickly men coughed and wheezed and groaned. Someone in the bunk above that of George and Aleck sneezed and blew his nose, and when he turned over in his bed, dirt and sawdust sifted through a crack in the boards and came down in a little shower on to George's blanket.

"I see why this lowest bed was unoccupied," he glumly remarked to his bunkmate.

"Yes, I suppose it is preferable to be in the topmost bunk," Aleck agreed. He asked George what he had been able to find out about life at Fort Delaware, and they discussed all they had heard from the prisoners who had been here a while.

"One fellow wanted to know about my regiment," said Aleck, "and after I told him, he asked me when I was killed. I wasn't killed, I replied. Yes, you were, he said, and now you are in hell."

"They're fond of their jokes, aren't they?" George observed.

"I suppose one has to keep a sense of humor in such a place."

It was a cool night, and the two men could feel the chilly air filtering through the spaces in the rough weatherboarding, and wafting in the stench from a nearby ditch.

"This blanket is sufficient for tonight," said George, "but it must have been devilishly cold in here during the winter."

He glanced over at the cast iron stove in the middle of the room, which was already going out.

"Do you think that stove was sufficient to heat this room in the coldest weather?" he wondered.

"I don't know," said Aleck. "But there are certainly enough spaces between the boards to admit a draft of mosquitoes!"

He slapped at his neck to remove one the pests, and George brushed one off his face, sighing, "This will only get worse in the summer."

Finding some comfort and distraction in each other's company, they continued to talk for a while, until most of the other conversations and noises in the room, except for the snoring, gradually died away. Eventually, the worst of the noisy slumberers quieted, and George and Aleck were able to sleep.

On his second day in the prison, George sat down to write some letters, the first for Marguerite, mainly reassuring her that he was still among the living, and afterwards, one to his brother, in which he gave some details of his capture. Knowing that his letters would be inspected by the prison authorities, he made no complaints about the conditions at Fort Delaware.

Ft. Delaware 17th May 1864

Dear Albert,

Though I am glad to be alive to write to you, I am sorry to be writing from this place as a prisoner of war. I was taken at Stony Creek on the 7th of May, along with an entire detachment of Holton Legion sent there to guard the railroad bridge and station. We were sent first to Fort McHenry, and then brought here.

We put up a sharp fight at Stony Creek for several hours, but with only fifty of us against a large force of Yankee cavalry, we could not hold them off indefinitely. After we were captured we had the sorry privilege of witnessing the enemy destroy the bridge, the station, a water tank, and some cars and track. The loss of all these will do a great deal of harm to our supply route to Petersburg. I had requested more men for the defense of the bridge. I don't know if any were sent; if they were, they did not arrive in time to be of help to us. Aleck Dwight received a minor wound but is doing well. He and I are bunkmates now, and are quartered in officers' barracks outside the fort.

We are allowed to receive food, money, and other necessities here, though there are rumors that some of these privileges will soon be taken from us. I am told that charitable persons in Baltimore and elsewhere send in needful things from time to time for the prisoners, but I should prefer to rely on you or some of Father's old friends in that city, or our cousin Mr. Jacob Taylor. I shall write them at once to let them know I am here. They can perhaps send me food, clothing, or something to read; from you I must ask for money if it is possible for you to remit some here. I have just written to Marguerite, and will send out her letter with this one.

I hope and pray my stay here will not be a prolonged one. It is generally believed, however, that prospects of exchange are very dim at present. As soon as the general exchange of prisoners recommences I should like very much to be exchanged, and if you know of anyone intimate with the Exchange Commissioner at Richmond, Mr. Ould, I wish you would mention my case (and that of Mr. Dwight) to him with emphasis. I have only one suit of clothes and hardly any money. Give my love to Susan and the little ones, and believe me to be ever

yr devoted brother,

George W. Taylor

P.S. Your letters to me must be no more than one page. That is the rule.

Aleck was also writing letters, and while George was still composing one to his brother, he noticed that the adjutant had begun fidgeting and looking very troubled. After they finished their letters and gave them to the barracks postmaster, with an odd urgency, Aleck drew George over to their bunk for a private conversation. The room was fairly empty at that time; it was a fine sunny morning, and most of the men had gone out into the prison yard.

"George!" he gasped, looking horrified. "Living dirt! The lice– the graybacks are on me! I found one in my sleeve–I know there must be more!"

"They're on most everyone here, I think," George replied in a matter-of-fact tone.

He had never seen Aleck so distraught, and was surprised that he seemed to be on the verge of hysterics.

"God, give me strength! I can't bear these–these things on my body!"

"Unfortunately, you'll have to get used to them, Aleck."

"Never! I could never do that!" he panted.

George thought Aleck might faint, and told him to sit down. The young man sat down heavily on the edge of the empty bunk.

"This is the worst," he groaned. "This is the worst of it all! I'd rather be wounded again than this."

"You don't mean that, Aleck."

"I do! This is unbearable!"

"You will have to bear it. Look here, we're alive and unhurt, except for these–things, as you call them, but there are many things much worse," George lectured him sternly, standing over his friend with his hands on his hips. "Compose yourself, soldier."

Aleck closed his eyes and took several deep breaths.

"General Lee himself couldn't command me to do that, George, but I will try," he said breathlessly. "I will try."

He opened his eyes and looked up at George with a sickened expression.

"Lie down and rest," said George.

Aleck did as he was told, shuddering with disgust as his head touched the surface of the wooden bed. He closed his eyes and lay still and rigid, slowing and deepening his breathing to calm himself.

"Heaven help him!" thought George, taking a last, wondering look at his friend before heading outside. "He can face the Yankee army without flinching, but is unmanned by insects on his body!"

Aleck kept to himself the rest of that day, and did not say much to anyone. The next morning, George woke up to find the adjutant calmly reading beside him, and showing no signs of the near-hysteria he had exhibited the day before. George asked him if he had slept well.

"Eventually," he answered curtly, not taking his eyes from a New Testament he held.

George climbed out of the uncomfortable bed and stretched his aching limbs. All the while, he was observing Aleck curiously.

"Well," said the adjutant, glancing up at him, "what are you expecting?"

"Nothing, I hope," George replied.

"Then you shall have your wish."

"You are feeling better?"

"I am feeling perfectly wretched, but I have no choice but to endure it. I am resigned. I am determined that I will endure, and bear up under this affliction. There is live dirt on my body, which will stay with me until I am out of this place. I believe there are bedbugs, too."

"Well of course there are!" said George. "They were eating me alive last night."

Aleck went on, very deliberately, "Finding those things on my body, came as a great shock to me, but the shock is over, and, I have realized, as you said, there are many worse things which could have befallen me."

He spoke with such a grave, resolute expression that George had to fight a strong urge to smile, even laugh, but he managed to refrain from both, and merely nodded in understanding. He could see that the peace Aleck had made with the disgusting creatures inhabiting his clothes and feeding on his body was a fragile one, and, feeling sorry for him, he had no desire to disturb it. He said nothing to anyone else about his friend's initial reaction to the body lice, and remained the only person who knew anything about it.

With his usual resilience, Aleck soon put aside his own troubles and tried to make himself useful to others by helping with the religious services some prisoners had organized in the barracks. When it became known that he had studied for the ministry, he was asked to preach and conduct informal prayer meetings. The services quickly became regular, and more popular, under his supervision. Besides this ministry to the other prisoners, it was not long before the adjutant found another absorbing undertaking to occupy his time and thoughts.

One afternoon, Captain Levy noticed that Aleck was reading from the Psalms of David in a large Bible borrowed from one of the other prisoners.

"Are you preaching from the Psalms today?" the captain asked with idle curiosity. He liked the young adjutant and found him interesting, and, feeling particularly dull and bored that day, he was hoping to strike up a conversation to pass the time.

"Yes," said Aleck, eyeing Captain Levy thoughtfully as he privately pondered whether it would be considered an impoliteness to invite him to the services.

"I am more accustomed to reading the Psalms in Hebrew," Levy remarked.

Aleck stared at the captain enviously.

"You know Hebrew?"

"Why, yes."

The adjutant continued staring at him, his mouth partly open in admiration.

"I have always longed to read the Scriptures in all their original languages! I already have some basic knowledge of the language, but our Hebrew instructor at the seminary was so often ill that I'm afraid I am still woefully deficient...I wonder, Captain Levy–I hesitate to ask such a favor of you–but I wonder if you would be willing to teach me Hebrew?"

Impressed by Aleck's reticence and boyish enthusiasm, the captain readily agreed to give Hebrew lessons. The young man thanked him profusely. Levy shrugged it off, and remarked that it was not as though he had much else to do in this place.

"When may we begin?" Aleck asked.

"Anytime," said Levy. "Tomorrow, if you like. I happen to have a few of the Holy Scriptures in Hebrew with me."

The next day, Captain Levy sat down with his pupil for a two-hour session that became a regular occurrence at least three times a week. After the Hebrew lessons, the captain sometimes continued his conversations with Aleck in discussions of other subjects. A well-educated man, Levy thrived on such intellectual stimulation. They talked of history, philosophy, literature, art, and even mathematics, and it did not take long for the captain to ascertain that he was dealing with an exceptional student in Adjutant Dwight. Aleck had long since mastered Greek and Latin, and his teacher saw that he was picking up the intricacies of the Hebrew language with amazing speed.

For George, the first week at Fort Delaware passed slowly. He found the boredom and tedium of prison life even worse than that of camp life in the army, but strangely enough, at least at first, despite all the unpleasantness of the situation, its novelty seemed to keep his melancholy at bay.

There were men from every state of the Confederacy imprisoned at Fort Delaware, some of whom were interesting types George had only observed from a distance before. Many of them had never heard the curiously pleasant accent of a native Charlestonian before, and would sometimes engage George in a conversation just to listen to him speak in his brogue.

Not all the captive officers were genteel aristocrats, but George found most of them well-mannered enough, except for one objectionable habit indulged in by quite a few–a tendency to be constantly spitting and spurting out a brown liquid whenever chewing tobacco could be procured. George was not unaccustomed to being around gentlemen who chewed and spewed tobacco, but he had never been forced to occupy close quarters with so many. One tall, lean mountaineer from North Carolina, a lieutenant in rank, almost always seemed to have a steady supply. He had a long, straggling beard the color of straw, and when it came time to expel the tobacco juice, he would carefully pull it aside so as not to soil himself. On one occasion in the prison yard, he accidentally spat on George's shoe. Seeing that he had offended the high-toned gentleman, the lieutenant apologized, but thereafter George tactfully but carefully avoided this particular officer in the pen.

Many of the officers were not as well educated as George, but rather than wasting away physically and mentally in prison, quite a few were eager to spend some of the long, endless hours of their incarceration in self-improvement. When it became known that George was an attorney, some of the officers who had been studying law before the war asked if he would devote some time to their instruction. He agreed to teach a small class, and soon found that he enjoyed imparting his knowledge and experience to these men. He had his brother send him a copy of the book he had written for law students before the war, and often taught from it. One evening, for their own edification and the entertainment of others, the law students conducted a mock trial in the barracks. The experiment went well and instructively for a while, but then degenerated into humorous nonsense, and ended with the defendant being found not guilty on a plea of insanity.

Time hung heavy on the hands of all the prisoners, but they usually managed to find ways to occupy and entertain themselves. If not working to earn a little money, they played chess and other board games, or a card game called whist, or spent their hours reading books or writing letters. There was also a debating society, a theatrical troupe led by Ned Wells, and a few other groups organized around an officer willing to teach a foreign language or some other art or skill. Outdoors, many of the prisoners played marbles as avidly as schoolboys, and once in a while, when the ground was not too muddy in the pen, some of the younger, healthier men amused themselves in a game of prisoners' base.

Those prisoners who had been on the Fort Delaware diet the longest, and had the least help from outside, had no excess energy for such activity. The scant rations eventually produced a chronic fatigue, and those suffering in this way tended to conserve what little strength they had during the day. Some of the prisoners seemed to suffer a mental as well as a physical strain from their captivity. One manifestation of this was a number of men who spent their days walking a constant, unchanging circuit around the prison yard. While some walked in pairs and talked, a few others rambled alone in a slow, aimless way, with blank expressions on their faces, seldom speaking to the other men, and sometimes scarcely acknowledging their existence.

One of the more popular pastimes among the prisoners was gambling. The king of this enterprise was a smooth-mannered, shrewd-looking gentleman from Mississippi. He never seemed to lose, except strategically in order to win the more, and it was said that he had even victimized some of the Yankee guards. A large, anxious crowd was always gathered around the table where he sat inside his division, and both here and outside, in the corner of the pen he occupied, the atmosphere was rather like that of a casino where card playing and other games of chance went on day after day, and large amounts of mostly Confederate money changed hands. The more religious prisoners disapproved of the gambling and tried to discourage it. Many of the officers had been raised to regard gambling as sinful, but in their desperate desire for distraction from prison life, some turned to the practice who might normally have avoided it.

As soon as George received some money from his brother, he went to the sutler's shop to purchase some food, and another item which came highly recommended, a frying pan. It was observed that Major Taylor and others in his mess were well-funded, and some of the less fortunate officers applied to them for small loans of money now and then. The applicants were usually scrupulous to offer some little item or service in barter, or to repay the money when they could, but no repayment was really expected. Though there were a few well-fed officers who were resented for their selfishness, George and his messmates were not numbered among those. They did what they could within reason to help the other prisoners.

One afternoon, while the Confederate officers waited for their mail to be distributed, some men who were veterans of the Seven Days campaign in Virginia were talking of their battle experiences. A small crowd had gathered around one particularly excitable, eloquent fellow who was holding forth.

"We had been fighting for hours!" he exclaimed dramatically. "We were exhausted, nearly dead, when then came Stonewall, like a meteor from heaven, and fell on the enemy and drove them off by the thousands!"

The man was obviously relishing the memory of that event, despite the serious wound he had received. He was waving his right arm expressively in the air as he spoke, but his left arm, which had been injured that day, hung uselessly at his side. As he began to go into more detail about this particular battle, he was suddenly interrupted by the cry of, "Mail!" His audience immediately deserted him and gathered around the division postmaster, who stepped up on a table to avoid the crush of eager men.

George heard his name called, and came close to tears as he was handed a letter bearing Marguerite's handwriting. He hid it in his coat, and when the mail call was finished, he hurried to his bunk to read it.

Greenville 23rd May 1864

Dearest,

Your brother received his letter from you and immediately sent word to us, telling us the joyful tidings that you are safe, in case the letter you wrote to me was delayed or lost. I had been perfectly miserable for many days, not hearing from you for so long, and rejoiced in thankfulness to know you are alive. I was so very glad to learn that you had not been wounded, and your friend only slightly. I am distressed, of course, to learn that you are in the hands of our enemy, but pray that they will treat you with some measure of humanity, and that friends will be raised up to meet your needs. Your brother says he is sending you some money as soon as possible.

Missing your letters, and being in suspense about your fate, I have scarcely been able to think of anything except the one whose life is so precious to me. Last night my fears prevailed and gave me bad dreams, but they were only that. I wrote at least two long letters to you which I am sure you must not have received. I anxiously await your letter from Fort Delaware, which I hope is not lost...

George read on greedily, devouring all the words on this one written page in much the same way a starving man devours food. After reading it several times, he pressed the letter to his lips, then carefully folded it and put it away in a breast pocket to peruse again that evening. Later, he added it to the precious collection of Marguerite's earlier letters he had hidden away behind a loose board in his bunk, along with her photograph. He had managed to keep a few of her letters, and periodically took them out to look at them again, and as he reread each one, in his imagination at least, he could escape for a little while from his situation and picture himself with Marguerite—take himself back to things as they were before the war, to the Finley household, where everything (or so it seemed to him now) was pure and perfect and pleasant–a veritable heaven compared to his present condition.

Persistent in his theatrical ambitions, Ned Wells had finally assembled a few awkward players willing to participate in a play roughly based on what he and a few others could collectively remember of *Nicholas Nickleby*. The novel was so lengthy and complicated in plot that he soon gave up trying to condense it into a play, and decided instead to narrate a simplified version of the story in speeches scattered among brief enactments of certain favorite scenes. Wells had an amazing memory, especially for the parts he loved the most, and had coached the other actors in dialogue and gesture, though with mixed results. His production turned out to be nearly incomprehensible to those who had not read the book, but everyone in the audience seemed to enjoy the characters nonetheless.

Captain Wells had been fortunate enough to find a few natural mimics who could produce a reasonable facsimile of various English accents. Two young cousins from Georgia reluctantly accepted the roles of the female characters, which they played rather woodenly at first, but after receiving their first laughs, they began to elaborate the ladies with more gusto and humor. A young man from Virginia was particularly impressive in his role as the pathetic Smike, but the audience's favorite was Captain Wells, who put on a false mustache and enthusiastically launched into the hilarious character of Mr. Mantalini, bringing the ridiculous rascal to life before their eyes. The men were wiping away tears of laughter whenever he spoke. This part, though, however brilliant, was brief, and when the actors plodded on through the clumsily connected melodramatics, before the more interesting climax of the piece, some of the spectators called for encores of the scenes which involved Mantalini, and another favorite, the cruel, one-eyed schoolmaster Squeers, also amusingly played by Wells.

The audience clamored for the scene in which the schoolmaster fed a scanty breakfast to his unfortunate pupils, and the actors, in dutiful compliance, reassembled themselves at a table.

"Here's richness!" Squeers boasted loudly, as he held up a canteen and poured out a thin stream of dirty, disgusting water into several tin cups.

Like before, he turned to the audience with a broad wink of his one good eye and hissed, "Fort Delaware slop! Beg yer pardon–soup!" And once again, the audience roared with hilarity.

After the play, which had been staged in the largest of the barracks rooms, the prisoners who had gathered to watch lingered in the place, and sat on the floors and bunks talking among themselves. A number of them were hungry, and they began reminiscing about the old days, when they were at home and enjoyed tables of plenty. One man described, in minute detail, a sumptuous feast served at a wedding he had attended. His listeners hung on every word, enthralled and tormented at the same time. When he was finished, other prisoners offered their favorite remembrances of lavish meals of holidays. This went on for a full hour before one officer jumped up and called for an end to such conversation.

He complained loudly, before stalking away, "What's the use of talking about such things now, when I would be happy to be my dog at home eating from the slop pail?"

His objection put an end to that particular line of conversation, but nothing could stop the universal longing for food. Many a man sat at wedding feasts and Christmas dinners that night in his dreams.

CHAPTER TEN

ONE MORNING, GEORGE WOKE UP to feel an intense itching under his chin. Clawing at it with his fingers, he immediately rose from his bed and went to the broken piece of looking glass mounted on a post near his bunk. He parted the hair of his beard, and even in the dim light, could see an angry red spot on his skin. He had scratched it and made it bleed. Exploring the rest of his face and neck covered by his beard, he found several more little red sores.

"Damn these things!" he muttered fiercely.

No matter how thoroughly he picked the lice off his clothes every morning (a daily ritual among all the prisoners), and no matter how carefully he washed himself off at the ditch afterwards, the creatures always reappeared. Lately, it seemed they were beginning to infest him with a vengeance. During the day, he could stop his scratching, but at night he could not and tore his skin.

George glowered at himself in the mirror as he came to the painful conclusion that the beard must go. He could not keep the lice out of his clothing, but at least he could remove what was becoming one of their favorite dining places. Besides, it was very difficult to keep his beard clean; he had found nits in it, and fancied it was becoming a nest and breeding ground for the repulsive little creatures. After breakfast he asked Aleck which men were hiring themselves out as barbers lately. Giving George a name, the adjutant stared at him in open-mouthed surprise.

"What are you contemplating?" he asked.

"I shall have this beard removed, and my hair cut shorter," George replied.

"I'll show you where he works," Aleck offered, very curious to see the outcome of this decision. Knowing how vain George was about his beard, he knew he had not come to it lightly. He led his friend out into the prison yard, where a man was cutting hair under a makeshift tent made from a blanket stretched over four poles. George stood and talked with Aleck as he waited his turn, there being several customers ahead of him. The barber, a captain from Alabama named Chisolm, was a tall, lanky young man who was rather ill-groomed considering his occupation.

When it was his turn, George took his seat nervously and made his request, then leaned his head against a rest–nothing more than a rough piece of wood nailed to the back of an old wooden chair and angled with a wedge.

"Don't move too much," the barber warned him, "or you're liable to get a splinter in the back of your head."

After he chopped away at George's hair with a pair of scissors, the Alabamian did the same to a large portion of his beard, and then lightly lathered it and picked up a straight razor.

"Mind the sores on my neck," George cautioned him.

"Oh," laughed Captain Chisolm, "I know all about those, Major Taylor. They bring me plenty of business."

Watching intently, Aleck was sitting on the ground with an elbow propped on one knee and his chin in his hand. Other customers in line were observing George, too, as well as a number of men who had nothing better to do than to watch the barbering. A man divesting himself of a fine, full beard drew considerable interest from the spectators. When the deed was done, the barber wiped his customer's face with a dirty towel, and, as a finishing touch, ran a tortoise shell comb through his hair to arrange it more neatly.

Aleck withheld comment until he and George had returned to their division.

"Well, George," he said, "I see you've been hiding a rather handsome countenance beneath that beard."

"I don't feel right without it," George complained, inspecting the red spots on his skin in the mirror. One was just under his chin, but fortunately none were on his face.

"You should have your likeness taken for Miss Marguerite," Aleck encouraged him eagerly. "This may be her only opportunity to see your face in full!"

George thought this was a good idea, and later, in the afternoon, he obtained permission to leave the officers' pen. Under the supervision of a guard, Aleck accompanied him to a nearby building where the visiting photographer was working, and they were directed to a sunny but dingy chamber furnished with a wooden bench, one spindly chair, a torn canvas backdrop, and a rack where some clothes hung. Here they waited in line again for an hour and watched the picture-taking of a number of other prisoners.

Though fussy over his better-paying customers, the photographer was not so particular about prisoners of war, and moved them in and out as quickly as possible, slowed down only by the necessary mechanics of his art. Watching him work, George wondered why an able-bodied man of his age (he looked about thirty) was not in the army.

The photographer's attire was dandified, his glossy dark hair and mustache pomaded and precisely curled, and his mannerisms so petulant and dramatic that Aleck nudged George and dubbed him in a whisper, "Mister Mantalini." George smiled but stifled a laugh, not wishing to antagonize the gentleman in any way.

While waiting he looked over the photographer's supply of clothes, civilian and military. He found a nice gray captain's jacket adorned with faded gold braid on the sleeves, but it smelled so strongly and repugnantly of body odor that he rejected and chose a plainer, fawn-colored frock coat. It seemed to be clean, at least, and fit him decently as he slipped it on.

When it was finally his turn George faced the camera standing up. The photographer asked him to strike a pose beside the chair or in it, but he begged a word with him first. Making an impatient flourish, the gentleman approached George to indulge him.

"I want a good likeness for my fiancée," he explained. "I don't wish to have a staring look, as I have had in other photographs."

"Lower your eyelids a little, then, or your chin," suggested the photographer. For a moment, losing his air of impatience, he paused and studied the symmetry of George's features with a kind of artistic satisfaction.

Aleck interposed with some advice.

"Perhaps he ought to lift his chin," he said.

The photographer noticed the unsightly sores on George's neck and did not think this a good idea.

"Have a seat, Mister– what is your name?"

"Taylor."

"Sit down, then, Mr. Taylor, unless you prefer to stand. We shall do our best."

George sat down in the chair, to which the photographer had attached a little device with a headrest. After positioning his sitter's head very precisely, he went to his camera to make the necessary preparations.

"Now, sir," he said to George, "look directly at the camera. Imagine that you are gazing into the eyes of your sweetheart, and think of how much you love her."

"That's good advice," Aleck commented approvingly.

"Now remember, Mr. Taylor, don't move until I say you may, unless you wish to be a blur."

George remained motionless as the photographer removed the lens cover and counted off the seconds.

A few days later, several copies of his photograph were ready. He showed one of the tintype images of himself to Aleck, who privately thought that there was more pathos than romance in his face, but told George he thought it an excellent likeness.

"Miss Marguerite will be very pleased," he added.

"She'll certainly be surprised!" laughed George. "She may not even know me."

"Don't worry, she'll know you."

George had run out of stationery, and asked one of the friendlier guards if he could be supplied with a sheet or two of paper. The next day, he was given a single sheet, but was mortified to see that it was adorned with an eagle and a U.S. flag in the top left corner.

"What impertinence!" he complained to Aleck later, showing him the offending piece of paper.

"Miss Marguerite won't mind the Yankee livery," his friend reassured him, "as long as the letter is from you. This should teach us not to ask favors of the guards. Next time find your paper elsewhere."

The following week, Marguerite happily received another envelope stamped "Prisoner's Letter, Fort Delaware, Del., Examined." She rushed to her room to read in private, and as she opened it, was surprised to see the letter's decoration, but even more astonished by the photograph that came with it.

Less than a week later, her reply arrived at Fort Delaware.

Greenville 18th June 1864

My dearest,

Words cannot sufficiently express the surprise and joy I experienced upon receiving your letter and likeness. My greatest joy is to know that you are safe and well, but I must tell you how delighted I was to <u>see</u> you. I have been so anxious for the sight of you, that since the image of your face first met my eyes I have scarcely taken them from it. I have never seen all of it, you know, and what I do see pleases me more than I can say, though I am sorry to note that you look a little sad. Under the circumstances, that is no surprise.

Your letter was very guarded, if you will forgive a poor pun. I know you must be careful of what you put into writing, as your letters are inspected, and I suppose I must be a little guarded, too, for fear you might be deprived of this communication. I certainly hope you will be able to find more satisfactory paper in the future.

I pray that you and your friends will be exchanged soon. My cousin Frank Gibbes was at Fort Delaware no more than a few weeks before he was exchanged, but that was a long while ago–in '62, I believe. I hope you are well, dearest. I am always wondering how you are and what you may be in need of.

Please write to me and tell me all the details of your capture. We all wish to know more of what has happened to you. Your brother informed me that he wrote to the Porters as soon as he heard from you, to make sure they had some word of you and Mr. Dwight. Miss Alicia replied to thank him with a very sweet note which he sent on to me. She says she is praying for both of you constantly (as I do, dearest). She has expressed a desire to know me and has extended an invitation to me to visit her in Columbia. If I do so, I shall have another likeness of myself made for you there, in case the one you had has been lost. You did not say. Oh, how I treasure the one you sent me! And how I yearn to see your face in person!

Yours most affectionately,

Marguerite Finley

The weather grew warmer, and though in June the heat was mostly tolerable, in July it became intense and nearly unbearable at times. There were no trees to give shade in the pen, and on hot sunny days the prisoners congregated in the shadows of buildings, or under a few blankets propped up by poles.

One cloudy afternoon, George and Aleck were walking in the pen to take a little exercise. As they paused to talk with another prisoner, George noticed that the sentries were not alone in their usual stations. General Schoepf, the commandant of the fort, was standing on a platform just behind the high wall around the pen, and there were several ladies with him. It was not unusual for civilians to visit Fort Delaware, and when they did, for purposes of entertainment, they always wanted a look at the "rebels."

George was standing very close to the wall, and one of the women looked down directly at him and smiled. He did not feel well-disposed toward curiosity-seekers who were regarding the prisoners as though they were exotic animals in a cage, even if the one simpering at him was an attractive young lady, and all she received in return was an icy stare. He turned away and walked on with Aleck, simmering with resentment.

As they came close to one of the gates, it opened to admit some new prisoners. One of the "fresh fish" who walked in was a short, fair-haired young man with a mild, beardless face.

"Robbie! Robert Porter!" Aleck yelled out, recognizing his brother-in-law.

The two young men were instantly together. They shook each other shoulders, embraced, and shook each other again, each excitedly interrupting the other's questions and answers. A small crowd formed around Robert before George could get to him, but once the other prisoners had pumped the new man for any important information about the goings on of the world outside, they left him alone with Aleck, and George stepped up to greet and embrace his cousin. The three talked of family, especially Alicia, and then inquired about mutual friends. Before all this, Robert announced that he was married now, and Aleck and George offered him their congratulations.

Robert and Aleck had not seen each other since the second year of the war. Both were anxious to learn any news of their fellow seminary students, but since they had left for military service at about the same time, neither seemed to know more than the other. They wondered what had become of their professors, and briefly reminisced about their days together in Camden.

Though it was uncomfortably warm inside the barracks that day, the three went inside to have more privacy as they talked. After Robert answered all their questions about his capture, the conversation again turned to Alicia. Robert had received a letter from her only the week before, and in it she reported that the Porters were doing well.

"I think Alice still likes it very much in Columbia," he said. "Everyone else is all right, too, except that they are worried about Willie. He is about to turn sixteen, and is itching to get into the army. Mother and Father think he is too young, but some of his friends who are sixteen have enlisted in the home guard, and Willie can't understand why he is not allowed to do the same."

"Sixteen is rather young," Aleck said doubtfully.

"Our cousin, Colonel Haskins, has told Willie that he is willing to arrange for him to join the Seventh South Carolina Cavalry in Virginia," Robert went on.

"What does Alice think of that?" asked George.

"She says that if she were a young man, sixteen or even younger, she would wish to go and fight, too. Willie has enlisted her to persuade Father to let him do that, but I'm afraid she has been rather half-hearted about it, as she is fearful for our little brother's safety. I myself am of much the same divided mind. I'm afraid I still think of him as a boy, a child–not a man. Has Alice written to you about it, Aleck?"

"She did mention it in her last letter," he said. "It is a difficult matter, to be sure."

George suggested that Robert's capture might affect his brother's fate.

"When your family learns you are here at Fort Delaware, I should think that Rev. Porter will be less inclined to grant Willie's wishes," he speculated.

"Perhaps you are right about that, George...," Robert responded thoughtfully. "But then again, perhaps not. I think if Father's health were better, he would join the army himself!"

"Yes, Alice has said that before," laughed Aleck.

During a silence that followed, as Aleck thought of his wife, pangs of homesickness wracked his heart.

"I don't suppose you have a likeness of Alice," he said to his brother-in-law.

"Don't you?" Robert responded, surprised.

"I did have one, but lost it when my bag was stolen in the Richmond depot, just as I was getting back from my last furlough."

"Bad luck! But I don't have Alice's photograph, and not only do I not have hers, I don't even have one of my wife! Things were stolen from me when I was taken prisoner."

"Yes, we've had some experience with that," George put in, remembering how Aleck's watch and Bible had been taken from him at Stony Creek.

Thinking of his bride, Robert expelled a long, pathetic sigh.

"Write to your wife today, Robbie, and ask her to send another likeness of herself to you," Aleck suggested.

Robert nodded, then cocked his head with an idea.

"All of us ought to have our likeness made here, and send it to Alice. Just think of it, the three of us together–her husband, her brother, and her cousin, all together! I think she would be very pleased to have it, though mortified at our situation. My wife will be happy to have one, too."

"We're not at all presentable," Aleck grumbled, picking at his somewhat ragged clothes in dismay, "but I suppose the photographer can provide us with suitable clothing."

It happened that the following week, a photographer returned to Fort Delaware. He spent the morning taking group photographs in the fort and the prison yard, and the afternoon he devoted mostly to individuals. Aleck, Robert and George cleaned and groomed themselves as best they could and presented themselves in the room being used as a studio. This time the photographer had better prop clothing, and all three young men were able to find gray uniform coats and pants which fit them well enough. They dressed themselves to look like proper soldiers again.

As they posed, Aleck stood in the middle, and the other two slipped an arm into each of his. A few days later, they received four copies of their photograph, and were pleased with the results.

"We don't look too bad, considering," George remarked.

Robert expressed an opinion that George was the handsomest of the three.

"What rot!" Aleck dissented facetiously. "Without question, the handsomest fellow is the one in the middle."

"Well," Robert laughed, "I'm sure Alice will think so."

One afternoon, just after the second meal of the day was served, the skies began to pour down a heavy rain, driving all the prisoners into the barracks. The rain and breezes cooled the air somewhat, and the temperature inside became tolerably mild.

A number of the officers were musical, and since everyone was cooped up for a while, they offered to provide some entertainment for the men. One officer from Tennessee owned a guitar, and another from the same state had preserved a fiddle, and several men joined them with harmonicas. Some of the tunes they played were mournful or spiritual, while others were lively and joyful, or, as one of the musicians put it, "sweet as candy." The livelier music frequently inspired the listeners who had enough energy to jump to their feet and dance a jig.

George liked this sort of music– it was a food and a balm for his soul–and he enjoyed it all until the musicians began a sad, heart-wrenching song about wives and children and sweethearts left behind at home. While they sang and played this tune George looked around him, and before long observed trembling lips and chins, sniffling noses, and fingers dabbing away tears. Thoughts of Mrs. Finley's musical soirees in Charleston had already led to thoughts of Marguerite, and pangs of longing and homesickness suddenly overwhelmed him. He left the gathering and headed for the relative solitude of his bunk.

George reclined in his bed and pulled out some of Marguerite's old letters, choosing one at random. It happened to be his least favorite, the one in which she had mourned the death of General Jackson. But being in a morose mood, George read it again, and was again struck with the same reactions and emotions he had experienced the first time he set eyes on it. Though only one page, and therefore brief compared to her other letters, the entire text was a torrent of grief. Though George had also been heartbroken over this horrific loss, he marveled at Marguerite's intense suffering.

She was so passionate! It was a side of her he had never clearly seen before this letter, which also made him realize how strongly she was inclined to hero worship. He feared this idolatry included him. George could tell by things she wrote to him in many of her letters that she had a rather ideal conception of his character, and this troubled him a little, as he doubted that he could ever fully live up it. He sighed heavily as he put the letter away.

He had tried to refrain from introspection since he arrived at Fort Delaware, and found it easy to do for a while. The constant struggle for proper food, sanitary water, cleanliness of body and clothes–for survival itself–had provided a distraction from the gloomy state of mind he had been suffering for some time. But having grown used to prison life, he went through all the daily routines and motions of survival almost mechanically now, and lately, found himself brooding more and more. It all began in earnest one day towards the end of June when something happened to dramatically remind him of his own mortality, and the precariousness of existence at Fort Delaware.

The prison outhouses, or "sinks" as they were called, were located at one edge of the pen in a low building with a flat roof. The building extended over the river embankment several feet, and as there had been a few escape attempts made by prisoners here at high tide, an armed sentry continually walked the roof. Late one afternoon, as George waited his turn at the latrine, the young guard on duty was particularly abusive to the prisoners below, cursing at them and shouting orders for them to move along faster in their trips to and from the sheds over the plank walkways. Displeased that some men were standing in groups as they waited, the sentry cried out from the roof several times, "Disperse that crowd!"

An officer who was lame from his wounds, a Colonel Jones from Virginia, was slowly hobbling past a few men standing together as he returned to his quarters. Seeing him, the guard shouted angrily, "Get along there! Trot, damn you, trot! Double-quick–double-quick, I say!"

Perceiving the menace in his tone, George and some other men instinctively, instantly ran for cover. The next moment, a shot rang out, and as the lame officer fell from the plank into the mud, he was heard to cry out, "Oh, God! Why did you shoot me! I didn't know you spoke to me!"

The prisoners closest to him pulled him out and began carrying him away, but the colonel was dead before they had gone a hundred steps.

The next day George and several other officers who had witnessed the shooting sent written complaints to the commanding general of the fort. They never received any response, and several days later, noticed that the murderous guard had been promoted in rank! All the letters going out of the prison at the time of the shooting were censored more carefully than usual, so that no word of the incident reached the outside world. During the following weeks, in the newspapers the prisoners were allowed to receive, they saw several advertisements inquiring after the colonel, but it was doubtful that a reply was made to any of them. Everyone wondered if the man's family ever learned of his fate.

There had been other senseless shootings of prisoners, and there would doubtless be more, and George reflected that he might have easily been the man killed by the guard, though it was possibly more likely that he would die of one of the various diseases that sometimes claimed lives at Fort Delaware. In late July, several of the officers in his division became very ill, and two who went into the prison hospital died. Even though George was usually able to purchase extra food from the sutler, his funds occasionally ran low. At such times his diet was barely adequate, and he noticed that he was beginning to lose weight and vitality. As he contemplated his chances of survival in this place, he felt his former despondency taking hold in him again, and threatening to grow worse, since things were of course much more bleak for him now that he was a prisoner of war. As far as any prisoner exchanges went, the situation was beginning to look hopeless, and on top of that, he was still harassed by a sickening despair about his country's chances of victory in the war.

The prisoners were allowed only one newspaper, one from Philadelphia, and that only when there was no news of any Confederate successes, so that the prisoners saw only the demoralizing reports of Yankee victories. Yet, gloomy as he was, George continued to struggle against his despair. Seeing that most of the other officers did not share his pessimism, he felt ashamed of it, and kept it to himself. He was not so hopeless that he did not hungrily seize on any rumor or report from incoming prisoners, no matter how fantastic, that the Confederates were close to winning the war, or negotiating some peaceful settlement, or that the two governments had agreed to exchange prisoners again in reasonable numbers. But when it happened that these rumors turned out to be false, as they almost always did, the disappointment left him a little more dejected with each successive disillusionment.

He observed Aleck, watched him preaching and praying and studying, and envied him for his buoyant temperament and strong faith. Though George had never had any doubts about the teachings of the church in which he had been raised, he was beginning to realize how spiritually feeble he was in himself. He had always considered his religious beliefs and practices sound, but knew that his faith had never really been tested by any great trial until this year, when he began to experience his terrible pessimism about the war. And now, besides that trial, one as terrible and more personal was upon him. He was a prisoner in the hands of the enemy, in a place from which there was little hope of escape, so that more than ever, he keenly felt the smallness of his spiritual strength. His melancholy seemed much stronger.

After making repeated requests for more than a month, Aleck had been given permission to visit the sick in the prison hospital as a chaplain. When he came back to the barracks from a trip there one morning, he told George about another prisoner he had met in the hospital, a Dr. Hardy. He was a Presbyterian clergyman who was also ministering to the sick and dying prisoners.

"Is he a chaplain?" asked George.

"Oh, no," Aleck replied, "though he is acting as one for the other prisoners. He is a political prisoner. There are quite a few here, he tells me. Dr. Hardy had a church in Portsmouth, Virginia."

"Why is a clergyman here?"

"He is a Delawarean, and some months ago, he was given permission to visit some relatives in Delaware City. A private conversation he had with another person in that place was reported to the military authorities, and he was arrested and brought to the prison, and has been here ever since. Dr. Hardy has been ministering to the prisoners here, and tells me there is lately great spiritual interest among our men. He even has a theological class for those who have decided to enter the ministry."

George was curious to know what Dr. Hardy had said in the private conversation which had led to his arrest.

"He said something to the effect that the flag of the United States had now become a symbol of coercion and despotism, and that it no longer meant what it used to."

"And merely for expressing this opinion," said George, "in private, he is thrown into prison."

"Yes."

"That fact alone demonstrates the truth of what he said."

"Dr. Hardy is very much against taking the oath of allegiance to the Federal government," Aleck went on. "He could be released if he took the oath, but to do so, he said, would be to give approval to the war. He says he will die in this place rather than do that, and I am afraid he may be speaking prophetically. He is ailing, and though I understand he is not more than fifty years old, he looks more like an old man."

"And yet they say that the political prisoners here have better food and shelter than we do," said George.

"Some of them do, but Dr. Hardy was moved out of the fort into the officers' barracks, and has been living as we do."

"That must be difficult for a man of his age."

Nodding in agreement, Aleck reached into his coat pocket and pulled out a little periodical he had folded to a small size to hide there.

"While in the fort Dr. Hardy was allowed to receive some Northern newspapers and journals, and he gave me this one."

The adjutant unfolded the small newspaper and showed it to his friend. George's interest waned when he saw that it was a religious weekly from Boston, but later, after Aleck had finished with the paper, George borrowed it out of sheer boredom, and despite his friend's warning that he would be displeased, George lay down in his bunk with the newspaper to peruse it. He had not had it in his hands very long, however, before he threw it down in disgust, having just read (in what purported to be a Christian publication) the editor's view that there could be no peace or compromise with the South, and that the end of the war could only come "by subjugation or extermination of the rebels."

Still seething with indignation, he rolled out of the bunk. Seeing the paper again on the floor, he picked it up and was about to tear it into pieces, when he was interrupted by the call of "Mail!"

That morning, George was disappointed by the postmaster. There were no letters or packages for him, though he had been expecting some. Aleck received one item, a letter from his father. He took it back to his bunk to read, and George followed him. He sat down next to the adjutant and watched him open the letter and begin reading.

After a little while, looking for some diversion from his low spirits, George asked, "Any interesting news from home?"

"My sister has a new baby, but I don't suppose you would find that very interesting," Aleck replied casually, keeping his eyes on the letter.

"Boy or girl?"

"Another boy. All her boys are fine little fellows, but invariably, for some reason, they all begin exceedingly ugly. I wonder if this one did the same."

"Do they resemble their father?" George inquired, as an attempt at humor.

"Well, my brother-in-law is not a bad looking man, but I suspect he had the same inauspicious beginnings. It must be a family trait."

"Good thing it's his family, then."

Aleck smiled vaguely.

"Yes...," he murmured, and his eyes became fixed more intently on the letter as he read on.

"Something else interesting?" George probed.

Aleck kept reading for a few moments before he answered, and when he did, he looked up with an expression of wonder and happiness.

"I...I have received an appointment as chaplain!" he stammered. "The Bishop has finally appointed me a chaplain!"

Almost as thrilled by the news as his friend, George congratulated him, breathing an inward sigh of relief.

"Something must have delayed the Bishop's letter to me. My family thought I already knew of the appointment! I don't know why they should have thought that!" Aleck puzzled.

"Perhaps they thought you were expecting it," George speculated.

"Perhaps, but I really didn't know whether I should expect it. I left that in God's hands."

"Well, now you know for sure. You're to be a chaplain, and I'm very glad of it."

"Thank you, George! I shall write to the Bishop directly, to see what is expected of me for my ordination. I suppose I can prepare for my examinations here. I have a Bible and a prayer book now. If only I could have more privacy and quiet!"

"There's no such thing in this place."

Aleck seemed not to hear this remark by George, so absorbed was he already in his own thoughts and plans.

"I must send in my resignation from the Legion, though I don't know how this business of my being a prisoner will complicate things."

"It may not complicate things, Aleck, but it does hinder. For both our sakes, I hope we are exchanged soon."

"You think we may be? What's the newest grape on that?"

"The grapevine is full of rumor and wishful thinking, and very little in the way of facts, I'm afraid. Say, does your wife know of the appointment?"

Aleck looked stunned. In his excitement, he had almost forgotten her.

"Why, I don't know! Father's letter doesn't say whether they wrote to her or not. Her father might have been informed, but I can't know that for certain. I must write to her this very moment to tell her the good news! She'll be so pleased!"

He scrambled to find paper and a pen or pencil and immediately sat down again in his bunk to begin a letter to Alicia. George was reclining beside him, a little soothed by the only good news he had heard in a long time.

"So Aleck is to be a chaplain now," he thought, slipping his hands under his head and staring up at the blankness of the boards above. "That's a blessing."

Though this change in the adjutant's status would probably do him no good as long as he was a prisoner of war, it would certainly put him out of most danger once he returned to the army. All he had to do now was survive Fort Delaware.

George turned his head and watched Aleck writing. Somehow even the young man's back expressed his excitement and happiness, quivering slightly as he eagerly jotted a letter to his wife. George reached up and squeezed and shook his narrow shoulder, and Aleck laughed and turned a joyous smile on him.

"Yes, I'm glad of your appointment, Aleck, very glad," George repeated.

When Aleck returned to the barracks from his hospital visits, he always told George about what he had seen and done there. Sometimes he expressed discouragement, and he was particularly disturbed by the patients who, suffering more from severe homesickness than any serious physical ailment, seemed to have given up the will to live.

"Dr. Hardy said that he has actually heard of men here dying of this nostalgia," Aleck remarked sadly. "Strange, he said, how despair can make men more susceptible to an early grave. It can kill as surely as smallpox."

Increasingly prone to despair himself, George was not happy to hear this opinion. He had no desire to help himself to an early grave, yet was finding it more and more difficult to fight against his low spirits. For him, everything seemed to militate against hope–until something extraordinary happened in August.

On a warm morning in the early part of that month, the relative quiet that prevailed in the officers' barracks was suddenly interrupted by a general uproar and tumult. George, who had been napping, opened his eyes to see dozens of men jumping out of their bunks and running past him. He quickly scrambled to his feet and followed them, hearing the command of "Turn out! Turn out!" loudly repeated by one of the guards outside.

In the pen, the crowd of men was rushing toward the fence, to face the Federal officers in charge of the fort who were standing above them on a platform. When the prisoners were all assembled and quieted down, General Schoepf looked them over, and then, in somewhat broken English and a heavy German accent, he made the announcement that he had received orders to send six hundred officers to South Carolina, to be exchanged for an equal number of Federal officers.

A rousing cheer went up from the pen. The prisoners could hardly contain their excitement. After they quieted again, they were ordered to form a line along the fence. The officers whose names were called were to step aside and form a new line. For what seemed a long while the men stood silently at attention, waiting for the roll call to begin in a torment of anticipation, anxiety, and hope, and George was praying to God as he had never prayed before, that his name was on that list. The thought that he might be going to Charleston soon, and that he would be exchanged and set free, almost made him feel faint.

The roll call began, officers of higher rank forming the first group. The first officer called out was a Major Adams, and as George watched this man's reaction, he thought he had never seen such utter joy expressed in a human face. The major fairly trembled with happiness as he took a few steps to the left to begin the line of the fortunates.

The names in this group were read off roughly alphabetically, and as they were called, each man was also given a number. As George finally heard his called, he felt somewhat dizzy again, and staggered a little as he made his way toward the second line.

The prisoners waited nervously, and when the names beginning with later letters of the alphabet began to be called, more and more men who knew they had not been chosen hung their heads in dejection. The expressions of those left in the first line became less and less hopeful as the second line grew into hundreds. Over three hundred names had been rattled off when Captain Wells' name was pronounced, as the last officer of that rank to be read off. He threw up his hands and head in dramatic gestures of gratitude and rejoicing as he crossed the yard. In the final group, as the names starting with latter part of the alphabet were called, Robert Porter heard his name. After this, a few additional names were called out of order and rank, and these included Adjutant Dwight and Captain Levy. These two men exchanged a look of amazement and relief as they stood next to each other at the end of the line of the chosen ones. A moment later, both were bowing their heads in prayers of thankfulness.

Many of the officers whose names had not been called that day were disconsolate. Some began weeping, and a few displayed anger and resentment, wondering if some of the richer prisoners had been favored by the prison authorities for some reason, or had used bribery to get themselves on the list. Fifty of the chosen men were wounded or sick prisoners, some of them amputees.

A week went by, and the six hundred officers selected for exchange were still at Fort Delaware, waiting to leave. Some ships which had not been seen before were docked at the wharf, but George noticed no preparations being made for their departure.

This unexpected, unexplained delay gradually extinguished the euphoria in many of the six hundred, and in some, joyfulness turned into tortured doubts. George began to grow pessimistic about the whole affair, especially after he got wind of one of the officers selling his place to another prisoner for a gold watch. He inquired further about the incident and learned that the officer originally selected did not believe there would be any exchange. George's heart fell when he heard this. It had all been too good to be true!

"Who knows what will become of us?" he wondered. "Better the devil you know...perhaps?"

He seriously considered selling his own spot, but eventually decided that if there was even the smallest possibility of getting home, he should take advantage of the opportunity. He knew that fifty Confederate officers had been sent to South Carolina just two months ago, in June, and had been exchanged there. If fifty could be successfully exchanged in South Carolina, George reasoned, why not six hundred? He later heard a rumor that the six hundred were being sent to Charleston for the same purpose as the former group of fifty–that of being placed under fire in retaliation for an equal number of Federal officers recently confined in the besieged city– but in spite of this disheartening prospect, he remained determined to leave Fort Delaware and take his chances.

Finally, on a Saturday morning, a Yankee sergeant came into the prisoners' barracks and made the fateful announcement to the chosen officers.

"Be ready at twelve o'clock sharp," he said.

Immediately a frenzy of activity followed, and rounds of goodbyes and farewells. About an hour later, a guard called for the officers who were leaving. It was almost noon, and time for them to go. Within a few minutes, six hundred officers were marching out through the gate of the prison toward the wharf, where a steamship awaited them.

CHAPTER ELEVEN

AN OLD SIDE-WHEEL STEAMSHIP named *Crescent City* was waiting for them at the pier, along with two gunboats which were to act as its escort down the coast. The steamer was manned with a civilian crew and two hundred guards, mostly inexperienced militia men of short enlistment. These soldiers were given little respect by their own army, and from the start of their assignment, some in turn treated the prisoners in their charge with scorn and harshness. Their insults would be the first of many unpleasant surprises for the prisoners.

The six hundred officers were marched on board the *Crescent City*, but instead of being allowed to remain on the upper deck as they expected, to their astonishment and dismay, they were ordered to line up at a hatchway and descend a ladder leading down into the second deck. This level, much of which was below the water line, was dark and very poorly ventilated. Here the ship, formerly a freighter, had been transformed into a prisoner transport by the construction of three tiers of shelves, or bunks, along both sides of the length of the vessel. The little light allowed in by the portholes was mostly obscured by the upper tier of bunks, and the passageway between the two sides of shelves was narrow, the space separating each tier being no more than two feet. Each bunk could accommodate three or four men at extremely close quarters.

George was one of the first to go down into the lower deck, and he immediately secured a bunk for himself and Aleck under the hatchway, where he saw that there would be some ventilation. Robert Porter and Captain Wells joined them as bunk mates.

Once the six hundred prisoners were all inside, there was little room to move around. One officer complained that they were crowded in like steers on a cattle car. A man next to him likened their situation to that of packed sardines.

A Virginia officer hazarded another comparison.

"I imagine it's rather like being the cargo on a Yankee slaver," he said.

"Hellfire!" a Louisianan drawled vehemently. "This *is* a damn slave ship!"

"I've seen quite a few of those," Ned Wells piped up. "And the Yanks are indeed well practiced in that trade. Before I left New York in fifty-nine, you could see the ships built there sailing out of the harbor every month, complete with their New England sea captains, bound for Africa, as in the days of old!"

Someone wondered aloud how long their voyage south would last. After some open speculation and debate, the general consensus was a minimum of three days.

"That long!" marveled a Texan. "How shall we bear it? It's already getting hot as Hades in here!"

"Another apt analogy for our predicament, gentlemen!" Wells observed laughingly, as they felt the ship begin to move.

Others quipped and made jokes for a while, but the initial high spirits of the men, inspired by the hope of exchange, soon faded before the harsh reality of their growing discomforts and misfortunes. The August heat was intense on deck, in the open air, but it was much worse below in the prisoners' place of close confinement, where a number of men were forced to occupy bunks near steaming boilers and glowing furnaces.

One officer who had long experience as a sailor characterized the *Crescent* as the 'most miserable ship to pitch and rock' he had ever seen, and hour by hour, more and more of the men grew seasick. Within two days, nearly three-fourths of the prisoners were suffering with nausea, and the stench of vomit became pervasive in their quarters.

Already enfeebled by months of prison life, the captives sweltered and gasped for water, which was doled out hot from the condensers. Perspiration dripped off them constantly and saturated their clothing. Fifty at a time were allowed to go to the upper deck for a brief period of relief, but each day the prisoners stood in line for hours waiting their turn to go up to relieve themselves in the wheel house, the only facility provided for them. Sometimes the sicker men were not able to control themselves, and had to leave the line to use one end of the hold for a privy.

On her fourth day at sea, after enduring some troubles and delays off Cape Fear, the *Crescent City* passed by Charleston and continued down the South Carolina coast. The following morning, the ship steamed into the harbor at Port Royal many miles south of Charleston, and while it lay at anchor there, the captive officers were forced to remain in their miserable hold for several more days without any explanation. They begged for their filthy quarters to be cleaned out, but the captain of the guards refused. Once or twice the prisoners were brought water from the island, but for some reason, this supply soon ceased, and for forty long hours they suffered for water in almost intolerable heat. When it rained one afternoon, George caught some rainwater in a piece of oilcloth and shared it with his bunkmates.

During the third day at Port Royal, there was a change of guard on the ship. These new men were from two New York regiments, and though battle-hardened, they were appalled by the conditions they found on board. After a visit below deck, a soldier reporting to the new captain of guards gasped, "Foul beyond belief!" Hearing this, the commander immediately set about giving the prisoners some relief, and within hours, the ship's hold was cleaned out. The luxuries of fresh water, coffee, and bread were provided, and the men were permitted some time on the upper deck. Some invalid and extremely sick prisoners, forty in number, were put on another boat and taken to nearby Beaufort.

On August 29th, the *Crescent City* set out to sea again with her cargo of prisoners, and two days later the ship arrived off Charleston harbor. Here the prisoners saw waters full of Federal monitors, gun boats, and blockaders, and witnessed repeated explosions of shells hurled from blazing artillery at the batteries and forts. The steamship proceeded a little way into the harbor and anchored near Battery Gregg, but almost another week passed before the Confederate officers were told that they would soon disembark at Morris Island, where a stockade prison awaited them. They believed this place to be merely a temporary holding pen until the exchange took place; most did not expect to be there longer than a few days–until they were informed otherwise. As the steamer approached Morris Island, a large, barren isle of sand, it was announced to the prisoners that there would be no exchange. Instead, they were told that they would be held in this place for an indefinite period, under the fire of their own guns.

Though the sky was overcast that morning, the prisoners emerged from the darkness of the ship's hold blinking, squinting, and shading their eyes in the daylight. They had not yet received any breakfast or water, and smacked and licked their parched lips with what little moisture that was left in their mouths. They moved slowly down the gangplank and were then marched from the wharf to the island, where they felt *terra firma* under their feet for the first time in nearly three weeks. Many heads immediately turned to look off in the direction of Fort Sumter, now reduced to little more than a shapeless mass of rubble after repeated bombardments, but still manned and active against the enemy.

When George and his fellow officers were assembled on the beach in the presence of their guards, he was struck with an extraordinary and strange spectacle as he looked about him. Five hundred and sixty Southern soldiers—pallid, hungry, some of them ill and tottering, and clad in all kinds and faded colors of garb, military and otherwise—faced orderly lines of black men dressed in identical, neat blue uniforms, all looking quite fit and well-fed.

To heighten the contrast, the skin of the prisoners had been bleached to the palest shade of white possible from their extended journey in darkness. What few worldly goods they possessed were wrapped in the remains of old quilts or other fabrics, or hung from their sagging shoulders in worn cotton haversacks.

At Fort Delaware George had used some of the money sent to him to replace his disintegrating uniform, and refusing anything issued to Federal soldiers, he had finally managed to put together an odd combination of old civilian clothes. After being soaked in perspiration for weeks, they were filthy, and torn in places. The seam of one of his trouser legs had split to a point above his knee, and the cloth flapped open in the sea breezes to reveal a muscular, ghastly white calf thinly covered with dark hair, the scar of his old Kinston wound plainly visible. As he stood on the hard sand beach, the surf in his ears, the wind whisking his hair in every direction, it occurred to him that he must look very much like Robinson Crusoe. All he imagined that he lacked was a full beard; he had the beginnings of one now, and his thick brown hair had grown longer, hanging over his eyes and ears in a tangled, shaggy mess.

The ship's guards were ordered to take away from the prisoners the blankets they had been issued earlier, and while this was going on, the black regiment went into a short demonstration of the manual, or rifle drill, following shouted orders from their white officers. Few things stirred the indignation of Confederate soldiers so much as the sight of black men in blue uniforms, since they assumed them to be fellow Southerners and therefore traitors to the cause–but now, in their situation as prisoners of war, they looked on these men with other feelings, mainly curiosity and apprehension. Some of the officers smirked derisively, amused, having never before seen black men deport themselves as soldiers in such a formal way, while those officers who had, earlier in the war, fought against the men of this regiment, in this very place, gazed at them warily, wondering if they were vindictive sorts. Other officers studied them with interest, and had to admit that they certainly looked soldierly and performed the drill skillfully.

Flanked on both sides by companies of enemy soldiers, the captive men began a march of nearly three miles along the beach toward the stockade pen. Some were so weakened and sick from the sea voyage that they stumbled and fell numerous times on the way, and the other prisoners raised them up and helped them as much as they could. After they had covered about half the distance to the stockade, it began to rain, and the thirsty men immediately set about catching water in their hands and hats, sucking in every drop for dear life. Seeing that a number of the prisoners were about to collapse from thirst, a few of the black soldiers brought them water from a spring not far away. For this kindness, they were reprimanded by their officers.

Soon the prisoners were within sight of a stockade composed of upright pine poles about twelve feet high, with sharpened tops. Passing into the stockade through a gate, they walked into an enclosure covering an area of an acre and a half, where tents housing four men each were set up in eight rows. Wishing to stay together, George, Aleck, Robert, and Captain Wells quickly claimed a tent for themselves, and Captain Levy became one of the occupants of the tent next to theirs.

After a brief rain ended, George and his three companions, joined by Captain Levy, sat in front of their tent taking in their new situation, observing first along each of the four log walls a "dead line" of coarse rope strung about twenty feet in. Atop the stockade walls, they could see parapets where armed black soldiers were stationed as sentries.

George wondered if the guards here would be as quick to pull the trigger on prisoners as the ones at Fort Delaware.

"Let's hope not," said Captain Levy, as he waved away a mosquito buzzing near his face, while Captain Wells slapped at a gnat biting into his bare arm, cursing such pestilences.

As their conversation continued, it was frequently interrupted or drowned out by the firing of the Yankee cannons in Fort Wagner, a fortification located only about one hundred and fifty yards behind the stockade prison.

"There will surely be some return fire soon," Robert ventured reluctantly. "Then things will get really interesting here."

"Yes, very interesting," Levy agreed, "to be fired upon by our own guns."

"Who would have believed it," Aleck marveled, shaking his head, "that we would be placed in such a situation!"

"It almost happened before, you know," said Captain Wells, "with the fifty officers who were sent down here in June."

"I heard those rumors," Aleck replied, "but I could hardly believe they were true."

"It was no rumor," said Wells. "Those men were lucky, and got exchanged. We, however, have jumped from the proverbial frying pan into the fire—artillery fire!"

His joke elicited some nervous laughter, until the booming guns of Fort Wagner suddenly put an end to it. Soberer reflections followed, as the five men speculated how long they might be kept in this place.

In the afternoon, all the prisoners were called to form ranks in one of the "streets" between the rows of tents, to be instructed on the rules of the prison camp. Afterwards, the men went back to their tents, and on the way, overhearing some interesting conversations, George made inquiries among a few officers who had gleaned some information from the ship's guards, and from newspapers, about the series of events and circumstances that had brought them to Morris Island. What they told him made him feel much less hopeful that any exchange was in their future.

General Jones, the Confederate commander at Charleston, had been forced to temporarily accept and incarcerate a large number of captive U.S. officers at several locations in the city. General Foster, the Union commander, knew that these prisoners had been brought to Charleston only out of necessity, but because they were quartered in parts of the city exposed to the continued Federal shelling, he decided to retaliate by placing a large number of Confederate prisoners directly in harm's way. After learning all these facts, George passed the information on to his friends, all of whom received it with the same dismay. Captain Wells angrily declared that he had given up all hope of exchange.

Just two days after George and his fellow prisoners arrived at Morris Island, an intense artillery duel began between the Federal batteries and Fort Moultrie, lasting from dusk until ten o'clock. The firing began from Fort Wagner, and in due time return fire came in from across the harbor. Startled and alarmed, the prisoners could only watch helplessly as the shells flew overhead, and hope that none of them fell into their area. A few of the shells burst from the guns at Wagner prematurely, scattering fragments throughout the prison pen, but fortunately, no injuries resulted.

After this episode, the shelling from both sides continued, in varying degrees of intensity, nearly every day. Even though the prison stockade had been strategically placed directly in front of the Federal batteries, it soon became apparent that the presence of the prisoners did nothing to shield those installations from Confederate fire. The gunners in the Confederate harbor forts and batteries seemed to know the exact location of the prisoners, and directed their artillery fire accordingly. A few guards were killed or wounded by the shelling, but none of the prisoners were done much harm. There was, however, an occasional close call, and it was enough to make some of the defenseless captives nervous.

The imprisoned officers were assigned to daily menial tasks necessary for the maintenance and cleanliness of the stockade. When these were finished they found other ways to pass the long, monotonous hours of their captivity, and to distract their minds from the constant threat of exploding shells in their midst. They played cards or chess, wrote in diaries, washed their clothes, read books and Bibles, chatted, and hatched a few futile schemes of escape.

Rules governing the inmates were very strict, and any violation, such as crossing the dead line, could bring on gunfire from the sentries on the parapets. As the officers settled in to their sorry life in the stockade, routines were established, and relationships, not always pleasant, developed between the prisoners and their captors. Though the guards were sometimes abusive and trigger happy, the Confederates were soon on friendly terms with the black sergeants who served as their wardens. Many of these soldiers had at least one thing in common with the Confederates–a healthy hatred of the commander, Colonel Hallowell, who treated his colored troops only a little less harshly than the prisoners.

During the first few weeks of their confinement in the stockade, Hallowell withheld the prisoners' mail, limited their drinking water, and fed them on a meager daily diet of a few crackers, a half pint of watery soup or rice, and two ounces of salt beef, often spoiled. During the fourth week of their captivity on the island, the prisoners' rations were reduced even further. Barely subsisting on such fare, many of the men began to grow weak and sick with intestinal disorders. When they first arrived on Morris Island, they had feared for their lives because of their placement as human shields, but as time wore on, they grew more concerned that they might slowly perish of malnutrition.

A few of the black wardens risked punishment to do kindnesses to the prisoners, sometimes doling out double or triple portions of food to those who seemed to need it the most, or now and then even smuggling in a better quality of eatables for them. Some of the wardens seemed ashamed of the paltry rations they gave to those in their charge. One day, when one of the officers complained of the poor food, a black sergeant agreed with him that they were hardly fit for a dog to eat.

"But it's all these Yankees are going to give you," he added contemptuously.

Aleck and Robert found particular favor in the eyes of one of the sergeants, an older man in the regiment who said he had been a barber in Boston. He was a religious individual, and when he found out that Aleck and Robert were seminarians, he brought them double rations every day, clear spring water, and portions of vegetables and bread whenever he could. Thanks to him, the two young clergymen fared reasonably well on Morris Island, though both steadily grew thinner, like every other prisoner. George's once muscular physique had certainly become leaner. His face had new concavities, and on different parts of his body, he began to notice the protuberances of bones he had never seen before.

In the second week of September, the prisoners were given the demoralizing news that General Sherman had captured and burned the city of Atlanta. The following week, one of the officers, a lieutenant from Tennessee, succumbed to malnutrition and dysentery. A few days later, another officer died of the same causes, and about two weeks after that, a third prisoner was dead due to pneumonia and complications of wounds that had never properly healed. It was not until mid-October that the prisoners were allowed to receive mail and packages, and given access to the post sutler, from whom they could buy food and tobacco. Rations also improved about this time, after Hallowell's cruelties were reported to a superior officer.

As soon as the mail resumed, George received a letter from Marguerite dated the tenth of September. He knew she must have written others since this one, but did not know if they had been returned or destroyed. Believing that George was to be exchanged, she had written to him in a hopeful, even cheerful mode. Some of her old friends had come to Greenville, and she wrote of their work and play together. Marguerite related that while she and her friends busied themselves sewing and knitting for the Soldiers' Aid Society, they reminisced about their girlhood together, and one afternoon, treated themselves to a picnic in the countryside. They had gone out on horseback, and after their meal, enjoyed themselves in races up and down the hills, during which Marguerite bounced wildly in the saddle and laughed so hard that tears came into her eyes. It made George smile to think of her having such fun, and finding such companionship.

That night he dreamed of Marguerite. He often wished that he had control over his dreams–too many of them turned out to be troubling, or nightmares of the worst kind, no matter how diligently he tried to think of only pleasant and comforting things before he fell asleep—but this particular dream, unlike most others, took him where his fondest desires wished to go. In it he saw himself in a beautiful and well-kept garden, a place of gracefully arranged greenery and flowers. Dressed in white like a bride, Marguerite was there, seated on the ground in a grassy area. She was reading a book of poetry, and looked up and held out her hand to George as he approached. He went to his knees beside her, tossed away the book, and gently pushed her back and fell with her to the soft, sweet-smelling grass. Face to face, their faces very close, she looked up at him and smiled, and he pressed a kiss to her lips.

"My wife," he whispered.

"My darling," she replied.

But his bliss was rudely and abruptly dispelled by a jarring noise in his ears from the real world. A loud voice was shouting just outside his tent. As usual at dawn, one of the sergeants was bellowing out orders to the prisoners.

What a dream he had interrupted! George sat up angrily and stumbled out of the tent.

"From paradise to purgatory," he was thinking, shambling into place for the morning's roll call.

As this first tedious routine of the day dragged on, interrupted only by the cries of sea birds, George looked up at the dawn sky. It was one of those soft, pastel skies more often seen in summer, a faint pinkish hue below giving way to a pale clear azure blue above, while the far western heavens were still a fading grey. A canopy of clouds overhead were formed in undulating rows that resembled the pattern left on a beach by the receding tide. Almost unconsciously, he had fallen into the habit of surveying the eastern sky each morning, to note its unique daily appearance, but he was really renewing an old habit, from a time before the war, when he almost always began the day with a walk along the Battery. Each morning, he recalled, there was a new exhibit to admire, always different from the last, and always beautiful in some way in its changing palette. On Morris Island, George could never see the horizon, which was obscured by the stockade wall, but he could see what was above it, and for a few brief moments, the beautiful and peaceful sight overhead offered a morsel of consolation in the face of a ruder sort of dawning—the roll call—marking the beginning of another miserable, deadening day of captivity.

That morning and afternoon passed in much the same way as every other day on the island passed, and just after sunset, the rumblings of artillery fire began again as usual. Most of the shelling took place after dark. George could never sleep while these noisy operations were going on, and, having nothing better to do, he would often sit in the door of his tent and watch the sky. There was a kind of grandeur in the spectacle after all, distressing as it was to him. At night, the firing guns resembled flashes of lightning, sometimes illuminating the whole sky, and the fuses of their projectiles made fiery streaks across the heavens like meteors.

It was not so pleasant when the shells thrown in by the harbor batteries and forts burst just beyond the prison stockade. With each boom from the Confederate installations in the distance, George would cringe and await the shell that was surely on its way, hoping it would not fall short but find its target at Fort Wagner, or at nearby Battery Gregg.

He remembered standing on the sea wall of Charleston before the war and gazing out on the harbor, where the mighty Fort Sumter appeared to be little more than a speck, not much larger than a hand's breadth in the distance. Yet from an even remoter distance, from the vicinity of Morris Island, shells were being thrown into the city by new, powerful artillery pieces. That these destructive projectiles could travel through the air a distance of five miles–five miles! he marveled–was a feat unheard of before this war. While watching from Sullivan's Island one evening, he remembered how his jaw had dropped in astonishment the first time he observed a shell hurtling across the harbor waters towards Charleston. Now, even after witnessing the same sight hundreds of times, he still looked on with amazement–as well as disbelief, sorrow, and indignation–unable to comprehend what military purpose it served to batter houses and shops and churches.

"My city," he whispered mournfully, hearing the dull, heavy explosion of a shell that had found its faraway target, "my beautiful city."

The next morning, George woke before dawn. Everyone else, at least in his hearing, seemed to be asleep. No one, and nothing, was stirring yet. It was so quiet, he could imagine himself alone. All that came to his ears was the ceaseless lapping of the surf, along with low roar of the sea breezes, constant and unvarying, and at times, a series of gurgling sounds from his empty stomach. It was so nice to imagine solitude, that he realized how much he missed it, as well as the luxury of privacy. They were privileges seldom if ever enjoyed by a prisoner of war.

He thought of Marguerite, and wondered if she were awake or sleeping at this early hour. He knew she was an early riser like himself; she had told him so. Was she thinking of him now? Perhaps she was dreaming of him. He had been dreaming of her again that night, though he could not recall the details.

The light of dawn began to show very faintly. Aleck was sleeping on the ground on a blanket directly opposite his, and in the dim light, George could begin to see his face in profile more clearly. The adjutant drew in a deep breath through his nose, and then opened his mouth to release it. His eyelids fluttered open, and he yawned, instigating a yawn in George. They talked a little while from their blankets before it was time to rise.

Before the men were dismissed from the roll call that morning, they were informed that their time on Morris Island would soon be coming to an end. After this announcement, the prisoners were kept in suspense for a number of days, but then, just before the beginning of the third week of October, they were told that they were being transferred to Fort Pulaski, which was located on the Georgia coast near Savannah. Many of them hoped an exchange awaited them there, but even if it did not, they were glad to leave Morris Island, certain that whatever awaited them there had to be an improvement on their present situation.

The morning they departed was much like the one on which they arrived, though the hour was earlier, and the air much cooler. Dark sheets of leaden clouds filled the sky to just above the horizon, where a narrow strip of opal daylight could be seen above the waters, also dark and gloomy looking. The Confederate officers were escorted to the wharf by the black soldiers and there boarded two old schooners.

The skies gradually cleared as the ships made their way down the coast, and the coolness and freshness of the air made the voyage almost pleasant, especially during the periods the prisoners were allowed on deck. They had been issued rations which were to last them for the three days of the trip, consisting of fifteen hardtack crackers and a piece of meat. Most of the men planned to consume a third of their ration each evening, but one ravenous officer could not resist devouring the entire amount on the first night.

George overheard a friend ask him, "What will you do for food for the rest of the time?"

The man replied sheepishly, "I reckon the Lord will provide."

The other officer looked scornful and said, "The Lord provided you with some sense. You should have used it."

Two days later, the prisoners arrived at their destination, one of them considerably hungrier than the rest. It was well after dark when the schooners anchored within sight of Fort Pulaski, so the captive passengers had to spend another night on board. The weather had turned extremely cold, and the officers huddled close together for warmth under their blankets that evening.

At a late hour, close to midnight, sudden confusion and uproar on the ship woke up the sleeping prisoners below deck. From above they heard cries of, "Man overboard!" and then, "Halt! Halt!"

Three Confederate officers had attempted to escape by swimming away. Somehow, they had made their way into the freezing cold waters before they were forced to return by warnings of gunfire. A few minutes after the shouting died down, the hatch opened, and the drowsy prisoners below deck looked up to see three forlorn, soaking wet, shivering men climbing down the ladder, their teeth rattling like castanets.

CHAPTER TWELVE

A PENTAGON OF RED BRICK, Fort Pulaski was similar in structure to Fort Delaware, but smaller. Like Fort Delaware it was surrounded by a moat, and situated on an island, between two channels of the Savannah River. Unlike the previous accommodations in Delaware, the prisoners' quarters here were inside the walls of the fort, in chambers with high, vaulted walls and ceilings of brick; these were casemates which had once housed pieces of cannonry poised to fire out of a single rectangular opening in the thick outer wall. The open windows, or embrasures, were now fitted with immovable iron bars. Larger bars of iron also filled many of the large, arched passageways between the casemates, and to complete the prison enclosure, the big archways of the inner walls which faced the parade ground were completely shut up with huge wooden doors.

Facing his new quarters while about thirty men were counted off as the occupants, George tried to gauge the size of the compartment; he guessed that it was about twenty-five feet wide and fifteen feet in length. As his eyes looked up and around, traveling over the curves of the brick arches of his cell, he visibly drooped, as though he could feel their heaviness settling down upon his shoulders. There was undeniably something of the dungeon about the place, and when the guards closed the iron gate behind him, the loud clanging noise, with its ring of finality and hopelessness, jarred his senses and his soul.

A good part of each casemate was taken up with a number of free-standing bunk beds, where two men could sleep on the top level, and two on the bottom. Other than this furniture, and a few rough tables and stools, there was little to be seen except the bare walls and brick floors. After claiming an upper berth for himself and Aleck, George went to the window and looked out. Beyond the flat, grassy expanse at the tip of the island, he could see a beautiful vista of water and marshes dotted with little barren islands. Through the embrasure there was a fairly strong, constant sea breeze blowing in off the river and the open waters which were not far away. He imagined that these winds would be refreshing and welcome during the warm months, but on this cold morning in late October, they were not so welcome.

Soon after the prisoners arrived at Fort Pulaski, the commandant visited their quarters, and the men were assembled to hear a short address he had prepared for them.

"Gentlemen," said Colonel Brown, a middle-aged man with a kindly face, "you shall be treated, while in my custody, humanely. You who have friends within our lines with whom you can correspond may write to them at once for money, clothing, and such other articles that will add to your comfort. I will do all I can for you, consistent with my duty, to make you as comfortable as possible. Myself and my regiment have seen service in the field and know what is due to a brave foe. I will make this the model military prison of the United States. I have already made requisition for blankets and clothing for you, and full army rations, together with plenty of fuel. All I shall ask is that you obey orders for the government of the prison, and such sanitary rules as shall be issued by me."

The men wondered if they were dreaming as they listened to Brown's words, which seemed sincere. Some of the prisoners were skeptical, having heard a similar speech from the detested Colonel Hallowell on their first day at Morris Island, but it soon became apparent that Colonel Brown was a man of his word. As he promised, they were given more food and allowed to send and receive mail, and purchase goods from the sutler. The rations, though not generous, were adequate, and even included some soft bread. The men were also permitted to take a weekly bath, albeit in cold water, and could spend some time in exercise on the parade ground in small numbers.

For the most part, the prisoners considered themselves better off at Fort Pulaski than at Morris Island. At least they were not under the constant threat of artillery fire, and the commandant and guards here, members of a New York regiment, treated them with respect. Gradually, to pass the monotonous hours, the men returned to some of the amusements and pastimes they had practiced at Fort Delaware. Gambling and card games became popular again, but the officers were never so active or high spirited as in their earlier days of captivity in the North. They were weaker, and cold all the time in their chambers of brick, with much less body weight now to insulate them since their deprivations at Morris Island. Aleck resumed his Hebrew studies with Captain Levy, Robert also joining him as a pupil, and both the young clergymen conducted religious services for the prisoners several times a week.

When rumors of an exchange reached the prisoners, their hopes soared again. The rumor turned out to be true. A large number of soldiers and officers, in fact, were to be exchanged near Savannah, but as the days passed, no word came that any of the men held at Fort Pulaski would be so fortunate. They waited for that news in vain for a week, but eventually began to give up hope.

As the weather grew colder, so did the prisoners' quarters. After complaints were made about this, some of the iron gratings separating the casemates were removed, and four stoves, one in every third compartment, were installed for heating and cooking. Within the dark, damp brick walls of their prison, however, the heat generated by four stoves was not sufficient to render much comfort. On the coldest days, the men kept to their beds to stay warm.

At the beginning of November, George woke up one morning to the sounds of sneezing and coughing beside him. He reached over and put his hand on Aleck's forehead, which was slightly feverish. George and Robert spent the next few days nursing the adjutant, whose cold they feared might turn into pneumonia. His physique, always slight, was not much more than skin and bones now. Robert, George, and Ned Wells gave up their blankets for his comfort, and shared their ration of warm soup with him.

When a box of luxuries arrived for Captain Levy, Aleck was treated to a meal of sweet potatoes, rice, and coffee. The next day, Captain Wells received a package containing two hams, bread, cakes, sorghum syrup, and a bottle of sherry. All this he shared generously with Aleck, and the food and drink seemed to have a reviving effect on him. He began to feel better very quickly, though his cough lingered.

One afternoon a guard came into their area looking for Adjutant Dwight. He was directed to his bunk, and there held a brief, hushed conversation with the young man. After the guard left, George approached his friend inquiringly.

Aleck was climbing down from the upper bunk with surprising energy.

"I am going to be exchanged!" he said to George wonderingly, almost in disbelief.

Some of the other prisoners overheard him, and a buzz immediately began and quickly passed from man to man. George's mouth fell open at the news, but he snapped it shut as he felt a lump rising in his throat, and a stinging fullness in his eyes. He turned his face away and said hoarsely, "I'm glad for you."

Aleck was also fighting tears.

"I'm very–very sorry to leave you in this place," he stammered, "and...all the others."

George turned back to him and saw that he looked ashamed.

"I'm very glad you're leaving us, Aleck!" he said, almost angrily. "And don't you even think of refusing this exchange. Not one man here would wish you to do that."

The adjutant looked at him gratefully, but his face still worked with conflicting emotions.

"I don't know why...I am one of only two chosen to be exchanged–only two! I wish with all my heart that all of us could leave this place together."

"Of course you do, Aleck. I know you do. But to know that you are going home, is the first real bit of happiness I've known in months, and–"

Robert came running up to them.

"Is it true?" he asked, wide-eyed. "I just heard you're to be exchanged. Is it true?"

Aleck nodded, suddenly shaking with nervous laughter, which brought on some coughing.

"Thank God!" he cried, rushing to embrace his brother-in-law. Both young men broke down into sobs as they held each other.

"Alice will be so happy!" said Robert, when he could bring himself to let go of Aleck.

"I was telling George, I wish we could all leave this place together," he said, wiping his eyes on a ragged sleeve.

"Well, that's not going to happen," Robert replied, taking on the something of the stern tone George had used. "But you are certainly going. This is God's will for you, and every one of us will be happy for your sake."

"When do you leave?" asked George.

"Very soon, I'm told," said Aleck. "Within the hour."

Other prisoners gathered around the adjutant to offer their congratulations. Captain Wells and Levy smothered him in embraces, and all the men expressed how pleased they were that the young "parson," as he was called, was gaining his freedom. As Aleck tried to groom himself a little and gather up his few belongings, a crowd of officers thronged the casemate like an audience. Some asked favors of him, to contact certain persons at home for them, or to carry a letter to the outside. A few wrote down their requests on scraps of paper, and Aleck promised to do all he could for them. One older officer offered him some medical advice concerning his cough. When nearly an hour had passed, someone asked the adjutant to say a final prayer with the men. His head hung low, Aleck could barely speak above a whisper; his voice broke several times with emotion, and his "amen" was curtailed by a cough he could no longer suppress.

After the prayer, Robert took Aleck aside and filled his ears with personal messages for his family in Columbia, and for the most important person of all, his wife Lily, who was with her family in Camden. Aleck realized that Robert took great enjoyment in telling him all these things because he felt he was, in a way, speaking to Lily. He let him go on, until his time and patience grew short.

"And tell her that–" Robert was saying, when Aleck stopped him.

"I can't possibly remember all these things you wish me to convey," he said laughingly. "And as for what you wish to say to your wife, you should have put it in a letter."

Robert smiled wryly and drew out a letter from his coat pocket.

"Will you see that this gets to her?" he requested.

"Of course! This will give my poor brain ease, and I won't have to write it all down myself."

In the last few minutes left to him, Aleck put his arm around George and spoke to him privately. The same guard who had brought the adjutant news of his release reappeared outside the gate with another prisoner–the other chosen man, a captain from Mississippi named Carson–and as the iron gates opened, the adjutant parted from George with an embrace and then passed—as he likened it in his own thoughts—out of death into life, darkness into light.

George pressed against the iron bars and reached out to Carson, who took his hand.

"Take care of him, Captain," he said. "He has been ill."

"I will, sir," the officer promised.

Robert, standing beside George at the bars, watched his brother-in-law until, after a final wave good-bye, he was out of sight.

"Two men," he murmured. "Two men out of hundreds, and Aleck was one of them. I have always felt there was a special grace on him. This is surely God's providence."

"I think you're right," George agreed quietly. "And none too soon."

About two weeks later, George received a letter from his cousin Alicia reporting on her husband's safe arrival in Columbia. His cough had disappeared, she wrote, and he was "eating like a horse." Later on, just before Christmas, Aleck wrote to George to tell him he had received his ordination and would be joining a South Carolina regiment in Virginia as its chaplain.

When the stoves were installed in the casemates, the prisoners were required to cook the raw rations they received themselves. One morning, George opened a package sent to him by Marguerite's relatives in Savannah to find ham, bread, potatoes, and rice, and immediately brought out the frying pan he had carefully and jealously preserved since its acquisition at Fort Delaware to prepare a little feast for himself and his closest friends.

November's weather grew colder and colder on the Georgia coast, during a winter which would be remembered as one of the most severe in decades. Although there were some brief respites of tolerable weather, on most days, blustering, icy winds whipped in through the open casemate windows, chilling the men inside to the bone, and many nights the temperatures fell so low that the sentinels who were on duty outside had to be changed every hour.

Towards the end of the month, conditions became a little more comfortable, or at least less crowded, when some two hundred of the officers were sent to another prison camp at Hilton Head. More than three hundred remained at Fort Pulaski, and despite the reduction in their numbers, they were still sleeping two or three to a bunk at night for warmth, for some still had no blankets. They were told that blankets had been requisitioned, but had not yet arrived. Some of the prisoners caught colds, and a few began developing signs of pneumonia and bronchitis.

November also brought the first death at Fort Pulaski. A young lieutenant who had grown sick during the last days at Morris Island did not improve within the cold, damp walls of the prison, and after lingering a few days in the hospital of the fort, he died and was buried outside its walls. The guards furnished a military escort for the body, and Robert Porter was allowed to conduct a brief service for the lieutenant in the presence of two of his closest friends.

In the middle of December, thirty more prisoners were selected for a special exchange. At the time of their departure, some of these officers published a letter to Colonel Brown in a Charleston newspaper to express their appreciation for the humane treatment they had received at his hands, but it would have been better for their fellow officers still imprisoned if they had never made this courteous gesture. When word of the letter reached the general in charge at Hilton Head, Brown was censured and ordered to cut the prisoners' rations and implement other harsh measures. He had no choice but to obey, but before actually enforcing these orders, the colonel warned the prisoners that hard times were just ahead, and all the men rushed to put in their purchases from the sutlers before that privilege was also revoked. Some of the Fort Pulaski prisoners had heard reports that such treatment was to be meted out to Confederate prisoners of war in retaliation for the alleged deliberate mistreatment of captive Union soldiers in the South.

December was made even bleaker by the news that Sherman's destructive army was moving across Georgia on its way toward the coast. On Christmas morning, the prisoners woke up to see a thick covering of snow on the parade ground. Later that day, they learned that General Sherman had captured the city of Savannah.

On the last day of 1864, on a gloomy, bitterly cold morning, Colonel Brown reluctantly spoke to an assembly of the prisoners to relate new orders that had been given to him. In a solemn, tremulous voice, he informed them that their new daily ration would consist of ten ounces of corn meal and a supply of pickles. The officers were then told that there would be no meat or vegetables in their diet, and hearing this, they realized that the specter of starvation had once again reappeared in their midst.

The barrels which contained the corn meal were stenciled "1861." When the prisoners opened them to inspect the contents, they discovered that the meal was rancid, soured, caked, and filled with weevils and wormlike bugs.

"It's moving!" observed one officer who was peering down into the barrel.

"A man can't live on that!" another cried out, horrified at the sight of what was to be their only food, except for an even smaller portion of bread that would be added later.

The prisoners broke open one of the kegs of sour pickles, but after consuming the stuff for a day or two, found that it did more harm than good. When it was discovered that the acidic pickles thinned the blood and caused digestive disorders, the rest of the kegs were left unopened.

Soon after the meager rationing began, the officers learned that two of their number had agreed to swear allegiance to the enemy, thereby disgracing themselves and betraying their loyalty to the Confederate States of America. Any of the officers could have secured better food and treatment, if they had been willing to take the oath of allegiance to the United States, but almost all of them preferred to suffer the rigors of their imprisonment rather than submit to the oath.

Each day, the prisoners made the corn meal into a mush with water and baked it in pans. Cooked in this way, without any grease or seasoning, it was a dry, repulsive mouthful to swallow, but it was all they had–until some prisoners began to catch rats and other animals to cook and consume. During the first week in January, two dogs, pets of the garrison, mysteriously disappeared, and soon afterwards, a small population of cats that lived in and around the fort began to dwindle.

The most kind-hearted of the guards sometimes risked reprimand or arrest to show pity on the prisoners, occasionally slipping a little bread through the bars for them. A middle-aged, gray-whiskered sergeant was most often their benefactor. One afternoon, as he was on guard duty outside a casemate, he stood closer than usual to the bars, next to a table where Ned Wells and three other officers, captains Douglas, Maxwell, and Morgan, were playing cards, their blankets wrapped around them like shawls. Seemingly observing the game, the guard lingered in this spot instead of pacing back and forth as usual.

The sergeant was a stout, almost corpulent man, and today he looked oddly more so than the day before, his big coat protruding open a little at his chest. After a while, having assured himself that no one was observing him, he stepped even closer to Captain Wells and, leaning over slightly, put a question to him in a whisper.

"Are you one of them fellers that eats cats?"

Wells looked up in surprise, but also glanced around the rooms cautiously before he nodded an answer. Then he noticed a decided bulge in the sergeant's coat. The guard unfastened a few buttons and pulled out the limp carcass of a large tabby tomcat.

"I'll shove him through the bars," he said, and Wells quickly stood and received the offering into his own jacket.

"I wrung his neck for ye. I wouldn't hurt a little critter, but it's hard to see you fellers starve, when there's food and meat aplenty in our stores."

As the guard buttoned his coat and slowly backed off to his usual post, the captain and his card partners hurried over to one of the casemate stoves to prepare a meal of the first meat they had seen in many days. All four captains had a naturally thin, wiry physique, and had only grown thinner in their captivity here and at Morris Island. While their dinner cooked they stood around the stove and cast lean and hungry looks its way, trembling with the cold, and in anticipation of at least a little portion of substantial food.

Soon another officer, a lieutenant from Kentucky, smelled roasted meat, and followed his nose to the corner where Captain Wells and his friends had taken their prize. They were crouched over a rough wooden table, about to dine. A fifth seat there was unoccupied, and the lieutenant approached with a demeanor of humble curiosity. The odor of meat rose in a little cloud of steam off a small white carcass, which Captain Wells was about to tear into to divide, and he paused and looked up when the Kentuckian drew near.

"How did you fellows get hold of meat?" inquired the curious officer. "It certainly smells good. What's that? A rabbit?"

Captain Douglas's nostrils exploded with a brief snort of laughter. Ned Wells chuckled and invited the lieutenant to take a seat and join them. He sat down opposite Captain Wells.

The captain tore a leg off the carcass, casting a sly glance at Douglas, who was trying to suppress his mirth.

"Well, it looks like a rabbit," the lieutenant remarked, looking rather perplexed.

"It's not a rabbit," said Wells.

"What is it, then? A squirrel? No, it's too large for that."

Wells had begun chewing on his piece of meat with obvious delectation, and made no answer. The lieutenant looked to the other men for one. Douglas was mute with suppressed amusement, and the others said nothing at first. As the Kentuckian turned back to Captain Wells with a quizzical expression, Captain Maxwell placed his hand over his mouth, muffling the sound of a drawn-out, "Me-o-ow."

The lieutenant's face fell, and all four of his table mates burst into laughter.

"It's a c-cat?" he stammered, recoiling a little.

The other men nodded and snorted in laughter as they began to take more portions and eat in earnest. The lieutenant could no longer look at the mutilated carcass on the table, though his empty stomach twisted painfully in disappointment.

"My mother...loved cats," he said quietly, with a strange expression of repugnance and astonishment. "We always had a yard full of 'em. I don't think I can eat a cat."

As he looked down at the carcass and smelled its aroma, his stomach ached again, tempting him to partake.

"Perhaps I could," the lieutenant murmured, but a moment later, he rose to his feet slowly and sadly.

"I just can't do it," he said, and, shaking his head, he turned and began to walk away.

"Suit yourself," Captain Wells said to his back, and when the Kentuckian was out of earshot he commented, "More for us, eh, gents?"

In reply Captain Maxwell mewed again, much to the amusement of his companions, who did not share the lieutenant's qualms about the consumption of domestic felines.

Since the coldest part of November, George had been having aches and pains in his joints, and as they became chronic and more intense, he assumed that he was suffering with an old man's disease–rheumatism. The only treatment, or rather relief, that the prison physician had to offer was opium. George used the drug very sparingly, and only when his pain was at its worst. A small amount of it would alleviate his discomfort for a while and let him sleep soundly, and though it gave him strange, vivid dreams, he relished these periods of oblivion, all the more so as the conditions in which he was forced to live worsened, and his suffering, and that of the other officers, grew more acute.

A few of the sickest prisoners had become addicted to the opium. The worst of these opium eaters was an officer from Virginia named Fitzgerald, who came from a good family and was a graduate of West Point. Once a fine figure of a man, he had been reduced to a physical wreck–a pitiful, filthy, loathsome skeleton in rags. He was nearly friendless among the captive officers, although some of them felt sorry for him, and would often feign a need for opium in order to obtain the stuff for Fitzgerald, or "Fitz" as he was known. Without it, he was in agony, and almost unbearable to look upon.

Robert Porter often spent time with Fitzgerald whenever he was in a reasonably lucid state of mind, trying to render him spiritual help and comfort.

"I am weak," Fitzgerald would say to him repeatedly. "I am so weak. Oh, will God forgive me?"

George and others observed the young man's tenderness with the pathetic invalid, and overheard some of his gentle reassurances.

"They that be whole have no need of a physician, but they that are sick," Robert reminded him, and Fitzgerald seemed to understand that it was not physical healing that he spoke of– it was becoming more and more obvious that there was no hope of that.

Seeing that the poor fellow was near the end, some of the prisoners who had ignored or shunned him tried to make him a little more comfortable and less lonely in his last days. Finally, he was taken to the hospital, and a few days later, word came of his death.

The news spread around the prisoners' quarters quickly, "Poor old Fitz is dead."

When George heard this, his only reaction was a vague feeling of relief that the man's sufferings were over at last.

One afternoon, one of the prisoners passed on some reading material to George, a magazine published in New York.

"I know you don't care for Yankee publications," said the officer, "but this magazine has an article about Charleston, and since you are from there, I thought you might wish to take a look at it."

George thanked him and took the tattered periodical to his bunk with him. After thumbing through a number of pages of little or no interest to him, he found the article about his native city and began to read it.

"Not many years ago," wrote the author, "Charleston sat like a queen upon the waters, her broad and beautiful bay covered with the sails of every nation, and her great export, cotton, affording employment to thousands of looms. There was no city in the South whose present was more prosperous or whose future seemed brighter. Added to its commercial advantages were those of a highly cultivated society. There was no city in the United States that enjoyed a higher reputation for intellectual culture than Charleston, and with it a refinement of taste, an elegance of manner, and a respect for high and noble lineage which made Charleston appear more like some aristocratic European city than the metropolis of an American state.

"The general appearance of the city was in keeping with the historical precedents of the people. Its churches were of the old English style of building, grand and spacious, but devoid of tinsel and useless ornament. Its libraries, orphanages, and halls of public gathering were solidly constructed, well finished, and unique as specimens of architecture. Its dwellings combined elegance with comfort, simplicity with taste. The antique appearance of the city and its European character was the remark of almost everyone who visited it.

"But all this is now changed. Except to an occasional blockade-runner the beautiful harbor of Charleston has been sealed for years; its fine society has been dissipated if not completely destroyed, while its noblest edifices have become a prey to the great conflagration of 1861, or have crumbled beneath the effect of the most continuous and terrific bombardment that has ever been concentrated upon a city..."

George paused here, remembering how he had watched the shelling from Sullivan's Island, and later, from Morris Island. He recalled the damage he had seen in the business district, and wondered how much worse it was by now. The writer went on to describe more details about the bombardment, but George soon stopped and closed the magazine; he could read no more, and returned it to its owner.

Under other circumstances, reading of his home, he would have felt many emotions going through his mind and heart, but reading about it now had left him mostly unmoved, and he experienced only a dull, momentary pang of homesickness. As his body had become weaker, there had been a corresponding waning of his emotions. He was growing apathetic about everything except his loved ones–and food. Food was always on his mind these days, just as it was the principal subject on the minds of all the famished prisoners.

Not long after the rations of the prisoners were cut, scurvy began to make its appearance among their ranks, and since the latter part of January, George had begun to notice unmistakable symptoms of this disease beginning in his own body. At the beginning of the year, he and a few other officers in his mess had spent their last few dollars in small purchases of food from the sutler, but in a little over a week, all their money was gone, and they were left with nothing to eat except their scant daily allowance. Though sutler privileges had been allowed again, after the first week of February, none of the prisoners had any money left.

Early in February, George received a letter from his brother which left him very anxious about Marguerite and her family. Albert wrote to him that General Sherman's large army had crossed the Savannah River, entered South Carolina, and was making its way through the state, burning and destroying everything in its path. What few Confederate forces there were in South Carolina could offer little effective resistance to this enemy army of sixty thousand, and were forced to continuously fall back. Charleston was to be evacuated, and Albert was making preparations to take his family to Darlington, South Carolina, a place he hoped would be safer than most, though it was difficult to ascertain what direction Sherman might take. Many thought he might march on Charleston, but Albert considered this unlikely. He had heard reports that the city of Columbia was his main object, and that his army was moving in that direction.

"After Columbia, then what?" George wondered. "Into the upcountry? Into Greenville?"

That night as he lay in his bunk he found it hard to fall asleep, and when he finally did, he had terrible dreams, seeing the Finley house in flames, and the family turned out into bitterly cold weather with nothing but the clothes on their backs. He was also in the dream, looking on in anguish, shackled as a prisoner of war, and unable to do anything to help them. He was being led away by enemy soldiers, and was crying out for Marguerite.

George woke himself from the nightmare with his own shouts, and though it was still hours before dawn, he could not go back to sleep.

CHAPTER THIRTEEN

"WHERE IS THE GLOVE PATTERN I was using earlier?" Alicia fretted, searching through a disorderly basket of material scraps, knitting needles, and other sewing supplies. She gave up looking and decided to read a book instead of crocheting.

Alicia turned up the flame of an oil lamp to read by, but her mother, who was seated next to her writing a letter, immediately objected, and she turned it back down.

"We can tolerate a little eye strain," said Mrs. Porter, keeping her voice low. "The oil is too expensive for luxuries."

"Reading, a luxury?" Alicia marveled to herself. She put her book away and sighed.

Everything was quiet and subdued in the household that evening. Rev. Porter was at a little desk near the fire writing a sermon in its light, his long legs crossed under the chair, and across the room, Dr. and Mrs. Crawford, her uncle and aunt, were seated in two identical armchairs separated by a spindly table, where they shared the light of a single candle. They had been reading, but the warmth of the fireplace had gradually lulled them into slumbers. The doctor had set aside his newspaper, and Mrs. Crawford's prayer book was spread open across her ample lap as she slept.

Their portraits, dating from several decades past, hung on the wall above their heads–the wife's over the husband, and the husband's over the wife. The young Mrs. Crawford had a long, smooth face and rosy patches on her cheeks, but she looked older than a bride of twenty. Her lips were prim and unsmiling, and her reddish hair was precisely parted and pulled up tightly at the back of her head in a chignon adorned with a high Spanish comb of ebony. The youthful Dr. Crawford had dark hair which curled below the ears, a long, lean face, and a very solemn, almost stern expression.

Alicia smiled a little as she studied the pictures of her relatives in contrast to the living subjects below them, wondering why the portrait painter had made them look so stiff. Perhaps he had not been a very good artist, she thought, or had meant to flatter his customers by rendering them excessively dignified. The Crawfords she knew were not so serious and formal, but were warm-hearted, good-humored people. Both husband and wife were considerably greyer and stouter now, and neither looked very dignified as they dozed, slightly open-mouthed, in their chairs.

She gazed wistfully at her book in disappointment, and wondered again that her mother had called reading a luxury. Alicia was inclined to regard it as a necessity these days, a needed distraction from all the worries and woes that threatened to overwhelm even the strongest minds. Reading and prayer had become her chief refuges, along with the journal she kept, and into which she poured her innermost feelings. Her eyes were tired, and since prayer required no external illumination, she took herself to her room to close them in that occupation, taking a candle to light her way. She had written two long letters that afternoon, one to Aleck in Virginia, the other to her brother Robert, and since her thoughts were still full of them, they became the main subjects of her petitions.

As she rose from her knees, she accidentally ripped a seam in her dress and sighed in frustration. Here was something else to be added to her sewing tomorrow–as if she needed more! For many months now she had been spending a good deal of her time making and mending clothes for herself and her family, and wondered how much longer it would be necessary for her to do so. Sometimes she became very tired of this chore.

For a moment Alicia thought she might go ahead and mend her torn skirt now, but then remembered her mother's frugality about the lights, and her own tired eyes, and soon gave up the idea. It seemed there was nothing else to do but to go to bed, so she began to take off her dress.

The underclothing she shed, as well as the night gown she put on, was made of somewhat coarse homespun, and her stockings were also made by her own hands. Her entire wardrobe now consisted of two calico dresses which had been patched and mended a number of times, a newer one of homespun plaid, and an old black silk mourning dress. The price of fabrics had become exorbitant, and a pair of shoes cost a small fortune, so she considered herself very fortunate to have one good pair of shoes, fine new English boots given to her as a Christmas gift by her Uncle William Beale, the owner of a shipping company in Charleston.

With a dreamy smile, Alicia remembered Christmas as she nestled herself under the covers of her bed. Despite the war and all its hardships, that holiday, and the weeks preceding it, had been one of the happiest times of her life. Her Aleck had returned to her, weak and wasted, but alive. By early November he was with her again, in the home of her family, where, under her loving care and theirs, he had regained his strength and health in a surprisingly short time. Just before Christmas, Mr. William Beale came up to Columbia with his wife and daughters, and their company made the season even more pleasant. Mr. Beale had with him gifts for the whole family, brought in on his blockade-runners, and food for a sumptuous feast, the likes of which had not been seen in the Crawford household in several years. Everyone had been so merry and affectionate, and Alicia recalled with particular fondness a beautiful day when they had all enjoyed a long walk in Sidney Park. The older people were hiding their fear and sadness after learning of the fall of Savannah, but Alicia could feel nothing but happiness, walking arm in arm with her husband, and cherishing every moment she had with him. A few days after Christmas, when he had to leave her, she was thankful that he was no longer a soldier but a chaplain now, and would therefore be in much less danger during the war.

December was nearly at an end now, and she had not yet heard from Aleck, but she knew he must be with his new brigade. She was expecting a letter from him any day, and was curious to know how he was handling his new responsibilities.

After a lovely Christmas, the new year did not begin auspiciously. The first hours of 1865 opened amidst terrible weather in Columbia. A violent thunderstorm kept many in the household from a sound sleep that New Year's Eve, and the next day, they received heartbreaking news from Mr. Beale. His only son, who had been a prisoner of war in the North for several months, had taken ill and died. In his last letters home, William Jr. had not been completely truthful with his family about his health, and so his death was cruelly unexpected. The grief of the Porter family for this young man was particularly acute as they thought of their Robert, also a prisoner, and grew even more anxious and prayerful for his sake. To add to the family's worries, their own William, Rev. Porter's youngest son, had just enlisted in Confederate service. He was only sixteen, and, having obtained permission from the governor to join the regular army rather than the home guard, he was preparing to travel to Virginia to join up with a cousin's cavalry regiment.

As January began, General Sherman was still in Georgia, but he had been uttering such threats against South Carolina that Rev. Porter was beginning to think he should take his family elsewhere, though certain circumstances kept him from doing this—even after it became known that Sherman's army had entered South Carolina and was making its way inland from the coast. In the second week of January, both Mrs. Porter and Dr. Crawford fell ill with severe colds, and neither could safely travel. Another consideration which kept Rev. Porter in Columbia was his belief that it was much more likely that Charleston would be targeted by Sherman. Most persons he talked to were of the same opinion—but it was not long before some of them began to change their minds.

In February, refugees from the South Carolina lowcountry began pouring into Columbia, telling tales of incendiarism, plunder, and outrage. Not long afterwards, people fleeing from areas as close by as Orangeburg District began to arrive in the city by the railroad and every other possible means of conveyance.

Rev. Porter then began to regret his decision to remain in Columbia. He was hearing estimates that the size of the invading army in South Carolina was anywhere from thirty to sixty thousand. Even if it were only the smaller number, he was certain that amount was far more than the total Confederate forces in the state.

As the days passed, he talked with a number of friends and neighbors, and several military men, among whom the consensus still seemed to be that Sherman's movement in the direction of Columbia was only a feint—that his real object was Charleston. One gentleman was very sure on this point.

"All these years, the Yankees have been trying with all their might to take Charleston," he said. "Now that it is within their power, they certainly will not pass up the chance! And they certainly cannot fail if their army is of such great numbers as reported."

The following week, this confident gentleman was proved wrong.

On Tuesday, the 14th of February, the whole population of Columbia was thrown into a state of excitement and terror at the news that Sherman's armies were only a few miles away across the river. Their exact numbers were not known, but Rev. Porter was convinced now that it was an extremely large army, and that any defense of the city by the greatly outnumbered Confederate forces would be futile. When he heard that a few thousand Confederate cavalrymen under the command of generals Butler, Hampton, and Wheeler were skirmishing with the Yankees about a dozen miles from the city, he reckoned that the only result of these actions would be delay. No matter how bravely or fiercely they fought, it seemed certain to him that they could not possibly stop the onslaught of an enemy army of tens of thousands.

That evening the clergyman sought solitude in a little sewing room upstairs, and there fell on his knees in front of a chair, praying as he had prayed only a few times in his life. The last time he had cried out to God in such anguish and supplication was when a young son, the last child born to him and his wife, had been ill. Despite his fervent prayers, the child had died. Now, his whole family was in danger, as well as relatives, friends, and neighbors. An entire city, populated mainly by women, children, and old men, was at the mercy of the enemy, and from what he had been told by some of the refugees who had already encountered these invaders, they were anything but merciful.

He prayed a full hour before he was interrupted. Alicia came to the door with a candle and opened it slightly.

"I have been searching for you all over the house, Papa," she said.

"Is something wrong?"

"No...I mean..."

"You wish to speak with me, my dear?" he asked gently.

"I don't wish to interrupt you."

She began to close the door, but he insisted that she come in. He rose from his knees with a slight groan and sat down in the chair he had been using as a prayer bench. She noticed her father wincing as she took the only other chair in the tiny room.

"Is your rheumatism worse today, Papa?"

"It's the damp weather, I'm afraid."

"You have been praying."

"Yes, dear."

"So have I, Papa."

Alicia suddenly clamped her mouth shut, and the delicate muscles of her jaw worked fitfully. She closed her eyes to prevent the tears that were welling up in them. After several deep breaths through dilated nostrils, she opened her mouth, exhaled forcefully, and then opened her eyes. They were moist, but no tears fell from them.

"I confess to you, Papa, I am afraid," she said. "For some reason, I seem to lack a measure of self-control lately. I have been feeling so weak and...well, I'm sure you have noticed. But I am trying to be brave, and calm."

"I know that you are, and will be, Alice. You have been a great help to me while your mother has been ill, and I have great confidence in you."

She nodded, and, realizing that she was slumping, drew herself up in stiff posture of self-possession.

"Is your Mama asleep?" he asked.

"Yes, thank goodness. I believe she will sleep a good long while now...if she is not disturbed. There has been a kind of ceaseless roar coming up from the streets today, but I read to her, and she was able to listen to my voice, and finally drift off to sleep. I hope she will sleep through the night. The rest will do her much good, but I really do not think that I shall be able to sleep tonight, Papa."

"You must try," he urged her.

"I do not think I can sleep alone in my chamber."

"Shall I sit up with you?"

"Would you, Papa?"

She looked so helpless and plaintive, so much like a little girl when she asked this, that he went to her and took her in his arms. That night, Rev. Porter sat in his daughter's room and read to her, just as her mother had read to her at bedtime when she was a child, and did not leave her to go to his own bed until she was asleep.

When Alicia opened her eyes the following morning, the room was so dark that she thought she had awakened very early, just at dawn, until she looked at a clock and saw that it was past seven. She went to the window and pulled back the curtains. A color of solid leaden gray met her eyes, beyond the blur of raindrops and streaks on the window panes. Shivering in the cold, she quickly dressed and went to see about her mother.

Her father was already up and about, and had just brought Mrs. Porter some breakfast. Alicia was happy to see her sitting up in the bed, eating with some evidence of appetite, and even smiling a little.

"Mama," she said, "you seem to be feeling better."

"I am! I slept so well last night–thanks to you, Alice."

"Your mother is looking well, is she not?" Rev. Porter observed from his chair beside the bed. "There are roses in her cheeks again."

"Yes, Papa," Alicia agreed. "I believe she is quite on the mend now."

As Mrs. Porter was finishing her breakfast, she was startled, and nearly spilled the last of the tea, when a loud crashing sound came to their ears. Rev. Porter went to the window and looked outside.

"It was only a trunk falling from the back of a wagon," he said. "Nothing to worry about."

Alicia came to her father's side and saw that the streets below were filled with an unusual number of people hurrying to and fro. A neighbor was loading a small mule-drawn wagon with boxes, trunks, and packages. In his haste he had let a trunk full of silver and china dishes slip out of his grasp and fall to the street, where it had shattered, along with most of the china. He and his wife were busy rescuing the pieces of silverware and stuffing them into a canvas bag, while his children, four teenage daughters, were climbing up to take their places in the back of the wagon.

Alicia eyed them enviously. She wished that she and her family could escape Columbia in the same way–in any way, really.

"Oh, Papa," she whispered, "I do wish we could leave the city."

Looking thoughtful, Rev. Porter glanced at his wife.

"Your mother is better," he said, also speaking in a whisper so that Mrs. Porter would not hear. "Perhaps I ought to go and see if it is possible to obtain some means of conveyance for us."

"Do you think we could take the cars?" asked Alicia.

"I shall go down to the Charlotte depot later, but don't–don't get your hopes up too much, Alice, and say nothing about this to your mother."

Later that morning, cannons could be heard in the distance, and as the hours wore on, their booming grew louder and more distinct. Just after breakfast Mrs. Porter had dressed and insisted on going downstairs. Taking on a few light chores despite her family's protests, she tried not to show any anxiety at these noises of war, but as they continued, and the day wore on, her strength flagged, and she had to sit down and rest.

Rev. Porter stood at the upstairs window and again watched the street below, which had only grown busier. On many streets he could not see, activity and panic were increasing. Government stores and supplies were being rushed in wagons to the railroad depot and shipped off on the last trains, and fearful crowds were filling the streets to escape the place, quailing at the booming of cannons not far in the distance.

In the early afternoon, for about three hours, the cannonade ceased, and the rain slacked off to a fine mist. Rev. Porter left the house and made his way to the Charlotte railroad depot, a crowded place where all was turmoil. There were many citizens, mostly elderly men, and women of all ages, who had come to seek a way out of Columbia for themselves and their families. Many looked panic-stricken as they were turned away. The government and the army were making use of the trains, and few private passengers were finding any accommodation. Rev. Porter saw at once that his mission was hopeless, and gave up before even attempting to obtain transportation.

As he was walking back to his house, the rain began drizzling lightly again. He pulled down his hat a little lower and tighter on his head, looking down for a moment, and as he looked up, nearly collided with another gentleman headed in the opposite direction. The man was carrying a valise in one hand and a stack of books under his other arm, and he dropped two of them as he avoided Rev. Porter.

"I beg your pardon," said the clergyman, automatically stooping down to pick up the books, one of which had landed in a tiny puddle.

"Oh, no!" cried the stranger, a portly, elderly man wearing spectacles. "Which one was that?"

Rev. Porter shook the water off the book in question and showed it to the man.

"Ah," he sighed in relief. "No harm done. I was afraid it was my brother's book. I thought I had put it on top."

"This one?" Rev. Porter held up the other book.

"Yes! Thank goodness. It looks unharmed."

The clergyman wondered why the volume was so valuable to the gentleman. It did not appear to be some rare antique; in fact, it looked rather new. The man noticed his fleeting display of curiosity and explained that the book was a treasured gift from his brother. While he spoke, Rev. Porter noticed the gilt title: *Post-Pleistocene Fossils of South Carolina*. He recognized the name of the author, a well-known professor and scientist from Columbia.

The clergyman carefully replaced the book under the man's arm and looked curious again.

"May I ask where you are going, sir?" he inquired. "Do you mean to leave the city?"

"I would certainly leave if I could, but I have no way to do so. My brother has insisted that I come to stay at his house in the college campus. He believes we shall be safe there, and I think he is right. Some of the college buildings are being used as hospitals, you know."

Just as he finished speaking, both men noticed a small procession of military wagons and ambulances rumbling down the muddy street toward them. The vehicles were bringing in the wounded from the fighting still going on not many miles outside the city. As they were passing by, Rev. Porter approached a mounted officer who seemed to be in charge. The slumping, bedraggled young man was wearing a heavy coat over his uniform, and the clergyman could only guess at his rank.

"Captain!" he called out, following beside his horse for a few steps. "The enemy—can they be stopped?"

The frowning officer only shook his head. In the meantime, the elderly gentleman with the books had struck up a conversation with one of the wagon drivers, and was offered a ride to the college. Rev. Porter helped him up to a seat beside the soldier and handed him his valise. He came very close to begging refuge for himself and his family with the stranger, but not knowing how many others might already be at his brother's house, or whether it was really safer at the college, he hesitated–and then it was too late to ask. With an oppressed, dismal feeling, he watched the officer and the wagons move on, until the rain suddenly grew heavier, forcing him to hurry home.

By the time Rev. Porter made it to the door of his sister's house his coat was soaking wet. He slipped off his muddy shoes and went inside. Alice met him in the entrance hall first, her eyes and expression full of one question. When she heard his answer, her little frame drooped, but otherwise she showed no disappointment or fear.

"Are you hungry, Papa?" she asked, taking his dripping hat.

"No, dear."

"I have just convinced Mama to take a little dinner, and tea. The tea seems to help her. It has been quieter for a while now, and I am glad she is not too nervous to eat."

"Very good," said Rev. Porter. "I am glad to hear it."

"I do think she is better physically, but the cannonading has made her nervous."

"We must all be calm and reassuring with her, Alice."

"Yes, Papa, I know."

In the middle of the afternoon, the noise of the cannons began again. It sounded closer, and along with it, the roar of musketry could be heard now. The noise continued for the rest of the day. There was no escape from it in any part of the house, except perhaps the above-ground basement, where thick shutters had been closed on all the windows, but no one ventured down into this cold, dark place to find out.

Mrs. Porter ate very little of her supper. In the evening, she clung to her husband. The two sat on a sofa together, his long arm around her plump little shoulders, and he squeezed and patted her arm comfortingly as they talked. After family prayers, Rev. Porter read aloud from the Psalter, choosing the psalms that he believed would bring the most solace and encouragement to everyone under the circumstances.

Husband and wife shared their bed again that night, and Mrs. Porter was able to sleep better with him beside her. Rev. Porter slept a few hours here and there, but his mind was overactive all night, either in waking thoughts or dreams, and he had to fight off apprehensive or despairing thoughts with prayers and reflections on the Scriptures.

The next morning, William came to the table that morning in his uniform, and after breakfast, he began saying his goodbyes to his family. He was only a boy, but he was a soldier now, and they tried not to weep or show fear for his sake. He was to leave Columbia with the withdrawing Confederate forces and later travel on to Virginia. After many drawn-out farewells, kisses, and embraces, Willie mounted his horse, said his last farewells, and rode off to join up with a company of dragoons.

About an hour later, the family heard the sounds of horses outside, and everyone went out to the piazza to see what was going on. A company of Confederate cavalry was passing through town to the front. They were fine looking soldiers, well-dressed, and mounted on well-groomed, spirited horses, and Alicia was filled with pride and admiration as they rode by.

"Oh, our brave boys," Mrs. Porter observed mournfully. "Is there any hope they can prevail?"

"They will do their best for us," her husband replied. There was conviction in his voice–he knew that they would do their best–but he also knew that however heroic their best might be, it could not be enough.

Alicia sighted a young man she knew and waved to him. The soldier lowered his head and tipped his hat to her, but offered no smile. He looked tired and meditative, like most of the men riding with him.

It was a chilly morning, and everyone soon went back inside except Alicia and her aunt. Wrapped in their shawls, they stayed on the piazza to watch the procession of cavalrymen as long as they could be seen.

"The cannon fire has not yet begun again," Mrs. Crawford remarked, then, after a pause, she wondered aloud with a shudder, "What if the Yankees should shell the city with those guns?"

"They would not do that," Alicia answered her. "They have not yet demanded the surrender of the city."

No sooner had the last of these words left her lips, than a shell went whirring directly over their heads. A moment later they heard it exploding not far off.

Alicia and her aunt exchanged a look of horrified astonishment, and both women rushed into the house to tell Rev. Porter and Dr. Crawford that a bombardment of the city had begun. Though his wife pleaded with him to stay home, Dr. Crawford left the house to see what he could find out about this turn of events. He returned an hour later and took Rev. Porter aside for a private conversation.

"Shells are falling into parts of the city," he said. "I heard that a man was killed near one of the depots. I think we should take ourselves down to the basement, and stay there as long as this continues."

Rev. Porter agreed. He gave out some instructions, and the ladies and servants began gathering up food, blankets, candles, lamps, extra clothes, mattresses, and everything else they could think of to make an extended visit to the basement more tolerable. While they did this, the two men removed clutter from two of the unused rooms and brought down some chairs and pillows. Within a short while they had all made themselves reasonably comfortable in this lower part of the house.

Despite her anxieties and nervousness, Mrs. Porter was feeling well again, and busied herself, along with her daughter and sister-in-law, in making pockets to wear under their hoop skirts, for the concealment of jewelry, money, and other valuables. Over the course of the next few hours, a number of pieces of shell landed in the yard of Dr. Crawford's home, and about a dozen fragments struck the house itself. In the afternoon, while Rev. Porter was upstairs fetching a few needed things which had been overlooked, the brass rim of one shell burst through the window of a bedroom. To keep out the cold, he covered the two shattered panes with part of a cardboard hatbox, pressing it in place with the back of a chair tilted against it.

As Rev. Porter was going back down to the basement, there was a knock at the front door. Someone called his name, and he recognized the voice of a neighbor. Seeing the damage to the house, the gentleman had walked over from next door to check on the family. Rev. Porter thanked him for his concern, and as he was speaking, a shell whistled overhead and exploded a block away. Cringing at the sound, the neighbor informed him that the Yankees were throwing in their shells from Lexington Heights, just across the river. They had burned the neighboring town of Lexington.

"I don't think we can hold Columbia," he opined. "Our forces are too few, and I don't believe reinforcements will reach us in time to do us any good–if there are any reinforcements. I imagine our troops will have to get out of the city tonight."

Darkness brought an end to the bombardment, and the family returned upstairs for their supper. While the meal was being prepared by Mrs. Crawford and her maid Mattie, Alicia opened the door to go out to the piazza, but closed it quickly, her eyes smarting. The air outside was heavy and stifling with the smoke of gunpowder.

Later that evening, the neighbor's prediction came true. Just before bedtime, the family was startled by the loud shouts of officers to the soldiers in the streets. In a steady rain, the Confederate forces were retreating, departing from the city, and leaving behind them many hearts aching with sorrow and dread.

Few in the household slept much that night.

At dawn on Friday, Alicia was drifting in and out of a troubled, fitful sleep after lying awake most of the night. Suddenly, something brought her bolt upright in the bed before she even realized it. The house had been shaken from the concussion of a terrific explosion in the city. The deep, resounding rumble of the blast was still in her ears as she scrambled to her feet. Thinking that a shell had struck the house, she threw on a robe and hurried downstairs, but as soon as she recovered from her sleepiness, she knew that no shell could have made such a noise. Her parents were already up and dressed. They were looking out a window, mystified as she was by the violent jolt and thunderous din simultaneous with it.

Later a neighbor brought the news that the South Carolina Railroad Depot had been blown up accidentally by poor people and plunderers who had gone there in search of valuables and food. The looters had taken lamps and torches to light their way, not knowing that kegs of gunpowder were also stored in the buildings, and had caused a massive explosion. The city's firemen soon put out the resulting fires, and afterwards brought out the bodies and remains of more than thirty men and women. There was no way of knowing how many more had simply been blown to bits or incinerated.

"Good heavens!" cried Mrs. Crawford, repulsed by the images the neighbor's descriptions created in her mind. "As if the Yankee cannons were not enough!"

Breakfast was served, but little of it was eaten. The women moved and spoke in a tense, subdued manner, sometimes betraying signs of fear. The men were energized, rather than unnerved, by strong protective instincts. Without his wife's knowledge, Dr. Crawford had cleaned and loaded a little pistol he owned, and was keeping it in one of his pockets.

While it was still early, Rev. Porter learned from a passer-by that the commissary and quartermaster stores of the city had been thrown open to the public. All their provisions were being given out to the people, said the man, hurrying on his way with several large packages in his arms. Dr. Crawford sent his manservant Nash to go and see what could be procured for the family. Nash, a large, strong black man, returned within an hour loaded down with parcels of flour, sugar, corn, and rice.

"Better that we have them," said the doctor, "than the Yankee soldiers who will soon be upon us."

He did not notice that his wife was entering the room as he spoke, and when Mrs. Crawford heard what he said she broke down into fearful sobs and swayed as if about to collapse. Her husband hurried to her side and helped her into an armchair. Seeing her reaction, Rev. Porter decided it would best for all the women to return to the basement again as soon as any enemy soldiers were seen on their street.

Within a few hours, a report spread about the town that the mayor and some aldermen had gone out to meet with the commanders of the Federal forces to surrender the city. Accepting their surrender, General Sherman had given assurances to these city officials that private property would not be harmed, and that the citizens of Columbia could rest easy that night, just as if the city was still under Confederate rule. Some public buildings would be destroyed, they were told, but only after the winds had subsided, to protect other structures from the spread of any fires that might result. Rev. Porter was happy for this mercy at least, and comforted to see the relief on his family's faces when he shared the news with them.

"Oh, thank God! Thank God!" cried his sister, trembling with emotion.

Though cheered by the news, Mrs. Porter felt weak, and Mrs. Crawford asked her maid Mattie to prepare a cup of strong tea for herself and her sister-in-law.

"Ain't but a little bit left," said the young woman, but she went to the kitchen to use the last of it.

As soon as the ladies finished drinking their tea, Rev. Porter instructed them all to go down into the basement. He suspected that enemy soldiers were likely already pouring into the town, and would soon be in their neighborhood.

It was not long before they appeared. Even through the heavy, bolted door of the basement, the women could hear the muffled shouts, hurrahs, and singing of the soldiers as they moved through the streets. They had entered Columbia in an orderly parade, but as soon as they were dismissed, most began to scatter and spread through every thoroughfare of the city. Some were moving in the direction of the Crawford house.

Mrs. Porter covered her heart with one hand and let out a nervous sigh.

"Don't worry, Mama," said Alicia. "They have been ordered to respect private property. They shall not come in the house."

"They did not respect private property in Georgia," her mother answered faintly, and then regretted her words when she saw the look of fear reflected in the faces around her.

"But as you said, dear," she added quickly, "we have the general's assurances to our mayor, and I do not expect to see soldiers in this house."

Finding a chair in a secluded corner, Mrs. Porter closed her eyes and breathed a silent prayer for strength and courage, and afterwards felt calmed.

Rev. Porter went up to the second floor of the house to get a better view of the street below, where he saw about a dozen soldiers, walking in groups of two or three. His blood began to run cold as he witnessed them entering private houses just a block down from his. He saw only one citizen of the town on the street, an elderly man. A burly soldier was shaking a fist at the old gentleman and holding out his other hand, palm up. The palm was soon filled with the citizen's gold watch.

"What idiocy to trust their word!" groaned the clergyman. "They will respect nothing!"

A few moments later, still watching the alarming scenes outside, he started when he felt the touch of a hand on his elbow. Rev. Porter swung around and faced his daughter.

"I'm sorry to startle you, Papa," said Alicia.

"Why have you come up here?"

"Aunt Delia wished me to tell you that Uncle Cecil has left the house."

"For what purpose?"

"He did not tell us. He came down to the basement to fetch his old medical bag and said not to worry, that he would return soon. He was in such a hurry that he would not stop to answer our questions when we asked him where he was going."

Rev. Porter peered out the window again. He soon spotted a man he was sure was his brother-in-law, hurrying down the street beside a young woman. They soon turned a corner and were out of sight.

"Some neighbor has need of him," the clergyman surmised.

"Perhaps it is poor Mrs. Cohen. Her baby is due anytime now. I hope she is not in trouble." As Rev. Porter continued to stare through the window, he reached out a hand and drew Alicia beside him.

"You are keeping a journal, are you not?" he said to her. "Perhaps you ought to see this, and record it."

As he opened the window a little, the loud voices of the soldiers in the street came more clearly to their ears. They were shouting, cheering, and singing. Soon a coarse, triumphant song began.

"Hail Columbia, happy land!" they sang. "If I don't burn you, I'll be damned!"

Rev. Porter quickly shut the window to muffle their words. Then, at a sudden, jarring noise from downstairs, Alicia jumped back and clung to her father. They heard a violent banging on the front door, as if a battering ram were being thrown against it.

"Papa!" she cried. "They are trying to enter the house!"

"Come with me," he said breathlessly, leading her downstairs.

He had hoped to get Alicia back into the basement before the door was broken in, but just as they entered the parlor, the door burst open, and a squad of seven or eight soldiers came through, nearly trampling each other as they piled in, their faces full of a fierce excitement. A few seemed intoxicated to one degree or another, and one was smoking a cigar.

Rev. Porter maneuvered his daughter behind him and faced the men defiantly.

"We have come to search the house for arms and contraband," announced a tall, rough-faced sergeant wearing a long overcoat, who then demanded, "Why didn't you open the door when we knocked?"

"We were upstairs," Dr. Porter replied, "and did not hear you until you began to beat down the door."

The man smiled and gave a short, scornful laugh. He motioned to the men with him, and they quickly proceeded upstairs. The sergeant was carrying a sheathed sword in his left hand. The weapon looked old, even antique, and Rev. Porter guessed that it was something he had purloined from one of the neighbor's houses.

"There are no arms in this house," he said to the sergeant.

"We'll see about that," the soldier answered sharply, brandishing a gun in his right hand. Then, in a sly tone he said, "Now, I am wondering what time it is. Won't you check your watch and tell me?"

Rev. Porter reluctantly drew out a treasured old timepiece from his coat pocket and the sergeant took it and put it in his pocket, then stepped forward to take a critical look at Alicia.

"This your daughter?" he asked.

Rev. Porter nodded. The sergeant spied the ring on her finger and demanded it. As she gave it to him, he asked her where her husband was, but received no answer.

"In the rebel army, I suppose," he sneered. "A bullet for him."

"My son-in-law is a chaplain in our army," Rev. Porter informed him. "And I am also a minister of the Gospel. We are poor, and have no guns or valuables for you."

"This is a pretty nice house for a poor man," the sergeant retorted.

"This is my sister's house. She is not rich, either."

"Shut up, you damned old rebel!" he snapped. Looking annoyed, he raised his gun again threateningly.

As they waited, not daring to move a muscle, Alicia and her father could hear the soldiers noisily rummaging through the furniture upstairs. Eventually, they also heard crashing sounds, the shattering of glass, and the thuds of heavy things being overturned. The soldier with a cigar in his mouth came back down to announce that one of the doors upstairs was locked.

"You had better give me the key, old man," said the sergeant.

As Alicia began searching her dress pockets for the key, Rev. Porter objected, "That is my daughter's chamber!"

"And what of that!" the man said disparagingly. "You think a woman's room is better than any other?"

He snatched the key out of Alicia's fingers and tossed it up to the soldier on the stairs, pointedly directing him to "search that room thoroughly." The ransacking continued for a while longer after this, but the soldiers eventually reappeared on the stairs, shaking their heads and cursing in frustration.

The one who seemed to be the most intoxicated said to the sergeant, "Ain't much worth havin' up there," adding with a malignant grin, "especially now."

The soldiers scattered into the rooms of the first floor and did much the same as they had done upstairs, while the sergeant looked on with evident satisfaction. When a soldier opened a writing desk which Rev. Porter used frequently, the clergyman involuntarily stepped forward and made a gesture of protest. Noticing this, the sergeant urged the soldier to examine the desk very carefully. The young man pulled out papers and notebooks and tossed them about on the floor. Confederate money and bonds he angrily tore into pieces and flung away, along with the drawers he had emptied. The last drawer he pulled out contained some family heirlooms, most of which he seemed to regard as valueless, until he came across an object which appeared to be made of gold.

"What's that?" asked the sergeant.

The soldier held up a handsome old seal between two fingers for the sergeant to see.

"That is my grandfather's seal," Rev. Porter replied anxiously. "It is my most precious family relic!"

"It's gold, isn't it? It's precious to me, too," laughed the soldier, slipping the seal into his pocket.

"Just who was your grandfather?" the sergeant asked derisively.

The indignant silence he received as an answer angered him again.

"Think you are better than I am?" he bellowed.

He stepped closer so that his face was only an inch or so away from that of Rev. Porter, and whiskey could be smelled on his breath. The clergyman continued to withhold an answer, but could not conceal a look of contempt that came into his eyes, and seeing this, the sergeant clumsily holstered his gun, dropped the sword, and seized the clergyman's coat collar roughly with both hands.

"We'll see how proud you are," he said, "when you are on your knees begging for a crust of bread from us!"

He shook the elderly man violently, then, deciding that this was not enough, picked up the old sword from the floor and smashed it across the clergyman's left arm. The excruciating pain of the blow caused Rev. Porter to collapse to his knees. Alicia immediately kneeled with her father and put her arms around him protectively.

"See? Humbled already!" jeered the soldier.

"How dare you!" she cried.

Though not afraid for herself, she was quivering with outrage and loathing as she glared at the man.

"Whoa-ho!" he laughed, rolling his head from side to side. "If looks could kill, I'd be a dead man for sure, boys!"

He turned away, still laughing, and joined in the general pillage. When the soldiers finally finished ransacking the first floor and taking whatever they wanted, Rev. Porter and Alicia were surprised and relieved to see them leave the house as abruptly as they had entered it. The raiders had seemed unaware of the basement, or uninterested in it.

"Oh, Papa," sobbed Alicia, "are you badly hurt?"

"He struck the bone of my elbow," Rev. Porter gasped hoarsely. "I don't think it is broken, though it may be fractured."

He managed to rise to his feet, and after taking a few deep breaths, felt well enough to walk.

"Papa, Aleck's letters were in my desk upstairs. Please, let me go and get them," Alicia begged him.

After nodding his permission, he waited at the foot of the stairway while his daughter went up. As soon as she reached the second floor, he heard a cry of "Fire! Fire!" and rushed up behind her. Smoke was drifting out of the door of her room into the hallway. Rev. Porter flung the door open and saw one of the curtains and the bed covers ablaze. Though the pain in his injured arm was almost intolerable, he quickly tore the quilt off the bed and used a heavy blanket beneath it to beat out the flames. After the burning quilt was smothered, he snatched down the burning curtain and did the same to it, then stamped out a small section of the carpet that was on fire. Papers from the desk, and clothing from the overturned bureau, were scattered all over the floor. Some of the letters Alicia had come to fetch were cinders now, but those away from the window and curtains were safe. She gathered them up and cradled them.

Rev. Porter looked for the wash basin, but found it broken in pieces on the floor. The water it had held had wet the carpet and prevented the fire from communicating to a large pile of papers near the window. The basins in the other bedrooms were also broken, so he continued to smother any smoldering remnants of the fabric with the blanket and the soles of his shoes. When he was satisfied that nothing was in danger of reigniting, they returned to the basement. On the way, Rev. Porter instructed Alicia to let him do the talking.

"Say nothing to your mother about my arm," he added.

Mrs. Porter, Mrs. Crawford, and the others had heard the strange voices and noises upstairs, and were nearly frantic. They all rushed up to Rev. Porter as he opened the door and entered with Alicia.

"Paul! There is soot on your hands and clothes!" exclaimed his wife. "What has happened?"

"Don't worry, dear," he said soothingly. "Everything is all right."

"Who was in the house?" asked his sister.

"Some soldiers came in, to search for arms and contraband, they claimed, but they were only here to steal our valuables. They are gone now."

"We heard such noises!" Mrs. Porter complained.

"They did some damage to the house, I'm afraid. One of them was smoking, and started a little fire, but we put it out," said Rev. Porter. "But at least they did not attempt to enter the basement. For that I am thankful."

Mrs. Crawford was fretting about her husband. Nash offered to go and look for him.

"Don't worry," Rev. Porter told them reassuringly. "The doctor will return shortly. I am sure he has not gone far. No doubt he has been summoned in a professional capacity."

"I thought perhaps he had gone to Mrs. Cohen's house, Aunt," Alicia suggested. "We saw him through the window with a lady who must have come to fetch him."

"Yes, yes, that must be the case," Mrs. Crawford sighed resignedly. "He is attending that good lady, or someone else in need. He could never refuse anyone in need. It must have been something urgent for him to leave in such haste. But how unfortunate for Mrs. Cohen if it is she! What a terrible time for a baby to be brought into the world."

Rev. Porter's arm was beginning to throb with a dull pain from his shoulder to his fingertips, and any movement of his elbow was torture.

"Alicia," he said, "come with me upstairs for a moment. I want you to gather up the rest of the food in the house and bring it down here, and also any other coverings and blankets and candles you can find. I think you should all stay in this basement for the night, as you have thus far been undetected here. Nash can protect you, and I shall keep watch upstairs and try to prevent more soldiers from coming in. If more do come, they can easily see that the house has already been pillaged, and will probably leave us alone."

"Oh, husband! Do not stay up there alone!" cried Mrs. Porter. "What if they should offer you violence?"

"They would have no reason to do that, my dear," he reassured her, glancing at Alicia.

As the afternoon came on, Rev. Porter paced back and forth in the front parlor of the house with a blanket wrapped around his shoulders, stopping now and then to gaze out the window. During this time, there were few citizens on the streets, but the clergyman witnessed once again the forcible surrender of valuables. As a Federal soldier accosted an elderly gentleman, the old man held one hand up to his ear as if hard of hearing, and the young man repeated his request more loudly. The befuddled old fellow unthinkingly drew out his watch, and the next moment, was without one.

Filled with indignation, Rev. Porter was suddenly seized with the idea that he must go out into the city and see all that was going on, in order to fix it in his mind, and later to make a written report of everything that passed before his eyes, but felt he ought not to do so until Dr. Crawford came home. He waited impatiently and more and more anxiously for his brother-in-law to return, troubled with apprehension for him. Another group of soldiers came into the house, but discerning that there was little left to steal in the place, they soon departed. Finally, about two o'clock, Dr. Crawford opened the door. He did not seem surprised to see that his home had been ransacked.

"The others are downstairs?" he asked immediately. "Everyone's all right?"

"None of the soldiers have gone down into the basement," said Rev. Porter. "And I believe we may thank God's providence for that. Some of them did come in while Alicia was up here with me, but she is all right."

"And are you?" Dr. Crawford asked, eyeing Rev. Porter as he took off his overcoat and hat. "You show signs of pain."

"One of them struck me on my arm. My elbow is perhaps fractured."

"Let me take a look at it."

With assistance from the doctor, Rev. Porter removed his coat and rolled up his sleeve. He groaned with acute pain as his brother-in-law touched the sorest spot.

"I'm afraid I have no anodynes to offer you," said the doctor, "but let me wrap your elbow with a bandage. That may be of some help to you."

"My whole arm aches terribly."

"Yes, well, I am not surprised. Your arm is black. It must have been quite a blow."

"It was."

After wrapping Rev. Porter's arm and helping him put on his coat and blanket again, Dr. Crawford fell into a chair. For a moment, he looked as though he were about to burst into tears. He put his hands over his eyes, rubbed his forehead, and let out a heavy sigh. When he drew his hands away from his face, his expression was one of deep despondency.

"Were you attending Mrs. Cohen?" Rev. Porter asked him, fearing the worst.

"No, though she will no doubt be in need of a physician soon. It was her daughter I attended today, a little girl of nine. She is very ill and feverish, I'm afraid. I did what I could, and if she is left undisturbed, I think she will survive, though her mother is beside herself with fear."

"Poor lady," the clergyman murmured. He closed his eyes and offered up a silent prayer for Mrs. Cohen and her daughter.

After a pause, Dr. Crawford related more bad news.

"The Yankees have raised their hateful flag over the State House," he said sorrowfully. "They are pouring into and through the city, bringing in immense wagon trains—wagons full of stolen goods, I'm told—setting up their camps in the outskirts of town. There are thousands of them, tens of thousands!"

"Do you still have your gun?" asked Rev. Porter.

"Yes, I was forced to give up my watch and wallet, but I still have the pistol."

"Now that you are home again, I shall go out."

"Why would you do that?"

"I feel I must! I must know what is going on. I fear there may be worse in store for us."

"What do you mean?" asked the doctor.

Rev. Porter cast a troubled look upstairs in the direction of his daughter's room.

"The first squad of soldiers who came here," he said, "tried to set fire to the house."

"My god!"

"Promise me you will not leave the house again until I return."

"I will not leave it, certainly not! But what shall I tell the others?"

"As long as possible, let them think I am still upstairs. Go let them know you are here, and then come back up as soon as you can."

While his brother-in-law went downstairs, Rev. Porter put on the overcoat the doctor had shed and looked for his favorite warm hat. He finally found it trampled in a corner as Dr. Crawford reappeared in the parlor.

"Do you want the gun?" he asked.

"No," said Rev. Porter. "I wish you to keep it with you here. Is everyone all right?"

"Yes. I told them I was going to stay upstairs–with you, I'm sure they assume. How long will you be gone?"

"I don't know. I shall try to return before dark."

"Take care!" Dr. Crawford called after him as went out the door.

Rev. Porter had hardly traversed a block before a soldier in blue stopped him and asked him for the time.

"I would gladly tell you," he replied, "but I have already had that question put to me today."

His sardonic look and tone drew a horse laugh from the soldier.

"Well, some other gentleman will be able to tell me, I'm sure," the young man chortled, walking on.

The clergyman continued down the street, and, turning a corner, caught sight of Mrs. Cohen's house. He walked up to her door and called out her name, announcing his own afterward. Soon a servant girl timidly peeped out and let him enter. Rev. Porter found the lady sprawled on a sofa, big with child, her face pale and haggard. She looked very nervous and fearful, but smiled faintly as she greeted her visitor. She was holding a handkerchief in one hand, and sniffled a little at times. She told the clergyman she was suffering with a slight cold. There was a cheerful fire burning in the fireplace, but he noticed some disorder in the room, and asked her if soldiers had been in her house.

She nodded, shuddering.

"A number of them were here not long ago," she said. "They took everything of value they could find on this floor. I told them about my sick child, and begged them not to go upstairs. One who seemed to be in charge took pity on me, and they all left."

"I fear they will go into every house before this is all over," said Rev. Porter.

"They came to yours?"

"Yes, more than once."

"Lord have mercy on us! Oh, thank God, my uncle and his wife and are on their way here. They are going to stay with us. They are trying to obtain a guard for this house. We were told that a number of persons in the city have that protection."

"Is your daughter any better?"

"Her nurse tells me that her fever has abated somewhat."

"That is very good!" the clergyman said encouragingly. "Very hopeful!"

"Yes, I have become more hopeful since Dr. Crawford was here. My daughter is asleep now."

"What is the child's name?"

"Sophie."

The name had barely left her lips when they were both startled by a loud banging at the door. Angry shouts could be heard from behind it. The servant girl shrieked and ran into the room, falling on her knees beside the sofa and clinging to it.

"They have come back!" gasped Mrs. Cohen, her face now paler than ashes.

Rev. Porter went to the locked door and opened it. A half dozen soldiers in blue pushed it wide open and came in. Mrs. Cohen recognized some of the same men who had been in her house before. The officer who had taken pity on her, however, was no longer among them, and several seemed inebriated.

"We have some unfinished business here!" one announced.

"Oh, please! I beg you, do not go up to my daughter!" Mrs. Cohen sobbed. "She is very ill!"

"We know your tricks," the same man muttered. He pushed Rev. Porter aside, and they all headed for the stairway. Still begging and pleading, Mrs. Cohen tried to raise herself up from the sofa, but fell back in a faint, and the servant crawled up beside her and put her arms around the lady. All this was ignored by the soldiers, who tramped up the stairs talking among themselves about the prospects of finding gold and jewelry hidden away on the second floor. Rev. Porter followed them.

The door to the child's bedroom was partly open. A thin, elderly black woman, the child's nurse, protested as the soldiers entered, shaking her bony fists in the air defiantly and calling down Biblical curses on their heads. They laughed at her, shoved her aside, and began to search the room. In the bed, the little girl woke and began to cry, and both Rev. Porter and the nurse went to her side protectively. He repeated her name in soothing tones.

"Sophie, Sophie! Be calm, child. We will not let them hurt you."

After the soldiers had rifled through all the furniture in the room, two came to the bed.

"You can take her up," one said to Rev. Porter, as the other began lifting the covers.

The frightened little girl grew hysterical.

"Don't you see how the child is agitated?" the clergyman objected. "Leave her alone!"

Hesitating, and noting that the child really was very ill, the soldier who had spoken signaled the other to stop, and they followed the rest into other bedrooms, but not before taking a look under Sophie's bed, where they found nothing of interest. As they left the room, Rev. Porter was amazed to see one of them pick up a beautiful little doll and stuff it in his haversack, muttering to himself as he did, "My little girl will like this."

Sophie did not see her toy being filched; she was clinging to the neck of her nurse, who had bent down to kiss and comfort her. Rev. Porter stayed with them as long as the soldiers were upstairs. When they had finished ransacking the other rooms, he followed the men downstairs, where they headed straight to the front door and left, slamming it behind them. Rev. Porter told Mrs. Cohen what had gone on the second floor and assured her that her daughter was safe. Unwilling to leave her alone, he waited with her for over an hour, until her uncle and aunt arrived, and then, entrusting Mrs. Cohen to their care and that of the guard they brought, he went out into the streets again. He spent another two hours or so checking on other neighbors and friends, many of whom had been intruded upon by soldiers. Even some who had Federal guards were robbed, and for this reason, Rev. Porter decided that he would put no confidence in their protection.

In the late afternoon, his empty stomach growled, and a wave of weakness and exhaustion passed over him. He realized that he had eaten nothing since a few bites at breakfast and decided to go home for a meal.

His brother-in-law sighed with relief to see him.

"Did any more soldiers come to the house?" Rev. Porter asked.

"A few came to the door, but after they looked inside, they did not stay. You look very tired, Paul."

"I am famished."

Dr. Crawford had just finished eating, and sent him down to the basement, where the others were still dining on a cold supper of bread, ham, and fruit preserves. Alicia interrupted her meal to prepare her father a plate and something to drink. She said they all must eat. They would need their strength.

The food refreshed him, and afterwards he sat down in a cushioned chair to rest, covering himself with a blanket. Wearily waving off questions and concerns from the ladies, he closed his eyes, and in the relative quiet that followed, he actually fell asleep for a while.

It was just before dusk when Rev. Porter woke. His wife came to his chair and kissed him.

"Are you feeling better now?" she gently inquired.

"I am. Thank you."

Forgetting about his injured arm, he extended it to pull off the blanket, and involuntarily winced and gasped in pain.

"Are you all right?" she asked anxiously.

"It's nothing, it's nothing," he said, producing a convincing smile. "Just my rheumatism. I shall go back up now."

Upstairs, despite his brother-in-law's protests, Rev. Porter insisted that he must go out again.

"But why, why?" Dr. Crawford demanded. "It will be dark soon, and therefore probably much more dangerous out there. I have seen many soldiers passing by."

"Help me put on this coat," Rev. Porter requested.

His brother-in-law reluctantly complied.

"Take the gun at least," the doctor urged him, but he refused.

Rev. Porter stepped outside and drew in a short, deep breath as the frigid air blew against his face. The weather had been windy all day. It seemed even more so as the evening drew on, and the temperature was turning bitterly cold.

As before, he saw few citizens in the streets, but many soldiers were strolling around, in groups or alone. As the clergyman watched these men, he sensed an air of expectation about them that filled him with an unaccountable dread. A fearful stranger who seemed to be wandering around aimlessly engaged the clergyman in conversation for a while, describing how he had seen the enemy army marching down Main Street in an endless blue column, all looking very well-fed, well-clothed, well-shod, and strong, and accompanied by at least a dozen bands playing at full blast.

"We are completely in their power!" the man lamented. "And some of the slaves are rejoicing to see them!"

He was looking for some consolation, and asked how long the soldiers would occupy the city, why they had not kept their word about respecting private property, and so on. Rev. Porter tried to encourage the stranger, but had few answers to offer him.

Leaving the fretful gentleman behind, he walked on a few blocks. It was beginning to grow dark. As he was turning on to Main Street, he noticed smoke coming out of the doorway of a saloon. A moment later, a man ran out of the building in a panic and cried out for help, and some soldiers gathered and approached the building. Rev. Porter heard the excited man shouting something to them about drunken soldiers and an overturned lamp causing a fire.

"It hasn't spread far yet!" the man cried, pointing inside the establishment. "If you will only help me, it can be put out!"

Within a little while, some firefighting equipment was brought in, and the soldiers began working a small hand-pump engine to extinguish the flames. Watching these men deal with this minor conflagration, which was soon put out, Rev. Porter felt a sense of relief. Perhaps his suspicions and fears had been unfounded, after all!

He began to cross the street, but suddenly, he was stopped in his tracks by the sight and sound of a sky rocket shooting high up into the air. It was red in color, and was promptly followed by two more rockets–the second white, the last one, blue.

He wondered what the meaning of that was, and before long, realized that it was a signal of some kind. The clergyman happened to be standing in front of a hotel at the moment. He hurried inside, rushed up several flights of stairs, and went out to the uppermost balcony, where a few other people were standing. From this height, he had a better view of the city, and within a matter of minutes he saw that fires were breaking out at several different points, simultaneously rising up in areas so widely separated from each other that none could have been caused by the communication of one fire to another. Rev. Porter heard wild shouts of exultation going up from the streets, and directly below, he saw that the soldiers who had been fighting the fire in the other hotel, after cutting its hoses, were smashing the hand-pump engine into pieces and abandoning it.

"God help us!" he whispered.

His heart was still beating fast from his exertions, but now began to pound even more rapidly and forcefully with horror. He went back down to the street. A building just a few doors down was on fire. The city fire engines had been brought out, but as soon as the firemen began pumping the water, soldiers axed and bayoneted the leather hoses, rendering them useless. Understanding now all too well that the city was doomed, Rev. Porter made his way home as quickly as possible. When he got there, he saw that the interior of the unoccupied house next door was in flames. The fire was just beginning to lick out through the windows on both floors, and the winds were picking up and carrying the sparks and embers toward his sister's residence. Parts of a wooden fence in the yard were already catching fire, ignited by sparks which had landed in dead dry grasses at its base. Another house not far away was also in flames.

Rev. Porter's brother-in-law was standing in the open door and gestured to him frantically.

"The house will surely catch fire!" he said. "We must get out of here!"

The two men went down to the basement. Dr. Crawford put his arm around his wife and held her tightly as Rev. Porter explained to them why they would have to leave the house. All were aghast as they listened, and Mrs. Crawford and Mattie began weeping. Mrs. Porter and Alicia also looked to be on the verge of tears.

"You ladies must calm yourselves. You must be strong. We must all be strong for each other, and trust in God to protect us," Rev. Porter exhorted them, though his voice was shaky. "Now, let us all wrap ourselves warmly in our coats and shawls and blankets. Take whatever you think we may need, certainly some food, but do not burden yourselves too much."

"But where shall we go?" Alicia asked her father.

"I don't know, I don't know," he answered. "But we cannot stay here."

"Perhaps we could go to the college, to the hospital there," she suggested.

Rev. Porter considered this a good idea, but his brother-in-law thought someplace closer would be better.

"What about the lunatic asylum?" he said.

"Yes! Yes! The asylum!" Mrs. Crawford agreed urgently. "Surely they won't set fire to the poor crazy people!"

At the mention of the state hospital, Rev. Porter remembered that it had been constructed as a fireproof building, and that it was surrounded by extensive grounds and a high brick wall which, if nothing else, would serve as a firebreak

"We'll try for the asylum, then," he said. "Now hurry, and do as I said."

CHAPTER FOURTEEN

THE WOMEN FRANTICALLY GATHERED up some bundles of clothing and food, along with a few cherished possessions they had secreted away in the basement, and followed the men up the stairs and out the door. Those who had been inside the house all day were shocked to meet the raw temperature of the air, but quickly became so frightened and dazed by the sights and sounds around them that they hardly noticed the cold. A growing din of human voices, mostly that of the soldiers, but also the cries of women and children, was added to increasing roar and crackling of multiplying conflagrations. The Porter ladies, Mrs. Crawford, and Nash and his wife Mattie moved down the broad avenue in a closely huddled mass, following the tall clergyman and the doctor—the wives holding on to their husbands' sleeves and coattails. Mattie let out a shriek when one wall of a burning building nearby suddenly caved in with a deafening crash, and Mrs. Porter could be heard praying aloud for God's protection.

As the little group passed by the house of a friend, a strong odor of turpentine met their nostrils. The dwelling was filled with fires on the interior of both floors, and Rev. Porter could see its owner, a widow named Keating, in the front parlor downstairs, engaged in a futile attempt to battle the flames threatening that room. He told the others to wait for him a moment and went inside to get her out, and as he approached her, asked about the smell of turpentine.

"The soldiers doused the furniture with it," she told him tearfully.

Flames were darting up over the two door sills, and the heat grew so intense that Rev. Porter could hardly bear it.

"I am sorry, Mrs. Keating," he said. "It is too late. I cannot fight such a fire. You must give up the house."

"No, no!" she lamented. "It is all I have!"

"Come, my good lady. Come with us. We'll do what we can for you."

She sighed pitifully and rolled her eyes, suddenly feeling faint from the heat and smoke, and the clergyman helped her gather up a few treasured belongings which had not been detected by the pillaging soldiery. As he wrapped a blanket around her shoulders, a stab of pain in his arm reminded him of his injury.

"Where are we going?" she asked anxiously.

"To the asylum."

"Oh, dear!" she cried, briefly looking more alarmed, but then said more calmly, "Well, a cousin of mine is there–the poor dear! Perhaps I may be able to comfort her."

Rev. Porter and those with him moved on, keeping close together. Mrs. Keating told them how she had obtained a guard that morning, and thought herself safe. A Corporal Morgan had stayed with her until nightfall, but then abandoned her.

"He told me he could no longer protect me," said the widow, "and warned me that the city was to be burned. He left me, warning me to get out of the house. Soon after, other soldiers came in and set fire to it."

As they came closer to the asylum, they began to hear the piteous shrieks and howls of some of the deranged, terrified inmates, and Alicia burst into tears.

"The poor things! The poor things!" she sobbed.

"Oh, Paul!" cried Mrs. Porter. "It is too distressing! Must we go there?"

"We must!" her husband answered emphatically, urging them on. "We have no choice."

The little group pressed on, and soon passed through the gate of the wall that surrounded the state hospital, a large, handsome building of classical design. As they approached the hospital, the clergyman looked up and saw that its roof of copper seemed to be glowing and moving with murky reflections of the surrounding fires. Rev. Porter had always been impressed with the beauty of the place, inside and out, when he had gone there a few times on ministerial calls. Many people were seeking refuge in the asylum tonight, and the clergyman and his party were preceded and followed by many others moving toward the grand portico, and then passing by massive Doric columns to enter the building.

Inside, the Porters saw a number of people they knew, and on every face, looks of bewilderment, fear, disbelief, and suffering. They found an open spot on one side of the wide main corridor and seated themselves on the floor to rest.

Later in the evening, one of Rev. Porter's closest friends, an elderly attorney long retired, took him aside for a private conversation and began to weep as he described his family's harrowing experiences that night. As he and his daughter and grandchildren were fleeing their burning house, two soldiers had attempted to take hold of his pretty teenage granddaughter. The old gentleman was fortunate enough to have a small pistol, which he pointed at them. One of the soldiers was about to draw his own pistol, when an officer suddenly interposed himself and ordered the men to desist and leave.

"If that officer had not been nearby," said the old man, "God knows what might have happened!"

Dr. Porter embraced his friend and could feel his trembling, and the heaving sobs rising up in him.

"My dear man," said the clergyman feelingly. "What a terrible ordeal for you! I am thankful that you and your family were protected."

"But others have not been so fortunate," said the gentleman, sniffing convulsively as he drew away. "Poor Mrs. Cohen, our neighbor, went into labor tonight. Her aunt begged the soldiers not to set fire to their house, but in vain. Some servants and others had to take her out into the street. They carried her out into the cold on her mattress! My god, she was in agony! We found a cart and put her into it, and brought her here. A physician is with her now, but he told me he thinks she will not survive."

"What of the little girl, Sophie?"

"We brought them all here. The child is not well, either. She is in the care of some friends now."

"I must go to the lady," said Dr. Porter. "Show me where she is."

When she saw her husband starting to walk down the hall with their friend, Mrs. Porter cried out to him, "Do not leave us!"

"I must, dear. You will be safe here," he answered her. "I shall return as soon as I can, but Mrs. Cohen is very ill."

"She is here? Oh, the poor thing!"

When Rev. Porter reached the room where Mrs. Cohen had been taken, he found her adult family and servants outside the closed door on their knees, all weeping. He could not keep back his own

322

tears. The door opened, and a man whom Rev. Porter recognized as a prominent physician of the town emerged, shaking his head.

"I am very sorry," he said, addressing Mrs. Cohen's elderly aunt and uncle. "Your niece is dead."

The old lady broke into piteous wails. Her husband asked about the baby.

"I'm afraid the infant did not survive, either."

Another heartrending wail went up from everyone in the group, and with this Rev. Porter broke down completely. He covered his face and walked off, staggering a little as he did.

In his whole life, he had given way to such emotion only a few times. He could not control it, and feeling so out of control, wanted to hide himself away, but looked for a long while in vain for a place of solitude in the crowded building. Refugees from the fires filled all the halls and every room he passed. Almost blinded by tears, he stumbled over young children on the floor, collided with passers-by, and turned away when he saw someone he knew. Finally he found a little empty room, no more than a closet, and closed himself up in it in complete darkness until he had exhausted himself with weeping. All the emotion pent up in him from everything he had experienced and seen that day–the unending scenes of suffering and destruction, which he knew must only grow worse as the night progressed–all those feelings burst out of him like an unstoppable flood.

Eventually, growing sober again, Rev. Porter took deep breaths to calm himself further and wiped his face dry with a handkerchief. But the sensation of emotional relief did not last long; it quickly gave way to his former feelings of outrage, and when he opened the door and left the room, he was more determined than ever to go back out into the streets of the doomed city, to witness its demise.

His brother-in-law, who had been searching for him, saw him as he emerged from the little room and ran up to him.

"The ladies sent me to look for you," he said. "They want you to stay with us."

"I must go out again," Rev. Porter replied.

Dr. Crawford was astounded.

"Are you mad? The whole city is burning down!"

"I am going out again," he repeated firmly, his expression solemn and set.

"But, but what shall I tell your wife–your, your–?" the doctor stammered.

"Tell them I am helping others. I shall try to return within an hour."

Rev. Porter left the building and walked across the grounds of the asylum, deliberating as to what direction to take. He thought of a friend who lived in a neighborhood he had not yet visited that night, and went that way.

As he had feared, the tumult and destruction in the city had only increased. As he passed through the gate of the asylum wall, a scene of pandemonium met his eyes. There were many terrified people in the streets now–men, women, and children–fleeing from burning houses and buildings, some of them carrying their sick and aged on litters, and some not fully dressed. Building after building was being consumed by the flames, the spreading conflagrations generated by the winds as well as the incendiaries who were running from house to house to pillage and then set fire.

Rev. Porter had never seen infernos of such magnitude. Their power and ferocity stunned and awed him. The flames seemed to reach the clouds, but they were clouds of smoke, up into which rose swirling sparks and small fragments of blazing shingles.

There were so many fires that many streets were as illuminated as daylight, except that this light was that of the lurid hue of a furnace. The orange glare the flames produced was so bright that it was casting black shadows like the sun; Rev. Porter could see clearly in it, except when the smoke and soot blew into his eyes and made them water. He later learned that people in the countryside thirty miles away could see the glow of the burning town, and the massive columns of smoke sent up by it.

More citizens driven from their burning homes surged through the streets, many of them trying to maintain a semblance of dignity and order in their flight, but numbers of soldiers, some of them reeling drunk, also filled the streets, and often accosted these people to interfere or block their way, at times fairly dancing with jubilation over their distress. Many soldiers showered the helpless refugees, old and young, male and female, black and white, with taunts and curses. At a corner, one of them gave Rev. Porter a shove and asked him mockingly, "Well, old man, how do you like secession now?"

Another intoxicated soldier climbed up to stand on top of a low brick wall to shout out a stump speech. Holding on to a post with one arm, and flailing his other high in the air, he began execrating the "original secessionists" and ranting about the preservation of "the glorious Union!"

"Tonight, Columbia," he roared, "you are privileged to see hell!"

Rev. Porter found himself agreeing with the man on this point. If ever a vision of hell had been revealed to human eyes, the clergyman felt this was it–demons and all. Only it was not a vision, but a hideous, terrifying reality all around him.

Worse than the insults and curses of the enemy, was the widespread, interminable robbery Rev. Porter continued to encounter. He observed soldiers and even officers stopping terrified individuals and families, mostly women and children, and wrenching from their arms the few belongings they had been able to salvage and carry with them, snatching away even such necessities as warm clothing and parcels of food, then tearing the blankets and shawls from their shoulders, leaving them little protection from the bitterly cold night. Quite often these stolen items of clothing and food were thrown into the flames or otherwise ruined by the bluecoats. Greedy soldiers who had found more valuable loot, and were already loaded down with it, would still stop to take more from the defenseless citizens.

Passing the cemetery of a church, the clergyman saw that even the dead were not being left unmolested in this orgy of pillage. Several coffins lay open beside open graves and tombs, and a small squad of bluecoats was pulling out a casket from another grave they had just dug up, looking for buried treasures, remembering that in other places they had plundered in the state, they had sometimes found gold rings on the withered hands of corpses, and once or twice, a coffin filled with silverware rather than a body.

Rev. Porter paused to watch the soldiers pry apart the coffin they had just pulled out of a new grave, then saw them laughing and gloating over it. They took the open casket and leaned it against a tree, so that the body inside–the ghastly, emaciated corpse of a young Confederate soldier–was propped up in a near standing position. A bluecoat put his face close to that of the dead man and said mockingly, "Poor lad! He looks hungry, don't he?" The soldier reached into his haversack, drew out a potato, and pushed it into the mouth of the corpse, eliciting raucous laughter from his comrades.

Trembling with indignation, Rev. Porter moved on. Rounding a corner, he caught sight of a young woman frantically stalking back and forth on the sidewalk in front of a burning house. She was wringing her hands and wailing piteously, then began screaming as a soldier emerged through the front door of the blazing dwelling.

The man, a soldier from Iowa who was apparently trying to help her, had gone inside to search for a lost child, and was now returning empty-handed.

The woman rushed up to the steps and tried to enter the house, but the soldier barred her way.

"There is no child in there!" he shouted.

"He is dead! He is dead!" she raved. "Oh, God, let me die with him!"

She struggled with him like a maniac, but he restrained her. After a short while she went limp in his arms, and he lowered her down to the street, where she collapsed in a heap, convulsed with sobs.

Dr. Porter approached the lady. Kneeling at her side, he was about to speak to her, when he heard the voice of another woman crying out wildly. A young black woman was rushing in their direction holding a child of two or three years in her arms.

"The child with me!" she was crying. "The child with me, Miz Bryan!"

The distraught mother looked up uncomprehending, her handsome face contorted in a mask of tragedy, and did not understand the girl until the child was brought close to her face. She seized the little boy, weeping and laughing hysterically. The child's nurse pulled on her sleeve and urged her to get to a place of safety, finding that the heat from the flames engulfing the house was becoming intolerable at such close proximity.

The soldier who had gone into the burning house to find the child lingered for a few moments, and as he looked down at the woman and her son, his rugged, soot-smeared face worked with pity and shame. Then, with a last glance at her burning house, he left her and hurried away. As Rev. Porter and the nurse helped the woman to her feet, some people who were passing by called her by name and took her under their care. He asked them where they were heading. An old gentleman, the only man in the group, answered that they were going to his sister's house.

"One of the Yankee generals has quartered himself there," he said, "so it will be safe. My sister sent word to us that she could offer us protection in her home tonight."

The strangers hurried on, and Rev. Porter continued on his way. As he turned down a street that was as yet apparently untouched by the flames, he saw some soldiers running ahead with bottles of turpentine and wads of cotton, then entering a house. Like most of the soldiers he had seen that night, these men were perfectly sober; none in this group seemed drunk in the least–except, he thought, with hatred. He watched through an open door a soldier setting fire to window curtains.

Rev. Porter reached the intersection of two streets where he recognized the friend he had been looking for, a foreign gentleman named Conrad who worked for Mr. William Beale's company in Charleston. Mr. Conrad had recently brought with him to Columbia valuable papers of the company, and of his brother, the Hanoverian consul, thinking that they would be safer here than in Charleston, but like many others who had sought security in the capital city, he had miscalculated.

Mr. Conrad, a slight, fair-haired man with a nervous manner, was standing before a group of women and girls. They were huddled together around an older, well-dressed lady who was weeping and holding her hands over her ears in a strange manner. As Rev. Porter drew closer he could see blood on her fingers, face, and shoulders.

"Oh, madame!" Mr. Conrad was saying in his thickly-accented but impeccable English, "This is an outrage! You and your daughters must come to my house. I shall afford you what protection I can."

"Mr. Conrad!" cried the minister. "What has happened?"

"Rev. Porter!" he was greeted vehemently. "Can you believe it? A soldier demanded Mrs. Richards' earrings, and before she could comply, the wretch tore them from her ears! The lobes of her ears are torn asunder!"

"A lady treated thus!" he gasped.

He removed a scarf he wore about his neck and placed it around the injured woman's head. She was in such a state of shock and fear that she could say nothing, but she quickly grasped the soft cloth and pulled it tightly around her ears with trembling hands. Her daughters, a group of five young women, three of whom were barely teenagers, thanked Rev. Porter as they sobbed in distress and commiseration for their mother.

"Come, ladies," said Mr. Conrad, urging them to walk with him. "Come with me. You will be safe at Mr. Beale's house."

Rev. Porter accompanied them, flanking the huddle of females who continued to cling to one another. At the house Mr. William Beale had rented for his employee, Mr. Conrad put his guests in the care of a trusted servant. Afterwards he begged a word alone with the minister, and took him into a parlor.

"I did not wish to repeat it before the ladies," he said in a low, confidential tone, "but the violence against Mrs. Richards was not the only reason that the ladies were so distraught. There was another woman with them a little while ago, a servant girl named Judith. Somehow, in the confusion and crowds, she became separated from them, and a little later, they heard a woman's screams, and they were certain that it was Judith's voice."

Mr. Conrad paused, and with a strange gulp, pulled out a handkerchief and held it to his mouth as he added, "I believe I heard those screams, too. Only think what that poor creature's fate must have been! I think–"

A wave of nausea swept over him, and, coughing and gasping, he ran into an adjoining room where a wash stand and basin could be seen through an open door. From the parlor, Rev. Porter could hear the sounds of his vomiting. He returned in a few minutes, wiping his mouth with a damp towel, and looking extremely pale.

"When I found Mrs. Richards and her daughters," Mr. Conrad went on weakly, "they had just spoken to some other ladies who had tried to take refuge in Sidney Park, but had to leave, because the soldiers were on a hill throwing down fireballs on the poor women and children trying to find safety there! Just before you met with us, there happened to be some officers on horseback nearby, riding along very calmly, like a patrol. I told them what I believed had happened to Judith, and they only looked at me and rode on. They said nothing–did nothing! I could not believe it! Mein Gott, mein Gott, I cried, why have you forsaken us?"

Rev. Porter experienced a sickly twinge in the pit of his own stomach, and suddenly felt so weak and faint that he had to sit down in a chair. He was trembling all over.

"Let me get you a little brandy," Mr. Conrad said anxiously.

He shook his head, waving off the suggestion.

"If you have any liquor, you had better get rid of it. The soldiers will be here sooner or later."

The foreign gentleman fell into a chair, panting with nervous exhaustion and distress.

"Yes, you are right, and well I know it. Just after dark I went to my office to bring home some important papers, and as I was coming back, an officer, a captain no less, stopped me and demanded to know what I was carrying in my satchels. It was very distressing to be accosted thus, as I had some of my brother's papers with me, as well as those of the company, and my own. I told the officer that I was the Hanoverian Consul, and was trying to save important papers from the fire."

Speaking very rapidly, Mr. Conrad had to pause to catch his breath, and then went on, "The captain ordered his men to take my baggage and go through it. Though they could plainly see the seal of the consulate on the documents, they took many of them and tossed the rest into a pile of burning debris. When I protested this robbery, the captain threatened to shoot me dead if I did not keep quiet. The soldiers also took my watch and every other valuable on my person, but those things I care very little for. The papers that were stolen or destroyed were of far greater value! There were drafts for great sums of money among them, our exchange on England, which I had made out for our stockholders! There is no way to stop payment on them to the thieves who have them now!"

"I am sorry for your loss," Rev. Porter responded faintly.

"In all my days in Hanover and America," Mr. Conrad groaned, "I never imagined I would ever behold such sights as I have seen in this city tonight! It appears that these men have been unleashed without restraint. When I tried to resist one of the soldiers who robbed me, he cursed me and said that he would drink up my heart's blood. Drink my heart's blood! Those were his very words! What kind of men are these? They seem to delight in the terror they inspire. And our women and children are at their mercy!"

When Rev. Porter placed his elbow on the arm of the chair, currents of agonizing pain shot up into his shoulder and down into his fingertips. At rest, he quickly became aware that most of his body was aching from both the injury and his chronic rheumatism, which had no doubt been aggravated that night by too much bodily strain and exposure to the cold. Glancing at a brandy decanter on a table, he changed his mind about a drink. Mr. Conrad got up and poured two glasses.

As they were finishing their brandy, they heard voices and noises which seemed to be originating from the house next door.

"Mr. Conrad," said the clergyman, "I believe there are soldiers in your neighbor's house. They will soon be in this one. You must get out. All of you must come with me."

"But where can we go?"

"My family has taken refuge in the state hospital. I shall return there. I must return now–I can take no more of this."

Mr. Conrad did not quite understand what Rev. Porter was talking about, but was so upset and so concerned for the ladies' safety that he did not bother to ask for any explanation. Realizing the imminent danger, he jumped up from his chair and called out for the servants. Within a few minutes the whole household was assembled at the door, and passed out of it just as soldiers were entering the yard.

The neighbor's house was igniting from several separate fires climbing up the exterior of the structure. On the piazza, Mr. Conrad noticed a wicker chair where he was used to seeing an old woman sit in the afternoons. It was being consumed, warping and melting away like the straw of a bonfire, and sending up sparks and glowing fragments that whirled around on the currents of convection created by the heat.

Toward the intersection, they had to cross the street to avoid the intense heat emanating from a house completely engulfed in flames, a two-story structure which seemed to be on the verge of collapse. Much of its facade had been devoured, so that much of its fiery interior was visible. When a wind gusted through, it breathed as if fed by a bellows, the flames whipping and swirling like tornadoes, then growing more furious, the ashes and cinders inside glowing a brighter red, like some great panting monster of fire. The winds had changed direction, and Rev. Porter thought they had diminished at least a little, but the fires continued to spread throughout the city in all directions regardless.

As they made their way back toward the state hospital, it became necessary to keep to the center of the street to avoid the debris falling from the structures all around them. At one corner showers of burning flakes and sparks rained down on them from a furious conflagration scarcely recognizable as a house or a building anymore, and the air was so hot and heavy with smoke at times that they could hardly breathe, and they quickened their pace in order not to suffocate.

Some of the frame edifices had caved in, others were about to, and the brick buildings were gutted by flames and sometimes looked as if they had partially exploded. Townspeople were still coursing through the streets, looking more and more panicked and desperate, while the soldiers continued to abuse and plunder them.

When they came within a few blocks of the asylum, Rev. Porter and his group had to stop to make way for a priest leading a procession of young girls, students of the Ursuline convent and school. All of them looked petrified with fear, but had been so well trained by the nuns, that they proceeded in a calm and orderly fashion, like disciplined little soldiers. Rev. Porter noticed the Mother Superior, a slender, pale woman who carried herself with great dignity. She was standing perfectly still as she watched her pupils pass. Her long, beautiful black robes were stained with ashes and bore the marks of burns and scorches. The clergyman motioned for her attention and spoke to her.

"Where are you taking these children?" he asked.

"For now," said the nun, "we shall take refuge in the churchyard, among the graves. I know not what else to do! Soldiers broke into the convent to loot it and it is now in flames and beyond all hope of saving. They took the chalice from the altar and drank from it, and then defiled the altar."

The lady went on, "We first went to our church, and two good officers protected the building from other soldiers who tried to set fire to it–more than once–but then we decided it was not safe for us there, either. Nowhere seems to be safe from these vandals! While our convent was burning, wicked soldiers taunted us, and asked us if we did not think that Sherman is greater than God."

"What blasphemy!" Rev. Porter exclaimed indignantly.

"Earlier today, that general himself promised us protection, but we see now what his promises are worth!"

"God will protect you, madam, and your charges," he said.

"May he do the same for you, sir, and yours," she replied.

He thanked her, and as the last of the procession of girls passed by, she stepped out to follow along behind them, holding out the flowing sleeves of her habit protectively, like the wings of a mother bird.

As the hospital came into sight, Rev. Porter noticed that a number of houses in the immediate vicinity of this building had so far escaped the flames. There were guards stationed along the fences every few yards, standing in front of residences which were obviously being protected as officers' quarters. In the same area, a group of what appeared to be very high-ranking officers was slowly riding along the street, looking all around and conversing among themselves. The clergyman felt sure that a certain tall, lean man on a fine sorrel horse must be General Sherman. Rev. Porter broke away from the others to try to get a better view of the general. He moved closer, but before he could get very far he was checked by an armed soldier warning him away. From this point, all he could see of the general's face–beneath the dark shadow cast by a wide-brimmed hat–was a grim mouth chewing on a cigar, the tip of a curving nose, and a strong, stubbled jaw.

Mr. Conrad called out to Rev Porter, begging him to come back. He and the ladies had paused to wait for him. The clergyman kept his eyes on the general as he rejoined them, his heart beating so fast—pounding with a murderous hatred and rage he had never known before—that he thought it must burst.

At some point in the very early morning hours, close to sunrise, the riotous soldiers were withdrawn. The arson ceased, and the fires soon died out.

Dawn broke in an eerie calm. In the hospital, many children were asleep, but most of the adults who were not ill or infirm were awake, and had been so all night, fearful that, at any moment, their place of refuge might also be consigned to the flames. They talked in hushed whispers and murmurs, speculating on what might happen today, and wondering how they would survive it, and all the days following. Mothers worried about feeding their children. All, in fact, were wondering where their next meal was to come from.

Rev. Porter went up to the roof of the hospital. There was a garden here. It was a place strangely beautiful and untouched, except for a dusting of ash visible on the leaves here and there, though the fresh scents of the greenery were smothered by the heavy odors of ashes and smoke which poisoned the air. He looked out, observing that columns of smoke were still rising up from smoldering pyres all around. Much of the central city was gone–half the buildings and dwellings, he estimated, if not more, had been destroyed. On block after block, except for numerous blackened chimneys and some remnants of brick walls and columns, little else remained standing.

Later in the morning, Rev. Porter conversed with a man who had gone out at daylight to see the results of the fires. The gentleman reported that the three railroad depots, as well as every house surrounding them, all the stores, several churches, a synagogue, the Ursuline convent and house, St. Mary's College, hotels, the old State House with its great library, and many other buildings–were now an indistinguishable mass of smoking ruins.

"What about Christ Church?" Rev. Porter asked the man.

"Also burned," he answered somberly.

Rev. Porter decided he would also go out and see all this for himself, so after his family and those who had taken refuge with them shared a carefully rationed breakfast of some cornbread and apples, the clergyman left the hospital alone and walked out into the desolated city. On the first street he went down he saw he saw a family gathered at the site of their former home, crying and mourning over it. They had perhaps thought to find something to salvage, but instead looked on nothing but charred timbers and ashes. On other streets, the same scene was repeated many times, and in the parks and common areas, bewildered, homeless families huddled close together, shivering in the cold without tents or any other kind of shelter except for the trees. In the burnt district, the trees and gardens were blasted and withered from the effects of the fires and smoke. Here a few poor souls were wandering about aimlessly, looking lost, nearly deranged, and more like ghosts than living beings. Amidst such devastation, even some of the living felt dead.

Several times Rev. Porter observed squads of soldiers busying themselves in a search for buried valuables. Directed by mounted officers, they were stabbing and boring into the ground with poles and rods, looking for the treasures that city residents might have hidden away in the earth. One group dug up a small wooden chest and smashed it open, and judging by their triumphant hoots and yells, he surmised that it must have contained a cache of gold or silverware.

As he reached the corner of Marion and Blanding streets, Rev. Porter glimpsed the remnants of his church, and had to cover his face and take in deep breaths to suppress his emotion. The large, once beautiful building was completely gutted. Its roof was gone, and its windows of gothic style were empty, their splendid glass panes shattered and melted. All that remained were the soaring, pointed arches of its outer brick walls. It was a sickening sight, yet somehow majestic; if not for the ugly blackening caused by the smoke and fire, the walls would have resembled some romantic ruin of an abbey in the English countryside.

While the clergyman surveyed the damage, a young Federal officer walking past stopped, turned, and approached him. His handsome face and his uniform were soiled with streaks of black soot.

"This must have been a very fine church," the captain remarked, nodding toward the remains.

"It was my church," Rev. Porter replied, barely audibly.

"You are a minister?"

The clergyman nodded, not taking his eyes off the ruined building. The officer also stared in that direction. After a few moments he spoke again, this time in a strained, tremulous tone.

"My father is a minister...and I wish to tell you, sir, that I am ashamed to own that I belong to the army which did this."

Rev. Porter looked at the young man, and their eyes met again. The captain's expression looked sincere and honest.

"Do you have a family here?" the officer asked.

"Yes, my wife, a daughter, and others..."

"I have a mother and two sisters," he said. "My god, what would I do if they were in such a plight as the poor women of Columba were last night, and are today! Stranger, if I were a Southern man in the sight of this burned city, I would never lay down my arms, not while the breath of life was in me."

He unbuttoned his coat and reached into a pocket. Drawing out a small leather wallet, he opened it and pulled out most of its contents–a considerable amount of gold coins and greenbacks.

"Take this," he insisted, holding out the money.

Rev. Porter hesitated, and before he could make any move to accept or refuse, the officer pressed the coins and cash into his hand.

"It will keep you from starvation for a while, at least," said the young man, and then, not waiting for an answer or a word of thanks, he turned and walked away at a hurried pace.

Rev. Porter was at first too stunned and sorrowful to fully comprehend what had just happened, to feel gratitude, or to have the presence of mind to express any, but possessing this unexpected fortune on his person, he automatically headed back to the hospital, fearing that it might be stolen from him by some less kindly soldier.

When he showed the money to his wife and daughter, they were astonished.

"Let me hide it in the secret pocket I sewed into my dress," offered Mrs. Porter. "There is room for it there."

Alicia agreed this was a good idea, and her mother took the money and hid it away under her skirt.

"God is watching over us!" she burst out tearfully, throwing her arms around her husband's neck. He embraced her and held her tightly for a long while. Later, Rev. Porter took Alicia aside and asked how long she thought their food would last.

"A day or two more," she answered, "if we are very careful. The doctor who is the head of the hospital told us he will try to provide some food for everyone as long as he can."

"I am glad to hear that, but still, we must be very careful. Even though we have the means to purchase food, there may be little or none to be purchased for a while, so we must keep to a strict ration. I don't think we ought to eat again until tonight–a late supper. I think we shall all be able to rest better with a little food in our stomachs, and we need to rest."

"How is your arm, Papa?" Alicia asked, touching his shoulder gently.

"It aches, and has become quite stiff, but the pain is tolerable. It is the least of my worries."

"You mustn't worry about us. We will bear up."

"I fear for your mother's health," he said.

"But Mama is over that illness, surely."

"Yes, but it weakened her, and I fear all this...will be too great a strain on her."

"She is stronger than you think, Papa," Alicia reassured him.

The next day was a Sunday. There were two other clergymen among the asylum refugees, a Baptist and a Presbyterian. Both were very elderly men. The first was too ill to speak; but the other offered to hold an informal service for anyone who wished to attend. Rev. Porter's body, especially his injured arm, ached severely that day, the coldest so far of the winter, and he did not accompany his family to the refectory, where they took the last seats available. Many others who came in after them stood along the walls, and children sat down on the floor.

Not having slept well the night before, Rev. Porter tried to sleep while they were gone, but the pain kept him awake. Having no distraction from it, nor the comfort of his family, he was glad when they returned. Reclining on a pallet, he asked his wife about the sermon, and she stroked his hair and face as she described it for him.

The following day they heard that the army of bluecoats was leaving the city, their vast mile-long wagon train gorged with even more spoils now. Having nowhere else to go, the Porters and the Crawfords remained at the hospital, while the others who had taken refuge with them managed to find shelter in the homes of friends and relatives who had not been burned out. On Tuesday morning Rev. Porter was feeling better, and decided to go out again. Alicia asked her father if she could accompany him.

"Do you think you can bear it?" he asked, searching her eyes deeply with his own.

"I can bear it," she answered, trying to stand a little taller before him. It was just dawning on her that she had been going about for several days with slumping shoulders and eyes often cast down to the ground in a blank, stunned, apathetic stare.

"Perhaps you ought to come with me, then," he said. "You can record what you have seen in your journal. I have begun one of my own, to record these horrible hours and days. I shall never forget what has been done to us, and I am determined that my grandchildren, and their children, shall not be ignorant of it, either."

The city seemed gutted from the heart. In the burnt district, Rev. Porter and his daughter walked along Sumter Street and saw only one house standing until they reached the last block before the college campus. Alicia was not as strong as she had imagined herself to be, and after several minutes of taking in the sight of ruin and rubbish, of hundreds of stark, blackened chimneys and columns, and other piteous remnants of once beautiful houses, she broke down into tears.

Her father stopped and put his arm around her as she wept. He said nothing, but waited for the outburst of emotion to pass, and then they walked on, picking their way over large and small heaps of debris.

It was a bitterly cold, overcast day. Few people were out. The leaden sky, the winds moaning through the ruins, and the absence of life in the once bustling city streets, added to the atmosphere of utter desolation.

Alicia was particularly distressed to see the ruins of the Gibbes mansion, knowing that it had contained an art and manuscript collection worthy of a museum, as well as the extensive collection of fossils and valuable library of Dr. Robert W. Gibbes, an eminent scientist. They heard that all his possessions had gone up in flames with the house, save one little statue, a marble bust of his son, the sole object of value which he had been able to carry out. The tall brick chimneys, and the roofless, scorched shell of the mansion's walls still stood, but they enclosed a nothingness now.

They went to view the ruins of the old State House, where so many valuable documents and books had gone up in flames with the building. After this they turned and went back to Sumter Street, retraced their steps several blocks, and then went down Blanding Street to see Christ Church.

Not far from the church, Alicia covered her eyes at the first glimpse of the ruined Clarkson family mansion, a home which she had always admired as one of the finest, most beautiful in the city, with a handsome, neoclassical colonnade surrounding the house. Now these massive columns were all that were left of the structure. The rest of it was ashes and rubble on the ground. Rev. Porter stopped to survey the destruction, and when Alicia uncovered her eyes, she saw an old gentleman standing a few yards away, also looking on the same dismal scene. After a few moments he approached them, remarking sadly, "What an admirable house this once was."

"It was indeed," Rev. Porter replied in the same tone.

"I watched it burn the other night. Terrible as it was, there was something awe-inspiring about it," he went on.

Rev. Porter eyed the man doubtfully.

"I am sure the fires of hell are an awe-inspiring sight, too, sir," he said brusquely.

"Oh, I did not mean to imply that I enjoyed the experience, sir, oh no, by no means," the man quickly rejoined. "I would have given my life to save the place. It belonged to a kinsman of mine. Do you know Colonel Clarkson?"

"No, I do not."

Alicia left her father's side and walked off a little ways to look at the gardens behind the ruins of the house. Strangely enough, the shrubberies, rose bushes, and trees looked largely untouched by the conflagration which had consumed the mansion.

The stranger, who introduced himself as Mr. Whilden, came closer to Rev. Porter and said in a confidential tone, "The burning of the house was not the only crime committed here that night."

The clergyman breathed a heavy sigh and steeled himself for what he was about to hear, but at the same moment, he began to feel a heavy malaise both physical and psychic, as though he were reaching the limits of his endurance.

"Before the house was set fire, some soldiers seized Mrs. Clarkson. She was spared, but her maid was not so fortunate," Mr. Whilden continued, but before he could say more he was suddenly interrupted by Rev. Porter, who waved a hand in the air.

"Enough!" he said brokenly. "Enough! I cannot hear more."

"Are you unwell, sir?" asked Mr. Whilden, observing his labored breathing.

The clergyman drew in a deep breath and exhaled slowly to calm himself.

"I have heard and seen too much, sir," he answered. "Too much."

Mr. Whilden gave a nod of understanding, and walked away just as Alicia returned. She was trembling. Her father thought she was cold, and reached out to put his arm around her, but she shrank away and put up quivering, fisted hands to her chin. When she spoke, there was a low pitch to her voice he had never heard before, startling in its virulence.

"How I hate those who did this!" she seethed. "I hate them all with a passion! I wish they had all burned with the city! I wish—"

She burst into tears again and shook with sobs, unable to finish what she had meant to say. Rev. Porter put his uninjured arm around his daughter and led her away.

On the way back to the hospital, they passed the city market. Its tall brick spire had collapsed, and the rest of the place was one great burnt-out shell supported by arches which looked as though they might crumble at any moment. As they paused to survey this area, Rev. Porter caught sight of a lady he knew making her way toward them. She was one of his parishioners, a highly educated woman who had taken to teaching to support her family after the death of her husband. Though Northern-born, she had lived in South Carolina many years and had cast her lot with its people. Her name was Reese, and she was a teacher at the ladies' college in Barhamville, just outside of Columbia.

"Mrs. Reese!" he called to her.

With very small feet, this plump, dark-haired lady of middle age was stepping over a pile of bricks, and nearly stumbled over the hem of her skirt. Rev. Porter rushed to her side and took her hand to assist her.

"Thank you!" she said, in a clipping, clear voice. "That is twice I have nearly fallen today."

"What of Barhamville?" he asked her.

"Not burned, thank God, though we did suffer some losses," she answered. "Dr. Marks managed to procure guards for us. Even so, they could not keep out the soldiers who kept intruding and offering us insults. I am very thankful all our girls were sent away to North Carolina before the Yankees took the city."

"Yes, that was wise. You are all safe?"

Mrs. Reese laughed mirthlessly.

"Is anyone safe these days?" she replied.

She could see that Alicia had been crying, and sadly patted her cheek with a look of commiseration.

"I know it is hard to bear, my dear," she said gently. "Is this the first time you have come out to see the city?"

Alicia nodded.

"I walked into town two days ago, while the army was still here, to ask for another guard, but was not successful. I wanted to weep the whole time, but, sir, I would not let myself. I would not let those devils see me weep. I think I shall never, never shed another tear."

"Oh, don't say that!" sighed Alicia, feeling her own tears rising up in her again.

Mrs. Reese stepped closer and studied her face.

"You look so pale, my dear," she remarked solicitously. "Are you unwell?"

Her father suddenly noticed his daughter's pallor, too, and took her arm on his own.

"I am fine," Alicia protested.

She had been feeling very weak and a little queasy for several days, but attributed this to the emotional ordeal she had been suffering, as well as the low quality and quantity of her food lately. Now the way Mrs. Reese and her father looked at her, made her wonder if there was some other cause.

"I shall take you back to the hospital now, Alicia," said Rev. Porter.

"Your house was burned?" asked Mrs. Reese, as she took hold of his arm to detain him. "Why don't you and your family come and stay at the college with us? There are plenty of unoccupied rooms there, and we even have vegetable gardens, and we hid away some chickens and a milch cow, if the stragglers do not steal them."

Rev. Porter grasped her hands in gratitude.

"Can you accommodate so many?" he asked.

"How many of you are there?"

"Including myself, there are five of us, and two servants."

"Seven of you will be no problem. We cannot guarantee that you will be well fed, but I believe we can provide better and more plentiful rations than those being doled out now to the citizens of Columbia. I'm told that the gracious Sherman left behind a few hundred head of starved, sickly cattle–stolen from farms in this state."

"Thank you, my good lady," said Rev. Porter feelingly. "Thank you a thousand times."

"It's a walk of nearly two miles to Barhamville," she reminded him. "Is everyone in your party up to it?"

"I think so, though my wife has been somewhat ill."

"And your daughter, it seems to me," said Mrs. Reese.

She glanced at Alicia again, then up at the sky.

"If the weather permits, you all ought to make the walk this afternoon. Most likely it will be warmer then."

"We will certainly do that, Mrs. Reese, if the weather permits."

"In that case, we shall expect you today."

Rev. Porter and Alicia hurried back to the hospital to tell Mrs. Porter the good news. She looked so heartened by it, her husband considered that it was the best medicine she could have received. The Crawfords were also very much relieved to hear of Mrs. Reese's offer, and everyone made ready for the journey.

In the early afternoon, the skies cleared, and bright sunshine warmed the little group as they walked the two miles to Barhamville. When the academy building came into clear view, Rev. Porter saw a lady standing in the circular driveway, well away from the school, talking to an elderly man on horseback, and he soon discerned that it was Mrs. Reese. She seemed to be holding a very animated conversation with the old gentleman, throwing up her arms expressively, shaking her head, and at one point, doubling over with her hands on her knees–but whether in laughter or distress, it was hard to tell. The man on horseback tipped his hat and rode off in a direction away from the city, and Mrs. Reese turned back toward the school.

Rev. Porter called out to her. She swung round, waved, and walked out to meet him. After some introductions, Mrs. Reese informed the group that the gentleman on horseback, a Mr. Carter, was one of the aldermen of the city. He was on his way to check on some relatives who lived in the countryside, and had stopped to inquire about the conditions at Barhamville.

"I told him we had fared better than many," she went on, in her brisk, energetic way of speaking, "and that I hope he finds his niece's family as well."

"Any other news?" Rev. Porter asked curiously.

"News? Oh! Oh, yes!" she answered in a sort of half-groan, half-laugh, putting a hand to her heart. "General Sherman and his officers are saying that the fire was accidental!"

"Accidental!" the clergyman repeated incredulously.

"Well they might wish to disown such a crime!" Dr. Crawford cried angrily.

As Mrs. Porter and Mrs. Crawford made similar exclamations, Mrs. Reese noticed with concern how tired and pale Alicia looked. As soon as the ladies finished speaking, she encouraged them all to come inside the school and rest.

"You must be fatigued from your long walk," she said. "Shall we go in now?"

They followed her along the drive. Alicia had visited friends at Barhamville before, and, glancing around as she walked, noticed how different things looked now. The school building itself, at least on the outside, looked largely untouched, but the formerly pristine lawn and grounds of the ladies' academy bore the impress of the invading army. It was marked with scores of blackened patches from numerous campfires, the debris of eating and drinking, the scattered trash of papers and other odds and ends, and the stumps of trees hewn down for firewood.

At the front door, the headmistress greeted Rev. Porter and the others, and Mrs. Reese showed them to their quarters.

That evening, in her own comfortable, cozy room, Alicia took out her most treasured possessions–her husband's letters–and, arranging them chronologically, she began to read them. A page was missing from one or two, and corners were scorched or burnt away here and there, but she had managed to preserve most of them, and most were intact. After she had read a few of the letters

Aleck had sent to her early in their marriage, she opened his last letter, in which he reminisced about their most recent time together in Columbia. Drifting into her own daydreams, Alicia remembered their walks in Sidney Park, the sweetness of their days and nights together, all their conversations—until the memory of that happiness became too bittersweet to bear, and she put away the letters in a flood of tears.

There was a knock at the door, and she heard her mother's voice.

"May I come in, Alice?" asked Mrs. Porter.

Wiping her face with a handkerchief, Alicia went to the door and opened it.

"What is wrong, dear?" her mother asked with concern.

"I was reading Aleck's letters," she said in a strained voice. "Oh, Mama, I miss him so."

Mrs. Porter put an arm around her daughter, and they sat down on the bed together.

"That is enough reason for tears, Alice," said Mrs. Porter. "But I think it is something more. It is all the strain of these past weeks, all we have been through. You have not been yourself in a long while, dear."

"I wanted to be strong, strong for your sake, and Papa's, but I'm afraid I have not," she lamented.

"Nonsense. You have been a great help and comfort to us."

"I should have been more of a help, but so often, I found myself crying for really no reason—"

"Good heavens! No reason for tears! You have certainly had many reasons for them," her mother protested.

"I tried to hide them from you and Papa, and everyone else, so that you would not worry about me."

"But I am concerned for you, Alice. Mrs. Reese says that you look ill, and I think so, too. Are you feeling unwell?"

Alicia admitted that she was. Mrs. Porter asked her more questions, some touching on very delicate and personal matters, and after hearing the answers, explained the reason for her weakness and malaise.

"I think there is no doubt of it," she said, lifting her lips in the first smile Alicia had seen on her face in many days. "You are expecting, Alice. You are going to be a mother, my dear."

CHAPTER FIFTEEN

THROUGHOUT FEBRUARY GEORGE LOOKED for a letter from Marguerite as anxiously as a castaway searches the horizon of the sea for a ship, but none arrived. He had only heard from his brother once, early in the month, and assumed that Albert and his family were in Darlington. Late in February news came that Columbia had been burned, as well as Winnsboro, Barnwell, Orangeburg, and many other towns and villages, but it seemed that General Sherman was now heading for North Carolina, and there was no hint that Greenville had been visited by his army. George convinced himself that Marguerite and her family must be all right, and told himself it was not reasonable to expect any letters from her soon. The enemy had been destroying the railroads wherever they went, and that fact, if nothing else, could account for the disruption of the mails.

Since January, the starving prisoners at Fort Pulaski had been slowly dying off, one or two each week, and George began to wonder if he would die in this place. On the meager rations, he observed himself growing weaker day by day, losing his physical strength as well as the exceptional health he had always enjoyed. Every week he inspected his arms and legs and saw that they were a little thinner each time. Then the symptoms of scurvy became more pronounced in his body. His gums were growing spongy, dark, and swollen, and bled sometimes. He suffered with a chronic fatigue and continued aches in his joints, and his formerly thick hair was thinning.

The effects of slow starvation, and all the ailments that went with it, were clearly visible among many of the prisoners now. In desperation, some began concocting schemes of escape, but most did not have the energy to begin the first steps of such drastic measures, let alone carry them to completion. Their bodies infested with lice, they moved around listlessly, aimlessly, or lay in their bunks, too weak or sick or cold to do anything else. There were vacant looks in many eyes, as time went on, one or two of the men seemed to be on the verge of insanity. So many of the prisoners had become so debilitated that they were no longer sent to the prison hospital. Even the sickest remained in the casemates with the others. Those with the more acute form of scurvy were marked with sores, knotted blood blisters, and livid patches where the blood had spilled out under the skin, as the tissues of their bodies disintegrated. Others suffered terribly with chronic diarrhea, dysentery, and other ailments.

So disturbing were the sights within the casemates now that the guards began to stay away. They walked their rounds of duty on the parapets and the parade ground, showing up in the prisoners' quarters only when necessary. Sometimes they tried to help, sneaking in a few pieces of bread or meat, and on one occasion, an officer of the guard took his men fishing in the river, and brought back a seine full of fish for the prisoners under the cover of darkness.

The weather in February continued bitterly cold, and the ration of wood for the stoves was barely enough to keep the fires going for more than a few hours. At night, the men without blankets paced the floors to generate a little warmth, and would sleep during the day under borrowed coverings.

The officers had given up asking for more food, but a few of them were permitted to go to Colonel Brown to plead for more fire wood. The quarters where he lived in warmth and comfort with his wife were located across the parade ground directly opposite the prison casemates, and when the little delegation of prisoners came to his door, they caught a glimpse of a well-furnished room with a cheerful fire burning in a grate.

After listening to their petitions, the colonel replied feelingly, "Gentlemen, I am very sorry for you. I have done all I could to prevent the enforcement of the orders under which you suffer, but I am bound to obey them, and I can do nothing for you."

They asked for some lumber to partition off part of their casemate for use as a hospital, but this request was also refused.

"Gentlemen, I can do nothing for you," he repeated somberly, "absolutely nothing."

With these words still ringing in their ears, the discouraged officers returned to the frigid casemates and reported the bad news about the firewood to their fellow prisoners.

Colonel Brown was obliged to make an inspection of the prisoners' quarters every Sunday, but as time wore on, and the men in his charge grew more sickly and emaciated, he found it more and more difficult to look at them. During each inspection tour he passed through the casemates as quickly as possible, with a fixed, constrained expression, the muscles of his clenched jaws working nervously, keeping his head lowered and facing straight on, as if not wishing to see or acknowledge what was around him. On the few occasions when he did glance at the prisoners, he seemed appalled.

The colonel was known to be a religious man, but upon emerging from the prison casemates one morning, he was heard to utter a fearful oath. Not long afterwards, a rumor about him began making the rounds. It was said that he had requested to be transferred back into field service rather than starve prisoners of war to death.

Increasingly despondent and obsessed with the thought of his death, George tried to determine some scientific method of calculating how much longer he had on this earth. He observed the progress of various diseases in the other men, especially those who seemed to be dying, but since each man's strength and constitution was different, he found no way to make an accurate prediction. Much of the time, what hope that was left in him rebelled against these morbid ruminations, and he refused to believe that God would allow him to perish so miserably, but hopeful or not, he began to think only of himself and his survival–until something happened that startled him out of his self-absorption. His cousin Robert, who had begun showing symptoms of dysentery, collapsed by his bunk one morning after returning from the latrine.

George and Captain Levy rushed to him and found him unconscious and feverish. They arranged a cushion of old clothes for him, lifted him into a lower bunk, and covered him with two blankets. George went to the gate and, seeing a passing guard, called out to him. The soldier reluctantly walked in.

"We need the surgeon," George pleaded. "Please, ask him to come to us."

The guard sighed, and though he knew it would be useless to bring a doctor, he did as George asked. The physician arrived within fifteen minutes. After examining Robert, he announced that there was really nothing he could do for him, but he ordered some hot tea and crackers. Robert was regaining consciousness, and as he smelled the aroma of the tea, his eyes fluttered open. George helped him sit up and drink it, careful not to let one drop go wasted. Robert drank a third of the tea, and the rest was used to soak and soften the hard crackers so that he could eat them.

For a day or two, though Robert continued very weak, with an unabated fever, he said that he felt better. It happened at that time that the guards provided the unexpected boon of fresh fish, and the sickest were given an extra portion. He felt so strengthened by the food at first that he sat up in his bunk and even walked around a little, but within a few hours he was found slumped over the tubs in the latrine, a bloody emission from his bowels pooling at his feet. Captains Wells and Levy cleaned him up as best they could, changed his clothes, and brought him back to his bed.

George sat by Robert's side for the rest of the day, and throughout the evening. His friend Captain Levy also kept close by, and helped George keep the sick man clean and comfortable as possible. One by one, other prisoners came to his bed to see him or inquire about him. Every officer respected the young parson, and many felt themselves indebted to him for the spiritual care and counsel he had always provided. Robert drifted in and out of consciousness, and when awake, seemed to be in great pain with abdominal cramps. George procured some opiates for him to make him more comfortable. Under their influence, he slept through the night peacefully.

The next morning, after George administered a smaller dose of the painkiller, Robert was able to eat a few bites of one of the corn meal cakes. It had been cooked in the same pan in which some of the fish had been fried the day before, and had more taste than usual.

George tried to cheer his cousin by reminiscing about happier days of their childhood together.

"Remember when Albert and I visited you in Beaufort for the summer?" he asked, smiling and patting Robert's hand.

"I remember," answered Robert, returning a weak smile. "You two got me into all sorts of trouble."

"We did, didn't we?" George laughed. "You were such a good boy, we felt it our duty to get you into at least a little trouble with our badness."

"Oh, it was only mischief. You and Albert were good boys, too."

"No, no, not half as good as the parson's son."

George kept on talking and reminiscing until he noticed Robert growing drowsy again.

"Do you wish to sleep now?" he asked.

"I am feeling rather sleepy," Robert yawned, but as George made a move to get up from his bedside chair, his cousin took hold of his arm. Something in his look made George lean closer, and Robert whispered to him, "I know I am dying. I can feel it."

"You don't know that," George promptly contradicted him.

"You've been looking so discouraged, George. From the things you say, you seem to think that we are losing this war."

George made no answer to this, but did not deny it.

"It's like the end of the world, isn't it? It's the end of this world for me, anyway. I know how much you wished that we would win this war, and I know how you feel. I used to feel that way myself. I don't anymore, though. I don't think I am long for this world...so it really doesn't matter...for me. I have been too much attached to worldly things, but I feel that attachment dissolving. That's how I know I shall be gone soon."

"Don't say such things," George responded irritably, adding in a more soothing tone, "Don't you worry about the war, Robbie. We're out of it for now, anyway. I'm sure they'll resume better rations for us soon. This can't continue much longer. Just hold on, hold on."

After a long nap, Robert woke up and asked for a pencil and paper. With what little strength he had left, he sat up and wrote a letter to his wife. When he was finished, he folded it and showed it to George.

"Will you see that she gets this letter?" he asked, handing him the folded cover addressed to Mrs. Robert Porter in Camden.

"I will do my best, Robbie."

"Thank you, cousin."

Robert seemed resigned to his fate, but there were moments when a small measure of physical strength seemed to return to him, and along with it, some thought that recovery might be possible. He asked George and others to pray with him for strength to submit patiently to God's will, whatever it may be.

Then, early one morning, Robert began throwing up blood. George put his hand on his wrist and could feel that his pulse was very weak. A wave of sickening dread passed through him, but he tried not to show what he was feeling, telling himself that there may yet be some hope. He begged the surgeon to do more for his cousin, but was told that the young man was beyond any medical help.

When, after taking a dose of opium, Robert exhibited signs of delirium, George lost control of his emotions and began to weep. Robert slowly came to his senses and saw his cousin covering his face.

"You mustn't mourn for me, George," he said gently, his voice barely stronger than a whisper. "You are taking this too hard. All is well with me. And do you know, I feel very happy, because I am sure that you will survive, and return home."

George looked up and wiped his face dry with a tattered handkerchief.

"Do you?"

"Yes," said Robert. "I feel certain that you will get back to your home, even if it is in ruins."

"I wish I had your faith."

"You have your measure. You must do with it what you can. God will help you."

"I haven't your faith, Robert...and what little I had, well, I fear I am losing that, too."

"You mustn't let that happen, cousin."

George glanced toward the casemate arch and noticed Captain Levy standing there. Robert saw him, too, and said he wished to speak with the captain. Levy remained where he was for the moment and made a gesture to indicate that he wanted a private word with George, so he left Robert's side and went to him.

"He wants to see you now, Joseph. He is sinking—"

George's voice broke on the last word and rose up in pitch approaching a wail. Covering his face again, he walked off unsteadily, shaken with sobs. Disturbed, Captain Levy hesitated, but managed to hide his apprehension as he walked in and took the chair beside Robert's bed.

"George said you are looking better today," he lied cheerfully. "I think he is right."

"I don't think I am feeling better."

"I have seen men much sicker than you recover," the captain pretended to scoff.

"I have never had a strong constitution," said Robert. "I suppose I wasn't cut out to be a soldier."

"Nonsense. You are young, and quite able to overcome this."

The young man shook his head slightly and stared up at the bunk floor above him.

"I am sure I shall never leave this place alive," he sighed.

"You will," the captain protested. "We will leave together, and go back to Charleston. You shall have supper with me at my father's house."

"A very fine supper I'm sure it would be," said Robert, looking at Levy with a glimmer of interest and pleasure.

"The very finest, Robbie. Whatever your heart desires! There will be no restraint to our gluttony."

"Ah-h, real food," he groaned longingly. He closed his eyes and tried to imagine it.

Remembering the farewell meal which had been prepared for him on the eve of his departure for Virginia, Captain Levy described in detail a sumptuous feast for his friend's imaginary delectation. He stopped when he saw Robert wince with pain and suddenly draw in a deep, rattling breath. The sound of it made Levy sick with fear, and he began to tremble slightly under his loose clothes. He stroked his friend's hair to comfort him. The young man opened his eyes and looked at the captain affectionately.

"I shall pray for you, Joseph," he said.

Robert's lips curved into a faint smile, and his eyes sparkled momentarily. Levy smiled sadly and nodded in response.

"When you are better, we must resume your Hebrew lessons," he said. "You are my best pupil, you know."

"As I am your only pupil, that is not a great compliment."

Levy laughed softly and stroked his hair again.

"If we do get back to Charleston, what will you do?" Robert asked him.

"If the war continues, and if I am able to do so, I shall go back into the army."

"You are a good soldier, Joseph."

Robert suddenly shivered violently, and then writhed in pain under his blanket, his face contorted in agony. After that, he grew calm, and his face took on a sleepy look. He sought Levy's hand and weakly pressed it.

"Tell the men, I love them all," he said.

Though Levy had fought hard against them, tears sprang into his eyes, and his throat was suddenly so strangled with emotion that he could hardly speak.

"I will," he choked out.

"I like to think, while I was among you, I was a chaplain of a sort, if not an official one..."

"You have served these men well. No official chaplain could have done better."

Robert closed his eyes and slipped into unconsciousness, or sleep–Levy did not know which. The captain rose and turned away from the bed with a sob, and left the room weeping uncontrollably.

When Robert woke up, George was sitting by his bed with a prayer book. There was no priest present to minister to him, but his cousin read to him from the order for the visitation of the sick. Robert kept his eyes closed as he listened, and George wondered if he had fallen asleep, but as soon as he finished those passages, the dying man asked him to read the communion of the sick. Less than an hour later, he was gone.

As darkness drew on, the prisoners placed a few of their candles around Robert's bunk and kept a kind of vigil there as long as they were allowed to do so. The officers were standing and sitting around the body, speaking their informal eulogies in hushed voices, or recalling to each other things Robert had said and done.

George had not slept more than a few hours in several nights. He sat by the bed quietly with a bowed head, nearly overcome with physical and emotional exhaustion. All emotion was wrung out of him now.

Eventually Captain Levy walked into the casemate and sat down at some distance, listening to the words of his fellow officers. One was saying, "He had a gentle, loving nature, and cared for us all."

The others nodded in solemn agreement. Then they noticed the captain, and beckoned him.

Captain Levy slowly rose and walked over to the bunk. His eyes were dry now, but red as fire from much weeping. His nose and lips were swollen and flushed, his expression grim.

"You were his friend, Captain," said Ned Wells. "Have you anything to say?"

Levy paused, looking down at Robert's pallid, lifeless face.

"What is there to say, when a man has been starved to death?" he finally answered very quietly.

His chest then heaved with a deep, tremulous breath, and a look of anger hardened his face.

"I only pray that God puts a saber in my hand again before this war is over. That is all I have to say."

He turned from them and walked out of the casemate. The mourners hung their heads and fell speechless. After a few minutes of this silence, an officer began to softly sing the hymn known to be Robert's favorite, and the others joined in one by one.

The unhappy duty of writing to Robert's wife and family naturally fell to George, but he found it very difficult to find any words. How did one begin such a terrible message? He had no idea if his communications would even reach them in the wrecked, dislocated, desolate condition of the state, but at last he composed two letters, folded them together, and addressed them to Rev. Paul Porter, Columbia, S.C.

One morning in mid-February, as George was chewing on his breakfast of a corn meal cake, he felt a sharp pang in his jaw. He swallowed what was in his mouth and put a finger inside to probe the sore spot, finding that one of his molars was cracked. The tooth was slightly loose to the touch, and when he unintentionally moved it he experienced an excruciating pain. He wondered if scurvy was now affecting his teeth, and grew anxious that he might lose some of them to the disease.

Eventually, his whole mouth seemed to ache and throb. George thought the torment would eventually diminish, but hours passed, and it only seemed to grow worse. When he could bear it no longer, he asked for permission to see the prison surgeon. Escorted by a guard, he left the prison casemate and went out into the open air for the first time in a long while, walking beyond the walls of the fort to a house that served as the post hospital. It was a frigid, windy day, and dark clouds were growing ever thicker overhead, portending rain.

The guard led George through the large front room which was the main ward. Here most of the beds were occupied with only the sickest officers from the prison, who had only lately been allowed hospital care. George waited impatiently while the soldier left him in a hallway to go and look for the physician. The soldier returned in a few minutes wearing an expression of disgust.

"You can go in now," he said, nodding toward a particular door.

The prisoners liked the surgeon for his kindness and friendliness, but he was given to spells of heavy drinking, and when George walked into his office, he saw that the doctor seemed to be suffering with a terrible hangover. He was still somewhat drunk as he sat at a desk with his head in his hands, and did not acknowledge his visitor until George spoke to him. A fire was dying in the grate, but the room was still comfortably warm, and George felt a slight thawing of his limbs. He felt faint, whether from the warmth of the room or the pain of his mouth, or both, and staggered to a chair in front of the desk.

"What is it?" asked the doctor, a balding man of forty-five who looked much older.

After his faintness passed, George explained about the broken tooth.

"Most likely it will have to be pulled, but...you will have to wait until I—until I am stronger. How did you injure the tooth?"

"I'm not sure. I think I bit down on something like a little stone in the cornbread I ate yesterday, but I didn't notice the damage until this morning," George replied.

"The same thing happened to me once," the doctor sighed. "I was grinding my teeth in my sleep, because of a bad dream, I suppose, and when I woke, my tooth was cracked in two. It had to be pulled, of course. Are you in great pain?"

George nodded. The doctor offered him opium.

"I will take that for the pain," said George, anxiously leaning forward, "but I am in need of something more, something for scurvy."

"It is all I can give you," answered the physician. "You know that."

He leaned back in his chair and studied George with a scowling expression.

"You think because I am drunk that I shall acquiesce?" he demanded irritably. "I am not as drunk as you may think. It's true I have remedies that would help you, but I am under orders not to offer such treatments to prisoners. I am not permitted to do anything but ease your pain."

"Why not?"

"I am not allowed to do anything but relieve your pain," he repeated dully, but after a few moments, studying George with pity, he momentarily roused himself from his semi-stupor, and drew closer to his patient to offer this piece of sober advice, "Save yourself, man! Take the oath!"

George's face flushed a bright red as he rose to his feet, and he answered in a voice husky with fury.

"I'll be damned if I'll swear an oath of allegiance to such a government that would do this to men—not while there's still hope I have one of my own!"

His whole face was throbbing violently, but George was hardly conscious of the pain as he walked away from the man in a state of shock. As his anger subsided, his mind was reeling with one idea—that his fate had just been sealed, and that a death sentence had just been passed on him.

"So I'm to die of scurvy," he thought, blinking convulsively in disbelief.

Just outside the door, suddenly feeling faint again, he swayed to one side. Black spots began appearing and multiplying in front of his eyes, and he leaned against a wall to keep himself from falling. A young man standing nearby saw him and helped him to a chair. George thought he recognized the man as one of his fellow prisoners, and his name—Lewis—came to mind. One of the youngest of the officers, he was a second lieutenant in rank. Masses of shaggy, curly blonde hair covered his head, and his lips were nowhere to be seen under a drooping mustache that was of a ruddier, darker color.

"Is that you, Lieutenant Lewis?" George asked, fighting the faintness trying to take hold of him.

"It is Lewis," the young officer answered. "I have been on parole here for a while as a nurse. Let me get you some water."

When the lieutenant returned with a tin cup, the surgeon stepped out of his office and spoke to George.

"You had better wait here, Major," he said. "I'll get to that tooth of yours in an hour or two."

After directing the nurse to put George in a bed and prepare some opium for him, he went back into his office, closing the door behind him. Lieutenant Lewis took George's arm and led him to a bed at the far end of the room. All the other patients were in beds on the other side. As soon as George finished drinking the water, the young man took the tin cup and left him again. He came back a few minutes later, this time with a cup full of steaming broth.

"This is good soup," he said, handing the cup to George, who began consuming its contents greedily.

"Our sick get better rations here," the lieutenant remarked. "And you're getting the best. It's what's fed to the sick soldiers of the garrison."

Lewis squatted down next to the bed and watched George finish off the soup, and when that was gone, he pulled a small yellow apple out of his pocket.

"Can you eat this?" he asked.

"I could eat it even if I had no teeth," George replied.

Though the chewing was very painful, he devoured the apple, gnawing away at the piece of fruit until there was nothing left except a tiny piece of stem.

"Thank you for the food, Lieutenant," he said gratefully, taking the young man's hand for a moment. "God bless you for it."

"I am glad to help. I wish I could give such help to all our men. I wish–"

The lieutenant stopped, cast a look around the room, then leaned closer to George and said in a low voice, "You could help me, Major Taylor."

"What do you mean?" George whispered.

"I am going to escape. I was born not far from here. My family's farm is less than twenty miles away. I don't know if they are still there, but there are certainly people in the area who know me, and would help me. You could come with me, Major Taylor. I can use your help. I was hoping at least one of our men in this ward would recover sufficiently to go with me, but they are all too ill and weak. Some are dying."

"How will you escape?" asked George, suddenly feeling more clear-headed and alert.

"I am simply going to walk out of this house after dark. The river is less than a quarter of a mile from here. I'm going to steal a boat."

"Aren't guards there?"

"There is usually one guard on duty at the pier, but there are boats on shore some distance away. Are you with me?"

George hesitated, remembering an attempted escape that had occurred Christmas night. In late November, an officer had discovered an old trapdoor concealed under his bunk. The door opened into a subterranean chamber, where he and seven comrades spent weeks digging into a casemate which was not part of the prison. Finally breaking through the floor of that room, they found themselves in the prison commissary. They made a long rope from blankets and clothes, lowered it out of the window, and under the cover of darkness and a dense fog, climbed down, swam the moat, and made their way to a point on the river where they knew that boats could be found. It turned out, however, that these boats were well guarded, and the eight prisoners were captured and returned to the fort. As punishment, they were put in close confinement without food for several days. George knew that if the lieutenant's plan failed as miserably, the same punishment would await them, and he was afraid that a stretch of days without any nourishment might be the death of him, or at least the beginning of the end.

"Are you sure there is only one guard?" he pressed the lieutenant.

"I said there is usually just one. Since Christmas, the boats have been chained and locked."

"Then how shall we get one?"

The lieutenant smiled, raising the corners of his big mustache.

"I have a file," he said. "I found one among the old medical instruments. So, I repeat, are you with me, Major?"

"When do you plan to do this?" George asked.

"If you pretend to be unconscious or delirious with the opium, I think the surgeon will allow you to stay here for the night, but no longer–so it must be tonight."

George began considering the matter, weighing the risks against the possible rewards, but then, remembering his earlier thought–that he was already under a death sentence anyway–he immediately made up his mind. If he had to stay in this place much longer, in close confinement or not, he would surely perish.

"I'm with you," he told the lieutenant.

When the doctor was ready to see George, the lieutenant administered only a minuscule dose of opium to him.

"If your tooth is already loose," Lewis had told him earlier, "you should be able to bear the pain. Afterwards, pretend that you are losing consciousness, and I'll tell the surgeon I perhaps gave you too much of the drug, and suggest that you spend the night here in the hospital. I'm sure he won't object."

George did as he was instructed, and after the surgeon pulled the tooth, he agreed to let the major keep his bed for the night, just as Lewis had predicted. His gums bled profusely for a while, and he felt so weak and groggy from the painful extraction and the loss of blood that he scarcely had to feign incapacitation, at least for a while. He drifted into a half-dozing, half-conscious state, losing the direction of his thoughts, which wandered to the past, until he finally fell asleep. A few hours later, when the doctor left the hospital, Lieutenant Lewis gave George another tin of beef broth, some soft bread, and several cups of tea. The pain in his jaw had diminished to a dull ache by this time, and he felt revived and strengthened by the food and drink.

Just before dusk it began raining. The winds blustered and blew raindrops against the windowpanes for about an hour, then died down, and after another hour of drizzling rain, the skies slowly cleared. The doctor returned to the house after a supper with the garrison officers, and after checking on his patients for the night, retired to his private rooms.

"He'll drink himself to sleep now," Lewis whispered to George.

They waited another hour. Making sure all the other men were asleep on his way out, Lieutenant Lewis left the ward for a few minutes. He returned with a canvas bag, a file, and two overcoats.

"Are you ready?" he asked.

George got up from the bed as quietly as possible and followed Lewis to a window.

"There is a guard out front," he said, lifting the sash slowly and carefully. "Keep low, and stay close to me. We'll have some cover in the high grasses until we reach the trees."

They climbed through the window and lowered themselves down outside. As George's feet hit the ground they slid a little on the wet, slippery grass. The soles of his old shoes were worn smooth and thin, and had several cracks and holes in them. The two men crossed an open area at a run, then slowed to a walk, and, moving at that pace, crouched behind the high grasses and weeds, until they reached the woods bordering the river. Briars and dead branches caught at their clothes as they slowly picked their way through the trees in the darkness. The moonlight was very dim behind a covering of clouds.

At the waters' edge, they stealthily moved along the bank, and soon the pier came into view. One sentry was there. He was smoking a cigar and doggedly pacing back and forth to keep warm.

"Where are the boats?" George whispered.

"Just beyond the pier," said Lewis. "We must cross the road and get into the woods on the other side."

They waited for the guard to change direction and begin pacing toward the pier, and as soon as he turned his back, they darted across the dirt road and entered the woods on that side. There was a covering of oyster shells on the road, and the faint noises of footsteps on them made the soldier turn and look around, but after a pause he promptly began his pacing again. Such sounds were not unusual to his ears out here at night; he had seen and heard deer, raccoons, and other animals quite often in the area.

George and Lieutenant Lewis kept quiet for a while. From where they sat they could discern the dark outlines of two boats on the shore, one a sail boat, the other a smaller open boat.

"We'll be in plain sight of the guard," George observed anxiously.

"No," said Lewis. "We'll take the skiff. The bigger boat will hide us while we cut the chain. It's the noise I'm worried about, but we have no choice."

As the pacing guard turned his back on them again, they rushed out of the woods and scurried down a slight incline, falling on their stomachs next to the smaller boat. Lewis felt around for the chain, pulled it close, and began scraping at it with the file. The noise seemed disturbingly loud to George, but the guard gave no indication that he heard it. He was grumbling to himself about the cold, and wondering about the hour.

"Half-past, half-past," he muttered, expecting his relief soon, and to pass the remaining time, he began singing a song out loud.

"Keep singing, brother," Lieutenant Lewis chuckled, filing at the chain with a vengeance.

George's heart began racing wildly with excitement and anticipation as he realized that they might actually have a chance of success. Only a small link of metal stood between them and their freedom now. Seeing that everything was so far working out according to their plan, he began imagining himself and Lieutenant Lewis in the little boat, silently paddling away down the river–but then something unanticipated happened.

Another soldier from the fort garrison was walking toward the river. During a brief pause, Lewis caught the sound of oyster shells being crushed underfoot, and stopped his work. The sentry abruptly stopped singing, and the two soldiers greeted each other and exchanged a few words.

The lieutenant tried the link he had been working on; it was nearly cut through. He hesitated, but resumed the filing. The low noise he was making muffled the sound of approaching footsteps in the grass, and neither he nor George was aware that the second soldier was moving toward the boats.

While Lewis kept filing, George put his head around the end of the boat to see if both guards were still present, and was shocked to see one of them walking in their direction. At that moment, the drifting clouds opened, and for a few seconds, a bright gibbous moon shed its light. As George tried to hide himself, he heard a loud shout, followed by footsteps trotting in their direction.

"They've found us!" Lewis gasped, dropping the file.

Both men grasped the chain and pulled on it with Herculean effort, but the weakened link held long enough for the guard to move within a few feet of them. His form was clearly visible in the light of the moon before the clouds covered it again.

"Halt!" he shouted, pointing a rifle down at the ground. "Halt, or I'll shoot!"

Lieutenant Lewis jumped up and bolted for the woods, thinking that the darkness would shield him. George's first instinct was to stay put, but almost instantaneously the thought flashed through his mind that the guard might not have seen both of them, and that he should follow Lewis. Even if one was caught, the other might still have some chance of escape.

George scrambled to his feet, following Lewis so closely that the lieutenant's coattails brushed against his hands once or twice. He ran as fast as he could, but at the edge of the woods, he nearly slipped and fell on the wet grasses. His right foot came down forcefully on something sharp, a rock or a root, and it tore through the tattered sole of his shoe and pierced deeply into flesh and muscle. Involuntarily, he cried out in pain, and the next moment, felt a hand seizing on his sleeve. For a split second he thought it might be Lewis trying to help him, but then he heard the angry voice of a guard shouting in his ears, and dimly made out the form of another soldier pointing a rifle at him. Lieutenant Lewis had disappeared into the woods.

The yells and cries had alerted other sentries in the area, and they rushed down to the pier to see what was going on. One of them asked if they should search the woods.

"There is no one with me," George told his captors.

"You're a lying dog!" the second guard laughed contemptuously. "I saw another, and we'll find him!"

A soldier carrying a lantern looked around near the boats. He soon found the file and the broken chain and held up both for the others to see.

"Well, look at this," he said. "They were nearly successful tonight!"

Limping and bleeding, George was taken back to the fort. The search for the other escapee began, and about two hours later, Lieutenant Lewis was brought in. Like George, he was stripped of his overcoat, questioned, and put into a small, bare, windowless cell by himself.

The night passed, and in the first morning light that filtered in under the door of the tiny cell, George examined his injured foot. The hole near his heel had stopped bleeding, but it looked inflamed and ready to open and bleed again at any moment. Hearing a guard just outside, he asked for the doctor.

"You'll get no doctor," a voice answered him roughly.

That day, the door opened only once, and a tin cup half full of water was placed inside his cell. George drank a little of it and used the rest to clean his wound. He made a bandage with a piece of sleeve ripped from his shirt and bound his foot with it. The hours dragged on, and as the guards changed and passed, he continued to beg for the surgeon, receiving no response.

Another day went by for the prisoners in their cold, dark cells, and then another, but on the morning of the fourth day, the guards opened the doors and, to their great surprise, ordered George and Lieutenant Lewis to come out.

Their punitive confinement had been shortened to three days. On their way back to the prison casemates, they learned that Colonel Brown and his regiment had left for the front and turned over Fort Pulaski to a new commandant and garrison. Either there had been some confusion or miscommunication during the changing of the garrison, or one of the guards in charge of George and Lieutenant Lewis had taken pity on them, and lied on their behalf. They never inquired about it.

Later that day the surgeon came into the prison to take a look at George's foot. The doctor was completely sober now and his expression looked wrathful at first. He was not kindly disposed toward George, since the escape from his hospital had gotten him into some trouble for his negligence and drinking, but he quickly put aside his personal feelings and did what he could for his patient, washing the wound with a little chlorinated soda, putting on a fresh, clean bandage, and leaving him with extra bandaging.

"Keep off that foot as much as possible," the surgeon advised, "and examine it often for–well, you know what for."

Just before the arrival of the new commandant and garrison, the rations of the prisoners were increased and improved, and there were hints and indications that something was in the works, most likely an exchange. Hearing these reports, which seemed to be more than baseless rumors, most of the imprisoned officers felt as though they had been snatched from the edge of the grave. They no longer had to fear starvation, and hopes of seeing home again raised their spirits. At the end of February they learned that they would all be leaving Fort Pulaski.

Two days before their scheduled departure, George asked for permission to see the surgeon a last time. The wound in his foot had still not healed. The doctor came to the prison, bringing with him an old crutch. He examined the foot again, but told George there was nothing more he could do.

"Use this," he said, and, handing the crutch to George he added, "Good luck to you, Major Taylor. You will need it."

In early March, George and his fellow captives boarded a ship and left the Georgia coast. At Hilton Head, the ship took on what was left of the two hundred prisoners sent there in November 1864. Having been fed on the same diet as the prisoners at Fort Pulaski, many of them were ill or disabled, and four who were too sick to be moved had to be left behind in the camp hospital, where they soon died. Despite the expectation of exchange, their numbers had been reduced a little more when, offered the enticement of freedom and an end to their sufferings, a few of the Confederate officers "swallowed the yellow dog" and took the oath of allegiance to the United States.

As the ship continued up the coast, an officer in charge of the guards came into the prisoners' hold one morning to make an announcement. There was to be no exchange. They were being returned to Fort Delaware.

Though the officers were of course disappointed and disheartened by the news, and had no desire to return to another Federal prison, they regarded Fort Delaware as at least a higher circle of hell than the places they had left behind.

CHAPTER SIXTEEN

THE SHIP CARRYING THE PRISONERS from Georgia and Hilton Head began sailing up the Delaware River at dawn on a Sunday and arrived at the fort just before noon. Disembarking at the wharf a little later, the men lined up to be counted, and while this went on, they watched a large number of the sickest officers being carried off in stretchers and ambulances to the hospital. One of the prisoners had died during the voyage and was buried at sea; others were at death's door.

As the returning men slowly filed into the officers' pen, the other officers waiting inside observed them speechlessly, shocked by their emaciation and the disfigurements resulting from scurvy. The prisoners who had remained at Fort Delaware had by no means enjoyed an easy time during their incarceration, but they were paragons of radiant health and fitness compared to the shuffling, limping scarecrows passing before their eyes. Many of those returning were unrecognizable to the men who had known them prior to their departure in August 1864.

Hobbling back to his old division building on his crutch, George took possession of a bunk next to the one he had shared with Aleck months before. The same old broken mirror was on a post nearby, but he avoided it, afraid to see what he looked like. His lips were cracked and tender, his face swollen and sore, and another tooth was causing him pain.

Many officers who had known him before came in to see him, offering what help they could in the form of a little food and a few pieces of clothing. The weather at that time of year was still bitterly cold, and an officer who had two blankets gave George one of them. Their attentions and kindness brought tears to his eyes, but he felt too weak and exhausted to converse with them at any length, and after eating the food they had given him, he wrapped himself in the blanket and slept for several hours.

Captain Allen, an officer from South Carolina who had been one of his old messmates, appointed himself George's nurse, and in the late afternoon, finding that he had a fever and a toothache, asked for permission to take him to the prison surgeon. Permission was granted the next morning, and Captain Allen was allowed to accompany George to the hospital. Examining his mouth, the surgeon noted that a tooth had been pulled recently. It was clumsy work, he said, and had loosened the adjoining tooth, necessitating its extraction. Before dealing with the tooth, the doctor also took a look at George's injured foot. The wound was still open and draining, and he thought it infected, but as long as there were no signs of gangrene, he considered it best to leave it alone for the time being. He changed the dressing and, like the doctor at Fort Pulaski, told George there was nothing more he could do for him.

After his tooth was pulled, the captain helped George return to his barracks bed where, under the influence of a powerful pain-killing opiate, he slept until the late afternoon. For supper, Captain Allen shared a meal of potatoes and onions with him.

"This is all I have for now," he told George, "but some of us are already raising funds for the Pulaski prisoners. We are allowed to receive packages, and we'll do our best to obtain some vegetables and better clothes for you."

George thanked him, and though his jaw ached and throbbed, he felt somewhat refreshed by the meal, and began asking questions about what had gone on at Fort Delaware in his absence. Evidently, not much had changed.

"Oh, it's as lovely as ever here," said the captain. "Yet we have not had it half so bad as you men who were sent away. Most of us envied the six hundred whose names were called that day, thinking that you were going home. Now that we know how you were treated, we're glad our names were not on that roster. Still, we have heard how y'all took care of each other. If you hadn't, I don't think as many of you would have come back here."

When George asked about the mail routes and learned that they were open, he begged some paper and a pencil and sat down to write to Albert and Marguerite. Both letters were brief; he mainly wanted them to know where he was and that he was still alive. He asked his brother to send him some warm clothes and bandages for his foot, and made no mention to him or to Marguerite of his physical condition, or what he had suffered at Fort Pulaski.

Two weeks later, a large box was delivered to George containing, among other things, a suit, a coat, fabric for bandages, and a supply of tobacco, which was as good as money in the prison. The same day, he received a letter from Marguerite, written from Greenville. She reported that she and her family were well, though very distressed for his sake, having heard nothing from him in many weeks, and that although Sherman's armies had not visited Greenville, they had destroyed many valuable records of Mr. Finley's bank which had been sent to Columbia for safekeeping.

She went on, "I wept with joy to hear from you again after such a long and painful interruption in our correspondence. What comfort to know that you are alive and well! I always pray for you, morning and night. You are my first thought when I awaken, and the last occupation of my mind and heart before I sleep. I hesitate to tell you this secret, and perhaps I ought not, but I already think of you as my husband. When I wonder if you are ill or hungry or cold, or if you have received my letters, or when I might receive one from you again, I am thinking of my dear husband..."

Though George was relieved to hear from Marguerite, and to know that she and her family were safe, her affectionate letter left him strangely unmoved. After reading it, he reluctantly went to the mirror near his bunk to take a look at himself. For sanitary reasons, he had shaved off his beard again, and the architecture of his face was plainly visible beneath the pale, drawn skin.

In his imagination, he could clearly see himself as he had looked his first day at Fort Delaware–not exactly well-groomed, but healthy and strong, his tall frame muscular and well-proportioned. Now he was only a shadow of that man. He pulled back his clothes to examine his emaciated arms and legs, and putting what he saw of his body with the reflection in the mirror, he could imagine the whole picture as one truly sorry sight.

"I am not fit to be a husband," he thought, looking into his dull, sunken eyes, "and likely never shall be."

In his weakened physical condition, he had for a long time been the easy prey of melancholy, and now this despondency was beginning to overwhelm him, blackening out a future he had hoped would be his reward after for years of labor and study in his profession, and nearly four years of hardship and sacrifice as a soldier. His hopes of love and marriage, the happiness he had foreseen, as well as his aspirations of an honorable career in the law and perhaps public life, seemed chimerical now. Along with his country, the war had destroyed them all.

In Georgia, March had brought mild, warming days and nights, but in Delaware the month was still bitterly frigid. George was soon sick with a cold, and attributed its onset to this sudden change of weather. Captain Allen nursed him diligently for more than two weeks; if not for his care, George was sure that his cold would have turned into pneumonia. For a few days, he had been on the verge of that condition, which, had it worsened, might have been the end of him.

Even though conditions were better at Fort Delaware than they had been at Fort Pulaski, George was more anxious than ever concerning his health. The symptoms of his scurvy were abating because of the better food he was able to obtain now, and he was slowly recovering from his cold, but his injured foot still refused to heal. As the surgeon had advised, he undressed the wound every morning to check for any signs of mortification. If the dreaded condition of gangrene set in, he knew that his foot would have to be amputated, and perhaps part of his leg, in order to save his life. At the end of March, the foot was no worse, yet no better, and when the doctor examined it again he was surprised to see that the wound had still not closed. He offered to operate on the foot, but George recoiled at the thought of surgery in the prison hospital, where he feared he would be exposed to all kinds of contagion. He had no wish to die among enemies and strangers.

In April, the devastating news came that General Lee had surrendered at Appomattox. Assuming that the war was at an end, the Federal authorities offered the prisoners the opportunity to take the oath of allegiance to the United States. Those who were willing to do so were promised an early release, and those who refused were threatened with hard labor. The commandant, General Schoepf, had the officers assembled in the pen and made a speech to them from a parapet on the fence.

Addressing the men in his loud, heavily accented voice, the general told them that their Confederacy was finished, and, speaking even louder, he urged them to swear allegiance "to ze pest government vat ever vas!"

A few of the officers did agree to take the oath at this time, but as it turned out, they were not released any sooner than those who held out to the end. Many refused to believe that all their armies would lay down their arms, but in early May, it was reported that General Johnston had surrendered his forces, and before long, the agonizing reality of their country's defeat became undeniable to all the prisoners.

As June began, the highest ranking Confederate officers at Fort Delaware, three generals, counseled their men to take the oath, and almost all of them did so by the end of the month. Day after day, in groups large and small, or one by one, they swallowed their pride, swallowed the dog, and were allowed to go home.

Feeble in body, but obstinate and defiant as ever, George was one of the last to give in. Though it was like dying for him to utter the words of the oath of allegiance to the United States, he felt no guilt afterwards for swearing falsely (as many had, he was sure). He felt so spiritually dead inside afterwards that he began to wonder if physical death might not be too far off also–his injured foot having become more swollen and much more painful lately. It helped him to rationalize this shameful act of capitulation, to regard it as the only way he could get home, possibly to die. But even if he did not die soon, he was afraid that his health was shattered forever–that he would never be strong and healthy again, and certainly never the same man he had been before. There were times now when he almost wished for death.

In the last week of June, he was finally given his freedom.

In March, the letters George had sent to the Porter family from Fort Pulaski made their way to Barhamville. Somehow, they had fallen into the hands of an acquaintance traveling by stage from Charleston. The man made inquiries in Columbia and found out that the Porters had taken refuge at the ladies' academy.

Rev. Porter received the letters with a sinking heart, recognizing his nephew's handwriting. After reading the one addressed to him, he gathered his family around him and read it aloud to them. He dissolved into tears just as they did, one by one, beginning with his wife, and he was unable to finish the last few lines. Later, when he was more composed, he made arrangements to send on the other letter to Robert's widow in Camden, along with a personal note of condolence that was agonizing to write. That evening, at family prayers, Rev. Porter conducted a kind of private memorial service for his son. Knowing that his body occupied an unmarked grave on the Georgia coast, the Porters had little or no hope of its recovery and reburial.

The sorrows of that month were followed by a series of joyful events, some of them expected, others earnestly hoped and prayed for. In April, Aleck Dwight rode home from North Carolina, where his brigade had disbanded. Zachary was still with him, and though the young chaplain's health was good, his entire worldly goods consisted of a lame horse, a watch, and a dollar and a half in silver in his pocket. Rev. Porter's older sons, Paul and Richard, also returned to Columbia at about the same time, and a week later, young William Porter came back to his family. They had not heard from him in over a month, and feared that he was dead or taken prisoner. With some delays along the way, the boy had ridden all the way to Virginia to fight, only to find out the day he arrived that Lee's army had just surrendered. In May, the family received a letter from Caroline Johnstone, the eldest daughter, who was in

England with her husband, young children, and her cousin Julian. They were destitute, but all alive and well.

Soon after the war's end, Rev. Porter received letters from friends and family in different parts of the state. Most of the letters were hand carried by friends and acquaintances traveling to Columbia from those areas, and they reported on the terrible condition of things, especially in the areas devastated by Sherman's armies. After a spate of such communications, the letters suddenly became more scarce, even as the mail services grew more regular. The ones that did trickle in were oddly restrained and muted in their reports and complaints, imparting mostly family news, and Rev. Porter realized that the mails were now perhaps being examined by the Federal military authorities in charge of the state. A cousin who came to Columbia from Charleston reported to him that persons who were known to have been strong supporters of the Confederate cause were being watched very carefully by the Yankees.

Four days after his release from Fort Delaware, George arrived in Charleston by steamship on a sunny summer afternoon. As he sailed by the crumbled ruin of Fort Sumter, he noticed a U.S. flag flying over the rubble left by the invader. He had sent a letter ahead of him to his brother, but in it asked him not to inform Marguerite or anyone else of his homecoming.

At the first sight of George, who hobbled toward him on a pair of crutches, Albert was shocked and saddened, but he concealed such feelings as best he could, and tried to show only his joy at George's return. Bringing him home in a buggy pulled by a drooping, elderly horse, Albert sat close to him on the leather seat, pressed his hand, and repeatedly shifted the reins into one hand to touch George again, as if to reassure himself that his brother's presence was reality and not a dream.

"You will stay with us," said Albert. "Everyone is very much looking forward to seeing you."

"What of my house?" asked George. "Was there any further damage?"

"Yes...but we'll talk of that later. We want you with us, anyway. We have only been back in Charleston a few weeks, you know, and have been hoping to see you soon. All of us were so happy when we received your last letter."

"About that," George responded, shifting awkwardly in the seat, "you have kept it confidential?"

"Of course! Just as you asked."

"Thank you."

Albert smiled, but scanned his brother's wan, rather lifeless face with hidden concern. Though George had greeted him with warm emotion, all that seemed gone now, and his expression and tone of voice were blank and dull. Except when he looked at Albert, he kept his eyes lowered and fixed on the dashboard opposite, not turning his head to glance out of the carriage windows. He had already seen too many blue uniforms in Charleston that day, and had no desire to see any more.

Albert's youngest children did not recognize their uncle, and seemed a little afraid of the thin, sickly stranger who walked into their house on crutches. The eldest daughter, George's favorite niece, burst into tears when she saw him and ran upstairs to shut herself away in her room. Seeing George again, Mrs. Taylor had the same reaction as her husband, but instantly put on the mask of a smile to conceal her distress.

After some conversation, George pled fatigue from his long journey and he asked if he could rest somewhere.

"We have a room prepared for you upstairs," said Albert, eyeing the crutches, "but if you are too tired to go up now, there is a comfortable sofa in my study."

"That will do."

"Would you like something to eat or drink now?" asked Mrs. Taylor. "Some lemonade, perhaps?"

"That is something I have not tasted in a very long while," said George. "Yes, thank you."

"It is so hot today!" she remarked nervously, quickly walking off to fetch the drink for him.

Albert went into the study with his brother and arranged some pillows on the sofa to make him more comfortable. The crutches were laid aside, and he helped him raise his injured foot, which was thickly wrapped in bandages.

"What more can I do for you?" Albert asked gently, leaning over him. "Does this foot need some attention?"

"I'll take care of it...later," said George.

"Do you need to see a physician?"

"Later," George repeated faintly, closing his eyes until his sister-in-law entered a few moments later with a tray containing a pitcher of lemonade and three tumblers. After Albert poured a glass for George, he gave his wife a look to indicate that they should leave him alone now.

Before closing the door behind him, Albert paused and asked, "Do you think you can handle the stairs? Your room is on the second floor."

"I believe I can," George replied "After I have rested a little."

As soon as he finished his drink, drowsiness overcame him with unexpected swiftness, and he slept until it was time for supper. To celebrate George's homecoming, Mrs. Taylor had spent a large and precious portion of her household money and prepared a meal that was sumptuous compared to the family's usual fare. The children were so excited to see meats and dishes and confections they had not enjoyed for several years that they forgot their misgivings about the gaunt, strangely unfamiliar family member seated at the table with them.

"You must come home every day, Uncle George!" cried one of the little boys, making everyone laugh except his uncle, who only smiled.

After the meal, George made apologies and excused himself for the evening. His brother helped him negotiate the stairs, which he went up slowly and steadily, turning himself slightly sideways, and being careful not to put any weight on his bandaged foot. On the landing, he rested, panting a little from the effort before following Albert into his room.

"I imagine I have displaced someone," said George, looking around the bedroom, which was full of his possessions and clothes.

"Certainly not," Albert disagreed. "This is a guest room, and you are much more than a guest in this house."

Once alone, George idled away some time browsing through old papers, books, photographs, and other odds and ends, but soon found himself growing drowsy again. The novelty and richness of a full meal and a glass of wine took effect, and within minutes of climbing into the luxury of a real bed, he was asleep.

The next morning, he woke early. After changing the bandage on his foot, George took a look at his old clothes and selected a favorite suit to wear. It had fit him perfectly before the war, but as he put it on, found that it was too large now for his attenuated form. He stood before a full-length mirror, and observing the way his clothing draped from his broad, bony shoulders, he thought he looked less like a man than a kind of framework resembling one. In the morning light he studied his pale, sunken cheeks and the dark circles under his hollow eyes with dismay. Before leaving Fort Delaware for Charleston, to more easily rid himself of vermin, he had cut his hair very short. What was left of it had lost its glossy sheen, and was not arranged in any fashionable or flattering style.

There was a knock at his bedroom door. His brother opened it and looked in. Albert smiled and surveyed George from head to foot.

"Well, that's certainly an improvement on the clothes you arrived in!" he remarked. "You're looking much better, much better."

"My clothes look better, yes," said George, not returning the smile.

"You look better altogether," Albert insisted. "Now that you have had a good supper, and a good night's sleep in a comfortable bed. And now it is time for a lavish breakfast we have prepared for you. I am very much looking forward to it, as lavish meals have not been the rule with us for quite some time."

George finished buttoning his coat.

"You mustn't go out of your way to provide me with such meals. I am not accustomed to them, and can do very well with much plainer fare."

"Well," said Albert, looking more serious, "this morning's meal is really mostly leftovers from last night. I'm afraid we haven't the resources anymore for such things as a rule, but nothing would have stopped us from celebrating your homecoming."

"How do you stand on resources, Albert?" George inquired.

"Not very well," he sighed. "But better than many others, I think. The night before we evacuated from Charleston, I went out alone and hid as many valuables as possible. Before that, knowing that Uncle John was too ill to travel, I left some papers and possessions with him, and many of yours. Fortunately he managed to avoid the pillage that went on when the city was occupied, so you see you still have your belongings. When we returned to Charleston, we found many things missing from the house, but thank God, the plunderers did not find the things I had hidden. I still have many of those things, but we've been selling them off piece by piece to get money. We've even sold some furniture and carpets–any luxuries which could be spared–and I imagine we shall have to part with more eventually."

"I wish I could be of some help to you," George said somberly.

"It is a help to us to have you back again. You don't know how we've worried about you, George. Losing father was bad enough–"

Albert broke off and covered his eyes, stifling a sob.

"Forgive me," he sniffed, and when he had regained his composure, he suggested that they go for a walk after breakfast.

Mrs. Taylor had suggested that some exercise and sunshine would be of benefit to George, and Albert agreed with her. He was anxious for George to see a doctor, but as yet had not pressed him to do so.

After the morning meal George and Albert left the house and wandered toward the nearby Citadel, the military college. As they stepped on to Meeting Street, George noticed that there was a large hole in the steeple of the beautiful Baptist church facing the Citadel square. He paused and gazed at it a while, discerning more damage to the sanctuary, and expressed some surprise that the shells had found targets this far uptown. Albert told him that shells had fallen even farther up the peninsula, as far as Spring Street, or so he had heard. George glanced across the street and, seeing many men in blue uniforms at the Citadel, where a New York regiment was headquartered, he immediately turned away. A lady dressed in black was approaching, and she slowed as she passed by; though her face was veiled, it was obvious that she was looking at George and Albert. Her scrutiny made George feel self-conscious, and he imagined that the sight of two crippled men—one lurching along with a cane, the other a mere scarecrow on crutches—must have excited her pity.

The two began making their way down Meeting Street, but before they reached Calhoun, George showed signs of fatigue, and suggested they return to the house.

"I certainly cannot walk much farther," he sighed, slumping into the rests of his crutches. "I am already tired."

"You've not recovered from your long journey," Albert replied. "Once you are rested, perhaps we can drive down to the Battery."

"Perhaps tomorrow," said George, "but you must prepare me for what I shall see. Perhaps you ought to tell me about my house now."

Albert reluctantly complied.

"A shell hit it, and caused a fire," he said. "The house was gutted. It is a complete loss."

"I feared as much," George replied in a strained whisper.

"It can be rebuilt, George," said Albert, attempting an encouraging tone.

"I'm sure I have no money for that."

"Not now...but someday you will."

When they returned to Albert's house, George went upstairs to his room and slept the rest of the afternoon.

That evening, before George came downstairs again, Mrs. Taylor found her husband alone in his study. Albert was sitting at his desk with a pen poised to write, but had paused, and looked up at her with a preoccupied, serious expression when she walked in.

"What are you doing, dear?" she asked.

"I am writing to our cousin Dr. Mitchell," he said, "about George. I shall send this note over now, and if he does not refuse, I shall take George to see him tomorrow."

"Isn't Dr. Mitchell retired? He must be very elderly now."

"He is, but George always liked him so much, I think he will see him. He was our physician when we were boys."

"Why not some other physician?" she wondered.

"I think he may at least listen to Dr. Mitchell. This morning, after our walk, I tried to persuade George to see a physician, but he put me off again. Something should be done about that foot. I can tell that it is giving him a great deal of pain. There must be some reason why it is not healing."

"His body has surely been greatly weakened by his long ordeal. Perhaps his wound will begin to heal once he regains his strength," Mrs. Taylor speculated.

"Well, that is possible, I suppose. Nevertheless, he ought to be in the care of a physician. If I can't persuade him, perhaps Dr. Mitchell will be able to do so. George is a stubborn man, but I don't understand why he won't seek medical care."

"He seems very depressed," his wife fretted, shaking her head. "Perhaps he–"

"What?"

"Perhaps he has lost the will to live," she ventured hesitantly.

"Nonsense!" her husband cried. "George is stronger than that."

"But bodily sickness can affect the mind, you know."

"All the more reason to get him to a doctor as soon as possible."

Albert put down the pen and folded up the piece of note paper in front of him. He had decided to go and see his cousin to make the request in person. Dr. Mitchell lived only two blocks away, and he told his wife he would walk over and be back home before dark.

The next morning, not long after breakfast, Albert asked George to walk with him before the day grew too hot and uncomfortable for such exercise.

"We don't have to walk too far," he said, "but I'll wager you will be able to walk farther today than you did yesterday. You are looking much stronger this morning."

"You certainly are, George," Mrs. Taylor agreed. "Sunshine and fresh air and exercise must be a good tonic. Your color is better today."

George received their opinions doubtfully, but consented to the walk.

As George and Albert approached Dr. Mitchell's house, they heard someone calling out their names. The doctor had risen from his chair on the piazza and was waving to them. He was a stooping, frail old man past eighty.

"Is that the Taylor boys?" he shouted. "Come here and let me have a look at you."

George reluctantly followed Albert to his gate, and they entered and walked up to the house. During the exchange of some pleasantries, Dr. Mitchell showed no surprise or concern at George's appearance.

"He has been prepared for me," thought George, glancing at his brother suspiciously.

His suspicions were confirmed when, after a long, reminiscent conversation, Dr. Mitchell finally remarked on the state of his health, and asked George if he would consent to a brief medical examination.

"This is why we are here, isn't it?" George asked his brother testily.

"What's the harm in it, George?" Albert pleaded.

"What's the use of it? I am a wreck, that's all. Dr. Mitchell can plainly see that, I'm sure."

"I have seen men in worse conditions than yours restored to at least a modicum of health," the doctor protested, "and go on to lead useful, if not comfortable lives."

"Let Dr. Mitchell look at your foot, at least," Albert urged. "What could be the harm in that?"

George hesitated, but then, looking at the old physician's trembling hands and squinting eyes, he refused. Dr. Mitchell seemed to understand, and reached over and took his hand.

"In cases like yours, George," he said gently. "Recovery is generally a matter of time and patience. Don't expect to get well overnight."

"I don't necessarily expect to get well at all," George muttered in reply.

The doctor suddenly looked surprised and indignant.

"Well!" he said. "Let me tell you something, young man, such a frame of mind is very dangerous. Are you aware of that?"

George declined to answer the question.

"Your brother tells me you are engaged to be married," Dr. Mitchell remarked after a pause.

"What of that?" George answered curtly.

"I should think that the prospect of matrimony would inspire some willingness, and hopefulness in you. A loving wife can soften the hard lines of life for a man, and the lines are very hard indeed for us these days. What was it the Romans used to say? *Vae victus* –woe to the vanquished. But vanquished as we are, we have no choice but to go on living. You must go on living, too."

George was unresponsive again, and kept his eyes lowered to the floor. Seeing that the young man was not very receptive to his philosophical musings, the doctor turned the conversation to more practical matters.

"Are you in pain?" he asked George.

"Sometimes," he said, at the end of a sigh.

Dr. Mitchell asked him about his most recent medical problems and treatments. George told him about the cold he had suffered at Fort Delaware, then remembered his other problem there.

"I also had a tooth pulled. I was in terrible pain, and they gave me an opiate for it."

"You are not in such pain as to require that now, are you?"

"No," said George. He suddenly shuddered as he remembered "poor old Fitz" and his awful addiction, and added, "I hope I am never in such pain again."

The doctor seemed to glimpse what was on his mind, and said, "A nephew of mine, a young man about your age, is wasting his life away with that stuff. He began taking it for a physical pain, but kept on taking it for quite another kind. It is terrible thing for his family to witness his slow ruination. He has been swamped, he tells me, and is being dragged down...but I think you are a stronger man, George. Your health can be restored, I am sure of it, if you will only make the effort."

"What about his foot?" Albert asked anxiously.

"Something can be done about that," Dr. Mitchell opined. "I imagine surgery will be necessary. Dr. Finley is the man for that."

At the name of Finley, George started.

"You know the gentleman?" the doctor inquired.

"I am acquainted with him," said George. Dr. Finley was Marguerite's uncle, and was often at her house, his own residence being next door.

"There is no finer surgeon in Charleston," Dr. Mitchell declared. "No finer physician, really. He was an instructor at the Medical College, and always kept up with all the latest advances in medical science. You could not put yourself in better hands. Now promise me that you will see him."

George scowled, and Albert looked at Dr. Mitchell apologetically. They did not stay much longer. On the walk home, George was sullen and silent. Albert was irritated that he had not allowed Dr. Mitchell to examine him, but even so, felt more hopeful now, since the old physician had managed to extract a promise from George that he would see a surgeon soon, though not necessarily Dr. Finley.

The mention of Dr. Finley led to thoughts of Marguerite, and Albert wondered when George was going to see her, or at least let her know that he had returned to Charleston. Wasn't he thinking of her? Why did he want to avoid her? Albert had his suspicions, and as they turned the corner of his street, he came out with a question about her.

"Have you communicated with Miss Marguerite yet?"

George scowled again.

"No."

"Why not?"

"I don't wish to see her—I should say rather, I don't wish her to see me."

"George!" said his brother, in a gently reproving tone. "Miss Finley is most anxious to see you, I'm sure."

393

George lowered his head, staring at the ground as they walked.

"When I do see her," he murmured, "I am thinking of breaking off the engagement."

"Surely not!"

"I am thinking that it was perhaps for the best that we did not marry during the war–that I was right not to. This," said George, stopping and pointing to himself with both hands, "is what would have returned to her as a husband."

"You'll get well, George," Albert argued. "Just as Dr. Mitchell said, it's only a matter of time and patience."

"I don't think I shall ever be well again."

"You don't know that for certain. Postpone the marriage if you like, but I beg you, for the sake of her happiness and yours, do not break with Miss Finley. Has she not been faithful and patient for five years? She must love you very much to have waited so long for you, when she might have–"

"Married someone else?" George finished for him.

"Well, yes..."

"I know that."

"Married someone much richer and better looking," Albert added with a smile, attempting some humor, but eliciting no amusement from his brother.

"She is so beautiful, I imagine it could have easily been done," George replied blankly.

Albert pretended to bristle with indignation.

"From what I know of Miss Finley, she cared nothing for your fortune or lack of one, and fell in love with you despite your looks."

This remark drew a little laugh from George, and for a few moments, his expression softened as he thought of the early days of their courtship. But the next instant, he realized that he was thinking of another man, not this wasted form hobbling along on crutches, and he frowned.

After the midday meal, the two brothers lingered at the dining room table talking. At first they spoke of family members. George reluctantly imparted more details of their cousin Robert's last days, and Albert offered up what he knew of various uncles, aunts, and cousins. When Albert mentioned that some relatives had been applying to him for legal assistance, the conversation turned to professional matters.

"They have no money to pay for such services, of course, and there is really very little I can do for them at present. Some of them are owed substantial amounts of money, but will probably never see a cent of it. I shall undertake to help the widows when I can–if I can–and it would be a great comfort and help to me if you could assume some of that burden, George. You have taken the oath, but there is as yet no amnesty for me, since I was a civil officer in the Confederate government. I shall apply to the president for a pardon, and I hope that if it is granted I shall be able to practice law again and support my family."

Mentioning the pardon, Albert colored momentarily and lowered his eyes to hide a look of humiliation and resentment, but quickly went on, "As for any legal work for you at present, George, there are a few paltry commissions of debt collection to be attended to, but I'm afraid most if not all will prove hopeless. We are under military rule, as you know, and on behalf of a few dispossessed clients, a few lawyers here have begun dealing with the Yankee general in charge of this district, but there is no other legal recourse for citizens here at present. Until the civil government is reestablished, there won't be any courts in operation, and consequently...very little for us to do."

Albert sighed, thinking of the situation he had just described, then concluded, "If nothing else, we must try to help the widows who have applied to us."

"I suppose...I ought to make myself useful to someone...while I can..," George said in a slow and disconnected way, staring off with an aimless, almost stupefied look.

Though disturbed by this look, Albert forced a smile.

"Of course you can, George," he said. "I know you won't let me down. I know you will be a great help, once you are feeling better."

George drew in a deep breath and let it escape in a weary exhalation.

"I am feeling very tired," he said. "I shall go up and rest now."

"Do that, George. The rest will do you good."

"Yes, yes, I'm sure it will," George answered negligently as he rose to his feet. A dark cloud began gathering before his eyes, and he had to steady himself by holding on to the back of the chair.

"Are you feeling faint?" his brother asked.

"A little...this happens sometimes when I stand up, but it usually passes. It is passing. I am fine."

"Let me take you to see a doctor," Albert urged.

"Not today."

"When, George?"

"Tomorrow is Sunday, but soon...soon–Monday, I promise."

Later that afternoon, Albert happened to glance outside through a window which looked out to a small, neglected garden next to the house. He saw George sitting there on a wrought iron bench, his elbows on his knees, his head in his hands. After a while he raised his head, sat up more erect, and fixed his eyes on a spot on the ground with a blank expression. Minutes passed, and he did not move except to blink a few times. David kept watching as he sat motionless and expressionless, simply staring. Finally, his chest heaved and fell with a deep breath, and he closed his eyes, but only to open them a moment later to stare again.

Remembering his conversation with his wife the previous evening, Albert wondered if was possible that George's mind had been affected by his physical illness, and by all the suffering he had gone through, but then reproached himself for such thoughts.

"No, no, my brother is a strong, rational man," he told himself. "He has been through a hellish ordeal, and is still suffering its effects in his body and mind, but he is still himself. He will come through all this, and be well again."

As he continued to watch, he saw George lace his fingers together and bring his clasped hands up to his chin. Then he bowed his head a little, closed his eyes, and kept them closed for a long while. Albert came to the conclusion that he was praying, and took this as a hopeful sign.

CHAPTER SEVENTEEN

WHEN GEORGE WOKE on Sunday morning, his foot was more swollen and painful than usual, but he said nothing of it to his brother, and about two hours after breakfast he asked his permission to take the buggy down to the Battery.

"Let me go with you," Albert offered. "We are not going to church."

"Why not?"

"Reverend Thomas passed away just before the evacuation, and no one has been found to take his place. Besides, few members of the congregation have returned to Charleston."

"I'd rather go alone, if you don't mind," said George. "I only wish to see the house. Afterwards, I shall pay a visit to Uncle John."

"I'm glad to hear it! I know it would cheer him to see you again."

Albert knew that George would probably pass Miss Finley's house on the way, and, noting a shade of preoccupation in his expression and manner, he wondered if his brother intended to call on her as well as their uncle. He hoped so.

Having observed the deplorable condition of the city streets, George traveled slowly toward the Battery, maneuvering the carriage around potholes and stretches and crisscrosses of deep ruts. Not all such hazards could be avoided, though, and after a few severe jolts along the way, his injured foot began to ache. Broad Street seemed to be in better shape, so he turned left at that corner, and then turned again to travel down East Bay Street the rest of the way.

During the war he had seen the burnt district–nothing but a forest of chimneys now–and that devastation was painful enough to see again, but when he reached the lower portion of the peninsula and came into the neighborhood where he had been born and raised, he felt even more sick at heart, knowing what awaited him when he reached his own house. The long artillery bombardment of the city had not been as destructive as the fire of 1861, but it had left most residences and buildings scarred and battered, and countless windows shattered. Near the Battery, all the houses appeared to be vacant, and almost all were visibly damaged to one degree or another. Some houses which seemed only slightly injured on the exterior by a small hole knocked in the wall had much more extensive injury in their interiors, where the shells had burst. The Yankee soldiers had cleared most of the thoroughfares of debris, and had filled the shell craters in them, not so much for the sake of the city's residents, but for their own purposes–yet the scene was still one of barrenness and desolation. Weeds and wild grasses of different sorts grew in and along the streets and throughout the once carefully tended gardens and yards.

George pulled up at his house on East Battery Street and got out of the buggy. What was left of the Taylor mansion was a broken, blackened shell. The roof was gone, along with the whole third floor, and several turkey buzzards were perched atop the highest remaining wall. Much of the facade of the second floor had collapsed, leaving the skeletal interior piteously exposed. Through one of the empty windows of the first floor, he could see what must have been his father's fine library, and a few shattered, empty shelves black as charcoal. The lovely piazzas where George and his brother had played so many hours as boys had collapsed into pieces, and the lawn and gardens were overgrown and shadowed by a few leafless, charred trees killed by the fire.

He stood transfixed, unable to take his eyes off the destruction, and turning his attention to the library again, he thought of his father.

"I'm glad you're not here to see this."

A moment later, a familiar voice called his name, and he turned to see his former neighbor and old friend, David Macbeth. Poorly dressed in an old suit, he approached with an outstretched hand.

"George Taylor, is that you?" he asked. "You are so changed I hardly know you."

They shook hands, and George noticed that David's handsome face was now marred by a long ugly scar down his left cheek. His left arm hung motionless at his side, but George did not ask the cause of that. He could guess.

"You see, I can say that to you because I am a changed man, too. My ruined face matches the city now," the young man laughed hollowly.

"Oh, it is not so bad as that," George protested politely.

"I was very sorry to see what became of your house, George. Terrible luck."

"I'm glad the fire did not spread to your father's house, or to our other neighbors," said George, and as he spoke, his gaze was again drawn irresistibly to the incinerated wreck of his home, and he remarked wonderingly on the extent of the damage in the shell district.

"There is even more damage than meets the eye. A friend who has viewed this part of the city from a church steeple says that it is hard to find a roof that has not been shattered by the shells–but are you surprised? The shelling went on day after day for a year and a half, George."

"Yes, I knew that, but I never understood for what purpose."

"Those proud rebels who owned these great houses had to be punished, you know," David answered sardonically.

A sudden wave of anger swept over George, and this emotion, coupled with his physical weakness, made him feel faint. He swayed a little, and David steadied him with his one good arm. The faintness passed quickly, though, and George assured his friend that he was quite all right. David suggested that they dine together that evening.

"My cousin has a farm on the neck. I am staying there. Won't you join us for supper? I'm sure my kinsman will be delighted to entertain a hero of the Confederacy."

"I? A hero?" George responded, surprised. "Surely you joke."

"I have heard what you and your fellow prisoners have been through in this last year or so, and I say you are all heroes."

George merely shook his head with a snort approximating laughter, and declined the invitation.

"I don't think I shall be up to another outing today, but I shall be glad to dine with you at your cousin's house some other time, and hear of what you have been about in the past few years. I'll wager your exploits were far more heroic than mine," he said, with a glance at his friend's useless arm.

After some conversation about their families, the two old friends parted, and George returned to the buggy. He drove on down the Battery, which, during the war, looked very different than it had in peace time, earthworks armed with cannons having been erected at a number of points fronting the harbor. The cannons were gone now, and the occupying military forces had returned most of the soil back to the empty lots from which it had been excavated. A steady breeze came from the gray water, and out across the harbor, battered Sumter seemed to brood and wait.

George rounded the tip of the peninsula, and passing by the park, turned up Meeting Street again. Marguerite's house was only a few blocks away. The horse had learned to avoid the holes and obstructions in the street, and picked its way along very gingerly. George pulled him up to a stop about a hundred yards from the Finley house.

The streets in this neighborhood were mostly deserted. Many of the houses were still unoccupied, but those where people dwelt looked no less neglected and bleak. Leaving the buggy, George took up his crutches again and walked toward the Finley house, moving even more slowly than his lameness necessitated.

Two elderly ladies in mourning clothes passed him with pitying looks, and he winced with a sudden, unusually sharp pain that shot up his leg. He passed the Finley gate, and almost kept on walking, but forced himself to stop and turn around.

"I must do this," he told himself.

George approached the gate again and waited, working up his nerve, but within a few seconds, he turned his head at a creaking sound, and saw that the large wooden doors of the carriage drive gate were slowly opening. He walked over and saw Marguerite's father pushing one of the doors aside.

"George Taylor!" he cried. "Is that you?"

He grasped George's hands and shook them vigorously, his expression a strange, alternating mixture of happiness and distress.

"Do come in! What a surprise! I am so pleased to see you!"

"You were on your way out," George suggested.

"Oh, but that must wait at least a little!" Mr. Finley protested. "Come to the house with me."

George made his way to the front steps, but they presented a difficulty for him, as his foot was throbbing painfully now. Mr. Finley perceived the problem and called out to his wife, who soon came down the steps to meet George in the walkway. The Finleys courteously refrained from making any comment on his appearance, but he could see the shock and pity in their eyes. What he saw only strengthened his resolve to do what he had come here for. After answering their questions about his family and some mutual friends, he mustered the courage to ask about Marguerite.

Her father and mother exchanged an odd look.

"Oh, she is well," said Mrs. Finley. "She will be so happy to see you! We did not know when to expect you."

"Is she at home?" he asked.

The odd look passed between the Finleys again.

"No, George," answered Mr. Finley. "She is not at home."

"Where is she?" he asked a little anxiously, puzzled by their strange demeanor.

"My daughter," said Mr. Finley, drawing in a deep breath, "is detained at the city jail."

"What!"

"She and two other ladies were arrested in church today, for refusing to offer up prayers for the president," Mrs. Finley explained tearfully.

George stared at them, speechless.

Mr. Finley went on, trembling with nervous excitement, "For omitting the same prayers just two months ago, General Hatch banished Rev. Marshall of St. John's Chapel and confiscated his property, and since then the other ministers have complied, but not our daughter! Oh, no! She and her friends returned to church today for the first time since we came back to the city, and when the rector began to pray for the government, the three ladies rose and left the church, and Yankee officers in attendance there arrested them on the spot. Oh, mercy, the girl is too headstrong! What obstinacy!"

George was fairly livid.

"Ladies—under arrest—at the jail!" he stammered in disbelief.

"We were not at church, but a friend who was there came by to tell us what happened," said Mr. Finley. "We immediately went to see the Yankee officer in charge, but it was to no avail. I was going to go down there again shortly. Mrs. Finley has insisted on it."

"I will go with you!" said George.

"Let us go immediately," Mrs. Finley suggested, glad for the reinforcement of George's company. "You shall ride with us in our carriage, and we shall bring them all home."

Mr. Finley advised his wife to stay home.

"I shall go with George," he told her. "We will handle this matter. I don't wish to see you so upset again, dear."

"Very well," sighed Mrs. Finley. "But do hurry and go. I shall have no peace until I have my daughter home again!"

While the carriage was being brought out by a servant, Mr. Finley began filling George's ears with what had been going on in Charleston since its occupation. After lamenting the pillage of his own house, he went on to tell him how, after gloating over their victory in a ceremonial flag raising at Fort Sumter, a group of Yankees ("The congregation of a Northern church!" he exclaimed incredulously) had taken an excursion through the city, entering unoccupied, unprotected buildings, public and private, even churches, and taking for themselves whatever they fancied. It had lately been discovered that they had made off with, among other things, valuable historic documents dating back nearly two centuries.

Hearing all this, George wanted to curse, but bit his tongue in front of Mrs. Finley. As he listened to Mr. Finley and focused more attention on him, he noticed that the old gentleman did not look well. Marguerite's father had aged considerably since the last time George saw him, and his eyes and face had a heavy, careworn appearance.

When the carriage was brought out, Mr. Finley took George's crutches and helped him into the conveyance. As they started down Meeting Street, George inquired about Frederick.

"Our son was wounded at Bentonville," said Mr. Finley, "but, thank God, is still with us. We were very anxious about him for a while, but under my brother's care, he has been doing quite well and should make a full recovery."

"What about the bank?" George asked him.

"I have closed it," said Mr. Finley. "I had no choice. If the bank is to survive, we must be closed, and for how long I do not know. If we opened now, we would have to liquidate all our assets in order to redeem our notes in circulation, and would then have to declare insolvency."

Lowering his head, he rubbed his fingers over the deepened creases in his brow and went on, "The week before Sherman arrived in Columbia, I transferred much of the bank property to Greenville by rail. I thought it would be safe there, and it was for a while. Sherman's armies did not visit Greenville, but in May, Yankee raiders who said they were pursuing President Davis came there, pillaged the town, and robbed the bank. I had taken pains to conceal our holdings, bricking them in the cellar, but the Yankee soldiers were apparently old hands at bank robbery, and tapped the brick wall until the sound changed, and found what we had hidden! Thirty thousand in gold and silver, almost all our specie, was stolen by them! We have less than five thousand now."

"That's very unfortunate," George sympathized.

"Very! And our liabilities are very great! I am buying as many of our notes as I can at a discounted rate to reduce them, through a connection in Liverpool who has made us a loan."

Mr. Finley hung his head lower and sighed, "I don't think any of the banks will survive this catastrophe, George, but I intend to do all in my power to save ours."

The carriage turned down Magazine Street, and soon they were in sight of the city jail, a large, impressive building which resembled a castle. It was now the headquarters for the United States troops occupying Charleston, and there were many men in blue uniforms in the vicinity. A soldier stationed at the main entrance recognized Mr. Finley from his earlier visit and spoke to him impudently, but allowed him to go inside with George, whom he eyed scornfully. The room they entered was filled with more blue uniformed men. A group of officers conversing among themselves approached on their way out, casting a few curious glances at the gaunt man on crutches, and as soon as they passed by, George caught sight of some ladies grouped together in a far corner. He tugged on Mr. Finley's sleeve and led him in that direction.

The women were dressed in black– and all three had dark veils draped from their hats, but George had no trouble distinguishing Marguerite from the others. Her shapely little figure and sprightly mannerisms were unmistakable. They stood facing an officer who was informing them, with an indignant, wrathful expression, that they were free to leave now.

Marguerite tossed her chin up and immediately turned her back on the man. Earlier, from this same officer, the ladies had received a long lecture on the sin of secession, along with stern reproofs concerning their lack of respect for a government they did not want, and vague but ominous warnings concerning any future misconduct.

The look on Marguerite's face transformed from contempt to wonder and tenderness when she saw George. Because of her veil, he did not see the change in her expression. The ladies with her quickened their pace to keep up with her as she rushed to George, and Mr. Finley instantly took her arm.

"Let's get out of this place!" he whispered urgently.

He kept a firm hold on Marguerite and led her outside, but when they reached the carriage, she escaped from her father's grasp, stepped closer to George, and lifted her veil.

He looked down at her speechlessly, stunned by her beauty. How was it possible that she was even more splendid than he remembered her in his dreams? Her girlish beauty had now matured into a full womanliness, and the curve of her cheekbone down to her chin was more delicate and elegant than ever. He could not master his emotions—he felt too weak. Seeing her radiant face again, he broke down and wept.

Disregarding proprieties, Marguerite flung her arms around him.

"Oh, George! I can hardly believe it! My dear George is home at last!"

For a few moments, he enjoyed the blissful sensation of Marguerite's arms around him, but then remembered what he had resolved to do that day. He also felt ashamed of his tears, which he thought she must surely consider unmanly.

"I am sorry, Miss Marguerite," he said brokenly. "I have been very ill and my–in my weakness, I am sometimes overcome."

She looked up at him. Tears streaked her face and overflowed from her eyes, but she blinked them away and smiled.

"Don't apologize for your feelings, George. I am glad for them."

When she let go he took out a handkerchief and wiped his face dry, and Marguerite did the same for her own face with one she drew out from her sleeve. She had to blow her nose, and laughed and blushed a little for it. George also felt a certain embarrassment now, and sniffed and cleared his throat awkwardly. Though he did not move away from Marguerite, she immediately sensed his attempt to throw up an invisible wall between them.

In the afternoon they were finally alone, seated on two separate benches in the Finley's garden. George felt it was time to broach the subject of their engagement, but he waited for Marguerite to finish a discourse she had begun about her cousin Harriott, a young lady who had endured a long engagement to an officer and was at last getting married.

"Her wedding is this Saturday," Marguerite was saying. "It will not be a grand affair, by any measure, but I should like to go. Will you accompany me?"

George shrugged in a noncommittal way. She had been talking about her cousin at such length that he was hardly listening by now, but casting about in his mind for some delicate way to bring up an unpleasant matter.

"If you wish, Marguerite," he added after a pause.

She studied him and began to smile.

"What is it?" he asked her.

"I see I shall have to take a less subtle tack with you."

"What do you mean?"

"What do I mean! Why, I sit here and prattle on and on about a young lady of my age who has been engaged to an officer lo these many years, and is now able to take his hand in marriage...and all this talk inspires no references from you concerning our own situation, which is very like, don't you think?"

"Ah, I see."

She rolled her eyes a little.

"Yes, at last!"

"About our situation...," he began, coughing from a sudden tightness in his throat.

"Yes?"

"Marguerite..."

He directed his eyes to the ground, unable to look into hers.

"You see my condition," he said, speaking with difficulty, his voice husky with emotion. "And...and because of it, I shall...I shall understand if you wish to be released from our engagement."

"Nonsense!" was her immediate and emphatic answer. George looked up in surprise. Her expression was resolute and indignant.

"My health is broken, Marguerite," he explained.

"What is broken can be mended," she countered.

"I should have said, my health is ruined, then. It is ruined. I would not ask you to be the wife of an invalid."

She looked at him with compassion, her expression softening.

"Oh, George, I know that you must have suffered greatly. I know that you feel very poorly now–but time will bring you better health, as well as nourishing food, and rest, and the care of those who love you."

"Marguerite," he groaned. "I won't do this to you. I cannot provide for you—nor protect you. I have no money, and no way of making any in my profession for who knows how long."

"You can find some other way of making a living," she responded in a matter-of-fact tone.

George threw his head up in frustration, thinking of friends and former comrades who had once been gentlemen of means, now reduced to the humiliation of menial work to earn a few dollars for bread, ruined men who had taken any kind of employment they could find, simply to keep body and soul together and feed their hungry families. He heard that an old school friend, the son of a once wealthy merchant, was working as a porter in a dry goods store set up by a Yankee. Another, a former high ranking officer in the Confederate Army, had a lowly job on the docks of Charleston. Other veterans who were amputees or invalids were mere beggars now, or living on the charity of family or friends.

"Marguerite, you don't understand," said George. "What am I to do? My body is so weak I am not fit for any sort of manual occupation."

"You can work for my father. He needs a trustworthy man."

"I don't know anything about your father's business."

"He will teach you."

"He has Frederick, who must also make a living. Besides, the bank has closed down for now, and it may be many months, or even years before it reopens–if it ever does."

Her eyes grew ominous.

"George Taylor," she said firmly. "You are the man I have chosen. I will have no other. If you do not marry me, I shall remain a spinster for the rest of my life."

This threat seemed to have little effect on George. He was not anxious, after all, to see her marry someone else. Marguerite rose to her feet and asked him to do the same. When he stood up she drew so close to him that her skirts covered his feet, and she held out her hand to him.

"Take my hand," she said. "I wish to feel your grip."

He took her hand lightly.

"Squeeze it!" she insisted. "I know you have more strength than that!"

"I don't wish to hurt you."

"Then grip it as though you were shaking the hand of a man."

He made his grasp firm and shook her hand.

Her verdict was, "That is not the handshake of an invalid."

George knew better; he had gripped her hand with nearly all his strength, and yet she had felt no discomfort. Marguerite studied his face carefully, noting the dark circles under his eyes, his flushed lips, and his complexion, which was pale except for a strange, patchy blush on his sunken cheeks.

"How long have you been so ill?" she asked.

"Quite a while...I suffered with scurvy while I was a prisoner. For a while I thought I would die of it. Some of my less fortunate friends who died of it were horrible to behold at the end."

A look of horror crossed her face.

"I am sorry to be so indelicate," he apologized, "but you did ask, so I told you the truth. I was fortunate not to lose my teeth to the scurvy, though two had to be pulled for other reasons."

"The truth is," she gasped, holding back tears, "the truth is that you have survived, and that you are a whole man. What is the loss of a few teeth? Open your mouth and let me see."

"Marguerite!" he protested in shame and embarrassment.

But she kept insisting on it, and he finally relented, realizing that it was probably for the best. A glimpse of the interior of his mouth might put a damper on her enthusiasm.

He bared his teeth for her and opened wide, feeling foolish and humiliated. She went up on the tips of her toes to get a closer view.

"You have lost a few jaw teeth," she observed. "But your smile is intact."

As she spoke, she realized that she had not yet seen him smile. She took his hands and smiled at him with heartbreaking affection. Tears suddenly sprang into his eyes.

"Marguerite," he faltered hoarsely, hanging his head. "For your own sake, let me go."

"I will not!" she cried. "Oh, George, I see that you are very depressed, and in this state of mind you do not see things rightly now, but I do."

As he looked down into the face of this determined little woman, he began to suspect that he might be fighting a losing battle. Still, he resisted and argued with her with what little strength and pride he had left, and the struggle continued. She stubbornly countered every argument and objection he could muster.

"You are so willful, Marguerite!" George finally exclaimed in exasperation.

"Then I shall will you to live, and be well again, and you will be," she answered compellingly.

"I...I don't want a willful wife," he muttered after a pause, looking away.

This was such a transparent and flimsy tactic that she actually laughed out loud, sighing his name affectionately as she quickly sobered herself. George sighed too and shook his head. He had run out of arguments.

He said nothing for a while, but the way his head slowly drooped lower and lower in dejection began to alarm her, and she began to grow fearful that he would break with her irrevocably if she continued to be so demanding. During the silence Marguerite pondered her options, and came to the conclusion that delay was her only hope.

"George, please, give us a little more time," she proposed. "If you still feel this way in a month's time, I shall release you from your promise, and never reproach you for it. But please, I beg of you, promise me that you will go to see my uncle, who is the best physician in Charleston. Let him help you. He will do it as a favor to me–I know he will. Will you do this for me?"

There was a look of desperation and suffering in her eyes he had never seen before, and it tore at his heart. Because of it, and because, in his own mind, he already considered their engagement broken, he glumly and reluctantly agreed to do as she asked.

Studying him again intently, Marguerite touched his face.

"You are feverish," she said with concern.

"It's the hot day," he replied, reaching into a pocket for a handkerchief. "Only the hot weather."

She put her hand up to his forehead and pressed her flat palm against his brow.

"No!" she insisted. "You are burning with a fever! Do you feel unwell?"

"I do feel rather weak today," he admitted. "More than usual."

"Come with me to my uncle's house," she urged him. "I believe Dr. Finley is at home. Let him have a look at you now."

George protested, but Marguerite took hold of his arm and began to pull him in the direction of Dr. Finley's house, which was just next door.

He waited at the foot of the front steps while Marguerite ran inside to see if her uncle was at home. She soon came out again and waved to George to enter. The effort of going up the steps on crutches left him nearly exhausted. Breathing heavily, he leaned against a pillar to rest. Until that moment he had not realized how feeble he really was.

Looking impatient, Dr. Finley came to the door to investigate the delay.

"Won't you come in, Mr. Taylor?" he said, rolling down a sleeve. He was a short, stout man, a few years younger than Marguerite's father. He had just received an urgent request from a neighbor whose child was ill, and was preparing to go out.

George put his weight on the crutches again and made his way into the house rather unsteadily. Dr. Finley immediately directed him to a chair. He touched George's face and briefly felt his pulse.

"You need some attention, Mr. Taylor. I must go out for a while, but I wish you to wait for me here. Will you do that?"

George nodded, submissive in his weakness.

"I shall return as soon as possible," he said, and on his way out the door, asked Marguerite to bring his guest some water.

Marguerite left the room, but George was not alone for long. She soon returned with a tumbler full of cool water. She noticed that George's hand trembled slightly as he took it from her, and after he drank the glass of water, she put it away and glided to the floor at his feet.

"I shall wait with you," she said, taking his hand, which she kissed several times. "My uncle will make you well again, George. I know it."

He let his head fall against the soft, comfortable padding of the chair, and though he made a feeble effort to remove his hand from hers, she would not let it go.

"It seems I am overruled by you and your uncle," he said. "I really haven't the strength to resist you."

"It's true," said Marguerite. "We have you in our toils, and won't let you go."

George almost smiled at this, but the next moment, Marguerite saw him wincing in pain. At the same time, he extended his bandaged foot and raised it a little from the floor. Seeing his discomfort, she quickly snatched a pillow from a nearby sofa and placed it under his foot as he lowered it.

"Thank you," he sighed. "That's better."

"Are you hungry, dear?" she asked.

George closed his eyes and shook his head from side to side a little.

"Let's wait for your uncle," he said. "Let me rest."

Marguerite let go of his hand and sat down on the sofa next to his chair. Both waited quietly until Dr. Finley returned. George was nearly drowsing when he heard the doctor's voice.

"Come into my study, Mr. Taylor. I wish to have a look at that foot."

Marguerite asked if she could be of any assistance, but her uncle advised her to wait where she was. George followed Dr. Finley into an adjoining room, and the physician closed the door as he took a chair, placing the pair of crutches on the floor beside him. While Dr.

Finley unwrapped the bandages, George answered his questions about the injury.

"More than four months," the doctor mused, studying the bottom of the foot intently, "and still the wound has not healed. There may be an infection in a bone, or some kind of splinter or other object inside your foot."

After a rather painful examination of the injury, Dr. Finley declared that surgery would be necessary.

"When?" asked George.

"Why not today? There is a great deal of inflammation, and it may only grow worse if we wait."

"But I am not feeling well today," George argued. "Perhaps it ought to wait until I am feeling stronger."

"This infection is sapping your strength, and may cause you to lose the foot, Mr. Taylor. As a soldier, I am sure you have seen what such wounds can lead to. I advise you not to wait. I have been fortunate enough to acquire a small supply of chloroform lately, so that the operation itself would be relatively painless."

After a long hesitation, George finally agreed to let Dr. Finley perform the surgery. The physician went to the door, opened it, and spoke to his niece in the parlor. He told her he was going to operate on Mr. Taylor, and asked her to fetch her mother.

"She is an experienced nurse, and I shall need her assistance," said Dr. Finley.

"May I be of some help?" Marguerite asked her uncle anxiously.

"Well, possibly–but I shall certainly need your mother. See if she can come here now. Oh, and bring one of your father's nightshirts. We must make Mr. Taylor comfortable during his recuperation."

"Must I stay here?" George asked, startled by the sudden preparations.

"Why not? It will be much more convenient for me while you are under my care. You will have to stay off that foot a good long while, you know. I have a nice, comfortable room for you on this floor, and I'm sure my niece would prefer to have you close by."

"Oh, George," Marguerite said pleadingly, looking in, "please do as Dr. Finley asks. Mama and I shall take care of you, and visit you every day."

"Another good reason to stay here, eh, Mr. Taylor?" the doctor chuckled, patting him on the shoulder.

CHAPTER EIGHTEEN

GEORGE'S MIND, TOWARDS MORNING, was tumultuous with dreams he did not clearly remember as he slowly came to consciousness. A faint, slightly unpleasant noise finally roused him, and he opened his eyes in the unfamiliar room with a deep inhalation. The little noise, a clicking sound, made him turn his head, and he saw Marguerite seated near his bed knitting. She had learned to knit at the beginning of the war, knitted endlessly throughout those years, and was still busying herself with it, to aid the poor of the city, and as an outlet for her overflowing energy.

Her head was bent intently over her work, and her slender hands worked with apparently effortless precision and rapidity.

"What is she thinking?" George wondered idly, watching her.

Marguerite had not yet noticed that he was awake, and kept knitting. Loose spirals of soft brown hair moved gently against her face where, drawn down by gravity, they obscured her lips and chin. He watched her with only a vague wistfulness, not much moved by her beauty. Though he had been very affected by it when he first saw her again, he was not so now. His heart felt hollow and cold. He was tired of all emotion, worn out from it, and he welcomed this sensation of numbness and detachment.

She happened to look over at him and was startled to see his open eyes.

"George!" she murmured breathlessly.

"How long did I sleep?" he asked, stretching under the covers.

"About fifteen hours," she said, with a glance at her watch. "Dr. Finley says he believes your foot will heal completely now."

She smiled, expecting George to show a similar happiness over the good news, but he only nodded and covered a yawn. When he moved his foot slightly, he experienced a kind of stabbing pain in it he had not felt before.

"You must keep still, George," Marguerite admonished him. "My uncle says you must make no unnecessary movement."

"It hurts too much to move," he complained.

"You must be hungry. Shall I bring you some breakfast?"

"I suppose I could eat."

She rose, put her knitting aside and, risking his displeasure, placed a light kiss on his forehead before gliding out of the room. While his breakfast was being prepared, George lifted his head and looked around his sick chamber. It was a pleasant, plain room full of handsome mahogany furniture. As Dr. Finley had been a widower for decades, there was no vestige of feminine finery anywhere in his house. George tried to make out the subject of a few small engravings that hung on the wall opposite his bed, and finally discerned that they were botanical drawings–medicinal plants, no doubt, he thought. He knew that Marguerite's uncle was not only a physician but a naturalist of sorts, and the author of a number of articles and books on medical botany and other subjects. The doctor had once proudly shown George his scientific library, which lately, to his great sorrow, he had been obliged to begin selling off, book by book, for needed cash.

Marguerite returned carrying his meal and a cup of tea on a tray, followed by her mother, who thought, for propriety's sake, that her daughter ought not to nurse George alone. After Mrs. Finley greeted him, Marguerite set the tray down on a table, and as George sat up in the bed, she piled pillows behind him to make a comfortable support, and served his food with a warm and complacent smile.

Now that she had him in her uncle's house and, as she saw it, under her power, Marguerite felt confident of his recovery and his eventual capitulation to a wedding, and George perceived all this as clearly as if he had read her mind. It made him feel resentful for a little while, until he reminded himself that he had agreed to this bargain, and so stoically resigned himself to it.

Later in the morning Dr. Finley rapped lightly on the door and stepped in to examine his patient. He pronounced himself very satisfied with the results of the operation. After changing the bandages, he told George that at least a month's bed rest would be necessary for the proper healing of his foot.

"You mustn't put any weight on it for a good long while," he said. "In a few weeks' time you may use the crutches again, but until then, you must mainly keep to your bed. Next week, it should be all right for you to sit in a chair part of the time."

As soon as Dr. Finley left the room, Albert came in, happy and relieved that his brother was finally receiving the medical care he needed, and bringing with him a dressing robe and some of George's nightshirts and clothes.

One morning, towards the end of the first week, Marguerite came into George's room to wake him, and found him talking and groaning in his sleep, and making strange grimaces of pain or anger. She approached him warily and reached out to gently touch his shoulder to wake him. He suddenly rose up, flailing his arms, roaring, "This is mine! Get away, damn you!"

One of his wildly waving hands struck Marguerite on the side of the head as she was backing away. She involuntarily gave a little cry, and his eyes opened wide.

"Did I strike you?" he asked, with a look of shock that matched her own.

"You didn't mean to, George," she said. "You were dreaming."

"Did I hurt you, Marguerite? Please forgive me!"

"I'm all right. But next time you are dreaming, I think I shall wake you with a broomstick."

She smiled at him, and he managed a feeble smile in return.

"Yes, perhaps you should," he said.

"What were you dreaming about?"

George hung his head.

"I'm not sure...," he muttered. "I think someone was trying to take something that belonged to me...food, I think...in the prison."

Mrs. Finley entered the room, and nothing more was said about the incident until the afternoon, when she left, expecting her daughter to follow her shortly. Lingering behind a few moments, Marguerite asked George about the dream, calling it that, and not a nightmare, thinking that he might rid himself of these bad memories if he talked of them. He would not talk of them. At the mention of his prison life he seemed to close up within himself, and grew sullen and morose. Undaunted, Marguerite suggested that it might do him good to write down his recent experiences.

"Perhaps if you put them on paper," she said, "it would take them off your mind, or at least ease your mind."

After considering her suggestion, George agreed that it might be a good idea, and that he ought to make such a record.

"At least it will give me something to do while I am penned up here," he added in a glum sigh.

This remark sent a sharp little dagger into Marguerite's heart. George saw that he had hurt her but, thinking it best to be honest with her about his feelings, he did not apologize, and turned away from her with a frown. Marguerites's pain quickly turned into resentment, and for the first time, she reproached him in anger.

"You should thank God that you are penned up here with me, George Taylor!" she blurted out, rushing from the room before she could say more.

She left him alone for several hours.

In the early evening, as Mrs. Finley was taking away his supper tray, George heard the sound of piano music from the parlor, and knew it must be Marguerite playing. He asked her mother to leave the door open as she went out of the room. Mrs. Finley left it wide open, so that he could see Marguerite seated at the keyboard, facing away from him.

George pulled on his robe, took hold of his crutches, and maneuvered himself into a chair next to the bed. Marguerite began to sing. He leaned forward and listened.

"Oh, come to me," she began, "and bring with thee, the sunny smiles of former years. If smiles so bright, will lend their light, to cheer a brow long used to tears."

She sang wistfully, sadly, but her voice was as beautiful as ever. It was just as he remembered it.

"I will not let one sad regret, one gloomy thought our meeting chill," she went on, "but for thy sake, I'll strive to make this altered face look cheerful still."

She hummed through a few bars, then sang, "Our theme shall be, the friends we love, not those we mourn; we'll not destroy a present joy, lamenting ones that never return..."

After this, she stopped abruptly, sensing someone's presence, and turned her head to see George.

"That was lovely," he said, with the beginnings of a smile.

Marguerite turned back to the keyboard, then slowly rose, turned, and walked to his door.

"I'm not sure I remember the words properly," she murmured, adding in a trembling voice, "But no matter—it is a sentimental song...the kind you do not like."

They looked at each other, and it was plain that they were both thinking of her earlier outburst, and the remark which had led to it. She had a contrite look about her, and saw that George wore the same expression.

"Will you forgive me?" she asked him, barely audibly.

"It is I who should ask your forgiveness, Marguerite," he answered. "None of this is your fault, but I am boorish enough to take it out on you."

"You will write your memoir, then?" she asked, smiling a little.

"Is that what we are to call it? Well, yes, I will write it."

The next morning Marguerite brought him an unused bank journal she had found among her father's things, and George began recording his reminiscences.

For as long as he was a convalescent at Dr. Finley's house, he spent several hours a day writing in the journal. He asked Marguerite and his brother for some of his old letters to them, and perused the correspondence for names and dates he found it hard to remember precisely. When he came to the end of the pages in the first journal, he asked for another, and Marguerite purchased a writing tablet for him. He continued in it, filling nearly every page before he was finished.

George usually wrote in the morning hours. In the afternoons, Marguerite would bring in a book or two from her uncle's library for the patient's amusement, drawing up a chair beside his bed, or sitting at a table with George next to her in his robe, and turning the pages as they perused them. They took turns reading the captions of illustrations of tropical birds, insects, exotic animals and plants, faraway places, and curious peoples. Some of the pictures actually caught his interest; he conjectured about them, and finally, after a while, began to make humorous observations, occasionally showing some of his old ironic tendencies. Marguerite was exultant when she told her uncle about George's returning sense of humor; the doctor agreed with his niece that it was a hopeful sign.

As much as possible, Marguerite was careful to protect the convalescent from anything upsetting or depressing. She kept newspapers away from him, and always changed the subject if politics came up in conversation. She was even tempted to censor his mail, but stopped short of that. A few letters contained very bad news, reporting the death of a relative or friend, and they left him somber and silent for long periods. In early July, George was especially distressed by a note sent over by his Uncle John Hutchinson concerning a favorite cousin. Injured late in the war, the young man had finally died of his wounds at his family's plantation in the middle of the state. George showed little emotion, except when reading or penning replies to these sad communications. Marguerite sometimes saw him covering and wiping his eyes as he wrote them, and was especially tender and deferential to him on those days.

One afternoon she brought George two letters, and when he recognized the handwriting of Aleck Dwight on the first one, he smiled and opened it with evident eagerness and interest. The letter came from Abbeville, where the young priest had recently been installed as rector of the Episcopal church. After a few lines about himself and his wife, Aleck wrote:

"Your letter from Georgia of course brought the awful tidings of Robert's death, but I assure you, it was a great comfort to all of us to know that he passed his last days and hours in the company of friends and the loving care of a kinsman. We rejoice in the confident hope that we shall see him again someday.

"Rev. Porter was very much relieved (as we all were) to receive your letter from Fort Delaware announcing your imminent release. We heard what the prisoners at Pulaski were forced to endure, and were praying for you every day. I am thankful to God that He spared you, but I know you must have suffered greatly. My dear friend, it pains me deeply to think of you as anything but able and healthy and strong, but I pray that your health will be restored to you completely. The mere presence of my Alice was always a miraculous, restorative tonic for me, and I trust Miss Marguerite will have the same effect on you.

"I recall that you were in low spirits when we parted, which must have only worsened, but I entreat you my dear friend, do not lose heart. I know that you looked forward to the end of the war as a commencement of a new life with brighter hopes, sweeter rewards, but now, instead, like so many of us, you find yourself contemplating desolation, standing as it were over the embers of a ruined homestead, hoping that something may be saved out of it for the comfort of those you love. It was not so long ago that I too was at the lowest point of my life—but mercifully, God did not allow me to stay there for long. I was with my brigade in North Carolina when word of the surrender came to us, and when I heard it, I knew it was the end, and that our fondest earthly hope would never be realized. The news affected me like a shock of death, and I could not sleep. At midnight I walked out beyond the camp, as you and I used to do together, but this time I was alone. There, in solitude, beneath the stars, I consecrated myself entirely to Christ and His kingdom.

"You must believe that you and I have been spared for a reason, George, so let us be strong for those who love us and need us. You know where to find the strength..."

Marguerite was seated near the bed crocheting a shawl. When she paused and looked up from her work, she noticed George's look of deep concentration as he finished reading the letter, and asked him about it.

"Is your friend Mr. Dwight well?"

"He is," George answered after a pause. "Would you like to read his letter?"

She took the paper, a single folded sheet, as he opened another letter, this one from an old friend, Captain Thomas Powell, from whom he had heard nothing for over a year. Like George, Powell was an attorney and the son of a once-wealthy and distinguished man. His father had died in the last year of the war, and not long afterwards, after enduring many months in the North as a prisoner of war, the captain had returned to his family's plantation on the Santee River, to a pillaged and vandalized home. To keep body and soul together, he had been hunting game and sending it down to Charleston to be sold, while at the same time working under very difficult conditions in an attempt to restore his rice plantation to some semblance of its former productiveness.

George was glad to hear from his old friend, and to know that he was still alive, though Captain Powell wrote that he found surviving the peace much more difficult than surviving the war.

Marguerite's eyes were moist as she finished reading Aleck's letter.

"I look forward to meeting Mr. Dwight someday," she said softly.

"He always wished to meet you."

"You did not tell me that your cousin Alicia was expecting," she remarked, handing the letter back to George.

"This is the first I have heard of it."

"I shall write to her," said Marguerite, "and see if I may make something for the baby–some warm covers for the winter, as the child is expected in September."

The patient improved steadily, without setbacks. He put on weight and grew stronger. Dr. Finley prescribed a little exercise after the long period of bed rest, and, using a new, more comfortable pair of crutches, George walked in the yard and the gardens with Marguerite and her mother, or next door to her home for a visit with her father. The monotony of his convalescence was also relieved by visits from family members and old friends. His brother came to see him three or four times a week, and beginning in mid-July, his cousin John Hutchinson paid him a call each Sunday.

After nearly two months had passed, George was looking more fit. His old clothes were still a little too large for him, but were wearable, and most of his old aches and pains had diminished to the occasional twinge. His appetite was good, and his emotions and expressions less subdued.

As Marguerite was serving his breakfast one morning, George asked her if she would like to read his reminiscences.

"Oh, yes!" she answered, a little surprised by the offer. "I should like very much to read them."

That afternoon, she took the two volumes he had written home with her, closed herself up in her room, and spent the whole of the evening with them. Her eyes were filled with tears at different intervals, and she had to stop several times to weep. George's censored letters from Fort Delaware and other places of captivity had given her little accurate knowledge of the true conditions and hardships of those places. It was only now that she realized what a terrible ordeal he had been through.

Marguerite slept very badly that night, and the next day, when she returned the books to George, it was all she could do not to burst into tears and lamentations for all his sufferings. She restrained herself, though, and quietly and solemnly remarked that she understood him better now that she knew all that he had been through. Then she complimented him on the literary qualities of his memoir.

"You are a very accomplished and expressive writer," she said. "As you are already twice a published author, I don't see why this work of yours ought not to be published also."

"I really hadn't thought of that," George replied, "but perhaps I shall look into it someday."

After a silence Marguerite asked, "I wonder, did you mean to discourage me by letting me read your memoir?"

"Not exactly," he said. "But I thought you ought to know...what has made me the way I am."

"Well, I was not discouraged," she told him firmly. "On the contrary, reading it only made me love you the more."

George studied her wonderingly.

"You are a stubborn little woman," he said, shaking his head.

Her face burst into a smile.

"I am indeed," she said. "You see, we have a fault in common."

That beautiful smile had its desired effect on him, and he returned it. He no longer felt cold toward Marguerite; like his body, his feelings were reviving. Her company had become charming to him again, and she began to notice this by little looks and hints he gave her.

Since the day he had come to live at her uncle's house, Marguerite had not uttered a word about their engagement. George had also avoided the subject, though it was obvious after his surgery that he was getting well. He began to think seriously again about the possibility of marriage. He had not committed himself to it, he reminded himself; he had only promised Marguerite that he would reconsider the matter after a certain period–but he found himself vacillating now, when before he had thought it best to part with her. What troubled him most now was how he would support a wife and family.

George took most of his meals in the dining room now, but Marguerite still pampered him by serving him breakfast and coffee in his room. One morning, while her mother was still in another part of the house, Marguerite was preparing his tray at the table, and happened to look up and see George's reflection in the mirror of a wardrobe. His eyes were traveling over the curves of her figure with unmistakable masculine interest, and when he noticed she was observing him, he immediately looked away. Though her heart was racing, she served him his breakfast demurely and, walking to the window, began their morning conversation with talk of the weather. It was raining.

The next morning, the two were alone again for a few minutes, and as George sat up in bed, he asked Marguerite to fluff his pillows before she brought the tray. He leaned forward as she began to arrange them and then suddenly fell back, pulled her down to him in an embrace, and kissed her.

Cradled in his arms, she looked up at him with eyes half-closed, their expression soft and yielding. He wanted to kiss her again, but refrained.

"I love you, George," she sighed.

"Rita," he whispered, "you're so beautiful. What do you want with a broken down old horse like me?"

"Don't talk like that, George. You're scarcely thirty."

"I feel a hundred."

"You're getting well again, George. You know that. And you'll only grow stronger and better, especially after we're married."

"Is that so?"

"Yes, I have it on good authority."

"Whose?"

"My own."

George drew in a deep breath, gently released her to her feet, and, expecting her mother to walk in at any moment, he cleared his throat to say somewhat gruffly, "I'd like my breakfast now."

Marguerite laughed and fetched it. Then, pulling her chair closer to the bed, she sat and watched him eat his meal with unconcealed affection.

Just after George finished his breakfast, his brother came by to see him. Marguerite yielded her chair to Albert, and she and her mother left the two men alone.

"I shall not stay long," said Albert, "but I wished to share some news with you. There is some new work, I am pleased to tell you, which promises to be one of the few hopes of income for our firm... eventually. Our cousin Mr. Pringle, who is the solicitor for the railroad, lost his partner last month. You might have heard of old Mr. Smith's death"

"Yes, I heard of it," said George.

"Mr. Pringle, who is not in the best of health himself, proposed an alliance with our firm when I told him that you were recovering and doing well again. He always held you in great esteem, you know. I have already accepted his offer on your behalf. I didn't think you would object."

"No, I don't object. The South Carolina Railroad is operating again?"

"On a very limited basis. They are slowly rebuilding–very slowly, and with great difficulty–but the routes will eventually be restored. Mr. Pringle told me that there was no other firm to which he would prefer to entrust the company's affairs, especially now that they are in such disarray."

Albert also told George he had received a letter from a gentleman in Washington, one of their father's old friends who had been advocating for him (and for George) there, and had been assured of a pardon from President Johnson as early as November, which would allow him to practice law again eventually. Speaking of the pardon, he turned his face away to hide a look of mortification, but George knew it was there without seeing it. He knew his brother well, and could see that Albert was bearing the same burden of despair that he carried in his own heart–yet even men without hope had to go on living, and working, to provide for themselves and their families.

Albert turned back to him with moist eyes.

"You and I shall be partners again, brother," he said feelingly, as he pressed George's hand. "Cast down, but not destroyed, eh?"

"Not destroyed," George echoed, gazing at his brother fondly and gratefully. "Not altogether."

Later that morning, after he dressed, George tried walking for the first time without his crutches, and discovered that his foot gave him very little pain. He left his room and found Marguerite in her uncle's library looking over the remnants of his finer books. He could see Dr. Finley seated at a desk in his office through a partially open door.

"George!" she said, surprised. "Where are your crutches?"

"I think I can dispense with them now, at least I hope so," George answered. "The doctor must advise me on that."

"There is no pain?"

"Hardly any."

She sat down on the sofa with a large book in her lap.

"It's raining again," she said, patting a spot on the cushion next to hers. "I thought you might like to read with me."

George obeyed, seating himself very close to her. She pointed out the handsome leather binding of the book, but he ignored her remark and broached another subject.

"Marguerite," he said, "since, as you say, and as you can see, I am doing well now, I think I ought to be going. I have imposed on your uncle's kindness too long."

Her shoulders drooped down a notch, and the corners of her lips sagged into a frown, but she quickly converted it into a neutral expression.

"Where will you go, George?" she asked.

"To my brother's, I suppose. He's insisting on it."

"When?"

"Tomorrow, I think."

"So soon?"

In the silence that followed, Marguerite looked at him with evident expectation, asking with her eyes, "*And what of us?*"

The answer now seemed inevitable to George, but the last, swiftly expiring remnants of his stubbornness and pride made him hesitate.

Marguerite finally broke the silence. Looking down at the book again and fingering its cover, she said, "Do you know, my uncle has promised me this house. He told me that he has put it in his will."

And she looked at George very frankly and brightly.

"No, I didn't know that," he replied.

"Yes, it's true!"

She opened the large volume on her lap to its title page. It was an illustrated work about the Birds of Paradise of New Guinea. After turning a number of pages, she paused to pull back the tissue paper from a vividly colored engraving of one of the gorgeous creatures. While Marguerite sighed and shook her head in admiration, George was giving most of his attention to her rather than the picture.

"Are you trying to put me in mind of paradise?" he asked, as if suspicious.

She laughed, but then said to him more seriously, "Don't you think they're beautiful? It is as though they are not of this world."

George shrugged and agreed, then looked away from the illustrations. His eyes slowly went over all the parts of the room. Pretending to study the library in detail, he looked off in different directions, and while he did, began to lean his weight against Marguerite a little.

The weather grew stormier outside, and as gusts of wind coming from the harbor threw raindrops against the windowpanes with emphatic pattering sounds, he remembered all the days and nights he had endured such storms in leaky tents and bleak prison quarters, and suddenly felt extremely thankful to be alive, to be home again, and sheltered among those he loved. The one he loved the most felt the warmth and pressure of his arm against her shoulder, and waited.

"This is a fine house," George remarked at last, nodding thoughtfully. "Yes, a very snug, pleasant house. A man could be comfortable here."

Marguerite smiled and turned another page.

END

About the Author

KAREN STOKES, an archivist with the South Carolina Historical Society in Charleston, S.C., is the author of several other books set in the Civil War and post-Civil War South: *Belles: A Carolina Love Story*, *Honor in the Dust*, and *The Soldier's Ghost*.

She is also the author of *South Carolina Civilians in Sherman's Path*, a non-fiction book released in June 2012 by The History Press, and is the co-editor of *Faith, Valor, and Devotion: The Civil War Letters of William Porcher DuBose*, published by the University of South Carolina Press in 2010.

Also from the Author

FICTION:

Belles: A Carolina Love Story

Carolina Twilight

The Immortals: A Story of Love and War

The Soldier's Ghost: A Tale of Charleston

NON-FICTION:

A Confederate Englishman: The Civil War Letters of Henry Wemyss Feilden (Co-editor)

A Confederate in Paris: Letters of A. Dudley Mann 1867-1879

A Legion of Devils: Sherman in South Carolina

Carolina Love Letters

Confederate South Carolina: True Stories of Civilians, Soldiers and the War

Days of Destruction: Augustine Thomas Smythe and the Civil War Siege of Charleston

Faith, Valor, and Devotion: The Civil War Correspondence of William Porcher DuBose (Co-editor)

Fortunes of War: The Adventures of a German Confederate

The Immortal 600: Surviving Civil War Charleston and Savannah

South Carolina Civilians in Sherman's Path

AVAILABLE FROM GREEN ALTAR BOOKS

If you enjoyed this book, perhaps some of our other titles will pique your interest. The following titles are now available for your reading pleasure… Enjoy!

THE FIELD OF JUSTICE
MOONSHINE AND MURDER IN NORTH GEORGIA
WILLIAM A. THOMAS, JR.

James Everett Kibler
Tiller

A FATAL MERCY
The Man Who Lost The Civil War
A Novel By
THOMAS MOORE

RANDALL IVEY
THE GIFT OF GAB

MAXCY GREGG'S
SPORTING JOURNALS 1842-1858
SUZANNE PARFITT JOHNSON, EDITOR
FOREWORD BY JAMES EVERETT KIBLER, JR.

CATHARINE SAVAGE BROSMAN
An Aesthetic Education and Other Stories

CHAINED TREE, CHAINED OWLS
POEMS
CATHARINE SAVAGE BROSMAN

Carolina Twilight
KAREN STOKES

SPLINTERED
Brandi Perry

TO Jekyll AND HIDE
MARTIN L WILSON

RUNAWAY HALEY
An Imagined Family Saga
WILLIAM A. THOMAS JR.

THE IMMORTALS
Karen Stokes

GREEN ALTAR BOOKS
SHOTWELL PUBLISHING

Green Altar (Literary Imprint)

CATHARINE BROSMAN
*An Aesthetic Education
and Other Stories (2nd Ed)*

Chained Tree, Chained Owls: Poems

Aerosols and Other Poems

Partial Memoirs

RANDALL IVEY
*A New England Romance:
And Other Southern Stories*

The Gift of Gab

SUZANNE JOHNSON
Maxcy Gregg's Sporting Journals 1842-1858

JAMES E. KIBLER, JR.
Tiller : Claybank County Series, Vol. 4

The Gentler Gamester

*In the Deep Heart's Core: Poems of Tribute and
Remembrance (forthcoming)*

THOMAS MOORE
*A Fatal Mercy:
The Man Who Lost The Civil War*

PERRIN LOVETT
The Substitute, Tom Ironsides 1

KAREN STOKES
Belles

Carolina Twilight

Honor in the Dust

The Immortals

The Soldier's Ghost: A Tale of Charleston

WILLIAM THOMAS
*Runaway Haley:
An Imagined Family Saga*

*The Field of Justice: Moonshine
and Murder in North Georgia*

CLYDE N. WILSON
*Southern Poets and Poems, 1606 -1860:
The Land They Loved, Volume 1*

*Confederate Poets and Poems, Vol1
The Land They Loved, Volume II*

Gold-Bug
(Mystery & Suspense Imprint)

BRANDI PERRY
Splintered: A New Orleans Tale

MARTIN WILSON
To Jekyll and Hide

JEFFERY ADDICOTT
*Union Terror: Debunking the
False Justifications for Union Terror*

*Trampling Union Terror:
Riders of the Second Alabama Cavalry*

MARK ATKINS
Women in Combat: Feminism Goes to War

JOYCE BENNETT
*Maryland, My Maryland:
The Cultural Cleansing of a Small Southern State*

GARRY BOWERS
*Slavery and The Civil War:
What Your History Teacher Didn't Tell You*

Dixie Days: Reminiscences Of a Southern Boyhood

JERRY BREWER
Dismantling the Republic

ANDREW P. CALHOUN
*My Own Darling Wife: Letters From A
Confederate Volunteer*

JOHN CHODES
Segregation: Federal Policy or Racism?

*Washington's KKK: The Union League During
Southern Reconstruction*

WALTER BRIAN CISCO
War Crimes Against Southern Civilians

DAVID T. CRUM
Stonewall Jackson: Saved by Providence

JOHN DEVANNY
Continuities: The South in a Time of Revolution

*Lincoln's Continuing Revolution: Essays of M.E.
Bradford and Thomas H. Landess*

JOSHUA DOGGRELL
Doxed: The Political Lynching of a Southern Cop

JAMES C. EDWARDS
*What Really Happened?:
Quantrill's Raid On Lawrence, Kansas*

TED EHMANN
*Boom & Bust In Bone Valley: Florida's
Phosphate Mining History 1886-2021*

JOHN AVERY EMISON
*The Deep State Assassination
of Martin Luther King Jr.*

DON GORDON
*Snowball's Chance: My Kidneys Failed,
My Wife Left Me & My Dog Died...*

JOHN R. GRAHAM
Constitutional History of Secession

PAUL C. GRAHAM
Confederaphobia

*When The Yankees Come: Former Carolina
Slaves Remember*

*Nonsense on Stilts: The Gettysburg Address
& Lincoln's Imaginary Nation*

JOE D. HAINES
*The Diary of Col. John Henry Stover Funk
of the Stonewall Brigade, 1861-1862*

CHARLES HAYES
The REAL First Thanksgiving

V.P. HUGHES
Col. John Singleton Mosby: In the News 1862-1916

TERRY HULSEY
25 Texas Heroes

*The Constitution of Non-State Government:
Field Guide to Texas Secession*

JOSEPH JAY
*Sacred Conviction:
The South's Stand for Biblical Authority*

JAMES R. KENNEDY
Dixie Rising: Rules For Rebels

*Nullifying Federal and State Gun Control:
A How-To Guide For Gun Owners*

*When Rebel Was Cool:
Growing Up In Dixie, 1950-1965*

*Reconstruction: Destroying the Republic
and Creating an Empire*

WALTER D. KENNEDY
The South's Struggle: America's Hope

*Lincoln, The Non-Christian President:
Exposing The Myth*

Lincoln, Marx, and the GOP

J.R. & W.D. KENNEDY
*Jefferson Davis: High Road to Emancipation
and Constitutional Government*

*Yankee Empire:
Aggressive Abroad and Despotic at Home*

Punished With Poverty: The Suffering South

The South Was Right! 3rd Edition

LEWIS LIBERMAN
Snowflake Buddies; ABC Leftism For Kids!

PHILIP LEIGH
*The Devil's Town: Hot Springs During
The Gangster Era*

U.S. Grant's Failed Presidency

The Causes of the Civil War

*The Dreadful Frauds: Critical Race Theory
And Identity Politics*

JACK MARQUARDT
*Around The World In 80 Years: Confessions
of a Connecticut Confederate*

MICHAEL MARTIN
Southern Grit: Sensing The Siege at Petersburg

SAMUEL MITCHAM
*The Greatest Lynching In American History:
New York, 1863*

*Confederate Patton: Richard Taylor and
The Red River Campaign*

CHARLES T. PACE
Lincoln As He Really Was

*Southern Independence. Why War? The War
To Prevent Southern Independence*

JAMES R. ROESCH
From Founding Fathers To Fire Eaters

KIRKPATRICK SALE
*Emancipation Hell: The Tragedy Wrought
By Lincoln's Emancipation Proclamation*

JOSEPH SCOTCHIE
*The Asheville Connection:
The Making of a Conservative*

ANNE W. SMITH
Charlottesville Untold: Inside Unite The Right

Robert E. Lee: A History for Kids

www.ingramcontent.com/pod-product-compliance
Lightning Source LLC
Chambersburg PA
CBHW071342020726
47502CB00001B/208